NEVERMORE

Nevermore

KELLY CREAGH

ATHENEUM BOOKS FOR YOUNG READERS

NEW YORK LONDON TORONTO SYDNEY

ATHENEUM BOOKS FOR YOUNG READERS
An imprint of Simon & Schuster Children's Publishing Division
1230 Avenue of the Americas, New York, New York 10020
ATHENEUM BOOKS FOR YOUNG READERS is a registered trademark
of Simon & Schuster, Inc.
For information about special discounts for bulk purchases,
please contact Simon & Schuster Special Sales at 1-866-506-1949
or business@simonandschuster.com.
The Simon & Schuster Speakers Bureau can bring authors to your live event.
For more information or to book an event, contact the Simon & Schuster Speakers
Bureau at 1-866-248-3049 or visit our website at www.simonspeakers.com.
The text for this book is set in Stempel Garamond LT.
Manufactured in the United States of America
First Atheneum Books for Young Readers paperback edition August 2011
2 4 6 8 10 9 7 5 3 1
The Library of Congress has cataloged the hardcover edition as follows:
Library of Congress Cataloging-in-Publication Data
Creagh, Kelly.
Nevermore / Kelly Creagh.
p.   cm.
Summary: When cheerleader Isobel Lanley is assigned to work with
goth, Edgar Allan Poe fan Varen Nethers on an English project, she is
swept into a horrific dream world that he has created in his mind.
ISBN 978-1-4424-0200-3 (hardcover)
[1. Horror stories. 2. Poe, Edgar Allan, 1809–1849—Fiction.
3. High schools—Fiction. 4. Schools—Fiction.] I. Title.
PZ7.C85983Ne 2010
[Fic]—dc22 2009050033
ISBN 978-1-4424-0201-0 (pbk)
ISBN 978-1-4424-0203-4 (eBook)

For Mom, who always encouraged me to dream
(even when it weirded you out)

Contents

Prologue   1

1. Assigned   5

2. Marked   14

3. After Nine   21

4. Entitled   31

5. A Note of Warning   44

6. Things Unseen   53

7. Maelstrom   64

8. Ligeia   75

9. Intangible Forms   87

10. Spirits of the Dead   96

11. Whispered Word   112

12. The Invisible Visible   121

13. Watched   135

14. All That We See   142

15. The Power of Words   148

16. Ultima Thule   162

17. Dead Air   168

18. The Other Half   174

19. Visitations   181

20. Uninvited   190

21. Motley Drama   201

22. Cheer Up   209

23. Dearly Departed   219

24. The Woodlands of Weir   234

25. Seeing Double   250

26. Freak 252

27. The Green Man 270

28. Ulalume 284

29. Driven 298

30. Projected 304

31. In the Flesh 318

32. Pinfeathers 328

33. Just a Bird 342

34. Caught 356

35. Tell-Tale Heart 366

36. No Return 383

37. The Grim Facade 388

38. Out of Space, Out of Time 404

39. Much of Madness 412

40. In a Vision 426

41. Alone 437

42. A Vow 443

43. The Oblong Box 454

44. Red Death 470

45. A Door 476

46. Bedight in Veils 487

47. Surcease of Sorrow 503

48. Invisible Woe 516

49. Obscure and Lonely 525

50. From Out That Shadow 535

Epilogue 542

*   *   *

Deep into that darkness peering,
                   long I stood there wondering, fearing,
Doubting, dreaming dreams no mortal
                        ever dared to dream before.

—Edgar Allan Poe, "The Raven"

*   *   *

Prologue
October 1849

Edgar opened one eye to a slit.

The passenger car jostled, and there arose from beneath, one long metal-on-metal cry. The sound squealed above the clatter of tracks, then faded with the hot sooty belch of smokestack steam. It merged, at last, with the staticky whispers that had awoken him.

"Does he sleep?"

Edgar felt his muscles clench. He took pains to stay calm, to not move, to keep his breathing steady, measured.

It had been during the passage through the last tunnel, when the world had once again gone black, that he'd first become aware of their renewed presence. The demons. They had returned. Always they returned. To drag him from this world into the other.

A shudder ran through him. He let his eye slip shut.

"Watch him," rasped another voice. *"He will take the next train."*

Edgar's hand on the armrest twitched. The sweat of his fever now became the cold sweat of fear, and it beaded on his broad brow until he felt a trickle slide down his temple.

He could *not* go back with them. Not when he had come

so close to severing his link with their world—*her* world—
forever.

He heard the sharp slide of the compartment door and
stealthily hazarded to raise his eyelid once more.

A stout man in a snug uniform pushed into the compartment.

"Arriving in Baltimore," he announced, his voice a mellow
drone. Edgar knew the man would not—*could* not—perceive
his pursuers, their grotesque grins, their fiendish claws.

The man brushed past. Edgar seized his chance. He
stooped low, making use of the conductor's wide frame to
shield his movement as he slid from his seat. Instinctively, his
grip tightened on Dr. Carter's malacca cane, the one he had
taken such care to switch out for his own. The one within
which slumbered a sleek silver blade.

The wheels squealed again. Without warning, the train
lurched to a halt.

Edgar faltered, crying out. He caught himself, gripping
the sides of the door frame, and turned in time to see the
hollow black gazes of his pursuers lift and capture his.

He broke into a run.

They slunk after him, their furious whispers now like a
torrent of rushing leaves.

Edgar dashed through the next compartment and the
next. His pathway ahead narrowed with travelers gathering
their belongings, blind to the monsters that followed in his
wake. Someone shouted as he shoved through, nearly toppling another man to the floor.

He closed in upon the nearest exit and stumbled out, almost losing his hold on the doctor's cane as he staggered onto the platform. He grasped the silver handle, itching to draw forth the sword concealed within, even in the midst of such a dense crowd.

With a piercing hiss, the train released a clouded burst of steam. Edgar slipped into its enveloping cover and raised the hood of his cloak.

He watched the creatures emerge from the train, their forms loosening into miasmic coils of black. They spilled forth from the doorway, curling with the steam before re-forming once more into wholeness.

Tall, gaunt, and rakish, the demons convened for only a moment, then dispersed in search.

Edgar merged with the assembly of fellow travelers. He made his way through the sea of the oblivious, his sights narrowed on the train that could return him to Richmond. To the singular hope that waited for him there.

Reaching the second platform, he lingered, hesitated, his back turned to the crowd. Then, with the conductor's cry of "All aboard!" Edgar grabbed the railing and hoisted himself up.

"*There!*" he heard one of them growl.

He hurried into the compartment, glancing behind him once—once only, peering through the darkened windows. Yes, they followed, dogged him like hellhounds!

Not until the first chug of the steam engine fell upon his ears did he fling open the closest door and leap from the moving train back onto the platform. Staggering to his feet, he rushed headlong into the crowd while behind him the train, puffing hard, picked up speed, his pursuers still aboard.

He knew that they would not be fooled for long.

No matter. There were other means of reaching Richmond.

Edgar pushed through the throng and found his way to the busy street, where he hailed a carriage.

"To the harbor," he called, and rapped the cane upon the rear wall as he shut the door behind him.

The carriage jerked, tottered, then rolled into action.

Edgar fell back within the coach, allowing himself a deep breath. He braced a quavering hand at his heated brow, where, behind his right eye, a dull ache began to throb.

The carriage swayed as it ambled through the narrow streets, and soon the pain in his head was replaced by a queer yet familiar tingling. It crept upon him, pervading his senses like the dull, faint prickle of a limb gone numb.

Slowly Edgar lowered his hand.

He turned his gaze to the shifting shadows at his right.

She sat beside him, her slight form draped in luminous white gossamer.

"*No,*" he murmured.

But the enveloping blackness had already begun to take its hold.

It wrapped him like a sheet, and as her hand, cold as marble, grasped his, he felt the pitch overtake him as it never had before.

In an instant, the blackness devoured him, leaving the coach vacant.

1
Assigned

By the end of fourth period, Isobel's espresso buzz from that morning's venti latte had long since worn off. She yawned, fast approaching crash-and-burn territory and shifted in her seat as Mr. Swanson droned on and on about the green-eyed monster, Desdemona, thus, thou, and yea verily. She traced and retraced the looping spiral design she'd all but ground into the front of her blue notebook.

"And with that," Mr. Swanson said, finally snapping closed his ultrathick teacher's copy of their text, cueing the rest of the class to follow suit with a unanimous *thunk*, "we'll leap into further discussion about Iago and his supposed honesty on Monday."

Isobel straightened in her seat, brushed her sheet of blond hair behind one shoulder, and shut her own book with relish.

"But hold on, hold on," he said above the rustling and scraping of chairs. He raised both hands and lowered them through the air, as if such a motion somehow held the power to still the room and reinstate the Elizabethan-literature-inspired stupor he'd managed to cast over all.

Kids jonesing for lunch and already halfway out of their seats sank back down again, their butts reconnecting with their chairs like magnets snapping together. All around, back-packs slipped from shoulders and chins returned to hands.

They should have known better, Isobel thought wryly. Swanson never let them out early. Never. *Especially* not as early as a quarter till.

"Don't go and get antsy on me yet, folks," he warned, now brandishing a stack of what looked suspiciously to Isobel like fresh-from-the-copier pages.

"Heads-up to the syllabus being passed around," he called, licking a finger and leafing through the first few. Then, rewetting his fingertips, he sent out the next stack, and the next.

Isobel blanched as she watched the papers make their way toward her, and she hoped she'd be lucky enough to snag one relatively free of Swanson saliva.

"We've avoided it long enough." He sighed in mock remorse. "Now, I'm sure the seniors all warned you about this one. Well, here it is. The big one. Better to get it over with early in the year, I say. You guessed it—the Swanson project." He announced this last bit cheerfully (if not maniacally), and a grin spread its way beneath his wiry gray-white mustache.

Groans arose from key points around the room, Isobel's own buried in the back of her throat.

Projects took time. A *lot* of time.

"This is to be a partner project," Swanson continued, "due the last Friday of the month. That's Halloween, for those of you who haven't got your iPhones or BlackBerries or Kicksides or whodiwhat calendars handy—which I hope for their sake no one does."

The boredom that had only a moment ago made Isobel's limbs heavy and her mind sluggish slipped away from her in a quick *whoosh*, like a magician's cloth.

Hold up. Did he say Halloween? Uh, yeah, where was *his* calendar? Did he not know that was the night of the rival football game against Millings? Lift up the rock, Swanson. Breathe. It's called air.

Isobel's grip tightened around her pen. She kept her gaze steady on her English teacher, all dials now tuned to the Swanson channel.

"This project," he said, "will consist of both a presentation and a detailed ten-page paper. I want you and your partner to select a famous American author—any American author. Though, in the spirit of Halloween, let's make sure they're dead, okay? In other words, no Stephen Kings, Heather Grahams, or James Pattersons. Also, this is an assignment to be completed outside of class, since we're currently in the middle of *Othello*."

Ten pages? Ten pages. That was epic. That was like . . . the freaking Gettysburg Address. Was Swanson really going to sit down and read all those papers?

Probably, she thought. And love every minute of it too.

She just didn't get it. Why did Swanson have to assign a huge project due on the day of the rival game? No one ever got any work done that week. He could have at least given them that weekend.

It always amazed her how teachers seemed to think that students didn't have lives outside of school. They couldn't

seem to grasp that by the time she got home from cheer practice, ate dinner, and scribbled down something on the mound
of homework she already had, it was practically time to go
to bed.

Isobel started an immediate scan of the room. This was
serious, and she needed to locate a brainer—stat.

She eyed Julie Tamers, marching band geek extraordi-
naire, and began to plan a strategic route to the open chair
next to hers when Mr. Swanson spoke again.

"FYI," he began, class roster poised in one hand, chin
tilted down, wire-rim glasses perched at the tip of his nose,
"I'm trying something different this year in hopes it will
both broaden your perspective and improve overall project
results. That said, I'll take a moment to include my little dis-
claimer that all pairings have been made at random. So after I
read your names off the list you can partner up, brainstorm
among yourselves, and then head to lunch. Starting with Josh
Anderson and Amber Ricks."

Isobel felt her jaw unhinge.

Wait, she thought. *Just wait.* Random pairings were so
third grade. He could *not* be serious.

"Katlyn Binkly and Alanna Sato," he continued. "Next
we have Todd Marks and Romelle Jenkins."

Around her, those whose names had already been called
rose from their seats to find their corresponding partners.
Isobel sat stunned at their willingness. For real? Was she the
only one who felt the burn of injustice? Wasn't anyone else
going to say anything?

"Isobel Lanley and Varen Nethers."

She felt her chest contract.

Oh.

Oh, no. No way.

She turned her head slowly and took a long, reluctant look to the opposite end of the room. He sat in the back row against the far corner, slumped in his seat and staring straight ahead through shreds of inky locks, his thin wrists lined in black leather bands specked with hostile silver studs.

This could *not* be happening.

Her hunger forgotten, a gnawing discomfort tugged at her insides instead as she wondered how many of the freaky rumors about him were true. For a moment she seriously thought about requesting another partner, but knowing Swanson, she realized that would probably fly about as fast and well as cafeteria meat loaf.

Isobel frowned and bit her lip. Maybe, just maybe, it wasn't going to be as bad as all that. Another glance at him, though, had her thinking otherwise.

Lost in the curtain of his dyed black hair, he hadn't even acknowledged her presence, let alone the fact that—*hello*— they were supposed to be using the time to discuss this monstrosity of a project.

She wondered if she should get up and go to him, since it didn't seem like he would be heading in her direction anytime soon.

Resigned, Isobel rose and collected her notebook. She fumbled for her backpack strap as her mind repeated all the whispers she'd ever heard linked with his name. There were rumors that he sometimes talked to himself, that he practiced witchcraft and had an evil eye tattooed on his left shoulder blade. That he lived in the basement of an abandoned church. That he slept in a coffin.

That he drank blood.

She approached him with steady steps, the way someone might inch up to a sleeping snake.

Slouched in his seat, one arm draped over the desktop, he was one long line of black, his well-worn, tightly strapped boots crossed at the ankles. Pinned beneath his arm dwelled the ratty black hardback book she'd seen him disappear into more than once during class.

In fact, it always seemed as though he was jotting or sketching *something* into its pages, though she could only guess at what. And maybe part of what made that whole thing so weird was that Swanson never called him on it, just like he never asked him to read out loud or answer questions. And that was weird too, because no one ever called Swanson out on *that*.

Isobel drifted to stand at a solid and safe four-foot distance. She waited, shifting her weight from one foot to the other. What was she supposed to say? Howdy, partner?

She glanced to the clock on the wall. Seven minutes left until lunch.

Aaawwkward, she thought as he continued to just sit there and stare off like she didn't exist. His enthusiasm was *almost* catching.

"Look, I'm not doing the work all by myself," she said at last, deciding to crack the rather thick ice with that little mallet of for-your-info.

He didn't move, but he spoke.

"Did I say that?"

Isobel felt a sting of surprise at the sound of his voice. It was as if she'd half expected him to be made of wax. His voice was calm and low and reasonable, not troubled and gruff like she'd assumed. He'd never spoken in class before, though. Ever, that she could remember.

"No," she said, stiffening, tempted to just bail. Nikki would never believe this, she thought. Her getting paired up with the king of goths? Talk about breaking news. "I just thought I'd let you know," she said, clearing her throat. "I mean . . . because, actually, you're not *saying* anything."

Feeling dumb for being the last person in the room standing, Isobel finally slid into the seat next to his, her gaze darting over the room.

A low murmur started among the pockets of groups, growing in volume as everyone went about exchanging ideas. After swapping scribbled sheets of notepaper, two groups even got up and left. And here she was, still stuck trying to commune with a member of the living dead.

Her jaw tightened. She was starting to think that Mr. Swanson's claim that all pairings had been made "at random" was a bunch of bull. This was probably his idea of a great joke, his way of getting back at her for not turning in that stupid paper on *Don Quixote*.

"As long as we're getting things out on the table, so to speak," he said, calling her attention back to their little space in the corner—it was so weird to hear him talk. "I'm not doing it on my own either."

He turned his head and caught her with his eyes.

She froze, locked by the intensity of his stare. His eyes were stark and cold, the concentrated green of pale jade. Outlined in smudged black kohl, those eyes focused on her, unblinking through the feathery strands of his jet-black hair, and it was like being watched through a cage by a complacent and calculating cat.

Discomfort welled in her, thick and black as an oil spring.

Who was this guy and what was his royal problem? Her gaze flicked briefly to the small metal loop that hugged one corner of his bottom lip.

He blinked once, then slowly lifted one hand and crooked a beckoning finger at her.

Isobel hesitated but then as though spellbound to obey, she found herself leaning in.

"What are you staring at?" he whispered.

She drew back, her face going hot. She swiveled away from him and put her hand in the air. *Mayday, Swanson. Do you read me?*

There came a slow, ominous clink of chains from behind her. Isobel went rigid. She lowered her hand and, looking up, found him towering over her, all tall straightness and stone pale.

She bit back a protest as he took her hand in his. She gawked as one long-fingered hand grasped hers and stared, unblinking, at the black pen that appeared from nowhere and began moving against her skin, the tip as cold and sharp as those eyes.

Oh. My. God. He was writing on her.

She tried to make a noise but couldn't.

His face remained emotionless as he made small, careful lines with the pen. The steady impression of the ballpoint tickled, creating knots in her stomach.

All she could do was stare at an enormous ring, molded into the shape of a silver dragon, as it snarled at her from his middle finger.

When at last he finished, he released her hand and, with one final almost admonishing stab of that razor gaze, turned away. Grabbing his black book, he slung his beaten leather satchel over one shoulder. "Don't call after nine," he said, and tucking the pen behind one ear, strolled out of the classroom.

Isobel's face burned. Her skin tingled where he'd touched her, with an almost imperceptible electricity that she couldn't be sure if she was imagining. Like the tips of her fingers had somehow fallen asleep.

She took a quick inventory, first of her senses, then of the people still in the room, afraid to see who had noticed, amazed that apparently no one had. Even Eagle Eye Swanson had just returned to his desk, where he now sat munching a sandwich and leafing through the school paper, the *Hawk's Call*.

Isobel looked down at her hand again.

In deep purple ink, he'd written "V — 555-0710."

2
Marked

"So are you going to tell Brad?" Nikki asked, an all-too-eager gleam in her pretty sapphire eyes.

Isobel dialed her combination, then kicked the dented bottom corner of her locker. The door popped open, sending her makeup bag toppling out to hit the floor with a muffled crack, contents spilling.

"*No,*" she muttered, and squatted to recover her eye shadow, the bronze cake of color inside having split apart into crumbles. She growl-sighed, shoving it all back into the pouch, yet again catching sight of the slanted, dark purple numbers that glared like an insignia against her skin.

"Why not?"

"Because," Isobel said, "I think Mr. Swanson likes the guy, and anyway, I have to pull off a good grade because of that paper I didn't do."

Isobel rose to stuff the pouch back into her locker when Nikki halted her, grabbing her by the wrist, shaking her own hand at her. "Izzy," she said, "look at this! He *wrote* on you. Like he was marking you as his next victim or something."

Isobel pulled her hand away. "Okay!" she said, tucking a stray strand of hair behind one ear. "We've already established that he's a weirdo. So let's just leave it at that. Brad doesn't need to know."

She jumped, cutting off Nikki's prepared retort, startled by a mysterious hand that, with a clink of bracelets, appeared from around the side of her open locker door. The hand held Isobel's runaway tube of Raspberry Ice lip gloss between a set of long fingers.

Isobel took the gloss and tossed it into her locker, about to mutter a quick thanks, when Nikki interrupted, snatching her wrist again.

"I mean, look at this!" she said, bringing Isobel's hand to her nose, scrutinizing the numbers as though they spelled some hidden message. "It probably means you've made his death list or something. I mean, the guy is a total Trench Coat Mafia wacko."

Isobel detached her wrist from Nikki's grasp once more and leveled a mordant stare at her friend. "Nikki, are you kidding me? It's a phone number."

"Yeah, I know. That's what I'm saying. You got hit on by Lurch, and now he's going to leave dead animals on your porch and cyber-stalk your Facebook page."

"It isn't like that." Isobel sighed again. "We just got stuck together for this . . . thing."

She stared into her open locker as she changed out her books.

To her, the presence of Varen Nethers, aka "that one guy," had always been like that of a fleeting shadow, an estranged entity that floated through the halls, never wanting to be bothered. In all truth, he'd probably crossed her mind no more than a handful of times and even then, only when someone chose to dredge up the latest crazy goth-centric gossip. She'd never had a class with him until this year, and Trenton was a big enough school that her day-to-day interaction with him had, before now, never amounted to more than the occasional hallway pass-by.

Isobel jumped again, shaken from her reverie, her breath catching when the mystery hand reappeared. This time it looped over the top of her locker door, the fingers clutching a familiar pistachio-green cylinder.

Cautiously Isobel took the tube of Pink Goddess lipstick and watched the hand of her locker neighbor slither away once more. She glanced at Nikki, who made a show of blinking before grasping Isobel's locker door and moving it aside. But the girl—Isobel thought her name was Grace or Gabbie—slammed her own locker shut, swiveled away without a word, and walked off.

"Creepers," Nikki muttered. She plucked the lipstick from Isobel's hand and, repositioning the locker door, stooped to use the mirror inside. "Back into the Middle Ages she goes."

Isobel watched the retreating back of the girl, whose too long, too straight brown hair swished in time with her floor-length broom skirt. With a final faint tinkle of bracelets, the girl swept around the next corner and out of sight.

"Anyway," Nikki said, finishing with the lipstick and tucking the tube back into Isobel's makeup bag. She blotted her lips and popped her mouth. "I still think you should tell Brad."

"Drop it, Nikki. I'm not going to *tell Brad*," Isobel snapped. "And don't *you* tell him either," she added, slamming her locker door shut. At this, Nikki's expression morphed, fading at once from scandalized coyness into wounded annoyance, and Isobel had only half a beat to regret her words before her friend twirled away.

"Nikki," Isobel moaned, starting after her.

"Whatever," Nikki shot over her shoulder. She fluttered one hand dismissively and quickened her pace. "You know," she called, "he's going to keep that stalker crap up if he thinks he can get away with it."

Watching the bounce of Nikki's ponytail, with its tiny blue and gold puff-ball hair tie, Isobel felt a tug of guilt. So maybe she'd been a little too insistent on keeping the whole phone number incident a secret. Then again, if she caught up to her, if she apologized now, Nikki might think it wouldn't be such a big deal if she *did* blab to Brad.

Isobel found herself hating that she'd told Nikki the truth when she should have just made something up. Of course, she hadn't wanted to play secrets, either. Nikki was her best friend. She was on the squad and part of the crew.

She slowed her steps and let Nikki walk ahead of her to lunch. When she was out of sight, Isobel ducked into the nearest girls' restroom. At the sink, she turned the water on warm and pumped soap from the dispenser into her hand. She lathered it thick over the numbers.

Like curls of smoke, the deep purple ink loosened into violet swirls and then slid down the drain.

*   *   *

At practice that day, she missed a jump.

She *never* missed a jump.

At the end of a round-off, back handspring, back tuck, she overrotated and had to catch herself on her heels. She hit the gymnasium floor hard, landing straight on her butt, bones jarring, teeth rattling.

Coach Anne ripped her for it, of course, blowing the dust off her old "no tumbling without someone spotting you" rant. Nothing made Coach more nervous than sloppy or botched stunts, especially with December Nationals looming. Their choreography was tight and sharp. Too tight and too clean to sit a hurt squad member in the stands and still expect to place.

Not surprisingly, Nikki didn't wait around to chat after Coach blew the final whistle. Isobel found she didn't mind too much, knowing that it was probably less about her still being peeved from earlier and more about wanting to catch up to Mark after football practice. Either way, she was grateful not to have to relive the locker argument and even more grateful that it was Friday. She needed a break.

It was good that they didn't have a game for another week, too. It would give the already purpling baseball-size bruise on the back of her thigh time to fade before she had to don her uniform again.

Isobel left the gym locker rooms and took her usual route through the hall toward the back parking lot, but slowed when she thought she heard Brad's voice. Had he come looking for her? She'd probably spent too long glaring at her bruised thigh in the locker room mirrors.

" —talk to her again. Do you understand?"

Turning the corner, Isobel halted.

A black-clad figure stood in a slump, his back pressed against a row of cobalt blue lockers, his tattered black hardback journal tucked beneath one arm. Brad hovered over him, wearing his blue and gold letter jacket, which bulked up his already hulking shoulders.

Varen, comparatively thin and frail-looking, appeared able to do little more than endure, his head hanging, his wispy black hair draped in his face.

An anger she couldn't explain flashed inside of her.

"Hey!" she called, closing in on them.

Varen's eyes lifted, locking on her, a look as stark as it was accusing, and it stopped her cold.

So help her, Isobel wanted to strangle Nikki till those stupid little blue and gold puff-balls popped off.

"What's going on?"

"Nothin', babe. Nothin'," Brad said, pushing away from the lockers, running a palm through his thick amber hair, glossy in the fluorescent lighting and still wet from the showers. He stuffed a hand into the pocket of his jacket and walked to meet her, slinging his other arm around her shoulders and planting a kiss on the side of her head with an audible *"Mmwah."*

Varen's expression remained blank, though his gaze chiseled into her, causing the world around her to smudge into oblivion, and she found herself unable to break away.

Did he think she ran off to tell Brad? Then again, what else was there for him to think?

Isobel opened her mouth to speak again, to set the record straight, but Brad's arm tightened around her shoulders, jostling her against him. This, combined with his deodorant and Zest soap smell, reminded her that he was there. Still in macho mode and still in reach of the strange boy who had asked her what she was staring at and who was now, intently, staring at her.

Isobel closed her mouth.

She let Brad angle her away. He dropped his arm to pat her tender rear.

"Don't," she said, wincing, but kept moving.

Anything to get away from those eyes.

3
After Nine

"You want to meet the crew at Zot's?" Brad asked as he pulled out of the school parking lot, joining the flow of traffic.

"I'm supposed to eat with my parents tonight," Isobel lied, shifting in her seat to stare out the passenger-side window. She knew she was doing the girl thing, the full-on "you should know why I'm mad" tactic straight out of the Petty Playbook, but she didn't care.

"Going to invite me?" he asked, not bothering to put on his turn signal when they reached the light.

"No."

"Oh," he said, "okay."

That was it. She jerked around in her seat to face him. "What did Nikki tell you?" she demanded, deciding to forgo the whole dance-around chitchat thing and cut to the chase.

"Nikki didn't say a thing," he said, making the turn. He reached up to pull down his sun visor, and a pack of Camels fell into his lap. Isobel sneered and turned to look back out her window. She hated when he smoked, and lately it had become more than just an after-school fix.

"Mark told me," he said.

Of course, she thought. It all made sense now. After lunch, Nikki, two shades short of bursting, must have told Mark, who, being Brad's best friend, must have then blabbed to Brad sometime before football practice. Just like preschool. Connect the dots.

"Listen," Isobel said, "we're paired to do a stupid project, that's all. He doesn't want to work with me, either, so just leave him alone."

"So he wrote his number on your hand?" Brad asked, his expression darkening. He took another turn, this one too sharply. Isobel gripped her seat. One of his hands left the wheel to slide a Camel from its pack.

"Never mind. Just take me home."

"Would you just chill out?" he growled. Finding his Zippo between the seats, he flipped open the metal lighter and held the flame to the cigarette. "All I told him was not to talk to you," he mumbled, the cigarette bobbing between his tightened lips. He snapped the Zippo shut and tossed it into the backseat, taking a long draw from the cigarette before returning both hands to the wheel.

Isobel hit the power button to crack her window.

"What?" he asked, an amused smile playing at his lips. "Excuse me if I don't like makeup-wearing fags writing on my girlfriend."

Isobel glared at him. He only shrugged again, like that excused him or something. She folded her arms and stared straight ahead, deciding it was best to give him the silent treatment, though her plan semi-backfired when he didn't say anything else. He only smiled away like he thought she was being cute.

After pulling into her driveway, Brad got out, like he always did, to get the car door for her. This time, though, Isobel threw open the door for herself. She slammed it shut behind her, the bang echoing through her neighborhood.

"Hey!" he said, arms spread. "What gives?"

She ignored him and marched up the brick sidewalk without a word.

"Izo!" he called. "Babe!"

It was the amusement, the underlying laughter in his voice that made her anger swell. Isobel stalked to her front door, refusing to let him cajole her into admitting that she was overreacting.

"All right. Fine," he called after her. "Then I guess I'll just leave your stuff on the porch?"

She paused on the front stoop of her house, then turned back to see Brad standing at the rear of his Mustang, trunk open, her gym bag hanging by its strap from one outstretched hand.

She was annoyed at herself for not thinking and annoyed at him for that big, churlish movie-star grin on his face. Abandoning the walkway, she stomped through the yard and jerked the bag from his grasp.

"Ooh," he said with a wink.

"Brad," she snapped, "you didn't have to do that."

"Aw, c'mon, Iz, I just talked to him. You heard what I said."

"I heard you threaten him!"

"I didn't threaten him." He laughed again, shaking his head like he thought she needed glasses or a hearing aid, or a head check.

"Good-bye," she said, and trudged once more for her front door.

"Okay, baby." He sighed. "Love you, too."

Isobel forced her lips to pinch together. As much as she wanted, she would not return the sentiment. She knew he was only probing for a response, trying to wriggle his way off the hook.

"All right," he called. "Tell Paps I said what's up."

Isobel flung open the screen door and stalked inside her house.

He yelled after her, "Change your mind, you'll know where we'll be."

She shut the door behind her and dropped her bag in the foyer. She stood motionless as she heard the slam of Brad's trunk, followed by the clap of the driver's-side door. She turned, ready to push her way back outside, to catch him before he left, but his engine revved, and he took off, music blasting, tires squealing.

"I don't understand what you see in this game," she mumbled, chewing on the crust of her last slice of pizza. Her parents had gone out for the night, leaving her alone with Danny, whose entire twelve-year-old existence revolved around his collection of video games, consoles, and online RPG empires.

"It's the same thing over and over, only with a background change."

"No, it's not," Danny said, and waggled the controller to the right, as if that would make the armor-clad figure on the screen jump farther.

Isobel narrowed her gaze on the back of Danny's school uniform pants, at his crack poking out just above the belt. She couldn't believe that he hadn't even bothered to change when he'd gotten home. Instead, like always, he'd plunked himself in front of the TV. "What's the difference, then?" she asked, only mild interest backing the question.

"Each level gets harder," he explained, leaning to his left while trying to get the figure on the screen to do the same. "Duh. And eventually you have to face Zorthibus Klax."

Isobel glanced down at her hand, at the pale purple lines that had somehow, very faintly, remained. "Sounds like some foul disease."

"Your *face* is a foul disease. Now shut up so I can concentrate."

Isobel rolled her eyes. She leaned her head against her hand, her elbow resting on the arm of the sofa, and eyed her metallic pink cell phone, which she'd set on the end table next to the TV remote. It sat there silent and still beneath the glow of the beige, fat-bellied lamp. She'd brought it down from her room after letting it charge just in case Nikki, the traitor, sent her a text.

Or in case Brad called.

She couldn't get it out of her mind, though. The way

Varen had looked at her in the hall. He probably thought she'd told Brad everything, just to get back at him. He must have thought she'd run right to him and told him what happened, showed him her hand and said, "Go get him!"

Absently Isobel ran her fingers across the back of her hand, over the place he'd written on her. If she concentrated, she could still feel the sensation of the pen, the weight of his hand, the sharpness of the ballpoint.

Hunkering down into the couch cushions, she hooked a thumb in her T-shirt, biting the collar, unnerved all over again by the memory.

Were they even still on for the project?

Her eyes fell to her phone and lingered there.

Finally she stood. "Don't burn down the house," she snapped at Danny, grabbing her cell.

She flipped open the phone as she wandered into the kitchen and scrutinized the digits on her hand—or rather, what remained of them. Was that last one a zero or a nine? She decided to guess, pressing the corresponding keys.

The phone rang on the other end. And rang . . . and rang.

"Hello?" a woman's light, sweet voice answered. This must be his mom, Isobel thought, admitting to herself that she'd half expected a gravelly tone and a chain smoker's cough.

"Uh, yes. May I speak to—" She glanced up, catching sight of the digital clock on the stove. Nine thirty. She gasped.

"Hello?" the voice asked.

"Oh, I— Sorry," Isobel sputtered, remembering what he'd said about calling after nine.

Automatically her thumb jabbed the end button. The phone went dead. For a moment she held the cell limp in her hand, staring at it. It was kind of a strange thing to say, now that she thought about it: *Don't call after nine.* What did he mean, *Don't call after nine*? What happened at nine? Was that when he retired to his tomb? Was it some bogus rule of his parents or his own thing? Why was he so *weird*?

Isobel wandered back into the living room, only to find Danny right where she'd left him, the TV screen flashing in bold biohazard orange while a high-pitched voice cackled evil victory in the background.

"Man!" He moaned, and threw the controller against the entertainment center.

"Hey!" Isobel shouted. "Watch it!"

He ignored her, collecting the controller again, like he wanted to make up with it. Isobel settled back onto the couch and watched as he restarted the game.

"Can't we watch TV or something?" she said with a sigh.

"*Nooooo!*" He groaned.

"Danny, you've been playing that thing nonstop." She reached for the TV remote.

"Don't!" He swung around and lunged at her, grasping for the remote. Isobel dropped her phone to grapple with both hands.

"For real, Danny, don't you have homework or friends or something?" She grunted, pulling the remote.

"Don't you?" he snarled, yanking it back.

Her phone rang. Danny let go of the remote and snatched up her cell. "Hello?"

Isobel grabbed for her phone, but Danny, with faster reflexes than she'd thought him capable of, slid out of her reach.

"Yeah, sure," he said, "hold on." Smiling, he waggled the phone. "It's your boyfriend!"

Isobel clambered off the couch and charged her brother, ready for battle. No one messed with her phone calls.

"Trade," he said, skittering back, holding the phone out behind him.

"Ugh. You're such a fungus!" She threw the remote down on the carpet. He tossed the phone at her and dove for the remote. The phone bounced between her hands before she caught it, and the video game music started up again.

She pressed the cell to her ear, blocking her other ear with one finger.

"Brad?"

"Not likely," said the cool voice on the other end.

A thunder started in her chest.

"How did you get my number?"

"Relax." His tone went from cold to glacial. "My folks have caller ID. You called *me*."

"Oh," she said, cringing. *Oh?* She glanced quickly at her brother, then slipped out of the room and out of earshot. "Well, listen," she said, groping for what she'd originally planned to say. "I just wanted you to know that I didn't tell Brad about the number thing."

"I wasn't hitting on you," he said, as if he were the one setting *her* straight. "If nothing else, you're not my type."

Her mouth fell open.

"Uh, *yeah*," she said, trying to ignore the heat that crawled its way up her neck. She felt like throwing the phone against the wall and curling up to die all at the same time. Who did this guy think he was? "I never said I thought you were—"

"Well, someone felt threatened."

"Look, I talked to him about it," she said, the words coming out quick and jerky. She hated sounding so spastic, especially when he seemed so unconcerned. "He just gets like that."

"Well, I guess it doesn't matter as long as he has you to make excuses for him."

Now he was making her mad. "You know what—" But he didn't let her finish.

"If you're not bailing on the project, I'll be at the main library tomorrow," he said, his voice hushed. She could hear a crackle on the other end, like he was moving around. "After one."

"But it's Saturday."

"*Christ,*" he hissed, "you've got to be kidding me."

Isobel started to say fine, whatever, she'd meet him. She paused, though, at the sound of someone calling for him in the background—a man. "Never mind," he snapped, "I'll do it myself." The line went dead.

Isobel bit down on the insides of her mouth hard. She drew the phone away from her ear and squeezed it. She wanted to scream. She wanted to smash the phone to pieces or cram it into the disposal.

"Turn it down," she yelled to Danny as she stormed through the living room. "I'm going to bed!"

"I can't hear you," he shot over one shoulder.

She mounted the stairs, her steps pounding hard enough to skew the picture frames.

What exactly *was* his type, anyway? Bride of freaking Frankenstein?

4
Entitled

Isobel checked her cell for missed calls first thing the next morning.

None.

Texts? None.

Apparently, the usual crew antics had all transpired without her and, perhaps worse, they had all gone on without a single "Hey, where are you?" or "How come you didn't show?" Nope. No Brad, no Mark. Not a single call from her squad—no Nikki, Alyssa, or even Stevie, who was usually the peacekeeper in their group.

Haters. All of them.

She set her phone aside, deciding to forget about the diss, but after taking a shower and downing a granola bar, she gave in to the itch to call someone. Still not ready to talk to Brad, she dialed Nikki instead.

Nikki's familiar ringer buzzed in Isobel's right ear, a bad pop song about some player sweating some chick. Isobel sat back against her headboard, listening as she stretched out. The song went on, and she rolled onto her stomach, facing her pillow. She grabbed the Magic 8 Ball off the bottom cubbyhole. Shaking it, she peered into the black circular window.

Will Nikki answer her phone?

The little triangle bobbed to the surface through the murk, bearing one of its cryptic one-size-fits-all messages. "Ask again later," it read. Isobel snorted. She was just about to hang up when the song stopped mid-chorus and Nikki's voice broke through, chipper and bright.

"Izzy!"

Isobel sat up, letting the Magic 8 Ball roll aside. "You're such a snitch. Did you know that?"

"Hey, where were you last night?" Nikki asked, her voice staying breezy. "Stevie finally beat Mark's score on Fighter Borg X."

"Nikki, I told you not to say anything about yesterday. Brad totally freaked out, and we had a fight."

Quiet fizz filtered through from the other side and Isobel waited, picturing Nikki in deep thought mode. No doubt she was using the dead air time to Photoshop, airbrush, and gloss-coat a good response.

"No," she said at last, "you told me not to tell Brad. And I didn't."

"So you did the next best thing and told Mark. Why?"

"Why not? What is *with* you, anyway? Brad said that all he did was talk to the guy and that you were the one who freaked out."

"Nikki, no one would have freaked out in the first place if you hadn't said anything!"

"Whatever," Nikki said. "Listen, we're going out for Chinese at Double Trouble. Brad's coming too." Nikki's voice adopted goocy sweetness as she said, "I'm sure if you *caaaaalllled* him, he'd swing by and pick you *uuuuppp*."

"I can't."

"Why not?"

"I have to . . . I have a dentist appointment." The lie was out before she could stop it.

"Eeww. Bummer," said Nikki after a beat, though Isobel could hear in her voice that she didn't buy it. No, Nikki knew her better than that, and Isobel knew that they both knew that it all boiled down to her keeping the holdout on Brad.

Of course, there was that little thing about not being able to tell Nikki that she'd made other plans. Or, more important, who she'd made them with. Even though she hadn't *really* made them per se.

Isobel shook her head, her brow creasing. This felt weird, lying to her friends, sneaking around over some stupid project.

"Oh, well," Nikki said, breaking the awkward silence.

Isobel frowned at the rumpled folds of her pink comforter. Since when had they ever had an awkward silence?

"Anyway," Nikki went on, "If you get out early or something, give me a ring on my cell."

Translation: *Call me if you change your mind or whenever you decide to stop sulking.*

"Okay, later," Isobel mumbled.

"Later."

There was a pause, like neither of them really wanted to end the call.

"Bye," Nikki said.

"Bye," replied Isobel, trying to sound more cheerful than she felt.

She waited, but this time, Nikki hung up.

That afternoon Isobel got a ride to the library from her dad. He dropped her off by the side entrance, near the old solemn-faced statue of Abraham Lincoln, saying he'd be back to pick her up some time around three, after his haircut appointment.

Isobel hurried up the stairs and barely waved good-bye to her dad before heading inside to begin her search for Varen. After spending nearly fifteen minutes scouring through the stacks and checking the study rooms, she finally found him on the second floor.

It was obvious he'd purposely picked a spot well out of sight, sequestered away in a far-off corner just beyond the 800s. Feeling more than just a little agitated by this, Isobel made a point of dropping her purse on the table right in front of where he sat reading, lost in the open spread of some gigantic tome.

He glanced up with his eyes only, glaring at her past the ridge of his leveled brow. A soft glint from the desk lamps ran liquid smooth down the curve of his lip ring.

She twiddled her fingers at him in a wave. *Ha*, the gesture seemed to say, *found you.*

He stared at her as she lowered herself into the cushiony swivel seat across from his, and in turn, she eyed the enormous tome he'd been absorbed in.

"So." She cleared her throat. "What are we doing?"

He did the prolonged silence thing again, like he needed the time to contemplate whether or not to banish her from his sight.

"We," he said at last, "are doing our project on Poe."

He shifted the huge book around and scooted it toward her, one finger indicating a black-and-white thumbnail photograph. The image portrayed was of a gaunt, deep-browed man with unruly hair and a small black-comb mustache. His eyes looked sad, desperate, and wild all at the same time. Sunken and pooled by enormous dark circles, they seemed to ache with sorrow.

To Isobel, he looked like a nicely dressed mental patient in need of a nap.

She sank farther into her chair, picking at the pages. "Didn't he marry his cousin or something?"

"The man is a literary god and that's all you have to say?"

She shrugged and grabbed a book from the stack on the table. She opened it, then flipped through the pages, glancing up at him. He leaned forward over the table and scribbled something onto a yellow steno notepad, which sat atop his black hardbound book. Her eyes fell to the book. She couldn't help wondering if it was some sort of journal or something and why he seemed to carry it with him wherever he went.

"Who's Lenore?" she asked, turning another page.

He stopped writing, looked up. Stared.

What? Had she said something wrong?

"His dead love," he replied finally.

"Poe's?"

"The narrator's."

"Oh," she said, wondering if there was a difference but knowing better than to ask.

She crossed her legs and adjusted herself in her seat. "So, how are we going to do the presentation part? Do I get stuck playing the dead chick?"

It was supposed to be a joke, something to help smooth down his prickly defense.

"You could never be Lenore," he said, returning to his scrawling.

At this, Isobel scoffed outright, trying to decide if she'd been insulted. "Yeah? Why not?"

"For one," he said, jotting along, "you're not dead."

"Oh," she replied, "so *you're* going to be Lenore, then?"

He looked up. Isobel smiled, swaying back and forth in her swivel seat.

His pen made a point of disconnecting with the paper, and there was another pause, followed by a slow blink before he said, "You do the talking for the presentation, I'll write the paper." He pulled off the top sheet from the steno pad and slid it in front of her.

Isobel picked up the paper. Leaning back in her chair, she watched him over the frayed top edge as he bent to extract a dark purple folder from his bag.

"Write these down," he said, setting the folder aside and returning his attention to the book with the thumbnail.

Isobel pulled her purse onto her lap, rustling around in the front flap until she found a pen.

"'The Fall of the House of Usher,'" he said, and Isobel started writing on the sheet of steno paper, right under where he'd already written "Major Works."

"'The Masque of the Red Death.' That's 'Masque' with a *q*," he said, and Isobel had to hurry up and write the word "Usher," only she ended up dropping the *e* and adding an extra *r* so that it slurred into "Ushrr."

"'The Murders' — "

"Hold on!" she said, her pen flying.

He waited.

"All right," she said, finishing up the *th* at the end of "Death." She crinkled her nose at the word. Why did it feel like she was inscribing someone's epitaph?

"'The Murders in the Rue Morgue,'" he continued.

"This guy had some major issues," Isobel murmured toward the paper, and shook her head as she wrote.

"'That's how most people choose to see it," he said. "Next is 'The Raven.'"

Isobel stopped writing. Lifting her pen from the paper, she looked up. "Well, how do you choose to see it?"

His eyes flashed up from the open book to stare at her again, a toned-down version of his death-ray glare.

"It's a legitimate question," she said. "And it totally has to do with the project." She gave a small, sly smile, but he didn't smile back. Isobel knew he wasn't exactly the Ronald McDonald type, but she wished he would lighten up. *Sheesh.*

"Maybe he just knew something the rest of us don't," he

said. He opened the purple folder, and his eyes shifted to the syllabus tucked inside.

"Like what?" she asked, genuinely curious.

For a long moment, he didn't say anything, and Isobel picked her pen up again, figuring he was ignoring her so she'd get back to work. Her hand poised and at the ready, she waited for the next gruesome title.

"I don't know," he said instead, surprising her.

She watched him thoughtfully as he stared down into the open book, like he hoped to fall in, the ends of his feathery black hair nearly brushing the words. There was something odd about the way he'd just spoken. Sort of like, maybe he *did* know, or at least had an idea.

"How did he die?" she asked.

"Nobody knows."

It was her turn to give the slow, patient blink.

Seeming to note her skepticism, he drew in a long breath before continuing. "He was found semiconscious, lying in a gutter in Baltimore. Somebody brought him into a nearby tavern—or some people say that they actually found him in the tavern."

Isobel listened, loosely twisting her pen between her fingertips.

"He was on his way home from Richmond, heading to New York, when he went missing for five days. Completely gone," he said. "He never made it, and some people say that for whatever reason, he tried to turn back. Then, when they found him in Baltimore, he couldn't say what had happened because he kept going in and out of consciousness. But he wasn't making any sense anyway."

"Why?" Isobel asked, her voice going quiet. "What did he say?"

Varen lifted his brows and cast his gaze toward one of the nearby windows, his eyes narrowing in the light. "Nothing that made sense. When they took him to the hospital, he talked to things that weren't there. Then, the day before he died, he started calling out for somebody. But nobody knew who it was."

"And then he just died?"

"After a few days in the hospital, yeah, he died."

"And nobody knows where he'd been or what happened to him? Like, at all?"

"There are a lot of theories," he said. "That's why we're covering it in the project."

"Like, what are some of the theories?" she asked.

"Well." Varen's chair creaked as he leaned back. His eyes went distant again, and for the first time, that iron gate guard of his seemed to lower an inch. "A lot of people stick to the theory that he drank himself to death."

Isobel's gaze trailed down to his hands. She'd never seen a boy with hands like that, with long, delicate fingers, beautiful but still masculine. His fingernails were long too, almost crystalline, tapered to points. They were the kind of hands you'd expect to see under lace cuffs, like Mozart or something.

"And it was election day," he said, "so a lot of people think he was drugged and used as a repeat voter. That's one of the most popular theories." He shrugged. "Some people even say it was rabies, just because he liked cats."

"Yeah, but wouldn't they have been able to tell if he'd been drinking?"

"The accounts got mixed up," he said. "And he had enemies. A lot of gossip got spread around."

"So what do *you* think happened to him?"

To Isobel's surprise, he made a face like that question bothered him. His eyebrows furrowed, his gaze darkened, and he frowned. "I don't know," he said. "I think a lot of those theories are too convenient. But at the same time, I don't have any of my own."

Moments passed. A balding man in a gray suit got up from a nearby table. Gathering his books, he passed them, taking a path through the stacks, leaving them even more alone than they had been before. A palpable silence took his place and seemed to condense the air between them.

Isobel flipped open another one of the books on the table, this one small and as thin as a magazine. She opened her mouth, ready to say something, though she didn't know what. Anything to break the silence.

He beat her to it, though, when without warning, he got up from the table, looming tall.

"Go through that one," he said, indicating with a stiff nod the book she held, "and see if you can find the poem 'Annabel Lee.' I've got to go check the shelf again."

Unable to help a small smirk, Isobel raised one hand in a salute. "Aye, aye, O Captain! My Captain!"

He turned. "Right era," he muttered, "wrong poet," then vanished between the shelves.

When he was out of sight, Isobel snapped closed the little book of poetry and leaned forward. She shifted away the yellow steno notepad and lifted the corner of his black hardback book. She peeked into the opening and peeled apart the pages, keeping the book open just a crack. She took a quick glance up to the row of shelves he'd slipped between. At no sign of him, she returned her eyes to the book, halfway standing to get a better look.

Its spine made a soft creaking noise as she pulled it open all the way. It went easily, as though the pages spent more time being pinned apart than clamped together.

Purple writing covered every inch of white paper. What was the deal with the purple ink, anyway? But it was the most beautiful handwriting Isobel had ever seen. Each loop and every curl connected cleanly to make the writing itself appear as perfect and uniform as a printed font. It baffled her how someone could sit and take the time to form letters so meticulously. She checked around her one more time before flipping the page over and there, her suspicions confirmed, she found still more writing. The guy was a regular Shakespeare.

In some places, there were big spaces where he had written around drawings. They were more like loose sketches, actually, the lines never certain but nevertheless making pictures. They were strange sketches too. People with crazy hair and with whole pieces of their faces missing, like they were made of glass. She leafed past another page, this time daring to read a little of what was there.

> *She stood in the mist, waiting for him again,*
> *always in the same place.*

Isobel glanced up, stooping slightly to try and see through the shelves and towers of books for any hint of moving black or silver. No sign of him. He must have gone all the way to the stacks at the far end of the library. Her eyes darted back down to the page, searching for the place where she'd left off. She'd read just a little bit more. It wasn't like it was a personal journal or anything, right?

> *He always asked the same question.*
> *"What do you want me to do?"*
> *She never answered. She couldn't. All she*
> *could do was stare, reaching toward him with*
> *her gaze alone, pulling him to drown in the*
> *sorrow of those depthless black pools.*

The black book thwacked shut. Isobel first stared at the silver-ringed fingers that pressed the cover down, then gradually her eyes traveled up the black-clad arm and then farther still until they met reluctantly with a pair of outlined eyes. They narrowed on her in disdain, and the way he looked at her made her feel like any second he was going to use the Force to choke her lifeless.

"I was just—"

"Snooping." He dropped the book he'd returned with on the table and snatched the black sketchbook journal, shoving it into his satchel.

"I didn't see anything," she lied, glancing at the title of the newly unshelved book. *The Secrets of Lucid Dreaming*, it read. But that, too, was quickly ripped out from under her eyes.

"I gotta go," he said, shouldering his satchel.

"Wait. What about the project?"

He pointed at her list of titles. "Start reading," he said. "You have a library card, right?"

Without waiting for an answer, he turned, once again disappearing between the shelves.

5
A Note of Warning

"Hey, Dad, what time is it?"

Isobel wondered if the crew might still be at Double Trouble's.

"Little after three," her dad said as the sedan rolled to a stop at an intersection. "Why?"

"Just wondering." She shrugged.

"You didn't say anything about my haircut," he said, lifting a hand from the steering wheel to primp imaginary curls at the back of his head.

Isobel tried to keep from grinning while she surveyed the cut. It was really more like a trim, though, a grooming of his usual style, which Isobel often referred to as shaggy à la hobo.

Isobel had not inherited her dad's dark brown, nearly black hair, like Danny had, though hers did have the same thin, almost straight texture.

"Oh, yes. Ravishing," she told him.

He watched her with a goofy grin until she said, "Light's green." Then he looked ahead again, both hands on the wheel.

"You're awfully glum today," he observed, making a turn west, toward their neighborhood. "Something going on with Brad?" he asked.

"No," she said, then thought better of leaving it at that. "Brad and I just wanted to hang out separately this weekend. That's all."

Her dad liked Brad because they could talk sports, Danny not exactly being the athletic type. What her mom and dad hadn't been too keen on was how "serious" they thought she and Brad had become since the beginning of junior year. "You should be thinking about college," her mom would say. Only problem with that was that Isobel wasn't sure where she would go yet, or what she would major in. It was an argument she didn't want to revisit.

"I see." After a beat, they came to a stop sign, and he asked, "So, what is this project about, anyway?"

"Poe." She sighed.

"Poe? As in Edgar Allan 'quoth the raven, nevermore'?"

"That's the guy," she said. She picked up one of the books in her lap and leafed through to find a picture. She found one of the bigger ones (they all looked the same to her) and held the book open in his direction.

He took a quick glance away from the road just before pulling into the driveway, then, putting the car into park, turned in his seat to look directly at her. He raised one eyebrow.

"Next time, maybe I should just let my hair grow out like that." He tilted his head to one side, eyeing her for a response. "And what about the mustache?" He draped an index finger over his top lip. "What do you think?"

She smiled at the visual and nearly snorted, because she hadn't expected to laugh. She pictured her father with a crazy crop of black locks and a neat little mustache. He looked, in her mind's eye, more like Charlie Chaplin than Poe.

A victorious smirk tugged at one side of his mouth.

Isobel slammed her locker closed.

"*Ah!*" she yelped, her notebook landing on the floor.

Varen. Right behind where the door to her locker had stood open. His eyes, calm to the point of emptiness, seemed to stare straight through her.

"Would you not do that!" she piped.

He said nothing, just stood there and stared, like she'd suddenly gone transparent or something.

"*What?*" she demanded.

He moved to walk past her and Isobel thought about telling him off right then and there, in front of the whole hall, for trying to pull this *Dawn of the Dead* crap with her.

That was when she felt his hand, which still held the morning's chill, slip against hers.

Isobel's breath caught in her throat, and her eyes widened. What did he think he was doing? What if someone saw?

He pressed something into her palm. Her fingers curled to secure it and, for the briefest moment, clenched his.

In the next, he moved on, and she felt herself turning to stare after him, rubbing her thumb over the smooth slip of folded paper.

She felt it crinkle in her hand as she watched his back, clad in a dark green mechanic's jacket. On a piece of white fabric, safety-pinned to the jacket, was the silhouette of a dead bird lying on its back, its legs crooked upward.

He walked to the group of goths standing in front of the window by the radiator and, lifting a hand, touched the shoulder of a dark-haired, copper-skinned girl. She turned, a sultry smile gracing her full, darkly painted lips. She had a red envelope in her hand, which she held out to Varen.

As the crowded hallway absorbed them, Isobel felt as though someone were lifting their finger off the slow-mo button.

She took a cautious look around to see if anyone had noticed, then casually pretended that there was something she'd forgotten in her locker and reopened it. It swung out without a fuss this time and she leaned in, unfolding the piece of notebook paper inside the darkened space.

They know you lied.

At first Isobel wasn't sure what it meant. When had she lied and to whom? And how would *he* even know? That thought in particular sent a chilling spark running along her spine and tingling through her shoulders. Maybe Nikki had been right. Maybe he *was* trying to freak her out.

As if on cue, Nikki strolled by.

"Hey, Nikki! Wait up," Isobel called, taking a moment to refold the cryptic note and slip it into the pocket of the periwinkle blue cardigan hanging in her locker. She'd worry about it later, she decided, and shut her locker door before giving her number dial a twirl.

When she turned again, though, Nikki had gone.

Had she not heard her?

That seemed unlikely, given she'd passed by less than six feet away.

Something must be up.

There was an ugly, twisty feeling in her stomach as Isobel began to piece the events of that morning together. Suddenly she realized exactly what the note meant.

Her lunch tray in hand, Isobel's heart hammered in her chest as she neared the crew's usual spot, a table near the long wall of big windows overlooking the courtyard.

"Here she comes," she heard Alyssa whisper. In response, all chattering at the table ceased. Nikki examined her nails. Mark swirled the end of his corn dog into a mound of ketchup. Alyssa, hiding her cell in her lap, tinkered with her messages, and Stevie, suddenly distracted by a group of pigeons in the courtyard, stared out the window. Brad just sat there, not looking at anything. He pursed his lips.

Isobel clutched the sides of her tray in an effort to steady everything from shaking. These were her friends. Why was she so worried?

The only one who looked up when she got right to the table was Brad. He watched her blatantly with those gorgeous, almost neon blue eyes as she edged onto the bench across from him. Nikki huffed and moved down to make room, slamming her tray around.

Nobody said anything.

Act normal, she thought. *Just act normal.*

Brad took a swig of his Coke. Eyeing her, he said, "So . . ."

Isobel squelched her smile and met his gaze, not liking his all-too-casual tone.

"Me and Mark were wondering, Izo," he continued. "Since, uh, you and I go to the same dentist . . . When did Dr. Morton start taking Saturday appointments?"

"Yeah," Mark chimed in from the other end of the table, gesturing at her with his corn dog. "Just curious."

Isobel took a deep breath and focused on Brad, pleading to him with her eyes to stop this before it started and just let the rest of lunch be normal. He could do that. He could have everyone laughing it off and talking about the upcoming game on Friday against Ackerman.

He looked away from her, chewing his burger like it was a chore.

"I had something I had to do," Isobel said, tearing open a ketchup packet. Maybe if she acted like it wasn't a big deal, then it wouldn't be.

"So you lied to us?" This came from Nikki, as she tossed her fork onto her tray. It clanged sharply, but the noise was lost in the surrounding cafeteria racket.

Isobel stared down at her food, her appetite replaced now by guilt-saturated nausea. Not knowing what to say, she squeezed her ketchup packet over her burger, still holding on to the slimming hope that they'd all just let it go. Yesterday on the phone, Nikki had acted like she'd known Isobel had been making it up anyway, right? So why did it matter now?

When she couldn't think of anything not incriminating to say, Isobel tried shrugging. She realized quickly, though, when Nikki made her *"Tch!"* sound, that that had been the wrong response.

Nikki stood, gathering her tray. "Something smells over here, I'm switching." And with that, she unthreaded her long legs from underneath the table and marched away to a distant, unoccupied table in the corner. No one dared try to stop her, least of all Isobel.

Without looking up, she felt the table shudder again as someone else stood. She could see varsity colors out of the corner of one eye, and she knew it must be Mark, moving to join Nikki, no doubt. Alyssa followed next, and finally even Stevie got up with what Isobel thought was an apologetic cough.

It was just her and Brad now.

"Where were you for real?" he asked after a long moment, ending the uncomfortable silence that had stretched between them. He'd asked in that soft and reasonable way that said all could still be forgiven.

"I can't tell you, because you'll just get mad."

"Then that's probably a good indication that you should tell me," he said with strained patience. She'd been batting zero ever since last Friday, and now she was striking out. Big-time.

A sharp sting started behind her eyes. She shouldn't have to make excuses to her boyfriend about doing her homework. Isobel lifted a finger to wipe a tear away before it could form.

She thought that everybody in the whole cafeteria had to be watching. The thought made her face burn, and she tried to shield her eyes with one hand.

Then, before she could summon up the resolve to answer, Brad rose from the table, taking his tray and moving away toward the others, leaving her completely alone.

Isobel felt her shoulders hitch when she tried to take a breath. She hadn't eaten lunch by herself since the fifth grade, when everyone had found out her mom had made her wash her hair the night before with mayonnaise.

The tears came freely now, to the point where she could be sure of mascara trails. She sat there, shielding her face from view with one hand and trying to convince the world with her other, by poking a fork through her salad, that she was just fine.

Everything turned blurry through the lens of tears, but she could still register the pair of black boots that stopped beside her table.

Oh God, she thought. *Anything but this.*

"Please," she murmured at her burger, her voice no more than a squeaky whisper, "don't do this."

"It's dead," he said. "I don't think it can hear you."

"You're making things worse!" she hissed, and still shielding her soppy eyes from the rest of the cafeteria, she angled her head to peer up at him.

"That's a good look for you," he said.

Isobel didn't have to look in the crew's direction to know they were watching. She could feel Brad's gaze on them.

And if he hadn't been able to guess who she'd been with on Saturday, he certainly knew now. Was this guy dense? Brad could pave the courtyard with him.

"He's going to kill you."

"Can't," he said. "Already dead. Remember?"

"You pick a funny time to adopt a sense of humor," she snapped, glancing back down.

"When are we meeting again for the project?"

Where did he get off? Did he not have a clue? "Go away. We're not."

"How about after school?"

"I have practice." It was funny how she could tell *him* the truth but had to lie to her friends.

"So I'm doing it by myself after all?" he asked in that cold, unaffected way.

"Mr. Swanson will give you a new partner. Go away."

And to her surprise, just like that, he did.

6
Things Unseen

Isobel had *not* wanted to come to practice today. Not after the episode at lunch. But with a pep rally and game on Friday, she'd had no choice. If she *had* missed, not only would the crew despise her, but so would the rest of the squad. They'd been working on their routine for months now, and she was the middle flyer for most of the big stunts. Plus, there was Coach's little rule of "Miss a practice, miss a game."

Isobel put one hand on Nikki's shoulder and the other on Alyssa's, shoving her sneakers into their awaiting grasps, literally handing herself over to people who currently hated her.

This was the only way to get the day's retribution, though, and she wasn't about to give that up. You had to be small and strong to be a flyer, and while Nikki had killer legs, they stretched the length of an ostrich's. Alyssa, on the other hand, had simply never been able to get up high enough.

Isobel prepared for the lift.

They hoisted her up, and the ground dropped away. She felt herself extend upward, like the stem of a flower shooting for the sun, her roots below her, stuck in the earth.

Coach screamed out the count as she went up. "Four,

five," and they dipped her down on five, preparing for the launch. "Six!" They popped her into the air. *Yes!*

Twisting once, twice, freewheeling. Her world became a spinning kaleidoscope of blurred faces, of blue and gold and bright white lights. An all-too-quick half turn, and she felt the catch. She dipped into her V position, one arm clamping around Nikki's back, the other wrapped around Alyssa. They set her to the floor.

"That was good, Iz," Coach said, sounding a bit more relaxed. "Let's keep it up—get it? Keep it up?" A collective groan arose from the squad. "Okay. This time with the music, boys and girls."

Isobel tugged her practice shorts down and got into position while Coach Anne went to fool with the CD player, her frizzy grizzly-bear hair springing with each step and her loafers squeaking against the gymnasium floor.

Nikki shifted into place directly behind Isobel, who could feel Nikki's eyes chiseling into the back of her skull.

When the pumping music started and the right beat came along, Isobel swiveled about-face to stare directly at Nikki, whose normally mirthful, cheer-ready blues glared ice.

"Why did you lie about it?" she hissed.

Well, Isobel thought, at least it seemed they were on speaking terms again.

The intro beat to the music thumped low, building in volume, and their arms lifted high while their heels pounded the floor. "Because! You run and tell everything!"

"Not when it's important!"

"Yeah, and you're the one who gets to decide when something's important!"

It really wasn't feasible to do much more talking than that. The electronic music sped up and every beat got a kick, a turn, or a flip. Coach liked flashy formation changes too, so they moved into a lot of shapes, breaking apart, fanning out, and making new configurations.

When it came time for Isobel's big flip, the bases stood ready for her.

Four, five, *up!* Two quick twists came right in time with the singer's "Woo-hoo!" but in the middle of her second revolution, for a split second, Isobel thought she saw something in the practice mirrors. A dark figure. She glimpsed it in a flash—someone standing in the gym doorway. She only caught the outline of the form in a quick blur, but whoever it was, he'd been wearing what had looked like a black hat and . . . a cloak?

She fell into the cradle and was brought to her feet again, facing the gym doors, which now stood empty.

Isobel glanced back at the mirrors, squinting, her eyes narrowing on the reflection of the vacant doorway, forgetting that she was supposed to be switching positions for the next formation when Stephanie Dorbon plowed into her. Isobel hit the floor hard and the pain from last week's bruise reawakened with a roar. She cringed, drawing in a sharp breath between her teeth.

All around her, the whole routine ground to a screeching halt. The music stopped.

"What the hell happened?" Coach shouted, her round

face blotchy red as she broke through to where Isobel sat and where Stephanie stood right next to her, hugging herself like she wanted out of the frame of blame that very second.

"I fell," Isobel said to relieve Steph's anxiety. She picked herself up to the grumbling of the squad, leaving her floundering dignity to choke to death on the floor. She folded her arms over her chest and shot a quick look back to the gymnasium doors.

Empty. She could have sworn . . .

"C'mon, folks!" Coach yelled. She cocked her wide hips to one side—always a bad sign. "This is dangerous stuff. Look. Bottom line. Pay *attention*! I don't want any broken bones, bloody noses, or sobbing parents, okay? Okay. We'll try it again tomorrow. Go home." She waved a hand of dismissal and everyone turned with a mumble and trudged to collect their gym bags and water bottles.

As Alyssa passed Isobel, she leaned in to mutter, "Great going, albatross."

Isobel kept her own comments in check. She slogged toward the bleachers to grab her bag, yanking it up from between two benches. She felt like chucking it out into traffic and watching an eighteen-wheeler plow over it.

"Isobel," Coach said, stepping up behind her, "you stay. We've got to talk." She brushed by and went to wind up the cord to the CD player while the boys folded up and stowed the practice mirrors. Isobel shut her eyes, keeping them that way for a full three seconds.

Could this day—could this *year* get any worse?

She released her gym bag and flopped onto the bleachers to watch everyone else file out the door. Nikki offered only a single backward glance before hurrying out after Alyssa. Isobel set her chin in her hands and focused on her tennis shoes, white with blue and yellow stripes.

She was more angry than upset. After crying at lunch that day, she'd had enough of being upset and letting other people see it. It was easier just to get mad.

Maybe she was losing her touch.

"What's going on, missy? It's time to talk," said Coach, settling on the bleachers next to her. The wood and iron squeaked as it compressed beneath her weight.

"I just got distracted," Isobel mumbled. She glanced toward the gym doors, which still stood vacant. She looked back down again at her hands, picking at the nonexistent dirt under her fingernails. Maybe she was just altogether losing it.

"Okay," Coach said. She looped her thumb through the yellow lanyard around her neck, jostling her whistle. "So whatever it was that distracted you today, could it be the same thing that distracted you last Friday? That's two falls in two weeks." Coach held up two fingers as though Isobel needed the visual as a reminder. "For you, that's not normal."

"I know. It—it's nothing," Isobel insisted. "I just . . ." She trailed off. She just what? Saw something that wasn't really there? Oh yeah, *that* wasn't begging for a call home.

"Well," Coach said, ending the stretch of silence, "I heard that you were upset at lunch today. Does that have anything to do with all this?"

Isobel felt her cheeks blossom into buds of fire, and she involuntarily braced a shielding hand at her brow. Did *everyone* know about the lunch saga?

"Listen, Isobel," Coach started, leaning forward, elbows on her knees. "You don't have to tell *me* anything. I'm just trying keep hold of my best flyer. That's all."

Isobel nodded at the floor. She appreciated the encouragement. It felt good to be recognized, but at the same time, she couldn't think of any way to respond. She could say she'd do better. She could say anything. But with Coach, words never went as far as actions. She'd just have to do better next time. She'd have to put all the crap aside, forget about everything for a while, and just think up.

"Hey." Coach nudged her.

Isobel lifted her head—and froze. Brad stood in the gym doorway, his letter jacket slung over one shoulder, his curly, thick hair wet and darkened from the showers.

Beside her, Coach stood, and the bleachers wobbled with a creak and a sigh. "Better let you go," she said. "Looks like there's someone here to see you."

"Go away."

Isobel forced herself to look straight at him as she said it. He'd followed her all the way from the gym to her locker, wearing that cocky grin, his lips curled up on one side, dimple displayed.

And that smirk combined with the way his wet hair hung in his face? So hot.

Isobel pivoted away from him, doing her best to remember her locker combination, but stopped when he reached out and began to turn the dial for her.

She swatted his hand aside and spun the rest of the numbers on her own, making a mental note to change the combination later.

When she tugged at the handle, the door stuck, and before she could stop him, Brad gave the bottom left corner a quick, rough kick. The door popped out.

"I said, go away!" she snarled.

First she got her binder, the one she'd left over the weekend, resolving to do her algebra tonight since she no longer had friends to go out with. Next she reached in to snag her cardigan, only to find that it had disappeared off the little hook inside. She blinked, then turned to find it draped by the collar off the tip of Brad's finger.

"Stop!" She snatched the sweater away and pulled it on, juggling her binder from arm to arm in the process. He stood there, watching, hands tucked into the pockets of his jacket.

Infuriated, she slammed her locker closed, shouldered her gym bag, and marched toward the front doors.

"Just so I have this straight," he called after her, "you don't want a ride home?"

"No."

Isobel shoved open the push-bar door with her hip. A rush of cool, moist air blasted her in the face, whipping her hair into a frenzy as she slipped out to stand on the concrete steps.

The trees in the yard tossed their arms around as if hailing a warning, their yellows and reds flashing. A few dry leaves skipped and tumbled along the empty bus drive as though heading for cover.

The sky, looming gray, emitted a low rumble.

She could call her mom, she thought, but Mondays were her yoga nights, so she probably already had her phone off. Of course, she could call her dad. He was probably already home from work, but then she'd have to field the barrage of Brad-centric questions, since he was usually the one who gave her a ride home anyway.

She looked over her shoulder at Brad.

Cocking an eyebrow at her, he waggled his car keys.

Isobel loved how Brad's face felt after he'd shaved that morning, smooth but still not completely soft. There was an underlying roughness to it that she liked to feel against the tips of her fingers and with her cheek while they kissed, a sensation like tempered sandpaper. She breathed him in as his mouth sought hers, savoring the smell of his cologne, musky and sharp all at once.

Outside, thunder rolled.

Steam coated the windows of Brad's Mustang. Light rain pattered against the glass while the radio softly buzzed on a pop station.

On their way to Isobel's house, Brad had pulled over into one of the vacant gravel lots of Cherokee Park. He'd said he'd wanted to talk, but so far they'd done more making out than talking. But that was okay with Isobel. She was ready for things to go back to normal, and if that meant just dropping the whole thing and pretending like it never happened, that was more than fine with her.

She felt Brad's hands slip to her shoulders, where they burrowed between the fabric of her sweater and her T-shirt, coaxing the cardigan back. Isobel shrugged and jostled her shoulders to aid the shedding of the outer layer. Despite the drop in temperature outside, it had gotten warm in the car.

"Mmm, Brad?" she murmured around his mouth.

He grunted in response, tugging her sweater free from her wrists before slinging it into the back. The leather seats creaked as he leaned in closer to her, his hands traveling lower.

"Mm—what time is it?" she asked, taking his hand and guiding it away from its original path toward her chest, placing it at her waist instead.

He made an "I don't know" sound, his hand venturing upward again.

"Brad!" She squirmed in his grasp, trying to sound stern, but she had to laugh at his sneaky persistence. He grinned through kissing her and lightly pinched her side, causing her to jolt and wiggle. "Brad, I gotta go home!" she insisted through giggles. "It's probably seven already, I know it is."

"You're just making that up," he whispered to her, all husky and soft.

She closed her eyes, clamping her lips shut, fighting the seduction.

" —just trying to get away to see your new boyfriend."

Isobel went still.

She knew he was teasing, but the words still managed to burrow beneath her skin. He wasn't going to let it go. She felt like a kite sinking back toward earth after flying high on a rush of wind. She frowned and pushed against him again. He lightened up and leaned back to look at her.

"I told you," she said, "it wasn't like that."

He watched her for a long moment before he sank back into his seat. Then he stared forward, out the steam-mottled windshield. "Well," he said, "then why the hell do you keep getting so bunched up about it?"

"I'm not. I mean—I just—" Isobel couldn't believe this. They'd been just fine two seconds ago. She reached for him.

He shook her off. "Would you wake up, Isobel? The way he stares at you, it's like he can't wait to tie you up!"

"Brad! Oh my God!"

"You just don't get it, Iz. He's a wing nut. A girl like you? You can't talk to a guy like that without him thinking he's won the freaking lottery!"

She thought about telling him that Varen had already cleared up the question of whether or not she was his type. That was probably a bad idea, though, seeing as it might throw Brad into Incredible Hulk mode, complete with bulging neck and psycho eyes.

"I'm not doing the project with him anymore, okay?" she said quickly, tucking her hair behind her ears.

"You'll forgive me if I'm not exactly torn up to hear that."

He reached to snap on the defrost. "Put on your seat belt."

Wrenching around, Isobel grabbed the belt and slung it over her lap. After the click of the buckle lock, Brad slammed his foot on the gas. Isobel braced herself. The back tires kicked a spray of gravel as he spun the Mustang toward the road.

7
Maelstrom

It was weird.

After not talking to Brad for the rest of that night, Isobel returned to school the next morning to find him waiting at her locker, and with help from a bag of Hershey's Kisses, they made up. Again.

After that, as long as no one brought up the "dentist" incident (or the *V* word), things appeared to go back to normal. The rest of that week seemed to slip past without any more nuclear meltdowns, and everyone ate lunch together again, complaining about terror tacos and boil burgers. Nikki had even warmed back up to Isobel, calling her on Thursday night to ask about borrowing her gold nail polish, then launching into a tirade about whether or not to ditch Mark and make her move on the cute chemistry guy.

She and Brad were better too. It seemed that all he'd really needed was a chance to cool down about the whole Varen thing. Of course, she hadn't yet figured out what to do for a grade in Swanson's class, but maybe if she talked to him on Monday, told him that her schedule conflicted too much with Varen's, then he'd give her a separate project or let her join one of the other groups. If she told him they'd tried to meet but that it didn't look like it was going to work out, well, that was mostly the truth. And that way, neither of them would take any blame.

It was better this way, she told herself. It was better for both of them if they just stayed away from each other. And whenever she caught herself thinking about him, about how he'd tried to warn her by slipping her that note, about how his voice sounded on the phone or about how concentrated he looked that day when he wrote on her hand, she pushed the thoughts away and tried to think of something else—anything else. It was her curiosity he'd piqued. That's all. Only that and nothing more.

She had to admit, though, she was a little baffled concerning the crew. She wasn't complaining, but at the same time, it was strange that everything could apparently be forgiven as long as it was never brought up again. She'd come to expect that sort of thing from Nikki, but even Alyssa was being super nice these days. In the end, Isobel chalked it up to everyone being psyched about the game—which, of course, Trenton won. Brad even made a touchdown in the second quarter.

Their squad's routine at halftime had gone off without a hitch too. Isobel had gotten her twist perfect with the glory of the stars spinning in the clear autumn sky, the blaring stadium lights and the filled stands all whirring into her kaleidoscopic swirl.

This was what high school was *supposed* to be like.

After the game, Brad suggested a round of victory ice cream, and they all piled into his Mustang, its windows decorated with soap words reading GO HAWKS and DIE BEARS DIE. Isobel took shotgun next to Brad, while Alyssa, Nikki, and Mark crammed into the back. Stevie, complaining about his ankle, stayed behind to brace it, saying he might meet up with them later.

"Hey, Nikki," Brad said, reaching an arm into the backseat. "Hand me that, would you?"

"I got it," said Alyssa, passing up a familiar blue sweater.

"Here." Brad glanced at Isobel pointedly, sweater in hand. "You left this in the backseat Monday."

"Oh," she said, blushing at the memory of how it had gotten there in the first place. She folded the sweater over her lap. "Thanks."

"Don't mention it."

Isobel sent him a curious sidelong glance.

He watched her for another moment, winked at her without smiling, then turned the ignition. The engine roared. "All right, people," he said over the rumble. "Let's go get some ice cream." He shifted the car into gear. "I know just the place."

They wound up at a little shop called Dessert Island. The sign outside depicted a pile of ice cream that looked like a tiny island sitting in a sea of chocolate sauce, a palm tree sticking out of the middle. Isobel wondered why they'd come here instead of going to Graeter's, which was the closest place to school, but shrugged it off as they strolled up to the storefront.

Tingling chimes announced them as they meandered through the door.

Inside, the shop was small with sparse seating. This, along with the do-it-yourself decorations and chalkboard menu, gave the place a very kitschy, family-owned feel.

Overhead, cheesy steel drum music warbled softly over the speaker system. All of the decor followed a tropical theme: quaint chairs with bamboo legs encircled wicker tables, a conch shell laid out on the center of each. Along the walls, a sprawling hand-painted mural depicted an ocean-side scene, complete with sandy beach, palm trees, and tropical birds, both perched and suspended in flight, plumage displayed.

There was no one behind the counter, but the neon OPEN sign in the front window blared electric pink, and the staff door leading to the back stood ajar, as though someone had propped it open.

It looked as though the five of them were the only customers.

"Heyo," Brad called across the counter. He tapped the service bell, and its ting rose shrill over the island music. "Anybody here?"

Isobel stepped up to the display glass, peering in to find all the usual favorites sharing quarters with more daring combinations like Macadamia Mocha Madness, Pineapple Bliss, and Go-Go Guava. For a moment she thought about taking a chance with the shocking pink Rum While You Can but in the end decided to default to her all-time favorite—Banana Fudge Swirl.

"Yeah, can I have a scoop of the Raspberry White Chocolate, in a cup?" Nikki asked sweetly.

"Chocolate malt," Brad added.

"Yeah, same here," Mark said. "Alyssa, what do you want?"

"Don't know yet, give me a second. It's got to be good."

"You know what you want yet, Izo?" she heard Brad ask. "Your usual?"

Isobel wandered down the long line of contenders to where her friends stood waiting, trailing a finger beneath the little rectangular plaques that listed a description of each ice cream. "Yeah, I guess so."

"And a scoop of Banana Fudge in a cup."

Isobel leaned her hip against the softly humming ice cream case. She stared through the glass, thinking about the game and about how well the routine had gone. In fact, all they really needed to do before Nationals was tighten the middle section, perfect the tumbling segment, and make a few adjustments on the ending pyramid. Of course, she could always sharpen her twists, and if she could work on landing her layout a fraction of a second sooner, she'd be in perfect sync.

Isobel heard the click of register keys, and her gaze drifted to stare unfocused at the store clerk's name tag.

VAREN, it read, in bulky Gothic lettering.

Isobel froze, her eyes locked on that name tag. Her smile fell away. Her mouth went instantly dry. A tingling sensation in her legs and arms snuffed the night's happiness, spreading its way into her lower stomach, where it congealed into a puddle of unease.

Reluctantly, she lifted her gaze.

Even though she'd read the name on the tag, it was still a shock to look up and see him staring back. For the first time, because of the green visor that he wore, she could see his face—his eyes—clearly. They remained fixed on her, holding an unreadable expression.

It would have been better, she thought, if he'd glared at her with hatred.

"Today?" Brad said, and tapped the counter between them, starting Isobel out of her shock.

Behind her, she heard Mark and Alyssa snicker.

Everything was playing out in slow motion again. Varen's gaze lingered on hers even as he turned away. She watched him as one elegant hand reached deftly into a bin behind the counter and pulled from a trough of water a single silver ice cream scoop.

Despite its thundering, she felt her heart plummet as she realized what was going on, what her friends were going to do—what they were *doing*.

"*Brad,*" she said, and pivoted toward him just in time to see him flick over a soda-shop-style straw canister. The multi-colored tubes went spilling across the counter and behind it, some of them landing in the open ice cream bins, the rest hitting the floor, making hollow little pop sounds as they bounced on the linoleum.

"*Oops.*"

"Brad, you klutz," Alyssa cooed.

"What can I say?" Brad shrugged. "I'm a hurricane."

Isobel glanced mutely up from the spilled straws to where Varen now stood, leaning over to scrape the very bottom of one of the ice cream canisters under the close scrutiny of Nikki, who stood on her toes to watch.

"Make sure you don't touch any of it," she said, her hands pressed flat against the glass, leaving huge hand-lotion smudge prints. He straightened, carefully packing the ice cream into a small paper cup adorned with palm trees. Just before he finished, Nikki tapped the glass like she would a fish tank.

"Hey. 'Scuse me," she said. "I changed my mind."

He raised his eyes.

"I want Cinnamon instead."

"We don't have—"

"Then I don't want anything." She shrugged and waved away what he'd already prepared.

Isobel could die. She could just *die*. But if she said something, if she tried to stop them, she knew everyone would just go back to hating her. Would Brad break up with her? At the very least, she'd have to quit the squad for sure.

The whir of the blender cut through the silence.

"Brad." She whirled and started for the door. "I want to go home."

"Sure thing, Izo," he called, "just let me get my malt." He knocked on the counter. "Can we step on that malt back there?"

Isobel turned her eyes to Nikki, only to see a smug Cheshire smile pasted across her face, arms folded, her gaze cast to the palm-leaf ceiling fans. The realization hit her then. They'd all been in on this together. The betrayal of it burned, and Isobel's fingers itched to form into fists.

Varen set the first malt on the counter next to the register. Brad snatched it up.

She watched in silent dread as Brad handed off the shake to Mark, who took it and tossed it on the floor. The plastic top popped off at impact, the brown ice cream mixture flying out to spatter across the floor and the nearby tables and chairs.

"*Hey!*" Isobel shouted, marching right up to shove Mark in the shoulder.

"Hey yourself, Iz! Relax. It was just an accident. Besides, Count Fagula's got a mop back there somewhere, I'm sure."

"Keeps it in his little green apron," Brad chimed in, causing both of them to explode into howls of laughter.

"Get out," Isobel growled, pointing them to the door.

"Can't." Brad sighed. As he spoke, he wandered to the store freezer, where he pulled open the door and tugged out a pint of ice cream. "We're still short some Banana Fudge and a couple of malts."

"Hey, Brad, over here!" shouted Mark, clapping his hands, raising them like he would for a pass.

A wild look came over Brad. "Go long!" he called. Gripping the pint like a football, he leaned back, preparing for the toss. Mark laughed and retreated as far as the front door, his eye on the pint.

"No! Don't!" Isobel screamed.

Brad threw the pint. Alyssa squealed and ducked. Nikki

flattened herself against the display glass. The carton hurtled through the air toward Mark, who dropped down at the last second, causing the pint to smash against the mural-painted wall behind him. The crushed carton slid down, then hit the floor, leaving a brown splat of Rocky Road right in the middle of a cockatoo.

Isobel spun in search of Varen, only to see Brad lift the hinged divider and invite himself behind the counter. He slid up to the register and, with practiced fingers, tapped a series of buttons that sent the cash drawer shooting out. He dipped a large hand in, and Isobel gaped as he claimed a wad of twenties.

That's when Varen moved.

He got close enough to reach for the money—close enough to almost snatch it back. As the scene played out, a sick terror seized Isobel's heart, tightening it in a fierce grip. She felt her entire form flinch as Brad shoved him. Varen stumbled backward, hands raised in an open-palm gesture of forfeit.

It wasn't what Brad wanted.

His face contorted and his fist balled. He reared back, his arm a python prepared to strike.

Without thinking, without knowing what she was doing, Isobel rushed him. She crashed hard against Brad, grappling for his arm. Knocked off balance, Brad dropped the money. Before he could steady himself, her hand struck. She slapped him, and the crack of her palm against his jaw split the room.

Everything went silent except for the quiet playing of

the steel drum music and the soft hum of the store freezer. Brad stared down at her, anger fixed in his eyes, causing them to burn unnaturally bright, like two supernovas ready to explode.

"Get out," she said, hissing the words between her teeth. She couldn't remember being this angry at anything or at anyone ever before in her life. She could feel herself trembling all over, like a time bomb. She swallowed, strangling the impulse to strike him again. "I said *get out!*"

Nikki was the first to scuttle out the door. Isobel knew this because she could hear that *tch* sound followed by the jingle of the door chimes. Someone else followed, but Isobel couldn't see whether it was Mark or Alyssa, because she was too busy staring holes into her *ex*-boyfriend. When she finally heard a third jingle of chimes, she steadied her voice and spoke quiet and slow.

"Don't ever talk to me again."

Brad stared at her long and hard, as though waiting for her to retract her words. She didn't, and finally he took the cue and broke away, brushing past her. He smoothed a hand through his hair as he made his way to the door, pulling a crumpled pack of cigarettes out of his back jeans pocket, like there was nothing the matter, like he didn't care one way or the other.

He paused before he reached the door, long enough to toss a folded piece of paper he'd dug out of his jacket pocket onto one of the little brown wicker tables.

The door chimes rang a fourth time.

Only when Brad was out of the shop did Isobel feel the shakes begin to subside.

She looked around, but Varen had vanished.

She bent to retrieve the money, stuffing it with trembling fingers haphazardly into the cash drawer and shoving it closed again, as though it could contain what had already gone awry. She gripped the sides of the register and stared at the numbered keys, trying to anchor herself, trying to decide if the here and now was too impossible to be real.

She flinched when Brad's headlights sliced through the front windows, as bright as search beams. They swiveled violently away, tires screeching. Isobel shut her eyes. She listened as he peeled out of the parking lot, the blast from his modified muffler sounding a roar before fading into the night.

Numb, she turned in a slow circle, opening her eyes again to pan the destruction around her. Chairs overturned, ice cream melting on the floor, and still no sign of Varen.

She shuddered, overcome with something akin to relief. She couldn't have faced him in that moment. She couldn't face him ever again. Not after this.

Moving on impulse, Isobel hurried to the door.

Her hands on the push bar, she stopped, her gaze catching on the table, on the folded slip of paper Brad had dropped there. Suddenly she realized what it was. It was the note from Varen, the note he'd written to warn her, the one that she'd tucked into the pocket of her sweater.

The sweater she'd left in Brad's car.

8
Ligeia

Her back pressed to the wall, Isobel lingered just outside the staff door. Finally, steeling herself with a shuddering breath, she pushed away from the wall and gave the door frame a timid double knock. "Hello?" she called into the pitch-blackness. "You—you back there?"

No answer.

Isobel reached a tremulous hand inside and patted the wall. Her fingers fumbled over a light switch and she flicked it upward, causing fluorescents to sputter on with a soft *clink*.

Inside, shelves packed with boxes of ice cream cones, packages of napkins, and cartons of paper cups lined the hideous lime green, cracked plaster walls. Her searching gaze traveled past a dark gray locker cabinet and the rear exit, stopping to rest on the door to the walk-in freezer. It stood ajar, mist whispering through a slim gap.

Isobel stepped into the room. She moved to the freezer and glanced down to find it propped open to a slit by a small wooden crate.

She put her hand to the latch and pulled, surprised when it opened easily, sending huge gales of cold air tumbling out over her sneakers. She peeked her head inside first, sliding in only when she thought she saw, through the veil of fog, one black boot.

"What are you doing in here?" was the first thing, the safest thing, she thought to ask.

He sat in one corner, lounging on a bench composed of shrink-wrapped ice cream canisters. She inched farther into the cold, suddenly glad of the turtleneck and the pair of blue sweatpants that she'd brought to throw on after the game. She let the freezer door thud back against the wooden crate, her shoulders hunkering, and wrapped her arms around her middle.

His visor sat on the floor between his boots, and his hair once again hung in his face so that she couldn't read his expression.

"I . . . ," she began, groping for the next thing to say, the *right* thing to say. "I'm sorry," she said, the words sounding lame in her own ears, and she knew that, on their own, they weren't enough. "I . . . didn't know they—"

"I know," he said.

She hugged herself tighter. "I—I put the money back in the—"

"Thanks."

Isobel pressed her lips together in a tight frown, a wad of frustration knotting itself in her chest. "Look—I'm trying . . . I said I was sor—"

"Why?" He looked up at her sharply, anger etched on his features. "Why did you do that?"

"I—," she stammered, entrapped once again within the force of those eyes. "What do you mean? I couldn't just—"

"Those were your friends, right?"

"Yeah, but—" Her gaze dropped to the frosted metal floor. She shook her head furiously, though more to combat his questions than to answer them.

"What do you think you proved, *cheerleader*?" He rose suddenly, and Isobel felt herself shrink back with an involuntary step.

"N-nothing," she stammered. "It just . . . it wasn't right."

"Why do you care?" he demanded, drawing close enough to stand over her, close enough for her to feel the anger rolling off of him, washing over her.

She paused to swallow, to think. She stared up at him, quivering from the cold and from nerves. She'd expected his anger, yes, but this blatant challenge? When she opened her mouth to respond, no words came. Why *did* she care?

She thought about it, then cleared her throat, all too conscious of his looming over her like a thundercloud. "Why— why do *you* care?"

"Who said I did?"

She flinched. There it was again. That blockade of his.

"You did," she whispered, her breath leaving her in a plume of white. Teeth chattering, she unfolded her arms and held out, between shaking fingers, the slip of paper Brad had left on the wicker table. "When you slipped me this note." She glanced up at him.

His face changed, uncertainty taking the place of resentment. He looked quickly at the note, then just as quickly away. He stepped back from her.

"Because," he started, but stopped himself. "I don't know," he amended, and turned to face the wall, shoulders stiff.

"How did you know, anyway?" she pressed. She watched his back, hoping the question would defuse his anger. And she wanted to know. "How did you know that they knew I lied about Saturday?"

"Someone—" Again, he checked himself. "I heard it through the grapevine, I guess. What does it matter?"

It mattered, Isobel thought, watching him, because that would mean he'd been listening in the first place.

"Never mind," she said, her teeth chattering. "Forget it. Can we just . . . ?" Her shivering worsened, and she waggled her knees to keep her blood flowing. How could he stand it in here? She shut her eyes for one elongated second. Opening them again, she said, "Look, can we please just get out of the freezer?"

He whirled and motioned in an offhanded *after you* gesture toward the door.

Hesitating only a moment, unsure if he would follow, Isobel slipped out.

Blessed warmth rushed over her as she re-entered the stockroom. As her nose thawed, she blew warm air into her fists, curling and flexing her fingers in an effort to regain feeling.

He came out behind her, kicking away the makeshift doorstop, letting the enormous freezer door ease shut and click into place.

She didn't wait for him to tell her to leave, and she didn't ask him where to find the cleaning supplies. Instead she went straight to the double-tub sink against the opposite wall and crouched to peer underneath. There she found an empty janitor's bucket and a stack of folded rags. She wrestled the bucket free, straightened, and turned on the hot water.

She glanced back at him. "Do you have a mop?"

"Who did you say this was again?" she asked, using a napkin to peel a wad of gum she could only assume had belonged to Alyssa off the display glass. She sprayed Windex in its place and wiped the case down with a rag.

"Cemetery Sighs," he replied, nodding his head to the grim beat of the churning, haunting music. Before they'd set to cleaning up the mess the crew had left, Varen had replaced the steel drum CD with one from his own collection, which he'd dug out of his car. He'd brought it in along with her gym bag, which Brad, gentleman that he was, had dumped in the parking lot before speeding off. She was actually grateful, though, seeing as the bag held both her phone and her house keys.

"This song is 'Emily Not, Not Gone,'" he said. "It's about a woman who dies and then rises from the grave to be with her true love."

"How romantic," Isobel scoffed.

"It is," he said, and dragged the mop through the last of the malt goo that had gone runny on the floor while they'd been in the freezer.

"It just sounds gruesome to me."

"Gruesome can be romantic."

"Sorry." She shook her head and made a face. "But that's just a strange thing to say."

He stopped mopping and turned to regard her. "Don't you think it's at all romantic—the idea that love could conquer death?"

"I guess." Isobel shrugged, but really she didn't want to think about it. The only thing that came to mind was the phrase "death breath." She grimaced at the thought of kissing a dead guy and walked to the sink behind the counter to rinse out her rag. Over the rush of cold water, the churning music broke to silence, and the female vocals crooned a cappella, beautiful and sad.

> Let this death shroud be a wedding veil,
> Though this skin is clay, my lips so pale.
> My eyes, for you, ever more shine bright
> Blacker than the raven wings of night.
> 'Tis I . . .
> 'Tis I . . .
> Your lost love, your Lady Ligeia. . . .

Isobel paused in thought as the haunting melody began again and then dissipated, the woman's voice trailing off, reverberating in a mesmerizing throb. She shut off the sink and swiveled around. "I thought you said her name was Emily," she said, her words seeming to pull him out of a trance.

He looked at her, lifted the mop from the floor, and

dunked it into the dingy water. "It is. Lady Ligeia . . ." But he stopped and shifted his weight from one foot to the other, as though considering whether or not to explain.

"What?" Isobel asked. Was she missing something? Did he think she was too stupid to get it?

"Lady Ligeia," he began again, "is a woman in literature who returns from the dead, taking over another woman's body to be with her true love."

"Oh, yes. *Lovely*." Isobel blanched. "I guess the other chick didn't mind at all?"

He smirked and, grasping the mop handle, wheeled the janitor's bucket behind the counter, guiding it toward the back room. "It's actually one of Poe's most famous stories."

Oh, she thought. So that's why he hadn't wanted to elaborate. She stood for a moment, arms crossed, thinking, one hip leaning against the display glass. Then, rounding the counter, she dropped her rag into the sink before going to stand in the doorway of the staff room. Hands braced on either side of the door frame, she leaned in.

"Hey," she called. "Speaking of, did you do the project yet?"

"No."

She watched him hoist the bucket and pour the filthy water into the tub sink.

"It's due week after next."

"Yeah, I know," he said. He set the bucket down and kept his back to her while he washed his hands. "Shouldn't you be the one worried about that?"

"I guess so," she mumbled, and cast her eyes to the polished floor. They'd scrubbed the place till it sparkled and she was convinced that it was actually cleaner now than it had been before Brad and the crew trashed it. If she had learned one thing for certain about Varen now, it was that he was thorough.

She looked up again and watched in silence as he opened the locker cabinet in the corner and brought out his wallet, strung with three different lengths of chain. He scooped something else out with his other hand, and when he made for the door, she stepped out of his way.

He brushed past her into the main room and deposited his wallet, coils of chains, and a handful of rings onto one of the wicker tables. Next he grabbed the plastic trash bag they'd filled during the cleanup and, pulling the plastic drawstring closed, tied it off.

"Give me a sec," he said. "I gotta take this out." Isobel watched him disappear into the staff room again, lugging the trash bag behind him. She heard the back outer door open.

She glanced down at the wallet on the table and the small collection of rings. One of the rings, she realized, was his high school ring. No one could have guessed by looking at it from a distance, though. The ring's boxy silver frame cradled a bulky, black rectangular gem in place of the traditional Trenton blue sapphire. A silver *V* stood in the middle of the onyx stone instead of a *T* and, on the side, where people usually had the school's hawk-head emblem, there was the profile of a crow or a raven or something that wasn't a hawk.

Her gaze drifted away from the rings to his wallet.

She glanced at the open staff door, then back to the wallet. Outside, the Dumpster banged.

Quickly Isobel snatched up his wallet and pried it open.

The first thing she found was a little plastic insert for pictures. It held a single oval photograph—the girl from Varen's morning group, part of the woe-is-me convergence that met at the radiator next to the side doors every morning. It was the girl who had handed him the red envelope, Isobel realized, and she thought her name was Lacy. Did this mean she was his girlfriend?

The girl wasn't smiling in the picture. She had a defiant expression on her round face, as though she were silently daring the onlooker to address her directly. She had mounds of thick black hair that fell past the cut of the photo, though Isobel knew that the black waves ended in coils dipped in red dye. She had full lips, too, painted a deep burgundy, and her eyeliner, drawn with sharp wingtips, made her huge dark eyes seem even larger. Those eyes, combined with her copper skin, made her look like an Egyptian goddess.

Varen's music ceased without warning. Silence pulsed. Hands fumbling, Isobel snapped closed the wallet and set it back on the table amid the rings, just as he'd left it. She dropped into one of the chairs and crossed her legs, trying to look nonchalant.

He emerged from the back room with his black booklet of CDs in one hand, his jacket in the other. He set the CD case aside and pulled on the worn hunter green jacket, the one with the silhouette of the dead bird safety-pinned onto the back. Stopping at the table, he stuffed his wallet into his back pocket and, turning halfway away, lifted his shirt to hook the chains through a front belt loop.

Isobel stole a glance.

A black silver-studded belt encircled his narrow hips. Beneath the baggy T-shirt, he was thin and pale but strong-looking. She tried not to go pink in the face when she suddenly caught herself wondering if his skin felt warm to the touch or vampire cold.

Isobel averted her eyes. She stared out the store windows instead, but she could still see his reflection in the darkened glass. She stared, watching his every movement as he set to putting the rings on his fingers methodically, one at a time. His arms, sinewy and graceful, moved as though conducting a ritual, and she blinked, unable to look away.

When he was finished, he snatched up his CD case and she snapped to.

"C'mon," he said. "I'll drive you home."

"It's the next right," she said, "by the fountain."

The headlights of Varen's car swept over the tiered fountain as he steered them into her neighborhood, Lotus Grove. He drove a black 1967 Cougar, the interior a dark burgundy, a nice ride.

The Cougar, rumbling, purring like its namesake, rolled to a stop in front of her driveway. Isobel took her time unfastening her seat belt. She stalled, remembering how Poe had come up again at the ice cream shop. That couldn't have been a coincidence, could it? He had to have been dropping a hint, right?

She'd thought about this the whole ride home. In truth, she'd been thinking about it ever since he'd introduced her to Cemetery Sighs. But she hadn't yet worked up enough courage to ask. Now that she was at her house and about to get out of the car, however, she couldn't ignore the now-or-never feeling churning in her gut.

"Listen," she began. She shifted in her seat to look at him, though he didn't return her gaze. Maybe he knew it was coming. She took the dive anyway. What did she have left to lose? "Are you . . . set on doing the project by yourself now?"

He said nothing, only continued to stare forward out the windshield. Isobel waited but, deciding not to hold her breath, took his silence as a yes. She grasped the door handle and pulled, not about to argue that she didn't deserve it.

"I get off of work at five on Sunday," he said, and she paused, one foot on the pavement. "Can you meet after that?"

"Yeah."

"Good," he said. "Nobit's Nook is a bookstore on Bardstown Road, you know where it is?"

She nodded. She knew where it was.

"I'll be there at five thirty," he said.

Sold, she thought. "Five thirty Sunday," she echoed, and grabbed her stuff, climbing out before he had time to change his mind. She shut the car door behind her, waved, and jogged up the slope of her lawn to her front door. She dug around in her gym bag in search of her keys, but when she tried the handle, she found the door unlocked. She slipped in, careful not to make any noise, since her parents had probably gone to bed sometime around eleven.

Once inside, she fished out her blinking phone and flipped it open. The LCD light lit up, showing seven missed calls— what? Oh crud, Coach always had them turn off their phones before a game, because she hated hearing them go off in the locker room. Had she left it on silent this whole time? Mom and Dad were going to—

"Where have you been?" A familiar voice broke through the darkness. Isobel's eyes flew wide. She turned and saw her mom sitting at the dining room table and her dad right next to her, neither of them wearing their happy faces.

"And who was that?" her father asked.

9

Intangible Forms

Grounded. That was her sentencing for the rest of the weekend, mostly because Isobel hadn't been able to come up with a satisfactory excuse as to why she hadn't checked her phone sooner. When her mom and dad had asked where she'd been, she'd done her best not to lie, saying that the crew had gone out for ice cream after the game and that they had lost track of time. To the question of who had brought her home, Isobel had only shrugged, saying that it had been someone from school. She could tell that her dad especially hadn't liked that answer, but he didn't interrogate her any further about it, either.

She wasn't ready to talk about what had happened at the ice cream shop. She certainly wasn't ready to tell her parents that she had broken up with Brad. Or even admit that the crew was no more. Not when she'd scarcely had time to process everything herself. Mostly, though, she felt reluctant about mentioning Varen's name at all, as if, somehow, that could only invoke further disaster.

And so, between bouts of sulking and trying not to think about losing all of her friends in one night, or about the crazy way Brad had acted or about how awkward things would be at school on Monday, Isobel spent most of that Saturday trying to devise a plan as to how she was going to meet up with Varen the next day. Of course, she already knew that it would have to involve sneaking out.

By late Sunday afternoon, when her dad had plunked himself in front of the TV, she also realized that, if she wanted to greatly decrease her chances of getting caught, she would also need to position a lookout.

Convincing Danny proved to be more difficult than usual. She started off the bidding by offering to do all of his chores for the week because, in the past, whenever she'd been desperate for a favor, that one had usually done the trick. This time, however, he passed on that proposal as well as on the prospect of collecting her allowance for the next two weeks. Normally one for immediate gratification, Danny surprised her by cutting an unusual deal, one that would involve Isobel putting on a part-time chauffeur hat after her birthday in the spring, after she finally got her car. The negotiation reminded her of a Mafia do-or-die session, complete with Danny threatening to make her life miserable should she "renege" on any one "clause" of their "agreement," and it made her realize how enterprising her little brother had become since starting middle school. But she figured that her parents would probably make her tote him around to some degree, anyway. And so, after reminding Danny how he watched way too much TV, Isobel reluctantly conceded.

"But I'm not picking your friends up or taking everybody home to ten different places," she said before taking his offered hand.

To this, Danny rolled his eyes, giving her hand a stiff shake. "That's why we have bikes. *Duh*."

"So what am I supposed to do if Mom and Dad try to go in your room?" Danny asked this while watching her load her backpack with a notepad, pens, and the books on Poe she'd checked out from the library.

"*Don't* let them in," she said. Honestly, hadn't they already gone over this?

"Yeah, but I can't keep them out. You and I both know that I can hardly keep *myself* out." He added this last bit while leaning against her vanity and opening one of the drawers.

"Well, you'd better," she said, shutting the drawer again. "You know the deal is off if they find out."

That ought to add a little extra incentive, Isobel thought.

She pulled on her backpack and walked over to her open window. Cool air breezed in, stirring her lace curtains, blowing in the scent of rusty leaves and that singed autumn smell that was almost spicy. So far it had been a nice day, if just a little bit cooler than Isobel liked. At least it didn't look like it was going to rain.

She straddled the window ledge, ducking her head down and out before climbing fully onto the roof. They lived in a split-level, so there had always been a little outcrop she could slip out to sit on if she needed to be alone.

Isobel steadied herself on the decline, the coarse shingles scraping and crunching under her shoes. She tried not to look over the ledge of the gutter. Instead she glanced over her shoulder to see Danny leaning out, looking after her.

"Remember," she said, but she didn't have to finish.

"If they start to ask questions, you have a headache, and you're asleep."

"And?"

"*And* keep a watch out at the garage door, because you'll be back by the stroke of seven thirty and in time for dinner or else you'll turn back into an alien and be deported to your home planet." Danny recited all this with his chubby face cupped in his hands, his elbows propped against the window ledge. He flashed a smile at the end.

Isobel rolled her eyes and turned to shuffle along the roof, careful to keep her footing square and sure against the sloped terrain.

"This may be none of my business," she heard Danny say from behind, "but can I ask *why* you're risking life, liberty, and limb to sneak out?"

"Normally," Isobel began as she reached the far edge, where she knew her mother's white wood lattice met with the roof, "that sort of information would be classified." She drew off her backpack and dropped it to the grass below. Then she turned and lowered herself, extending a leg over the ledge, feeling around for purchase. The tip of her shoe slid into a slot on the lattice. "But since you asked . . ." Gaining a foothold, she began to descend. "I've got to go do my homework."

*   *   *

The door creaked, and a belt of rusty bells clanged as she entered the old bookstore.

From the outside, Isobel could tell that the building had once been someone's house, the painted bricks chipping green paint, a crumbling chimney visible on one side of the roof. Inside, the musty air held an antique thickness, and the scent of dust and aging books combined to make breathing a chore.

The front room stretched before her long and narrow, lined with rows of tall, sturdy bookshelves that reached almost to the ceiling. Overhead, the tired light fixtures burned a dull gold, adding little relief to the accumulated shadows.

Isobel inched in. She didn't see Varen anywhere, but then again she couldn't see much of anything yet. Carefully she stepped around a mound of ancient-looking tomes gathered near the door. She thought that this place must be in violation of at least ten different fire codes. She moved between two shelves and thought about calling out but for some reason, couldn't bring herself to break the dead silence.

Isobel's gaze passed up and over the marked spines of countless books, every item categorized by its own number and date, and it made her feel almost as though she were walking through catacombs.

When she reached the end, she peered around the shelf to see a counter. Well, really, she saw a lot of books piled on top of something that at one time must have been a counter. Behind it sat an old man with crazy, flyaway white hair sticking out every which way around his head, like he'd caught his breakfast fork in a wall socket that morning.

He scowled at her with one large, piercing gray eye, the other eye pinched shut. In his lap was an enormous leather-bound book, open to a page somewhere in the middle.

"Oh, ah . . . ," she said, and jabbed her thumb over her shoulder, as though he'd need to know she'd come in through the front door. "I'm just looking for someone."

He kept staring at her with that one eye, and it made her think of how a bird eyes a worm.

"Uh. You don't . . . happen to know . . ." She trailed off, transfixed by that eye.

Creepy much? He didn't even blink.

Isobel took a step back and pointed over her shoulder again. "I'll just let myself—"

He snorted, loud and abrupt. She jumped, ready to turn tail and scuttle outside to wait for Varen on the street. They could just go to Starbucks and study, because this was too freaky for her. Before she could take so much as a single backward step, though, the man's pinched eye flew open. He stirred in his seat, blinking rapidly, sniffing.

"Oh, oh," he grunted. He straightened in his armchair and squinted at her with both eyes, one of which she saw was a dark muddy brown, though it looked almost black in the dim lighting. "Where did you come from, young lady?"

Isobel stared at him, having to break her gaze away to glance back at the front door—to the sunlight and the side-walk and the sane people walking their dogs.

"Oh, don't let this get to you," he said, aiming the tip of one finger at the large gray eye. "It's glass." He wheezed out a haggard laugh. "Glad you came along." His laugh dissolved into a loose cough. "Or I'd have slept the day away," he added.

"I'm—I'm supposed to meet someone here," Isobel murmured, and then was sorry she'd opened her mouth. All she really wanted to do was go back outside and stand on the sidewalk. She'd passed a nice café on the way that would maybe work as a compromise, and they could work there instead. She didn't even see anywhere to sit down in this place.

"Oh, yeah?" He coughed again, though he might have been laughing. She couldn't be sure. She watched him coil one wrinkled fist against his mouth. His shoulders shook as he wheezed into his hand, his cheeks puffing like a blowfish.

When he stopped coughing, he let out a relieved sigh. "He's upstairs," the man grunted, and pointed one knotted finger toward an archway, which led into a back room that Isobel could see was (surprise, surprise) filled with still more books. "All the way to the back and up the stairs. Ignore the sign on the door."

"Uh, thanks," she said, but he'd already bent his head and gone back to reading. Or sleeping. It was hard to tell.

Turning, Isobel passed through the archway and into the back part of the store. She found the door he'd told her about against the back wall. Tall and narrow, it looked like the lid of a coffin. Her first thought was that it must be a broom closet, but she didn't see any other doors around, and this one did have a sign on it. Actually, it had two.

DO NOT ENTER

That was the first one. The second sign, written by hand on a yellowing slip of coarse paper, bore another warning.

BEWARE OF BESS

Who, or *what*, was Bess? she wondered. More important, which sign was the one she was supposed to ignore? Isobel glanced over her shoulder toward the front room. She didn't really feel like going back to ask grandpa-coughs-a-lot, and he *did* say to go upstairs.

Isobel grasped the tarnished brass knob and turned. The door squeaked open, revealing a long, narrow staircase that stretched steeply upward. Square shafts of white sunlight shone down from a window at the top, a million dust motes dancing in and out of the beams.

All right, she thought. If these were the stairs she was supposed to go up, then where was this Bess?

"Hello?"

Her voice sounded quiet and small in her own ears. She didn't receive an answer, but she thought she could hear the shuffling of papers, so she mounted the stairs, leaving the door open behind her.

There was no banister leading up, so she held her arms out at either side and braced her hands along the dark wood-paneled walls. The stairs groaned and creaked underfoot, as though murmuring secrets about her.

She took one step after another, and as she drew closer to the top, an odd feeling began to creep over her. She felt it in her stomach first, a queasy sensation coupled with the slightest hint of vertigo. It made her skin prickle and the tiny hairs on her arms stand at attention. She drew to a halt on the steps and listened.

Crack!

Isobel yelped. Her knees buckled, and she dropped down to clutch the stairs.

Whipping her head around, she saw that someone had slammed the door shut.

10
Spirits of the Dead

"What are you doing?"

She knew that voice, languid and calm, with that faint hint of irritation. Isobel slowly turned her head until she found herself focusing on a pair of dusty black boots positioned at the top of the stairs, less than a foot from her nose. Tilting her head back, her eyes met with the cool greens of one Varen Nethers, the great-and-jaded.

He stared down at her, a Discman in one hand, spinning a CD, his other hand poised on the buzzing, squealing headphones draped around his neck.

"That crazy old guy slammed the door on me!"

He shot her an admonishing glare before turning away, moving into the room, which was small—tiny really, an attic, or so it had probably once been. His boots made hollow thumping sounds against the dried-out floorboards as he made his way toward a small, café-style table, which sat at the other end of the room, swamped with papers. In the center of the space, an ugly, threadbare, brown and orange throw rug lay stretched out on the floor, like the severed scalp of some balding monster. Aside from a few obligatory stacks of books in each corner of the room, there was nothing else.

The table sat beneath a window, the only other besides the one above the stairs. This window was smaller and round, and it overlooked the street.

"Bruce hates noise," Varen said, "so I can't picture him slamming any doors."

Isobel pursed her lips. She watched him resume his seat at the table, setting the CD player aside before he began sifting through the mess of papers. She eyed the Discman, thinking that it was really old-school that he still carried one, that he didn't have an iPod or some other MP3 player. She thought better about commenting on it, though.

Instead she folded her arms and said, "So you're calling me a liar."

"Did I say that?" he asked without looking up, and she couldn't help but recall how these same words had been the first he'd ever spoken to her.

"Well, you insinuated it."

"You're jumping to conclusions."

"Yeah, so then who slammed the door?"

"Bess," he said, as though this were the logical conclusion for anyone to make.

"Who the heck *is* this Bess?" Isobel's arms went up and landed at her sides in an exasperated flop. She hadn't even met Bess, and already she was starting to despise her.

"The poltergeist."

"The what?"

"Pol-ter-geist," he said again, enunciating each syllable.

"You mean, like what?" Isobel scoffed. "A ghost?"

"Sort of."

"You're serious."

His eyes lifted from the table to fix on her—seriously.

"Whatever," she said, brushing off a patch of gray grit she'd spotted on the front of her jeans, dust that she'd probably picked up from those grimy stairs. It was evident that he was just trying to weird her out again. Probably.

Isobel ignored the goose bumps that prickled all the way up the back of her neck, like tiny spiders with electric legs. "So we're working up here? I don't get it. How do you know that guy?"

"Bruce owns the ice cream shop."

"He's your boss?"

"More or less," he said, and scribbled something onto his notepad.

"I was kind of wondering why you were there all by yourself," she said, using her dad's probing trick, trying to make it sound more like a casual observation than prying.

"Yeah, well, he's short on help. And speaking of that, I'd appreciate it if you didn't mention anything to him about . . . what happened." He didn't look up at her, just kept writing, his pen moving in slow, careful strokes.

"Why? Would you get fired?"

"No. He's just got enough to worry about."

"Do you work here, too?" she asked, looking around. She shed her backpack and let it drop to the floor. Then she took a seat in the chair across from his.

"Not really," he said.

"So what, you just hang out here? With Bruce? And Bess?" she added, trying not to smile.

"Did you read?" he asked.

She paused. Oh, yeah. The reading.

For the first time since she'd written them down, Isobel thought back to the list of titles he'd given her. So much had gotten in the way between then and now. She grimaced. "Mm. About that . . ."

He sighed. A soft sound, like a dying breath.

"Well, have *you* read them?" she asked.

"Multiple times."

"Of course," she said, realizing she might as well have asked the pope if he'd read the Bible.

"You know, you can find most, if not all, of Poe's tales and poems on the Internet," he said, in a very distinct and warning "you'll have no excuse the next time" tone.

"Oh, sure. Let me just ask my geek brother to stop slaying zombie ninjas for a few hours so I can borrow the PC and catch up on my Victorian horror lit."

"Doomed Kingdom One or Two?"

"Huh?"

"Is he playing Doomed Kingdom One or Two? It's the only series with zombie ninjas."

Isobel stared at him, incredulous. "How should I know?"

"Hm," he said, eyes dropping, as though she'd just ratcheted herself down yet another slot on his respect scale. "Never mind." She glared at him as he leaned over to pull something out of his satchel. "Here. You can borrow this for now." Carefully he laid a large, black, gold-embossed book on the table in front of her. Its title read, *The Complete Works of Edgar Allan Poe*, in shining gold letters. "But if anything happens to it, I own your soul."

"Uh, *thanks*," she said, handling it with care while under his scrutiny. "It's so nice and portable."

"We'll have to meet again tomorrow," he said. "After school."

"Can't. I've got practice." Though she hadn't even begun to figure out how she was going to deal with school yet, with facing Brad or Nikki, she still had to stand her ground where practice was concerned. She didn't dare miss, not this close to Nationals.

"Whatever," he said. "Tuesday, then."

"Fine. What time?"

"Sometime after school. But I have to work, so you'll have to come by the shop."

Isobel bit her lip and thought about that. She hadn't realized how tricky this was going to be. On top of being grounded, now that she and Brad were broken up, it was going to be tough to get around. "Can I hitch a ride there with you?" she asked.

He shrugged. Okaaay, she'd just go ahead and take that as a yes. Now all she needed was a way to get home afterward. She probably could walk home, as long as she thought up a good excuse for being gone.

She turned her attention back to the *Complete Works*. On the bottom, she noticed a thin silk ribbon, sticking out like a beige tongue. Following her fingers along the top edge, Isobel pried the book open to the marked page. "Dream-Land," the title read. Isobel skimmed over the first stanza:

> By a route obscure and lonely,
> Haunted by ill angels only,
> Where an Eidolon, named NIGHT,
> On a black throne reigns upright,
> I have reached these lands but newly
> From an ultimate dim Thule—
> From a wild weird clime that lieth, sublime,
> Out of SPACE—out of TIME.

Yeah, well, that made about as much sense as Cracker Jacks.

Isobel flipped forward until she recognized one of the titles that Varen had told her to write down at the library: "The Masque of the Red Death." She thumbed through the story, counting six pages. That didn't seem so bad. She began the first paragraph:

> The "Red Death" had long devastated the country. No pestilence had ever been so fatal, or so hideous. Blood was its Avatar and its seal—the redness and the horror of blood. There were sharp pains, and sudden dizziness, and then profuse bleeding at the pores, with dissolution. The scarlet stains upon the body

and especially upon the face of the victim,
were the pest ban which shut him out from
the aid and from the sympathy of his fellow-
men. And the whole seizure, progress and
termination of the disease, were the incidents
of half an hour.

Isobel glanced up from the page with her eyes only. She
stared at Varen from over the top edge of the book while
he remained absorbed in his notes. Was he serious? The first
paragraph alone was like reading the synopsis of a bad low-
budget slasher flick remixed with nineteenth-century flair.
Either that or a physician's death report. Reluctantly she let
her eyes fall back to the story.

But the Prince Prospero was happy and daunt-
less and sagacious.

Isobel's head popped up. "What does 'sagacious' mean?"
"Sagacious," he said, writing, "adjective describing someone in possession of acute mental faculties. Also describing
one who might, in a bookstore, think to get up and locate an
actual dictionary instead of asking a billion questions."
Isobel made a face at him. When his pen paused, she
ducked her head down and dove back into the page.

When his dominions were half depopulated,
he summoned to his presence a thousand

hale and light-hearted friends from among the knights and dames of his court, and with these retired to the deep seclusion of one of his castellated abbeys. This was an extensive and magnificent structure, the creation of the prince's own eccentric yet august taste. A strong and lofty wall girdled it in. This wall had gates of iron. The courtiers, having entered, brought furnaces and massy hammers and welded the bolts. They resolved to leave means neither of ingress or egress to the sudden impulses of despair or of frenzy from within.

She stopped, thinking that must mean that, no matter what side of the door you were on, there would be no checking in or out of the Prospero Hotel. She had to admit that was a little dooming right there, and it made her kind of want to know what happened. How was Poe going to write his peeps out of this if there was no exit? She skimmed to the bottom of the paragraph.

Buffoons...improvisatori...ballet-dancers... musicians, there was Beauty, there was wine. All these and security were within. Without was the "Red Death."

Yadda yadda. She turned the page.

"Are you skipping?" he asked.

"Nope," she lied without missing a beat, "I just read fast."

> It was a voluptuous scene, that masquerade.
> But first let me tell of the rooms in which it
> was held. There were seven—an imperial suite.

It was here that Isobel first felt the twinge of an inward pull on her mind. Slowly the words started to get out of the way and let images of courtiers revolve, in slow motion, through her mind's eye. It was as though she had somehow adapted to the density of the language. Soon the words smudged away from the page, and in their place, she was left with the sensation of gliding through the scene, like she'd become a movie camera, sweeping through the sets of rooms and over the heads of costumed actors.

Each of the seven rooms, she read, had its own color, with tall, Gothic windows to match. First was the blue chamber, then the purple, then the green, the orange, the white, and then the violet. The last chamber, however, was black, with heavy draperies and bloodred windows.

> It was in this apartment, also, that there stood
> against the western wall, a gigantic clock of
> ebony. Its pendulum swung to and fro with a
> dull, heavy, monotonous clang; and when the
> minute-hand made the circuit of the face, and
> the hour was to be stricken, there came from

the brazen lungs of the clock a sound which
was clear and loud and deep and exceedingly
musical, but of so peculiar a note and emphasis that, at each lapse of an hour, the musicians
of the orchestra were constrained to pause,
momentarily, in their performance, to hearken
to the sound; and thus the waltzers perforce
ceased their evolutions; and there was a brief
disconcert of the whole gay company; and,
while the chimes of the clock yet rang, it was
observed that the giddiest grew pale, and the
more aged and sedate passed their hands over
their brows as if in confused reverie or meditation. But when the echoes had fully ceased,
a light laughter at once pervaded the assembly;
the musicians looked at each other and smiled
as if at their own nervousness and folly, and
made whispering vows, each to the other, that
the next chiming of the clock should produce
in them no similar emotion; and then, after the
lapse of sixty minutes, (which embrace three
thousand and six hundred seconds of the Time
that flies), there came yet another chiming of
the clock, and then were the same disconcert
and tremulousness and meditation as before.

Isobel skimmed ahead until she reached midnight in the
story. Having seen plenty of horror flicks, she knew enough

to expect the major drama to start then. And Poe didn't disappoint. When the black clock chimed twelve, so began the real freakiness. Left and right, everybody started to flip out over some stranger-danger creep who had come out of nowhere.

> The figure was tall and gaunt, and shrouded from head to foot in the habiliments of the grave. The mask which concealed the visage was made so nearly to resemble the countenance of a stiffened corpse that the closest scrutiny must have had difficulty detecting the cheat. And yet all this might have been endured, if not approved, by the mad revelers around. But the mummer had gone so far as to assume the type of the Red Death. His vesture was dabbled in *blood*—and his broad brow, with all the features of the face, was besprinkled with the scarlet horror.

Gross, she thought, *but also kind of cool.* Isobel flipped the page and scanned to the very end, to where Prince Prospero, peeved to the max, started charging through all the chambers.

> He bore aloft a drawn dagger, and had approached, in rapid impetuosity, to within three or four feet of the retreating figure, when the latter, having attained the extremity of the velvet apartment, turned suddenly

and confronted his pursuer. There was a sharp cry—and the dagger dropped gleaming upon the sable carpet, upon which, instantly afterwards, fell prostrate in death the Prince Prospero. Then, summoning the wild courage of despair, a throng of the revellers at once threw themselves into the black apartment, and, seizing the mummer, whose tall figure stood erect and motionless within the shadow of the ebony clock, gasped in unutterable horror at finding the grave-cerements and corpse-like mask which they handled with so violent a rudeness, untenanted by any tangible form.

And now was acknowledged the presence of the Red Death. He had come like a thief in the night. And one by one dropped the revellers in the blood-bedewed halls of their revel, and died each in the despairing posture of his fall. And the life of the ebony clock went out with that of the last of the gay. And the flames of the tripods expired. And Darkness and Decay and the Red Death held illimitable dominion over all.

Hold up. Wait—what? That was it?

Isobel traced over the last sentence again, even though she knew she hadn't missed anything. Or maybe she had?

She swallowed hard against the lump that had formed thick at the back of her throat.

"Okay." She slammed the book shut, causing the table to rattle, which must have caused Varen's writing to skip because he looked up, eyebrows raised. "So can we talk about how I just read this Masque with a *q* thing and how at the end the bad guy totally wins?"

He drew his pen away from the page and sank back into his chair, regarding her with something like amusement. "I assume that when you say 'bad guy' you're referring to the Red Death, implying that Prospero is the good guy?"

Her jaw jutted to one side as she took this into consideration. She saw his point and, eyes rolling upward, lashes fluttering, she sighed. "So, whatever, he locked out all the sick people and threw a big party for his rich buddies. Not cool, I get it. But that aside, why would Poe write a story about some lavish palace and take so much time talking about all these different-colored rooms and build up all of this stuff about this chiming clock and some sagacious prince and his drinking pals if he's just going to kill everybody at the end?"

"Because," Varen said, "in the end, Death always wins."

At these words, Isobel recoiled. She took her hands from the table and put them into her lap, shoulders hunching. "You know," she said, "no offense, but it's when you say stuff like that that people start to worry about you."

His expression fell.

She cringed on the inside, admitting to herself that she hadn't meant to sound so blunt. He stared at her, but she couldn't meet that kohl-etched gaze, half-hidden behind his hair yet still able to pierce her straight through.

"I mean . . . ," she began, gesturing with her hands, as though they could help with the damage control.

"So," he said, "are *you* worried about me?"

Her eyes lifted. He watched her steadily, all too serious and, again, she found herself floundering in that penetrating stare.

Was he being for real? Or was he just mocking her again?

He blinked once, clearly waiting for an answer.

"Um . . ."

She was saved by the sound of a low creak. His focus broke away. She followed his gaze, realizing that it must have been the downstairs door reopening.

"Is somebody coming?" she asked.

"Just Bess," he murmured. "What time is it?"

Isobel felt that prickling sensation on the back of her neck again, only this time it wasn't so easy to shake off. The spider legs came back, trickling electric cold right down her spine. She reached for her backpack, still flustered, her fingers fumbling for the heart-shaped silver key-chain watch.

"Oh, no." She felt her gut plummet. "I've got to go," she said, her chair scraping loudly against the floorboards as she stood. She pulled on her backpack and made her way to the stairs.

"Wait," he called. She heard his pen smack the table.

"Can't," she said. "Sorry." She knew he was irritated with her again but decided she couldn't help that. He could just add this to his (no doubt full) list of things to brood about.

She hustled down the stairs, through the back room, and onto the main floor, past Bruce, who sat slumped in his chair, his glass eye wide open, seeming to follow her as she went. Isobel pushed out the front door, the bells clanking hard as she let it bang shut behind her. Outside, the temperature had dropped, and the air had turned crisper, so much that Isobel could see her breath. Next to her, a streetlamp snapped on.

That was when she realized she'd left the Poe book upstairs.

With a growl, she swiveled, marched back into the shop, and hurried past a snoring Bruce to the back of the store. She started when she found the "Beware of Bess" door closed. Again.

She reached for the knob but paused when she heard voices—one deep and low, another soft and mellow. Who was he talking to? Had someone been hiding up there while they'd been working? She thought of Lacy and immediately opened the door and climbed up, calling, "I forgot—"

She stopped when she reached the top landing. He was gone. His black book was gone too, but his notepad lay on the table, next to his Discman and the Poe book. Isobel turned in a quick circle, but there was no sign of him or anyone else. But how could that be? How could he have left so quickly?

She surveyed the room again to confirm that there were no other doors, no closets to hide in.

Then whose voices had she heard?

With a frigid spike of unease, she realized she was up there alone. With a ghost.

She shot forward, grabbed the Poe book, and scuttled down the stairs, grateful when the door did not slam shut on her this time.

Shoving the Poe book into her bag, she scurried to the front and outside again, the weirdness vibe clinging to her until a brisk breeze whisked past her and blew it away.

Outside, the horizon between buildings blushed a deep peach, while the glow of the streetlamps and storefront windows seemed to brighten by the second. She started in the direction of her house but began to realize, as dusk continued to make its gradual descent, that a fast walk wasn't going to cut it.

Isobel started to run.

11
Whispered Word

The sidewalk raced by beneath her pounding feet, the chilled autumn air stinging her lungs. As she ran, Isobel felt her body enter that uncomfortable place of being warm on the inside but cold with sweat on the outside. She knew she'd pay later for not having warmed up or anything before launching straight into a full-out run.

She tried to picture Danny still holding down the fort, doing whatever he could to direct attention away from her unusually quiet room, which her parents, by now, would have started to wonder about. And if they hadn't, well, they would when they sat down to dinner and she wasn't there.

She swung around a crosswalk pole, stopping to tap the silver button. The light changed, and with only a moment's hesitation to check for traffic, she jogged across the street to Willow Avenue. She slowed, however, as a new thought entered her mind. She stopped and stared down the road where, just ahead, she could see one of the side entrances to the park.

She hesitated, taking a moment to breathe, to debate. She pulled the straps of her backpack forward, bringing the bag flush with her back, and she felt the weight of the Poe book as it pressed into her spine.

Even though the park was huge, with forest patches split by lots of twisty, turny roads and steep rolling hills, it *would* be a lot faster to cut through. And getting past the closed-off entrance and into her subdivision would be as simple as climbing over a low wooden gate. Growing up, she and Danny must have done it every weekend in the summer.

She glanced skyward. Through the smattering of clouds, three early night stars shone in the deepening blue, but it wasn't completely dark yet. If she went through the park, if she ran the whole way and managed not to get lost, she'd make it in time for sure. She knew it.

Her mind made up, she darted for the park entrance.

On either side of the street loomed tall and haughty window-faced Victorian homes. They seemed to watch her as she veered past, taking the one-way blacktop road that curved upward into the park. Soon, the houses and build-ings and streetlights fell away. Her path narrowed to a single, twisting lane of asphalt. Rows of trees and thick underbrush emerged on either side of her. The farther into the park she ran, the denser the surrounding forest grew.

Overhead, the interlocking patchwork of hanging boughs worked to transform her pathway into a darkening tunnel. Through the lacework of limbs, thick clouds inched by.

Isobel ran on, listening to the soft beat of her sneakers as they pounded the blacktop. She couldn't wait to get home and into a hot shower. She thought about making herself some peppermint tea and maybe even going to bed early, even though she couldn't say it was because she was looking forward to tomorrow.

Darkness crept in around her, spreading its fingers through the trees, working to smear them into a single black blur.

As she approached a fork in the road, she slowed, but only long enough to decide that she should keep going straight. She'd somehow forgotten that the city didn't keep the park roads lit, and she hoped that if a car came up, it would have its lights on, that she would hear it, and that the driver would see her.

She kept running, her breath the loudest sound in her ears. The only sound.

She frowned, at last admitting to herself that something had felt funny since she'd entered the park. Only now, however, could she place her finger on what.

She slowed her run to a jog, listening to the lonely, hollow clap of her sneakers.

Quiet.

Everything around her stood really still and really . . . quiet.

The breeze that had greeted her outside the bookshop had vanished somewhere between there and here, and she looked up now to find the tree limbs motionless, their leaves immobile.

Or were those leaves at all?

A black shadow moved in one of the trees, and Isobel registered the silhouette of one huge black bird. It made no sound, though it seemed to watch her from its perch. One of the leaves at its side moved. Another bird. Soon, with a ruffle of feathers, she noticed another and, on her other side, another.

One of them broke the silence with a caw, the sound falling harsh on her ears, rasping and raw.

Spooked, Isobel picked up the pace again, glad that cheerleading had kept her in such great shape. True, she wasn't the world's best runner, but she could keep going if she needed to, and right now, she needed to.

She wondered, an ice-water sensation rushing through her veins with the thought, if Bess could have followed her. Could poltergusties—or whatever they were—could they follow someone? Stick to them like parasites?

Isobel shook off the convulsive shudder that rattled its way through her shoulders. Stupid idea. No such thing as ghosts. Only stupid boys with morbid fascinations and old men who liked to slam doors.

Maybe the stillness was just her imagination. After all, this was a park. Parks were supposed to be placid. Serene. Maybe she just missed the sounds of traffic and people and the glare of artificial light. Besides, everything died in the fall anyway, right? All the little crickets had chirped their last sometime back in early September.

Still, she couldn't help feeling that there should have been some sounds. Like a dog barking. Or a foraging squirrel. A rabbit or *something*.

She slowed to a stop again, this time so she could catch her breath. She leaned forward, clasping her knees, her own huffing all but reverberating in the silence. She glanced over her shoulder at the darkening stretch of road behind her, black, like a ribbon of ink. She looked forward once more. She wasn't sure, but she thought the entrance to her neighborhood lay straight ahead from where she stood right now. If she was right, she'd enter a block behind her house and be home maybe even with a few seconds to spare.

But something else felt wrong now, and it wasn't just the stillness.

Since she had stopped running, the air around her had seemed to compress, to grow denser. She couldn't explain it, but it felt as though the night itself, unnatural in its calmness, had begun to move in on her, to close in tight.

Her nerves prickled. Along her neck and arms, all hairs raised to stand on end.

The idea that you could feel like you were being watched had always sort of struck Isobel as being corny in a Scooby-Doo kind of way. Now, though, as she turned and looked around at all the black trees with their skeletal arms tangled in a silent fight for space, she couldn't help the sudden feeling that, somewhere among them, something watched her, waited for her to move again.

The birds were gone now. Which was weird, since she hadn't heard them take off.

She listened.

Nothing. The silence grew, feeding on itself until it became a dull roar in her ears.

She continued on the road, though at a slower, quieter

walk, and just when she started to think that listening to the eerie nothing might be worse than actually hearing something, a hushing sound—a fast *whoosh*—broke through from the line of trees at her right. She jumped, an ice pick of fear stabbing her through the middle so that, for a moment, she forgot how to breathe.

Whatever it was had been big. As in person big.

"Who's there?"

Skoooshh!

Isobel whirled. This sound had come from the trees directly across the road. It came again from behind. She heard the pop of a branch and the crush of dry leaves. She spun in a circle, and despite the cascade of sudden noise, the rustling and crackling, she could not sense so much as the slightest movement in any direction.

Isobel felt her throat constrict and her chest tighten. Her heartbeat sped to triple time. She turned and broke once more into a run, taking the road as hard and as fast as her legs would carry her. Her palms, cold and sweaty, tightened around the straps of her backpack, and she felt the Poe book pound against her.

Whatever it was in the woods, it followed her. Out of the corner of one eye, she thought she saw the edge of a dark something. Then there was another at her left. Figures, tall and long, rushed through the black gate of trees on either side of her, their movements too fast. Impossibly fast.

As she sped up, so did the dappled forms.

They seemed to multiply as, out of her periphery, she

spotted yet another. This one glided away from the others to rush along the group of trees directly beside her. It moved *through* the trees, through undergrowth, dashing over the dry ground—a rippling form. She risked a quick glance, head-on, but saw nothing, only blackness and tangled branches and stillness. But that was impossible!

"Go away!" she screamed. She couldn't outrun them, whatever or whoever they were. She couldn't gain even the slightest bit of distance, and already a stitch the size of a softball had begun to knot itself in her side. She blocked out the pain, pushing through. Run. Run. Run!

"Run!" she heard someone hiss. A man.

It had come from the line of trees beside her.

Isobel tried to cry for help but couldn't find the breath, able only to choke out a low sob. She couldn't stop to scream, but she couldn't keep going like this, either. She couldn't breathe anymore. Her lungs stung from the cold while her sides ached with stiffening pain.

Why hadn't she gone around the park like before? Why hadn't she just—

The gate!

Straight ahead. There! She could see it.

Dizziness wafted in around her temples, but she wouldn't stop now. Somehow, she knew that if she could just clear the gate, she would make it home. She'd be all right.

Reaching the gate, Isobel clasped a hand to the wood and, as she vaulted over, felt the stabbing reward of a thick splinter as it entered her palm. Her feet hit the dust and gravel pathway beyond. She teetered forward from the weight of her book bag and slammed to her knees. She picked herself up again, stumbling, scrambling, running even as her body begged her to stop.

The chains that held the swinging gate shut rattled behind her. Whispers and hisses. Someone laughed, but the sound morphed into a high-pitched shriek. She heard a splintering shatter—like a crash of plates.

She dared not turn around.

To her left and right, familiar houses zoomed by, looking like shocked faces in the low street light. She tore past them, and even as her own house drew into view, she did not slow. She willed her body to keep moving in spite of her screaming muscles, the torturous ache in her lungs.

"Isssobel."

The sound of her name whisked by her, caught by the wind and then lost in the rush of leaves scattering around her feet. She had heard it, though. Her name. Someone had whispered her name.

That, at last, stopped her and brought her stuttering to a halt at the edge of her front yard. She wheeled around, eyes scanning. She gasped for breath, sucking down air in huge gulps.

She peeled her backpack off and, mustering every bit of strength she had left, threw it onto the ground. It made a dull thud sound as the book within slammed to the cold, hard turf.

Whoever it was had said her name. That meant they knew her.

As though triggered by the flip of a switch, rage replaced her fear.

"Who's there?" she shouted, heaving. "Who is it? Why don't you just come out?"

She wiped her running nose with her sleeve, not caring.

"Brad?" she roared toward the oak in Mrs. Finley's yard. "Mark? I know you're there!" This she turned on a row of shrubs lining Mr. Anchor's white fence.

"Brad, if that's you, this isn't funny, I swear to God it's not! Wherever you are—*whoever* you are—!" As she shouted, Isobel bent down despite her wooziness and hauled up from the leaf-strewn grass a thick and gnarled branch. She swung it, teetering. "Come out already!" She waved the limb through the air again, swiping. "Come out so I can take this stick and shove it straight up your—"

"*Isobel!*"

Whirling, Isobel dropped the stick. It cracked against the asphalt.

Her mother leaned out the front door, her form cast in the buttery glow of the porch light. Arms crossed, tucked in against the cold, she squinted at Isobel, her expression undergoing a strange battle between concern and outrage.

12
The Invisible Visible

In that moment, all Isobel wanted to do was run to her mom, cry on her, and tell her everything. She wanted her dad to search the yard, call the cops, and have them shut down the park. And right then, with her mom watching her like that, and the energy draining from her limbs, making her feel so tired, Isobel found she didn't care anymore about getting in trouble. Maybe she *wanted* to stay inside for the rest of her life.

Just as she was about to collapse onto the grass, release the waterworks, and let the confessions fly, Danny's voice broke out from the side of the house. "You tell 'em, Iz!" he shouted. Her head jerked up, and she saw him trudging toward her, huffing, his belly wobbling beneath his white T-shirt. Behind him, like a disobedient dog, he pulled along one of the large plastic trash cans they kept on the back porch. Isobel watched, only vaguely aware that her mouth had dropped open.

Danny sent a cheerful wave toward their mom, who had stepped out onto the porch. Snorting, he said, "That raccoon again."

"What are you two doing?" her mom said. Her arms remained folded. She shifted her weight from one foot to the other, eyeing them both. "Somebody better tell me what's going on out here."

Isobel's numb gawk shifted away from her brother, to her mother, and back to her brother.

"It's all good, Mom," Danny assured her as he drew the huge trash can to sit right next to the mailbox, grunting and puffing. He patted the lid. "Just taking out the trash. Thought we'd do it before dinner so we wouldn't have to in the morning." He beamed.

"Isobel?" Her mom's voice sounded as though it were coming from inside a bottle.

Isobel tried to work her mouth, feeling like a fish that had flopped out of its tank.

"She's helping me," Danny answered for her.

Isobel found it easier to nod than to talk.

"And," Danny continued, "that stupid raccoon came back again. *Damn raccoon!*" he shouted, his voice echoing through the neighborhood.

"*Danny!*"

"Sorry, Mom. Darn raccoon!" he yelled.

"Both of you," her mom snapped, "get in here. Right now. You can finish taking out the trash after dinner, Danny. Not you, Isobel. You look like death warmed over. Get inside before you get sick."

When their mother turned away to open the screen door for them, Isobel felt Danny's elbow shoot into her side, causing her to jump with a residual jolt of adrenaline. *Where the hell were you?* he mouthed. But he didn't wait for an answer.

KELLY CREAGH — 123

Instead he scowled and, shaking his head, hustled into the house and past their mom. Isobel drifted toward the open door and her worried mother. She wiped her nose on her sleeve again, sniffing.

"I hope you two weren't out here fighting," her mom said, leaning down to brush the chalky dirt from the knees of Isobel's jeans. "You're both getting too old for that. You especially, Isobel."

Stepping in, Isobel glanced over her shoulder and into the darkness one last time.

Perched in the branches of Mrs. Finley's oak, she noticed a single black bird, swiveling its head around. Its gaze seemed to stop on her.

They had turkey and mashed potatoes for dinner, but Isobel hadn't been able to force down more than a few bites. Between her dad repeatedly asking her if she felt all right and her mom reaching over every three seconds to feel her forehead, Isobel couldn't concentrate on her food anyway. Eventually she excused herself and went to take a shower.

There was something about warm water and being alone that made it easier to think.

Isobel could feel the tension slide off her shoulders and swirl down the drain with the grime and the sweat. Her muscles relaxed, and closed up in the small warm space, she felt safe.

Shutting the water off and stepping out of the shower, she wrapped her hair in a towel and pulled on the fluffy pink robe her mom had given her last Christmas.

She guessed she had Danny to thank for not getting in trouble. The raccoon story had been pretty swift, since something had been coming around and knocking over the trash cans at night. Of course, she knew the reason he'd come to her rescue had nothing to do with any brotherly sense of duty, but because of the pact they'd made. If she didn't get a car in the spring, then he didn't get a chauffeur.

Isobel gathered up her dirty, sweat-stained clothes. She left the steamy, warm bathroom, huddling into her robe as she passed through the frigid hallway and made the ten-foot trek to her room. She shut her bedroom door behind her and, looking around, noticed that Danny hadn't bothered to close the curtains like she'd told him to do after she'd left. With a grunt, she dropped her clothes in her hamper and went to draw the shade down. She stopped, peering into the night. That bird. It was still there, still sitting on the same branch of the knot-limbed oak across the street. It seemed to be staring right at her.

Isobel pulled her shade and yanked the lace curtains closed.

Sitting on the edge of her bed, she unwrapped her hair from the towel-turban and patted it to soak up the extra moisture. She set the towel aside and reached for the metallic green hair dryer on her nightstand (which she seldom unplugged or put away) and flicked it on to the lowest setting. She turned her head to one side, idly waving the blow dryer back and forth through her hair. With her free hand, she picked up her cell from the bedside table where she'd left it to charge. She flipped it open and checked for missed calls. None. She checked for texts. Again, none.

She sighed. All things considered, it didn't surprise her.

She stared at the wall, and her eyes went unfocused. The warm air felt good against her scalp, and combined with the low drone, it began to make her drowsy. She wouldn't have guessed she'd be able to sleep tonight, but now that she was home, surrounded by normalcy, the memory of her terror began to subside, as though it had been something that had happened a month ago, and not an hour.

Like she'd done a dozen times already, she replayed the run in her head. If she hadn't been so scared, so completely out of it, she might have seen who it was. But she hadn't wanted to stop long enough to wait for someone to appear. While the thought had made sense outside, when she'd been swinging a stick at nothing, she now tried to come to terms with the idea that she'd been chased by someone who knew her. And if that was the case, then more than anything, it had probably all been just a sick joke, right?

She frowned, knowing that it didn't make much sense. In fact, nothing about it made sense. It didn't seem likely that Brad or any of the others would do something like that. She couldn't picture it. Besides, Brad would have to have followed her to the bookstore, then waited for her outside. And while she could picture him spying, something about the idea of him chasing her through the park at dusk just didn't add up. He was too straightforward for that. Not to mention too proud.

No, even if he had been anywhere around, even if he'd been spying, she thought she knew him well enough to say that he would never try to scare her so badly. In fact, even if he had followed her, breakup or not, she knew he wouldn't have let her go into the park by herself to begin with. It had been a stupid move—she knew that now. He was always getting after her for doing stupid, impulsive things.

Isobel bit her lip. Her hand tightened on her phone as she battled the sudden wave of longing to dial Brad's number. She wanted to call him, to tell him what had happened.

But she knew what he would say. First, he'd be smug because she'd called him, because she'd caved after only a day. Then he'd ask all sorts of reasonable-sounding questions. Then, finally, he'd say it was Varen and go into an all-out "I told you so" blowup. And then . . . then what? Do more of what he had already shown himself capable of?

Isobel scowled at the thought. There was something about the memory of Brad slamming Varen around that made her whole body wince, like someone breaking a Ming vase just to prove that they could.

Then again, she thought, pausing—what about Varen?

Could he have followed right behind her after she'd left the bookstore? It would have been easy to do. But why would he? To play a joke on her? Prove some morbid point? She *had* heard voices upstairs after going back to get the Poe book. Was it something he'd planned? Revenge for the ice cream shop? With some of the dark stuff he said sometimes, she didn't know if she would put it past him.

Over the whir of the hair dryer, she thought she heard a quiet tap, a knock on her door.

Isobel shut off the hair dryer. Glancing at her door, she gathered her still damp hair in one hand and said, "Come in."

Her door remained shut. She stared at it, waiting. "Mom?" she said. "Dad?"

There was no answer.

She set her phone aside, left the dryer on her bed, and went to open her door. Poking her head out into the hall, she heard the blare of the TV from downstairs, the distant roar of a crowd over her dad's enthused "Go, go, go!" The bathroom light was off, and she could still smell the remnants of the cherry blossom shower gel she'd used. Danny's door stood ajar at the end of the hallway, blasts of blue-white light issuing forth, each burst accompanied by a zombie's scream of anguish. Other than that, there was nothing.

Confused, Isobel shut her door again, then went to her dresser, pulling open the top drawer and rifling for her favorite pair of pink-and-black-striped pajama shorts, and matching T-shirt.

She got dressed, tossing her robe onto the floor, but paused after pulling the T-shirt down over her head because she thought she had heard the tap again, this time from behind.

Isobel looked up. She stared past her reflection in the dresser mirror, her gaze fixing on her window. She waited, and the sound came once more. A soft and quiet tap. It was accompanied this time by a low scuffle, like the scrape of rough fabric against wood.

She twisted around to stare at her window, ears straining.

The rustling came again, louder this time. There, beyond the lace of her curtains, under the tiny slit at the bottom of the shade, something moved.

Her heart rate quickened.

For a moment she thought about going to her door and calling downstairs for her dad.

Then the scraping shuffle seemed to shift. It became continuous now, and at this angle, she thought she could see a bit of black cloth, like the shoulder of someone's shirt—somebody angling to try and get a good grip on her window.

In one quick move, Isobel reached out to her dresser, snatching the "Number One Flyer" trophy she'd won freshman year. It left behind a polished square of wood in the layer of accumulated dust. Clenching the trophy by the fake-gold cheerleader figurine, she held it upside down in one hand, brandishing the hard granite base like a club.

Each footstep soaked silently into the carpet as she drew closer to her window.

A long rustling *shhirrk-sruuffshh* sounded from just outside. Squinting, she thought she could see what looked like a set of long, thin, black-gloved fingers trying to reach under the sill.

With a quick step forward, Isobel yanked down on the shade. It rushed upward with a loud snap. Something screeched. Blackness, like spattering ink, spread across her window. With a short scream, she fell back. She hurled the trophy toward the window, missing the glass by inches, knocking a dent into the wall.

An angry flurry of dark feathers splayed against the glass, followed by the tap of a pointed beak and a low, grating croak.

"Stupid bird!" Isobel shouted, her heart pounding so hard that she could feel her pulse thudding in her temples. She pulled herself up from the floor, a stinging bite of rug burn chafing the back of her thigh. She ignored it, rushing to pluck two pink throw pillows from her bed. She chucked one right after the other at the window. The huge beast of a bird gave one giant flap of its black wings. It let out a squawk when the first pillow hit, and then, after the second, it swooped off into the darkness.

Isobel yanked the shade down again, pulling the lace curtains closed.

She made her way back to her bed. Fighting the shivers, she grabbed her robe along the way, throwing it back on over her pajamas. She chucked her dryer off her bed and onto the floor, swiping up her phone.

She paced. The view screen of her phone read 8:52 in electric blue. Cutting it close to nine, she thought. Well, he'd just have to deal.

Isobel punched in the number. The dial tone rang once . . . twice . . . three times. She'd give it one more—

"Yeah?"

Isobel blinked in surprise. She hadn't expected *him* to answer. "Yeah, hey," she said, trying to sound businesslike.

"Hey," he said, but she could hear the underlying question in his tone: *Why dost thou, O simplest of mortals, summon me from my grave?*

All right, then, she'd get right to it. "Listen," she said, "I need to talk to you. You weren't in the park tonight, were you?" Okay, maybe that sounded a bit more accusatory than she'd meant it to. She winced but decided to wait and see how he reacted.

Nothing from the other end. Didn't he even breathe? Jeez.

She let the quiet fizz of no response go until it reached the point of making her uncomfortable. "If it was you," she said, breaking the silence, "then I don't think it was funny, but I think you should just tell me." There. She'd said it. It was better to make sure that it hadn't been him first before she started spouting off about invisible pursuers, right?

She found herself waiting through another long stretch of silent phone-buzz before, finally, she heard him draw a breath to speak. "I don't know what kind of acid you dropped between six thirty and now," he said, "but I don't know what the hell you're talking about."

"The park," she said, though with less oomph. She was starting to think that maybe there had been a better way to go about this. She hadn't been trying to say it *had* been him. She was only trying to figure out *if* it had.

"What about the park?" he said, impatient.

"Someone chased me," she blurted.

"And you think it was me."

Uh-oh. Isobel folded her free arm across her chest, linking it with her other at the elbow. Head down, she began to pace again. "I didn't say that."

"You insinuated it."

Isobel cringed, hating to hear her own words turned around on her.

"I—"

"First of all," he said without giving her a chance to finish, "if you were in the park by yourself tonight, you should realize that was stupid."

"Yeah, thanks."

"Consider yourself welcome. Secondly," he continued, "you really must be on something to assume that *I* would follow *you*, let alone chase you. I'm sorry, but my existence isn't that sad."

Ouch.

"Okay, listen. I'm sorry," she said, shaking her head. "I didn't mean to accuse you. That wasn't why I called."

"But you did accuse me." His tone dissolved into a patronizing drone. "And why else would you call? Certainly not to chat, I hope."

Well, this had all gone straight to hell in a fat, flaming rocket.

"You know," he said, plowing on, sounding more venomous by the second, "despite what everyone has always told you, the world does not revolve around you."

"*Look,*" she growled, "I said I was sorry! You don't have to be a jerk about it."

"I'm only telling you what nobody else will."

"Yeah?" she said, her voice rising. If he wanted to pull out the artillery, that was just fine with her, she had her own guns. Bring it. "Why don't you speak for yourself?" she hissed. "I mean, what screams 'cry for attention' more than walking around looking like the grim reaper and scribbling creepy, tortured messages into some book?"

"Please," she heard him scoff through a thin scratch of phone fuzz—he was probably using a cordless handset, she realized, and it made her wonder if he even owned a cell. "I don't have to explain myself to you, of all people. Aside from the fact that you wouldn't get it, you—"

"Hey," she cut in. She'd had enough of his more-competent-than-thou condescending crap. If anyone went around thinking themselves superior, it was him. "Just because I live in the sunlight, enjoy being blond, and wear a cheerleading uniform, that doesn't mean I'm stupid. I'm so sick of that."

"Just because I wear black and keep a *private* journal, that doesn't mean I'm going to blow up the school. Or terrorize mindless cheerleaders, for that matter."

"You're so mean."

"Like you care."

"What if I do?"

Isobel immediately covered her mouth with one hand; she could feel her cheeks growing hot beneath her palm. Where had *that* come from?

"You don't," he assured her. "You care about your fluffy pink ego."

"That's not true," she said, walking to plop back down on the corner of her bed, frowning at the hem of her fluffy pink robe. She shut her eyes and ground her fingers into her forehead. When had this gone all screwy? Hadn't they been fine in the attic? What about the ice cream shop? Didn't that count for something? "I didn't know how else to tell you, is all."

"Tell me what?"

"About the park." She sighed, raking a hand through her damp hair. "Just—never mind. I'm sorry, okay? I didn't really think it was you. I just didn't want you to think I was crazy or something."

"By telling me that someone chased you through the park and that I should confess? Crazy? No. Experiencing visions of grandeur? It's possible."

"I just thought it might be your idea of a joke or something. I couldn't see them, whoever it was," she said, her voice going small and weak, her conviction having since curled under like a withering plant.

"Well, as rousing as that sounds," he said, "I was still at the bookshop an hour after you left. I should also let you know, by the way, that I pawned my invisibility cloak last week. You might want to check with the shop to see if someone bought it."

"I just," she began softly, "I just needed to tell *somebody*."

The line went quiet again. She heard a crackle of movement. His voice lowered as he said, "Are you sure you didn't just imagine it? I mean, you were reading right before you left."

Did he think she was in kindergarten? "I know the difference between a story and reality. Besides, I heard voices, and the gate rattling behind me after I got out of the park."

"And aside from the obvious choice that is me, you can't think of anyone else?" His tone dripped sarcasm, and she didn't have to guess to know who he meant.

"He wouldn't," she said.

"I can see there's a lot you assume he wouldn't do."

To this, she remained silent.

"You didn't see who it was at all?" he asked.

"No, that's just the thing—"

"Hold on," he said.

Isobel went quiet and listened. She could hear him moving around on the other end again, a door opening, and then a man's voice.

"Varen, it's nine," the voice said. "No phone after nine. You know that."

Uh, say what? He had a *phone* curfew? Horrors.

"Who is that? Who are you talking to?" asked the voice.

Isobel heard Varen mumble some kind of a response, though she couldn't hear what he said because it sounded like the phone had been wrapped in cloth.

"Well, time to say good-bye," the man's voice said. "Tell them you'll talk tomorrow."

Isobel heard the shuffle of movement again, and then Varen's voice returned.

"I gotta go," he said.

"Okay. . . . Uh, I'll see you at school tomorrow?"

Silence.

"Hello?"

"Yeah," he said. "Sure."

13
Watched

Isobel sat at the kitchen table, staring down into the floating bits of cereal in her breakfast bowl, feeling not unlike day-old roadkill—soggy, drained, and flattened. She was achy and congested, too; like little magic bunnies had visited her sometime during the whole four hours she'd slept and stuffed her head full of wet cotton. Every noise—the clank of dishes in the kitchen sink, the shuffle of footsteps in the hall, the crinkle of her dad's newspaper—sounded as though it was coming from somewhere deep underground.

She glanced up from the table, chewing, and squinted down the hallway, to where Danny's backpack lay beside the umbrella stand. Vaguely she wondered what she'd done with her own. Then she remembered.

Isobel dropped her spoon. It clanged loudly against her bowl.

She launched up from her seat.

"Isobel?" her dad asked from the other end of the table. She didn't bother to answer. She raced down the hall, then burst through the front door.

The morning air hit her cold, its moisture flooding her lungs, reawakening all the pangs from last night. A deep ache seeped from her bones and resurfaced in her muscles as she forced herself to move. Wet grass whipped at the hems of her jeans.

Oh, please, be okay. Please be okay!

In the grass—it was still there. Thank God.

Isobel ran to crouch beside her backpack. It was covered in a spray of dew, the nylon wet but not drenched. Fingers anxious and fumbling, Isobel pulled open the zippers, pried the bag open. Fixing her hands on *The Complete Works of Edgar Allan Poe*, she drew the book carefully out, turning it over in her grasp, feeling along the spine. She inspected the pages. It felt dry. It felt whole. She breathed a sigh of relief.

Isobel jerked the zippers closed. That was when she noticed the glittery goop on the front of the bag, right under her embroidered initials. Her eyes narrowed, following the trail of glitter that led up to her heart-shaped key-chain watch.

"Oh, *no*," she moaned, picking the silver watch up with her fingertips. The glass in the middle, right over the face of the watch, had shattered, leaking decorative pink glitter goo from inside onto the face of the watch and down the front of her bag, like fairy guts. She must have broken it when she'd slammed her bag down last night, the weight of the book crushing her watch.

Isobel unclipped the watch from her bag and held it in her palm.

She stood, pulling her backpack onto one shoulder with her free arm while staring down at the broken trinket in her hand. She walked slowly back inside the house and dumped her bag by the front door, then wandered into the kitchen, where she slumped once more into her chair.

"What've you got there?" her dad asked, not bothering to fold down his paper.

"My watch. It's broken."

"Ohhh," he said, "I'm sorry, sweetheart."

"Yeah," she muttered, setting the watch aside on her place mat. She picked up her spoon and prodded her cereal.

"Well," Danny said from his end of the table, half the milk in his spoonful of Lucky Charms sloshing back into his bowl, "next time you'll know not to look at it."

Isobel didn't have the energy to quip back. It was already going to be a long day. She had practice that afternoon and with half of the crew, too. And if that wasn't bad enough, she was certain the day wouldn't end without her running into Brad at least once.

Oh, no, she thought, looking up. *Brad.* How was she supposed to get home from practice?

Isobel glared down at the table, bracing a hand against her forehead. She felt like just giving up. Could she do that? Where was the eject button on life? It wouldn't have to be this way if her parents would just go ahead and let her take her driver's test instead of making her wait until she turned seventeen in the spring. Unfortunately, waiting and keeping a permit longer had been part of the deal when she'd first asked them for a car.

"Dad?"

"Mmm?"

"Can you pick me up today after practice? Around four thirty?"

"Don't you usually catch a ride home with Brad?" he asked.

"He—his car is in the shop."

"Oh? I thought he was pretty good with cars."

Oh, come on, Dad.

"It's just one of those things. Can you come?"

"Well," he said, "I guess I could drop by on the way home from work. Does Brad need a ride home too?"

"No."

That did the trick, and her father put down his paper. He eyed her before asking, "You two still getting along okay?"

"Fine, Dad." She sighed, slouching. "Fine."

"You sure you're feeling all right, Izzy? You don't look so good."

"Hundredth time, Dad, yeah."

Apart from losing all her friends in one weekend, being chased by phantom stalkers, and feeling like a sock puppet personified, she was just peachy, Dad, thanks for asking.

"Humph," he said, flipping his paper back up. He leafed noisily through a series of pages before snapping the paper straight again. "You've been acting kind of funny lately."

"Hormones," she murmured.

Danny slammed his spoon on the table. "Gross!" he shouted.

Her dad's only response was a short "Mm."

Then her mom came in. "You two ready to hit the bricks?"

Eager for an excuse to bolt, Isobel scooped up her broken watch. Pulling on her brown corduroy jacket from the back of her chair, she started for the door. She grabbed her backpack along the way.

"It's still early. Who wants a ride to the bus stop?" her mom asked. "I think we even have time for drive-through lattes."

"Me," Isobel growled in coffee lust, while Danny shook his head and groaned.

At her locker, Isobel tucked a strand of her half-blow-dried, half-air-dried, pillow-crimped hair behind one ear and leaned down to pick up her binder. Next to her, she heard a furious rustle of papers, followed by books clunking. She looked over to see the weird skinny girl, her locker neighbor, on her knees, rooting through an impossible tangle of papers, bracelets clanking.

Wispy and long-necked, she reminded Isobel of a goose. She always wore long, flowing, flowery broom skirts with black leotard pants underneath and fitted sweaters layered over tank tops. She also wore oval-framed glasses and had straight, mouse brown hair so long she could sit on it. The girl usually secured her hair with a bandanna or a low ponytail tied at the nape of her neck.

She wasn't someone Isobel would normally talk to, but for some reason, at that moment it struck her as kind of funny how they saw each other every day and had never spoken.

Didn't having lockers together make you at least

acquaintances? It was one of those situations where you had to be around someone you wouldn't normally hang out with.

Like being paired for a project.

"Hey," Isobel said before she could stop herself. "What are you looking for? Did you lose something?"

"She speaks," the girl said, "imagine that." Using both arms, she shoveled the pile of papers into her locker, then rose, angling, using her foot to stomp down the contents. "And she, who drops everything, asks *me* if I've lost something. No, I haven't lost anything. Except, perhaps, my ability to be surprised."

Isobel couldn't help but stare as the girl gripped the sides of her locker, switched feet, and stomped again to compress the papers. She had some sort of New York accent, short, sharp, and a little brutal-sounding. Not at all what she'd expected. Suddenly the girl looked at her. "What did you do to your hair?"

Isobel felt her mouth open and a draft float in. Nice. The most fashion-challenged girl in school had just noticed her hair issues. "Slept on it sort of wet," she murmured. She set her backpack down and crouched to scrounge through her emergency pouch for a hair tie.

So much for making acquaintances.

"Looks good," the girl said, shutting her locker door. "Makes you look a little less stuck-up." With that, she turned away and floated off in a swish of hair and skirts.

O-kay, Isobel thought. Despite the dig, she couldn't keep from smiling just a little. She took the hair tie and looped it around her wrist. Maybe today wasn't going to be so bad after all.

That's when she saw *them*.

Brad. And Nikki. Walking down the hall—*together*—in her direction, holding *hands*.

Oh. My. God.

Isobel looked away quickly. She slammed her locker shut and wrestled to get her combination lock back in place and snap it closed before they got close enough to see her. Giving the combination pad a twist, she risked another glance and, sure enough, Brad was staring straight at her, his hand linked with Nikki's—fingers intertwined.

And Nikki. Just look at her, smiling away at everything around her, like she just won Miss America or something.

Well, they could have each other.

Isobel spun away to take an alternate route to class. She wasn't going to give them the satisfaction of a public display. She knew that was what Brad wanted.

But when she entered the stairwell, out of their sight, she felt her swollen sense of pride deflate. She had to fight down a whole swell of emotions she hadn't expected to feel. She was mad—*really* mad—but she was confused, too. Then again, she hadn't expected to see Brad practically welded to Nikki not two days after she'd broken up with him.

But maybe she should have.

14
All That We See

Isobel wasn't sure why she hadn't stopped to think about it before now, but as the end of the lunch line drew nearer, it dawned on her. Where was she going to sit?

The last thing she wanted was to be seen floundering around in the lunchroom, especially since the crew would be watching. No doubt they'd already been broadcasting her downfall.

She moved forward out of the line, taking a few slow steps into the cafeteria, like she was trying to be extra careful not to spill her lemonade. She could see the crew out of the corner of her eye, sitting at the usual table. Even though she didn't look at them straight on, she could tell they were staring, waiting for her to try and sit with them—to try and sit anywhere.

She scanned the room.

As usual, everyone sat within their designated social sphere.

Computer geeks near the far wall. The hippies in the corner, some of them on the floor. The jocks at the tables overlooking the courtyard. And there, in the corner farthest from the windows, like a gaggle of dark, exotic birds, sat the goths and the weirdos.

Among them, she saw Varen.

Before she knew what her feet were doing, they started moving her in that direction. Her pathway chosen, she bypassed the opportunity of an empty table and walked straight for the black gathering, trying to ignore the sacrificial lamb feeling she was getting.

As though they had some kind of sonar or radar built in, a few of them glanced over. She stepped closer and heard someone make a hushing remark. Then, like in a creepy painting where all the figures seem to stare at the onlooker, they turned their heads. All those outlined eyes chiseling into her almost made her veer off course.

Isobel ignored the impulse to steer away. She kept going, her steps taking her ever forward until she drew to a slow stop, standing no more than three feet away.

Everyone stared at her now—the whole cafeteria—she could feel it, a scarcely perceptible vibration coming at her from all angles. It was like they were watching the series finale of some major drama show and were all waiting to see who would die.

Amid all the icicle stares, Varen's was the only gaze she sought in return. Why, though, did it seem like he was the last person to look at her?

"What do you want, Barbie?" the girl sitting next to him asked.

Isobel's mouth pinched tight. She heard the girl, registered the words, but for some reason, she couldn't respond. She was too focused on waiting for Varen. For him to say something. To intercede on her behalf.

All she could do was keep her eyes locked on his while she stood there, waiting—waiting for him to clear her name and a place for her to sit.

"Hey," the girl said again, waving a hand between them, breaking the spell.

Varen turned away. Dazed, Isobel looked at the girl, recognizing her instantly as the one who had handed Varen the red envelope, the girl he kept a picture of in his wallet. Lacy.

"I don't know if you're lost or something," she said, her voice deep, mellow, and full of disinterest. "Or, like, if it's too hard for you to remember which table you're supposed to sit at?" A snicker trickled through the others. "But you can't sit here."

Isobel looked back to Varen. *Tell them,* she thought. Why didn't he just tell them?

He sat staring straight ahead, his jaw hard.

Like an electroshock, Isobel felt a surge of fear, mortification, stupidity, and liquid anger. It all shot through her spine, a deadly mixture that filled her from the inside out.

With every second that ticked by, the knot in her stomach expanded. She could feel everyone staring at her, and her face burned.

So this was how it would go?

"I can't believe you," she said, her voice scarcely above a whisper.

But she was talking right to him. Right at him. Why wouldn't he look at her?

Slowly, one by one, the rest of them followed his example.

They each turned back to their lunches, chains clanking, black lace rustling—a few dark smiles gracing painted lips. *Dismissed,* they seemed to say.

No, Isobel thought, it wasn't going to be that easy.

"You think you're different." Her voice wavered, and she hated sounding so weak. "You think you're all *so* different," she went on, louder this time. "You do everything to be *different*," she spat.

The silence of the table—of the whole cafeteria—was reclaimed in an instant. "But you're not," she said at last. "You are just like every. Body. Else."

Pivoting, Isobel swung away. She dumped her tray onto the vacant table she had passed earlier, where it landed with a loud clatter. Refusing to meet anyone's eyes, she stormed out the cafeteria doors, using both arms to shove them wide.

Alone in the hallway, she bit down on the inside of her bottom lip, hard—hard enough to taste the copper sting of blood. She pounded her fist against a locker door.

Stupid.

Stupid, stupid, stupid!

She kept walking, straight to the nearest girls' bathroom.

She pushed through the door and dabbed the sleeve of her sweater against her eyelids, hating the tears that soaked it, hating that she'd have to hand wash the fabric later in Woolite to get the mascara smudges out—hating most of all the thought that he might know she was crying.

Isobel grabbed the trash can, piled high with wadded paper towels and tissues, and hauled it over. It toppled onto its side, its metal body clanging against the tiled floor.

She *really* didn't care. It was just embarrassing, was all. Humiliating. But then what had she expected? It shouldn't be this big of a surprise. None of it should be. Not Brad, not Nikki—least of all *him*.

I don't care. She said it over and over in her mind, pacing the floor, trampling wet towels.

All he'd cared about was the project.

All that had mattered to him was the grade.

She was expendable.

"I don't care!" she screamed at the trash can, kicking it. The crash echoed, and the can upchucked more wadded paper towels onto the floor.

She was stupid for shouting. She was stupid for crying, and most of all, she was stupid for believing, for even a second, that they might have been friends.

Isobel grabbed a handful of paper towels from the metal dispenser. She would *not* go back out into the hall with her makeup smeared and her eyes puffy-red.

Drawing in a shuddering breath, she turned on the faucet and brought her gaze up to her reflection.

A dry croak caught in her throat.

He stood in the doorway of the stall behind her. A man, cloaked in black. He stared at her, a tattered fedora hat shading his features, a white scarf swathing his mouth and nose, hiding his face.

She opened her mouth to . . . to what? To scream? To say something?

Suddenly, in the mirror, the door to the bathroom popped open. The skinny girl, her locker neighbor, poked her head in. Isobel whirled around.

"Talk about crash and burn," the girl said. "You all right or what?"

Isobel stared at the open space where she had seen the man. Behind her, she gripped the cold sink. Her eyes darted to the girl and then, her head whipping around, she looked back into the mirror. In it she could see her own face, drained of color, and the stall behind her—empty.

Her lips formed words. "Did you . . . ?" The question withered in her mouth.

"I . . . ," the girl started, "well, I thought I'd better, I dunno . . . check on you?"

"You didn't just see . . . ?" Isobel turned, pointed at the stall.

The girl shrugged. "Well . . ." She gave a quick glance over one bony shoulder back into the hall. "Hate to break it to you, but I think it's pretty safe to say everybody saw."

15
The Power of Words

"All right, ladies, take five!"

The shrill blast of Coach Anne's whistle pierced through Isobel's head, ringing in her brain like a fire bell, sending her headache officially into migraine status.

Without turning to talk and stretch with the others like she normally would, Isobel broke away from formation and trudged to the bleachers, where she'd left her gym bag. She tugged down on the hems of her blue practice shorts and plopped onto the bottom-most bench. She grabbed, opened, and drained the rest of her Gatorade in one smooth motion, then screwed the cap back on and stuffed the empty bottle into the bag between her street shoes and jeans.

Sitting there, she couldn't seem to bring herself to form a single coherent thought. Not since she'd had to order her brain to stop its relentless attempts to assign a rational explanation to what she'd seen in the girls' bathroom earlier that day: the dark figure that had stared her down and then vanished.

Deciding that she would do better to wait until after she'd had more than ten cents' worth of sleep, Isobel tried to think of something else. That, however, only left room for her brain to play and replay the agonizing scene from lunch.

Again and again she saw Varen look up at her from the crowded lunch table, those stony green eyes fixing on her, at first in mild surprise, then slowly melding into two pools of nothing—until he was looking at her with only vague recognition, like he might have seen her on a milk carton somewhere.

And that girl. Lacy.

Isobel thought back to the way she had glared at her—territorially.

She pictured them together, hands linked, and she couldn't help but wonder what kind of boyfriend he was.

He could be so cynical. So dry and acidic. As blank as a page. Could he be tender, too?

She flinched at the thought, angry at her mind for letting it venture so far beyond what she already knew to be true. He wasn't any different from the people he pretended to be above. He'd proven that much at lunch.

She sighed, keeping her eyes closed, trying to release some of the day's stress in one long exhale.

To top everything off, she was now doomed to be kicked off the squad, too.

And she would be. As soon as next Friday zoomed by and left her with a big fat zero on Mr. Swanson's English project.

She would be a Trenton High cheerleader nevermore.

Not showing up for today's practice, though, would have been admitting defeat.

If nothing else, it would have been her way of personally paving a path and rolling out the red carpet for Alyssa to take over her spot as center flyer. And despite the fact that nobody on the squad liked her anymore, Isobel still loved cheerleading. She was good at it, and in spite of everything, she was not prepared to make it easy for Alyssa, or anyone else who wanted her little slice of sky, to take her place.

"All right there, Iz?"

Isobel popped one eye open to see the whistle around Coach's neck swinging back and forth on its yellow lanyard like a clock pendulum.

"Yeah," she said, blinking slowly, putting on a smile until Coach passed. "Headache," she said. At least it wasn't a lie.

"You looked good out there today, Izzy," Coach called over her shoulder.

Isobel watched Coach's back as she stepped into the hall, where she stopped to fill her water bottle at the fountain. Normally she would have welcomed the encouragement. Especially after a day like today. With the rest of the squad standing by, however, watching and listening, she wished Coach hadn't said anything, because now they'd started to whisper.

Isobel pretended to ignore them by searching for something in her bag but paused when she heard the squeak of approaching sneakers. She looked up enough to count eight pairs of gold-and-blue-accented tennis shoes. Raising her eyes, she saw that it was Alyssa who led the pack, Nikki only one step behind.

"I'm surprised you decided to show up today," said Alyssa, loosing her platinum hair from its tight ponytail.

Isobel lifted her chin. "If only to save everyone from having to watch you try to do more than a single twist for the rest of the season."

A trickle of giggles ran through Alyssa's buddy patrol. Isobel let a cool, subdued smile tease up one side of her mouth. Alyssa's cheeks flared pink and her whole face pinched together, as though she'd just chomped down on an extra-green crabapple. The laughter at her back dissolved quickly into sniffs and coughs.

"So what happened to your leg?" Alyssa asked.

Feeling that this must be of some sort of trick, Isobel resisted the urge to check her legs. "I don't know what you're talking about," she said, looking away. She wished Coach would come back already. What was taking her so long?

"Oh, I think you do," said Alyssa. "I'm talking about that mark on the back of your thigh. Why don't you stand up and show everybody?"

Isobel kept her seat. She tried to guess what was going on, tried to remember having done anything that would have put a mark on the back of her leg.

Had they left something for her to sit in? *What?*

Then she remembered.

"Rug burn," she murmured, not liking that she couldn't guess Alyssa's game. And too late she realized it would have been better to have said nothing.

Isobel turned away to zip up her bag as giggles erupted from the group. She stopped and slowly raised her gaze

again to the faces of her squad, wondering how these people
had ever been her friends.

"Oh," Alyssa said, her mouth on the verge of bursting
into one of her radiant, blinding, too-much-whitener smiles.
"That's funny. We thought it must have been something like
that, what with your new undead boyfriend and all. Bet
you're sorry now, though. Gosh. Especially after putting out.
Tell me, how does it feel to realize you're a skank *and* get
dumped twice in one day?"

Isobel launched up from the bleachers, the sudden action
spurring the collective squeals of backtracking sneakers
and cheerleaders. She shoved Alyssa hard, hard enough to
send her stumbling backward through her backup party and
straight to the floor. She hit with a jolt, landing on her backside, her glossed mouth fixed in a shocked O.

"Hey!"

The shriek of a whistle split through Isobel's throbbing
head again and in her peripheral vision, she could see Coach
bustling up to them, her oval face reddening to a ripe beet
color. Isobel trembled with fury. Her eyes remained locked
on Alyssa, who stared up at her from the floor, her hands
clenched. Coach seized Isobel by the arm and with a strong,
yanking grip ended the hate-stare between them.

"What the hell is wrong with you two?" shouted Coach
Anne, this time focusing her attention on Alyssa. "You know
I don't tolerate fighting on my squad!" She swung around to
glower at Isobel again, her face purple. "In my office! Both
of you!"

Then she spun on her heel and stormed toward her office door at the far end of the gym.

Alyssa smiled at Isobel as she picked herself up from the floor. Revolving in a slow turn, she followed after Coach Anne.

Scalding heat crawled up Isobel's face. She couldn't bring herself to take so much as a single step in the direction of that office. Not with everyone staring again. Not when she wanted so badly to put her fist through Alyssa's flawless teeth, to crush that perfect button nose flat and permanently erase that conceited smile from her stupid face.

The heat of rage coursed through her veins like a deadly poison.

She had to get out of there. Now. Or she'd blow up.

On impulse, Isobel grabbed her gym bag. She looped the strap over one shoulder and started to walk hard and fast for the gymnasium doors.

"Lanley!" she heard Coach howl after her. Isobel, her head down, plowed forward. She had to keep moving. She *had* to, or she'd look back. She'd see everyone staring at her, thinking whatever they wanted about her, and she knew she would explode.

"Lanley, stop right there!"

Isobel cringed, covering her ears.

"You walk out that door, you're walking off the squad! You hear me?"

She heard. But she was on autopilot now and couldn't have stopped herself anyway.

Once out of the gym, she started to move faster, nearly jogging down the deserted hallway, her sneakers making quiet claps. She rounded a corner and would have run right past her locker if she hadn't noticed the little piece of white folded paper sticking out of the top vent. Isobel stopped, knowing all too well whose handwriting she would find on that slip of paper. She let the strap of her heavy gym bag slip from her shoulder, and jerking the note out of the slot, she opened it.

Even though she'd known what to expect, there still came a blunt stab of hurt at the sight of dark purple ink.

We need to talk.

"No," she said aloud, tearing the note in two. "We don't." She'd shredded the paper again, again, and again, finally letting the flecks flutter to the floor like ash.

Isobel twisted her locker combination in, kicked the dented bottom corner of the door, and stood back as it popped out. She delved inside and withdrew her backpack, dragging it out by one strap. She set the bag on the floor in front of her feet and jerked open the zippers, extracting *The Complete Works of Edgar Allan Poe*. Then she spun around, strode to the nearest trash can, and tipped the book in, letting it fall onto a bed of papers and plastic soda bottles.

Something inside her winced, begged for her to pull it out again.

But something else rejoiced.

She ignored the urge to rescue the book and, walking to a

nearby stand, picked up several school newsletters. Wadding them up, she made her way back to the trash and tossed them in, sprinkling them over the book. Like flowers on a coffin.

Thankfully, Isobel's dad got to school a little early to pick her up that day, so she didn't have to worry about waiting around with anyone else from the squad, or about Brad showing up and her dad finding out she'd lied about his car being in the shop.

The ride home was a quiet one, and for once her father didn't try to pry, asking questions like, "Why so quiet?" or "Did something happen today?" She knew he wouldn't realize it, but she was grateful for this. The last thing she wanted to do was talk about what had happened that day.

When she got home, Isobel went straight to her room. She fell onto her bed, buried her face in her pillows, shut her eyes, and blessedly, mercifully fell asleep, her body seeming to agree with her mind that she had had enough. She didn't wake up until hours later when her mom, having returned from a PTA meeting at Danny's school, came to check on her.

"Izzy?"

Isobel rolled over onto one side, feeling herself pulled on opposite ends by wakefulness and sleep. She felt hot and kicked off some of the blankets. "Mm?" she murmured.

"Do you want to come down and have some supper? Soup and grilled cheese?"

"Rrrrrrg," Isobel managed. Soup didn't sound too bad,

but it did if it meant she had to get up, walk downstairs, and lift a spoon to her mouth.

She felt her mother's soft, cool hand press against her forehead.

"I think you've got a fever," Isobel heard her say. "Daddy said you looked like you didn't feel well."

Isobel thought her mom said something else after that too, maybe asking her if she wanted some ginger ale, but that hazy feeling returned, like something tugging her down into deep, dark waters. The sensation overtook her, and she slept once more.

When Isobel opened her eyes again, it was with the feeling that something was wrong. She sat upright in bed—then froze at what she saw.

Trinkets from her dresser, as well as other objects from around her room—her "Number One Flyer" trophy, a tube of lipstick, her stuffed bunny Max, her pom-poms, and her portable CD player—were all floating around, drifting slowly through the air, as though her entire room had somehow been transported into the farthest reaches of outer space.

Isobel sat up wide awake, staring, unable to blink. At least not until her hair dryer came hovering right up into her face, its cord dangling behind like a tail. She lifted a hand and batted the dryer away, then watched it reel, handle over snout, in the direction of her closet.

Swinging her legs off the side of her bed, she stood,

turning in a slow circle to survey the asteroid field that her room had somehow become. When her gaze fell on her open doorway, she stopped.

In the hallway, a blinding white light flickered in short bursts, like flashes of lightning, interspersed with moments of blue-tinted darkness.

Standing on the stairway landing, right in front of Danny's door, Isobel saw the outline of a tall figure.

Terror seized her as the form began to move toward her, seeming to glide just over the carpet. Another brilliant blaze of white light flashed through the space beyond, revealing the figure's black cloak, his tattered fedora hat.

Isobel backed away, somehow knowing that it would do her no good to rush forward and slam the door. She felt her back meet the wall.

As the figure crossed the threshold, she saw that he wore a white scarf over the bottom half of his face, and she recognized him instantly as the man from the bathroom—the figure from the mirror. He brought with him a scent both sweet and musty, like wilted roses, and the odor of perfumed decay permeated the air.

Her heart pounding, she watched wide-eyed as, behind him, the door eased closed by itself, blocking out the flashes of white light. When the door clicked into place, Isobel's floating belongings dropped to the floor with a collective, carpet-muffled thud.

"Do not be alarmed," the man said, his voice dry, husky, and low, like the sound of a match striking. Above the white scarf, his eyes glistened like sharp flecks of coal, and they seemed to chip right into her. "This is a dream."

Isobel stood still and silent for another moment, her hands pressed flat to the wall behind her, as if its tangible presence held the power to ground her.

A dream?

Well, Isobel thought, taking a moment to consider the situation—her floating stuff, the hall lightning, followed by the entrance of creepy mystery man. Yeah, she could probably buy that this was a dream. It was the not-feeling-alarmed part she wasn't so sure about.

"Who—who are you?"

"My name," he began, as though he'd expected the question, "is Reynolds."

She edged away from him, trying to put a greater distance between herself and Creepy McCreeperson. She bent down, careful not to let her eyes leave him, and plucked up a hairbrush from where it had fallen on her floor. She held it at arm's length in front of herself, a stupid weapon feeling better than no weapon at all. At the very least, she could give him style.

"If this is a dream," she said, "then there's a good chance that—that I'm imagining you. Like the way I imagined you in the mirror. And that day at practice. If that was you. You're . . . a manifestation of repressed childhood . . . traumas." Isobel crunched down hard on her brain, trying to squeeze out whatever vocabulary from her psychology class she'd managed to soak up.

"Your friend is in grave danger," he said, cutting her off, his words coming clipped and short. "You would be wise to be quiet and listen. I haven't much time."

She stared as he made his way farther into her room. A glance toward her digital clock showed the numbers twitching and randomly changing on their own, as though her clock couldn't make up its mind on what time it wanted to be.

"Then it sounds like you're in the wrong dream, because I don't have any friends."

"Then it is a pity," he said brusquely, his cold gaze narrowing on her, "that he has put you in so much danger. Because it is *you* she is after."

She blinked as he turned, his great cloak swirling after him. Isobel lowered the brush. *She?*

Her eyes remained trained on him as he drifted toward her nightstand, dipping a long-fingered hand into the folds of his cloak. As the fabric moved aside, Isobel thought she caught sight of the decorative hilt of an old-fashioned blade. The folds of dark, heavy fabric fell again, though, and she saw that he now held a book—one she knew, with its gold-leafed pages and thick black binding.

"Hey!" Stepping away from the wall, she dropped the brush. A thrill of something drummed up from inside her— a mix of relief and confusion. And fear. "I thought I . . ."

He set the book gently on the nightstand and passed a gloved hand over the gold-embossed title, his fingertips lingering over the words—*The Complete Works of Edgar Allan Poe.*

"I believe that this book has been given to you for a

reason," he said, turning his coal eyes once more onto hers. "I would not be so careless with it again."

Isobel stared down at the book in disbelief. The very one she'd tossed into the school trash earlier that day. She could see the beige tonguelike ribbon sticking out of the bottom, and the gentle crease etched along its spine. And yet somehow it was here, safe.

"Mark these words," he said, "The only way for you to gain power over what happens to you in the dreamworld is if you are able to realize that you are dreaming. If you cannot do this, you are beyond my help."

Isobel shook her head, trying to fight her mounting confusion. The more this guy talked, the more he sounded like a fortune cookie. "What do I have to do with any of this? Who's after me?"

"That name is best left unsaid. Words, Isobel, have always held the dangerous power to conjure things into being. Remember that."

"Speaking of names, how do you know mine? And why is this 'she'—whoever it is—why is she after me?"

"Because," he said, choosing to answer only her second question, "he dreams of you. . . ."

"Who?"

"Come." With a sweep of his cloak, he turned to her bedroom window, one spidery hand drawing back the white lace.

Isobel drew nearer to the black square of her open window. A cool breeze filtered through, stirring the curtains. She felt the brush of her hair against her cheek.

How could a dream feel so real?

When she reached the window, she glanced first at Reynolds. Standing this close to him, she could see his eyes above the white scarf—really see them. They were void of pupils. Black, coin-size holes bored into her before turning away and gazing out the window into the space beyond.

Isobel followed his gaze.

As she looked, the darkness cleared. A scratchy gray image, fuzzy around the edges and frayed through the middle, like an old-time movie, came into view. In the distance, she could see the outline of a dark forest. A dim violet light radiated through the arrangement of thin black trees. And there, standing just outside the forest boundaries, Isobel recognized the angular shoulders of a familiar form. A tall, slim figure clad in a dark green jacket.

"Varen . . . ?"

16
Ultima Thule

Isobel blinked up at the ceiling. An unfamiliar tingle prickled along her limbs, like the faint buzz of static electricity. Somehow she'd skipped right over her normal waking-up routine of rolling around and punching her pillows and had just opened her eyes.

She'd been dreaming about something. Something important.

Him. She'd seen him.

Oh no, *him.*

She groaned, a dull ache creeping up from her spine to settle in her chest. Ugh. She didn't even want to *think* of his name. She rolled over, squeezing her eyes shut, stuffing her face into her pillow. She wasn't ready to remember what had happened, to recall the nightmare that had been the day before.

The faint pins-and-needles sensation, still there, buzzed through her like a soft vibration, though the closer she drifted to full consciousness, the faster it seemed to fade.

Isobel's gaze slipped dazedly to her window, where she watched the half-naked tree limbs quiver and sway, waving in and out of her view, like clawed hands snatching at the sun.

The sun.

"Oh, crap!" she croaked.

Isobel sat up and pulled her alarm clock from the top of her headboard.

"Eleven thirty-five, oh my God!"

She'd slept through the rest of yesterday and into the next morning. She hadn't set her alarm! She was supposed to be in Mr. Swanson's class right this very second! Why hadn't anyone woken her up? Why hadn't . . . ?

Isobel stared at the clock, clutching it between her hands. Her eyes went slowly unfocused as the memory of last night's dream struggled to resurface. Why did remembering feel so crucial? The blue numbers of her clock blurred against their black backdrop, burning into her eyes. She thought about the way they had gone haywire when—

"*Reynolds,*" she whispered.

She dropped the clock. It cracked against the wood of her bed frame, then thudded onto the carpet. Like a jolt of electricity to her brain, the image of her floating things seized her. She sat frozen, clutching the comforter beneath her. Her eyes scanned her room.

She saw her hairbrush, not on the floor but on her dresser, and behind it, her "Number One Flyer" trophy.

"Mom?" Her voice grated in her throat.

She swallowed against the pain and pulled herself out of bed, then padded to her door and opened it.

Isobel went very still, her hand tightening on her door handle. She stared down the length of the empty, silent hall, afraid to turn around. The book. Would it be there if she looked?

Slowly, her grip easing, she turned, her eyes trailing to her nightstand. She saw her dusty photo album of last year's cheer events. Next to it sat her lamp, the shade trimmed in a skirt of pink and white beaded fringe, and a couple of hair ties.

No book. No Poe.

Realizing she'd been holding her breath, Isobel exhaled in one long rush that turned into a laugh at the tail end.

She stepped out into the hallway and down the stairs, past the collage of family photos. It made her feel silly, the idea that she'd taken something from her subconscious so seriously.

Cold white daylight streamed in through the front-door windows and through the lace curtains in the living room, but around her, the house seemed dim and dead. "Mom?" Isobel called out again, her throat now feeling slightly less like a cat's scratching post.

One by one, she flicked on light switches as she reached them even though it wasn't that dark inside. The false light afforded her little comfort. The silence was too thick. Her fingertips brushed the walls as she passed through the hall, moving toward the kitchen, where she knew she could find a cold ginger ale and maybe something to eat. She opened the fridge, opted for a Sprite, and drank half before closing the door again.

Isobel figured her fever last night had probably caused

her mother to call the school for her that morning. So where was her mother now?

No school today. She couldn't say that she wasn't grateful. There was no way she'd have survived a repeat of the day before.

Isobel shut her eyes, trying to block Varen's smooth, pale features from forming in her mind, but that only caused him to materialize more vividly. Grasping the handle of the fridge, Isobel rested her forehead against the cool surface. The cold felt so good against her skin. She turned to press her cheek there too. *Wake up, Isobel. What's the deal? Why can't you get over it already? He's just some guy.* Some guy who'd she'd dreamt was having dreams about her. How completely whacked was that?

Why did he have to be so . . . so . . .

Isobel let out a growl of frustration, pushing off from the fridge. She took a noisy slurp from her Sprite and made a beeline straight for the pantry. She was going to pull a major Danny and find some Chips Ahoy to scarf down for breakfast.

She reached for the cabinet door and stopped.

A glint of gold on black caught her eye.

She looked, and the Sprite slid out of her grasp. It thumped onto the floor, and soda spread across the tiles with a quiet hiss.

There, on the kitchen table, sat the large, familiar black book, autumn sunlight gleaming off the gold-lined pages and the embossed title that read *The Complete Works of Edgar Allan Poe.*

"No!"

She grabbed the book and swept it from the table. It hit the floor, falling open on the kitchen tile.

Isobel drew back, her arms huddled against her body, her fists balled into tight knots beneath her chin. She could feel herself shaking. This couldn't be for real, she thought. This couldn't be happening. She'd thrown it away. She'd gotten rid of it. Last night had been a *dream*.

She stared down at the book. She watched a trickle of soda crawl across the floor toward it, and despite everything in her being telling her not to, she inched forward. Her shadow settled over a picture in the open book, a large black-and-white image of a pale-faced, sunken-eyed man.

A neatly tied cravat laced his neck like a fancy noose. A rumpled jacket, so black it nearly blended into the portrait's background, was fastened in the middle by a solitary button. The man's wide forehead gave way to sorrowful, downward-slanted brows. And then there were the eyes themselves. Dark wells.

Crouching, Isobel lifted the book out of the soda, which had begun to pool at its edge. She found herself at once entrapped by those eyes, transfixed because they seemed to stare right back at her, pleading with her in earnest for . . . for what?

Her gaze trailed down to the caption: *"Ultima Thule" daguerreotype of Poe taken November 9, 1848, less than a year before the poet's mysterious death.*

Ultima Thule. Why did that sound familiar?

Isobel stared once again into his eyes. There was something about them, the way they pulled her in, the way they only dimly reflected the light, the way they resembled two black, coin-size holes.

She slammed the book shut.

17
Dead Air

Isobel sat staring vacantly at the video game images that flashed in front of her eyes. She hadn't the slightest idea what she was watching—some overdramatic vampire slayer game Danny had switched on when he'd gotten home from school. Blades swiped, blood splashed, and zombies screamed.

She'd spent the better part of the day right there on the couch. She'd turned on the TV initially for the noise, for some kind of normal sound to surround her until her mom returned from the grocery store. That, and she'd needed something to ground her, to let her know she was really awake and not still asleep—that she wasn't locked in some perpetual dream within a dream.

But she hadn't found much comfort in knowing that she was, indeed, awake and in the real world. Not given what had happened, what she'd seen in her dream—what she'd found in the kitchen.

"Isobel!"

She jolted, looking up to see her mother standing behind the couch, holding a hand over the mouthpiece of their portable phone. "Isobel," she said, lowering her voice, her brows knitting. "Did you really not hear me calling you?"

Isobel stared up at her mother.

"I said, 'Telephone.' Isobel, are you sure you don't need to go to the doctor? Ever since yesterday you've been acting like you're on some other planet."

"I'm fine, Mom," she muttered, reaching out for the handset. "Just tired is all."

Isobel held the phone to her ear, staring blankly at her mother's back as she disappeared once more into the kitchen. "'Lo?"

"Don't hang up."

Her insides flared.

Maybe it was because he'd told her not to, or maybe it was because she couldn't bear the sound of his voice so close in her ear. She hung up.

For a moment she stared at the phone in her hand, impressed with herself yet shocked at her own gall. It was like hanging up on Dracula. At the same time, an intense regret coursed through her. *Why* did she wish more than anything that she could tell *him* (of all people!) about everything that had been happening to her?

Maybe because Reynolds said he was involved. Or maybe because that freaky book had been his to begin with.

The phone rang again, its little red light flickering in urgency. Isobel stared down at the caller ID screen until a name popped up on the display. DESSERT ISLAND it read, with the phone number listed below.

Her thumb twitched toward the talk button.

Why was he even calling her? Surely he hadn't expected

her to show up for their planned meeting at the ice cream shop. He was arrogant and callous, but he wasn't dense.

"Danny," she said, rising, the phone ringing for the third time now. She tossed the handset to the floor beside where her brother lay on his stomach. "Five bucks says this is the wrong number."

"Eez-oh-bel?" he said in a corny fake Spanish accent. "I don know no Eez-oh-bel."

She turned and moved quickly into the kitchen, where her mother stood in front of the stove fixing dinner. She ignored, as best she could, Danny's leisurely *"Heeelllooo?"* from the next room.

One look at the Poe book sitting where she'd left it on the kitchen table, however, had her turning straight back around.

"Isobel," her mother said, stopping her. "You're not mad at me, are you?" Her tone was curious, probing.

"No, why?"

"Oh, well." Stirring what Isobel thought smelled like mushroom rice (one of her favorites), her mom shrugged. "I thought you might be upset that I cleaned your room this morning while you were still sleeping."

"What?"

"I just picked up the floor a little. I didn't think you'd mind, since you were still asleep. You must have been tired. You didn't even wake up when I took your shoes off. But I was just making sure," she chattered on. "I didn't know if I'd put something back the wrong way. Oh, and I hope you don't mind that I borrowed the book from your nightstand.

Where did you get it? I didn't see a library bar code. Dad said you were reading Poe for school."

Isobel couldn't register the question. Her gaze drifted again to the Poe book. Rushing forward, she snatched it off the table, then marched out of the kitchen and back into the hall, fixing her sights on the stairs. It had to be the book, she thought. Nothing freaky had happened until after she'd set eyes on it, and now she had to get rid of it. She couldn't throw it away again, of course. Maybe if she dug a hole and buried it? Or would she have to burn it? Then again, Reynolds had told her to keep it, that it was important. But who, or *what*, was Reynolds in the first place?

What would happen if she just . . . gave it back?

Danny's voice floated out to her from the living room. "Yeah, but the original Transylvania Wars is kind of old-school, don't you think?"

Isobel paused outside the living room archway, her head turning slowly to see Danny cradling the phone between his shoulder and ear, his thumbs flying over the controller, a digital vampire slayer executing an elaborate string of sword blows to a group of manic undead.

"Okay, so I'm at the Nosferatu Dungeon door," she heard Danny say. "Now how do you get Gothica's Gate to open again?"

Isobel felt her clenched jaw fall slack. No way. She stalked into the living room and glared at the back of her brother's head. "Who are you talking to?"

"Hold on." He tossed the words at her from over his

shoulder, scooting in closer to the TV, close enough for his nose to touch the screen. "Ohhh," he said, "I see it now! Jeez! How did you ever figure that out?"

"Danny, give me the phone." Isobel thrust her hand out for the receiver. "And you can forget the five bucks."

"I was only gonna charge you three-fifty anyway," he said, holding the phone just out of her reach. "He knew he hadn't dialed the wrong number, so I had to tell him you were on the crapper."

"What? Danny! Oh my *God*." Isobel lashed out, wrenching the phone from his hand, her face scalding. Storming out of the living room, she contemplated hanging up again, this time on the grounds of mortification. But then she realized she couldn't avoid him much longer and lifted the receiver to her ear. "*What?*" she growled. With the Poe book tucked under one arm, Isobel mounted the stairs and stomped each one as she climbed. She headed for the last place she wanted to be but the only one in which she'd find herself alone—her room.

"Your brother," the soft voice said, a hint of laughter behind it.

"Is a little jerk," she snarled. "Now what do you want?"

"Would you relax for a second?"

The hand holding the phone quivered in fury. "No!" she seethed, "I will *not* relax!"

"I need to—"

"You need to just drop dead, okay?"

"Isobel, listen—"

Could this really be the first time he'd ever used her name? She shoved the thought aside. "No!" she shouted, "*you* listen! You are *such* a hypocrite."

Silence. Was he even still there?

She plowed on, not caring. "What?" she said. "Shocked that the dumb blond cheerleader actually has a vocabulary beyond 'Go team'?"

He came back with a note of defense. "I never—"

"You have done nothing but condescend to me. I stuck up for you! And after what you did yesterday, you think you can just leave me little notes and call me up and be all, 'Hey, we need to talk,' and expect me just to say, 'Hey, okay'? What kind of acid are *you* dropping?"

"Isobel—"

"No, *Varen*. Don't call me again. You can just take the stupid project and do it yourself."

"I didn't call you because of the project."

"Well, I'm flattered," she said, unable to keep the waver out of her voice. Hesitating for a fraction of a second, she jammed her thumb on the end button, severing their connection.

18
The Other Half

Isobel came downstairs for dinner, but only for her mother's sake. She was not hungry in the least, and even felt a slight pang of nausea. Under her parents' scrutiny, however, she lifted her fork, took another bite of rice, chewed.

"Feeling any better?" her dad asked, finally breaking the silence. Isobel saw her mother shoot him a wary look. Apparently, they'd been discussing whether or not to commit her while she'd been wallowing upstairs in her room. "Yeah," she said, "a little."

Her mom rose from the table. "You finished, honey?" she asked, her hand pausing on Isobel's plate. Grateful, Isobel nodded and set her fork down.

"Think you'll go back to school tomorrow?" asked her dad in that tone that expected a yes. Sports geek that he was, he didn't like her to miss cheer practice. Too bad she was going to anyway. Isobel nodded in response. She slumped in her chair, mulling over how to tell her parents she'd quit the squad.

"Well, that's good," her dad said, dragging his fork through the wilting leaves of his salad. Isobel glanced down to the empty place mat in front of her and traced the floral imprint with the tip of her finger. She opened her mouth and drew in a breath, deciding it would be better just to blurt it out now and get it over with. They'd have to go easy on her since she'd been sick, right?

In the kitchen, the phone rang.

Isobel's back shot into a straight line. "Hello?" her mother answered.

She sat rigid in her chair, hoping it was a wrong number, or Danny's troop leader, or her dad's boss—or hell, even Coach Anne.

"Expecting a call?" asked her father.

Isobel's attention snapped back to her dad, who sat eyeing her curiously, an odd smile on his face. *Oh God*, she thought, knowing exactly what that expression meant. He thought he had this all figured out, that this all must be over Brad.

"Isobel," her mother said, and poked her head out of the kitchen. She held out the cordless handset. "Phone."

He wouldn't dare, she thought. She rose, took the receiver, and retreated with it into the kitchen. Her back to her mother, she answered with a quiet and warning, "Hello?"

"Oh, good," a girl's blunt, clipped voice said, "you're not dead."

"What? Who is this?"

"It's Gwen."

"Gwen? Gwen who?"

"Gwen Daniels. Our lockers are next to each other? Let me guess, you never knew my name to begin with, did you? Again, I fail to be surprised."

"Uh, how did you get my number?"

"I looked you up online."

"You can do that?" Isobel asked with a twinge of unease.

"Internet White Pages. Duh. What the heck is going on with you? Are you okay? Half the school thinks you've killed yourself." There was a pause before Gwen added, "The other half thinks you and Varen eloped."

"*What?*"

"Wait . . . Nobody told you what happened?"

"Happened? No. What happened?" Who exactly did Gwen think would tell her? Hello, news flash. Had she not witnessed firsthand her social demise in the lunchroom?

"Hold on," Isobel murmured. Quickly she left the kitchen and went up the stairs. In her room, door closed, Isobel didn't have to prompt Gwen to continue.

"So did you know your boyfriend knows your locker combination?"

"You mean Brad? We broke up. I thought that was obvious." It irked her that people at school might still think they were together, or worse, just on the fritz.

"Oh, you know what I meant. That's not the point. Did you really tell him your combination?"

"He knows it," Isobel grumbled, getting more annoyed by the second. Was it any of Gwen's business who she gave her locker combination to? They were locker neighbors, not locker roomies. "What does that have to do with what happened?"

"It was right after last period. Your big football player ex-guy—did you say his name was Ben?"

"Brad."

"Right, well, for some reason, that guy was in your locker. Now, I wasn't there yet, so I can't say *exactly* what the deal was. I sort of figured out this much after the fact—from what other people said they saw."

"Other people?" She cringed.

"Well, apparently, this Brad guy was getting stuff out of your locker, planning to take it with him, it looked like."

Isobel tried to remember exactly what she'd stored in her locker. All she knew she had in there was her binder, some books, and a box of tampons—what could he want with any of that? Evidence, she realized at once. He must be looking for some kind of proof about her and Varen. Maybe. What else would it be?

"But then guess who shows up."

"*No.*"

"Yeah."

Something in her middle turned a wobbly somersault. Varen approaching Brad? Bad. Very bad.

"What happened?" Her voice almost cracked.

"Well, this is the part that I saw. Apparently, Varen wanted Brad to give him all your stuff. Then Brad grabbed a fistful of Dr. Doom's shirt and slammed him into the lockers. Hard. I mean, I saw his head bounce. One-handed, too—Bruno never even had to put your stuff down."

Isobel gasped. Suddenly she couldn't breathe. The room around her seemed to tilt. She cringed, and the hand holding the phone felt weak.

"And *that's* what triggered it, I think."

Oh God. There was more? Isobel needed to sit down. She sank onto one corner of her bed, waiting for the worst. How bad could it be? she thought. If Varen had called her from work, then he had to be at least somewhat okay. He couldn't be in traction if he was at work, right?

"Well," Gwen said, her voice flattening out, "let me just say that when he banged into the lockers—the lockers banged back."

"What do you mean they banged back?"

The line went quiet and fuzzy for a moment. Isobel squished the phone in hard against one ear, blocking her other ear with a finger. She turned her head to one side, and another roll of static fizzed against her eardrum.

"All the lockers . . . they knocked back," Gwen said. "One right after the other. Everybody hit the floor, because it sounded like gunfire—I *swear*. I saw some of the locks jolting around. It happened so fast—and it wasn't like some sort of crazy chain reaction that had been set off or something," she interrupted herself to say, as though she'd already wrestled with this theory in her own mind, "because it started at the total opposite end of the hall, on the *other* side. It only stopped when it reached *your* locker. Which slammed shut—by *itself*. And even though he tried, Goliath couldn't get it open again."

"Gwen," Isobel said, standing, a note of hysteria in her voice. Her eyes fell to the Poe book still sitting on her carpet where she'd left it. She kicked it under her bed. "You're making this up."

"Sorry, but I'm not that creative."

"Did somebody set you up to call me and say all this?"

"Look," Gwen said, "I didn't call because of some prank. I called you because there's something really freaked out goin' on, and since it transpired in the direct vicinity of *your* locker, I thought you might like to know."

A scuffling noise had Isobel turning to face the window.

"Of course," Gwen prattled, "if I'd known I'd be accused of conspiracy on top of lying, I'd have written about the whole ordeal in an article and submitted it to the school newspaper instead."

"Shh!" Isobel hissed. "Gwen, shh!"

The sound came again. A low, grating noise.

"I don't think I should have to shush. You know, I didn't have to call you. I had better things to do. My trig homework, for example."

"No, Gwen," said Isobel. She dropped her voice as the dull, scraping noise grew louder. "I hear something."

For a moment the line went silent.

"Gwen?" Isobel said, afraid she'd hung up.

"I'm here, though I'm startin' to wonder why."

"Listen," said Isobel as another long scratching noise issued from behind her drawn shade. "I believe you. There's been a lot of weird stuff happening, actually. But I can't tell you about it right now, because I think there's something outside my window."

There was a moment of tense silence. Isobel strained both ears, listening.

"You want me to call the police or somethin'?" Gwen whispered.

"No, not yet. Listen, I want you to stay on the line with me while I try to get a look. It could just be . . . y'know—a bird or something,"

"A *bird*? Are you kidding me?"

"No," Isobel murmured, distracted as the scratching continued, closer this time. Something shuffled right up against her window ledge. Whatever it was out there, it sounded a lot bigger than a bird.

"Hold on," she said. She crept forward, the phone held tight against one ear, her other arm outstretched, fingers reaching toward the shade.

"Isobel? What's going on? Are you there or what?"

Transfixed by the large, moving black shape shifting in and out of the visible edge around her window shade, she watched her own hand as it drifted closer—remarkably steady—toward her window. Touching a finger to the edge, she peeled back the canvas ever so slightly, squinting, trying to peer past the glare and into the dusk.

A thin, spidery hand, almost glowing white in the twilight, slammed against the glass. Isobel shrieked and stumbled back, tripping and falling on the carpet. The shade flew up. The phone jumped from her grasp and landed out of her reach.

On and off, she could hear Gwen's distant, frantic voice calling her name.

Isobel stared up in terror through the dark square of her window, at the pale, luminous face that stared back.

19
Visitations

"Varen!" Isobel launched herself from the floor. She rushed to the window. Finding the clasps, she snapped the locks back, fixed her fingers in the grooves, and heaved upward.

He crouched precariously on the slanted roof, watching her, his calm, expressionless face level with hers. With every glimpse, every meeting of their eyes, those cool, kohl-rimmed jades bored into her, causing little electrodes to zip through her insides.

"Isobel! Isobel!" came a tiny, strained insect voice from somewhere behind. "Isobel, I'm calling the police!"

"Oh!" Isobel whirled, throwing a *Hold on!* gesture toward the window before diving for the handset.

"Gwen," she said, "it's Varen. I gotta go."

"Omigod. Okay—but you better call me baa—!"

Beep.

Isobel flung the phone aside and sprang to grapple once more with the window. She tugged and jerked until it shimmied up half an inch, allowing in the cold evening air. She slipped her hands under the bottom, ready to lift, but froze when she felt his fingertips, cool from the October air, slide in next to hers.

All breathing ceased. And there was that static sensation again, a soft buzz where their skin touched.

The quiet knock at her door made her jump. She spun, slamming her back to the window. There was a shift and a shudder from outside, a quiet curse, and then a long, scraping scuffle.

"Isobel?" Her father.

"Not decent!" she yelled, her voice ridiculously loud, erratic. "Just a second!" She turned and faced the window again, only to catch sight of Varen sliding backward, headfirst down the slope of her roof, some sort of bag trailing behind him, still clutched in his white-knuckled grasp.

"Oh!" Isobel's hands rushed to cover her mouth, so her suppressed scream came out as a high-pitched squeak. She fought the urge to shut her eyes and watched, horrified, as he careened toward the ledge. The strap of his bag snagged on the corner of an upturned shingle and ripped from his grasp. He skidded to the end of the roof, managing to reposition himself at the last second, just in time for the heels of his boots to catch against the gutter, hands braced out on either side of him.

He stopped. Isobel breathed again.

The knock at her door was more insistent this time. "Isobel, is everything all right in there?"

"Fine!" she called. Putting a foot on her window ledge, she hoisted herself up and grasped the shade, pulling it down. "Just . . . give me a second, okay?" She undid the ties on her curtains and drew them together. Turning, she tore across her room and barreled into her closet. She yanked her pink robe from its hanger, threw it around herself, pushed her arms through the sleeves, and tied the belt haphazardly around her waist. Gripping the collar closed so her dad wouldn't see her T-shirt, she scuttled to the door and opened it a crack.

"Yeah?" she asked, trying to make her breathing seem normal.

Her dad stepped closer and put the toe of his shoe between the door and the door frame. Isobel pushed in on the door. He squinted down at her suspiciously, then peered past her, over her head.

"*Dad*," she said, "I am *trying* to get ready to take a shower."

"Oh," he said. The lie worked, and her father leaned back again, removing his shoe. "I thought I heard you yell."

"I was on the phone," she answered, having had the excuse ready.

"Everything all right?"

"Yep!" She flashed a smile.

"Okay." He shoved his hands into his pockets, but didn't turn to leave.

"Okay," she echoed, and pressed the door shut.

"Listen," he said, jamming the door with his foot again, "you didn't hear anything on the roof, did you? Mom says she thought she might have heard that raccoon again."

"No!" Isobel answered quickly—maybe too quickly. She tried to wipe her face clear of any knowing. "No," she repeated. "Nothing."

"Well," he said, "do you mind if I take a look?"

"Dad!" she screeched. She pushed his foot out with her own, then clamped the door shut in his face. "Just wait till I'm in the shower! I am *naked!*"

"Okay! Okay! I'll wait, I'll wait!"

Isobel stood another moment at the door, her ear pressed against it, listening. After the sound of quiet shuffling, she cracked it again and saw him tromp down the stairs, muttering to himself.

She shut the door and turned the lock, then padded back to the window and heaved it open.

"What are you doing?" she hissed into the darkness.

She could see him at the roof's ledge, inching backward toward her window crab-style, until he had at least a foot between him and the drop-off.

Isobel pulled herself out through the window. She crouched on the sill and leaned out into the sharp air, a chilly wind whipping through her hair as she watched him rise to a standing position.

He stepped sideways up the slanted roof toward her, one foot carefully following the other as he moved with all the agility of a tightrope walker.

Varen said nothing as he drew nearer, his jet-black hair stirring ever so slightly in the wind. He bent down along the way and scooped up the small nylon satchel that had snagged on the upturned roofing tile. When he came near enough, he grabbed hold of the window ledge and pulled himself forward. For the briefest moment, they came face-to-face. Their eyes locked.

Then he broke the stare, swiveled, and sank into a sitting position, chains clanking, with his knees up.

She watched him speechlessly as he set a cooler bag between his boots, like he was settling down to a picnic or something. An image of the contents as hospital blood bags, complete with juice-box straws, flashed through her mind.

Unfolding her legs, she made herself as comfortable as she could on the cold outer edge of the sill.

An intangible and unnameable charge electrified the space between them, and at first, neither one of them said anything. Another breeze rustled past, shaking the tree limbs and lacing the air with the spicy scent of dead leaves and chimney smoke.

Finally she heard him unzip the bag and watched him pull out a small cylinder.

"I thought you might like some crappy ice cream," he said.

As Isobel's eyes fixed on the carton, something inside of her broke. She felt it, a landslide. A flood of warmth followed, causing the tips of her fingers to burn against the cold frost of the carton as she accepted it with one hand.

In the dim light streaming from her room, she could discern little monkeys swinging on vines across the package. BANANA FUDGE SWIRL, the label read, and she felt a twisty sensation that came from the realization that he'd actually remembered.

Next he held out a spoon for her, staring at her from behind the curve of white plastic with such intensity that it frightened her. She felt an unfurling sensation through her whole body, like she was experiencing the first drop of a roller coaster—one that was sure to have a lot of loops up ahead.

Isobel took the spoon slowly, a gesture that seemed to carry with it some sort of immense weight that she didn't exactly understand yet. His eyes fell away, releasing her.

A curious smile threatened to crack at one side of her mouth as she watched him pry open a carton of his own. He pulled another spoon from the nylon bag, then wordlessly dug in.

Isobel took a bite too, savoring the combination of banana and chocolate.

She couldn't keep her eyes off his hands, those long fingers that, in their movement, held a grace all their own. His silver rings glinted in the light from her window, and she focused on his knuckles before clearing her throat to speak.

"That was Gwen Daniels on the phone," she blurted, shattering the silence that had become, at least for her, unbearable. "She told me that you tried to keep Brad from taking stuff out of my locker. Is that why you called me?"

"Partly," he admitted.

"Is that why you're here now?"

"No."

"Oh." Her stomach clutched. She waited for him to say something else, but he didn't. She looked down into her carton of ice cream, pushing her spoon through, creating little paths and mountains. "She, uh, said that he, um . . . Are you okay?" she asked.

He scowled up at her, looking genuinely affronted. She

returned his stare, refusing to take back the question even though it seemed as if he was just as stubbornly going to refuse to acknowledge it.

"Gwen said"—Isobel tried out these waters tentatively— "that something strange happened with all the lockers. Did . . . did you see it?"

His face darkened. He glanced away from her. "I don't know what you're talking about," he muttered, taking another bite of ice cream.

Ooookay, she thought. She wouldn't go there just yet, then.

"Do you know why he wanted my stuff?"

He stopped picking at his ice cream and looked back up at her through the jagged edges of his hair. "I figured you would know that."

Isobel shook her head. She took another bite of ice cream, then, shivering, set it aside on the sill next to her. She slid off the window ledge and, easing down, settled on the roof beside him, all too conscious that now a space of mere inches existed between them.

"I need to tell you about something," she whispered.

He stuck his spoon into his ice cream and, reaching over her, set it on the window ledge next to hers. He raised his eyebrows expectantly, maybe even a little curiously.

"I had a dream last night," she continued, half surprised he'd given her his full attention sans his usual dry remark or disparaging comment. "About Poe—*I think*," she added.

His cool expression didn't change. "Poe?"

"Yeah." She nodded, biting her bottom lip, afraid she might be alone in this after all.

"What happened?" he asked, seeming to take her seriously enough, though that could have been because of the way she'd been staring at him—wide-eyed, thirsty for him to believe.

His question was the waving checkered flag she'd been waiting for. "Your Poe book," she said, then stopped when she realized that in order to tell him the rest, she would have to admit to tossing it in the trash. Maybe she could modify the truth a little and say she'd lost it instead.

Then something else stalled her. From inside her room came another quiet knock at her door.

"Isobel?" her mom called. What was this? Parent-daughter conference night?

"Ugh," she growled, poking her head over the windowsill. Between the two ice cream cartons, she could see her locked door handle jiggling.

"Go," he said.

She glanced at him, just in time to watch him sink into the shadows, lying back against the roof. His legs outstretched, he crossed them at the ankles, the toes of his boots now the only visible part of him within the line of light streaming from her window. "I'll wait."

"Isobel?" her mother called again. "Why is this door locked?"

Trying to be ladylike about it, Isobel crawled back through the window, shutting it as quietly as she could manage. She pulled down the shade once more to hide the ice cream cartons, then opened her door.

"Isobel, what are you do—?"

"I've been *trying* to get ready to take a shower."

Her mother regarded her strangely for a moment, a basket of Danny's laundry tucked under one arm. She smiled halfway, then said, "I guess you really are feeling better now that you're snapping at me."

Isobel frowned, feeling guilty at seeing her mother's only lightly masked relief at the return of her daughter from Zombie World. "I'm not snapping," she said. "What is it?"

"Brad's here. He brought your homework."

20
Uninvited

She found Brad at the kitchen table. Her dad sat across from him, the now infamous books and binders from her locker in a pile between them.

After shedding her robe and throwing on an oversize sweater, Isobel had crept down the stairs, her ears tuned to the murmur of Brad's voice. Above the noise of the TV, however, she hadn't been able to make out specific words, and now, as she stood in the doorway to the kitchen, glaring at them, she wondered how much Brad had said. Had he mentioned Varen? By the look on his face, that jerky fake smile of his, he'd just been yukking it up with her dad. Listening while her father relived his football days, and maybe that was all.

"Isobel," her dad started, his tone guarded because he must have read the look on her face.

Her scowl hardened as it became apparent to her that Brad's year and a half of kissing her father's butt were about to pay off. And Brad, sitting there with that gleam in his eye, had known this would be the case. He'd known that she wouldn't have told her parents about their breakup. The thought of Brad being able to read her so well infuriated her to the point of wanting to snatch something off the wall and throw it at him. The feeling only got worse when her dad said, "Simmer down. Brad just brought your homework."

"Yeah." Her eyes fixed on Brad's deceptively handsome face. "Thanks, you're a real good person. Now please go."

"Isobel," snapped her dad in warning. Before, he'd always referred to Brad as "a real good kid," and perhaps she'd taken a step too far with her sarcastic play on his words. "Now, I don't know what's going on with you two," he said, and rose to lean across the table between them, like a referee calling a foul. "But, Isobel"—he pointed an accusing finger at her, something she *hated*—"you don't talk like that to any guest in this house, no matter who it is."

"But—"

"I don't want to hear it," he said, holding his hand up. "Now I'm leaving the kitchen, because whatever this is about, it's something you guys need to iron out." He gestured loosely between them. "But you two have been together long enough to do it in civil tones. If I hear any yelling," he said pointedly to Isobel, "then Brad'll go home, and it'll be another week of house arrest for you. Understand?"

Staring stubbornly at nothing, chin up, Isobel nodded, not trusting herself to give a verbal reply.

With that, her father breezed past her and into the living room, where she heard the volume of the TV spike a few notches, and then she was alone with Brad.

They stared at each other and Isobel waited for him to speak first. She wanted to know exactly what this was about before making any assumptions. After a moment, Brad scooted his chair back and stood, his letter jacket still on, she was glad to see. Maybe that meant he hadn't planned on staying long.

"I figured you hadn't told them," he said, grinning.

"Don't worry, I'll get around to it."

"I came to talk."

"I have nothing to say to you." She folded her arms close against herself. She didn't like the way he was looking at her, like he was assessing her for damage.

"*Hey,*" he said, louder, anger flashing in his features, those sharp blue eyes blazing. "I'm trying to warn you about that freak you're screwing."

Isobel felt her face flame. She rushed him, pushed him toward the back door. He stayed rooted to the spot, smirk in place. She spared a worried glance over her shoulder into the living room, then scowled at Brad. She gave up, knowing she'd have better luck in displacing a tree, and strode past him. She snapped on the porch light, then wordlessly opened the back door and stepped out into the brisk night.

Folding her arms, this time against the cold, she huddled into her sweater, waiting for him to follow. He took his time, making a point of closing the door behind him as he ambled out. She watched him thumb a cigarette from a half-crushed pack he'd pulled from the inside pocket of his jacket. As he lit up, she sneered.

"So now you're smoking at my parents' house?"

"You going to tell on me?"

"What do you want?"

He took a long draw from the cigarette, which he kept pinched between his thumb and fingers, his eyes crinkling in thought. He held the smoke in his lungs for a moment, then exhaled in a sigh. "This is getting really old, Izo," he said, and leaned his back against the brick wall beneath the porch light. "You need to just friggin' forget it already."

"Forget what exactly?"

The smirk reappeared as he tapped a few ashes onto the porch. "He dissed you in front of the entire school, Iz," he said. "Face it, he basically told you to get lost yesterday."

Her eyebrows shot up in disbelief. "Is *that* what this is about?"

"Look," he said, "why don't you just sit with us again tomorrow, and I'll let everybody know we can forget the whole thing."

"*What?*"

"I won't even bother the little faggot anymore, if that'll make you happy."

"We are *over*. You of all people should realize that. And, anyway, what about Nikki?"

Putting the cigarette to his lips again, he took another long tug, as though only to keep from smiling. He shrugged, blinking down at her in lazy indifference.

"You're such a jerk." She turned, ready to stalk back inside the house.

"I'll tell Alyssa to back off. I'll tell her to chill out so you can get your spot back on the squad."

Isobel turned to face him again. "Would you listen to

yourself? You're trying to bribe me into being your girlfriend. Don't you think that's just a little pathetic?"

"You belong with us," he said, "whether you're my girl-friend or not."

"No, Brad. No, I don't." She shook her head, half in denial, half in disbelief. Did he even know how he sounded?

"You think you belong with him?"

"I'm not with anybody."

"That's not what I heard."

"You hear what you want to."

At this he frowned. "Izo." He dropped the cigarette and ground it out with the tip of one shoe. He stepped in closer. She stood her ground, eyeing him suspiciously as he drew nearer, close enough for her to catch the smell of his cologne mixed in with cigarette smoke and the spearmint gum he always chewed to keep his mom guessing. "The guy is a total freak."

"Stop calling him that."

"Listen," he said, inching in, his expression hardening, "there's something not right about all of this. He's got you brainwashed or something."

She felt herself bristling all over from his closeness, and she wanted to step back, away from his familiar scent and his low, protective tone, but that was exactly what he wanted. She could feel it. He wanted to know he could still affect her like that, that he still held that power over her.

He leaned down and kissed her neck.

She went rigid. "Stop," she warned.

The smell of tobacco filled her nostrils as his mouth trailed up to her jaw. She felt his arms slide around her lower back, clamping her to his solid frame. "No, Brad," she was scarcely able to squeak. She raised her hands, palms pressed against the front of his jacket. She pushed, angling back, but not far enough. "I said stop!" He pressed his mouth over hers.

She made a muffled sound as close to a scream as she could manage, even though she knew there was no way her father would hear over the blare of the television. If only he would walk into the kitchen and look out the window. He'd see—he'd know how Brad could be sometimes. She thrashed against him, preparing to bite down on his bottom lip, when suddenly, tensing, he stopped and pulled back.

"What was that?"

"Let go!" she growled, prying herself away, shoving him as hard as she could, though she only succeeded in rumpling his jacket. "What is *wrong* with you?"

He shushed her, tilting his head to listen. From above came the sound of heavy scraping. "There it is again," he muttered.

Her eyes widened. Varen. He must have heard them arguing from the roof. What was he doing? Was he coming this way? Was he *crazy*? Her mind raced for a distraction.

"You're such a jerk!" she shouted as loud as she could. Brad's head whipped back around to her, his eyes, that angry, electric shade of blue, searching.

She staggered a few steps back. "Go away!" she shouted again, knowing someone would be there any second.

Brad did too, it seemed, because he wasted no time in

stepping down off the porch. He raised a finger, pointing at her as he backed away. "You'll see," he said. "You'll see. In the meantime, why don't you tell that little faggot I'm gonna kill him. Tell him I'm gonna beat the livin' piss out of him for what he did, 'cause I know it was him. Tell him that for me, would ya, Iz?"

Isobel stared after him in horrified disbelief, her confusion mounting. Did *what*?

She heard the porch door open behind her and her mother's voice. "Isobel, time to come in now. You shouldn't even be out here after being sick."

Isobel stood frozen, staring after Brad as he turned away and headed around to the front of the house, no doubt to wherever he'd parked his Mustang.

His Mustang. Why hadn't she heard his Mustang? Turning, she rushed in past her mother, through the kitchen and into the living room, right up to the window. Parting the draperies, Isobel watched Brad climb into another car, one she recognized as his mom's sleek black BMW.

She turned to see her father sit up from reclining in his easy chair. The TV on mute, he glared at her.

"Where's Brad's Mustang?"

Her father's gaze narrowed. "I didn't ask," he said coolly, "because yesterday you told me that it was in the shop."

"I forgot," she muttered, and swiveled for the stairs. "I'm going to bed."

"I was just about to suggest that," he said, then snapped the TV volume back on.

Isobel stomped upstairs once more, averting her gaze from Danny, who stood leaning halfway out his door. "Ooh, somebody's in trouuuuuu—"

She shut her door, cutting him off, then stopped, her heart tripping over itself at the sight of Varen Nethers perched on one corner of her tousled pink bed, last year's cheerleading album draped open across his lap.

"What are you *doing*!?" Undiluted panic spurred her forward, giving her enough nerve to snatch the album away.

Oh God, she thought, looking down at the page the album had been opened to. He'd seen the one from last year's squad sleepover, the one of her stuffing an entire slice of pepperoni pineapple pizza into her mouth.

"Impressive," he said as he lay back against her bed, propped up on his elbows.

Clutching the scrapbook to her chest, she turned away, not wanting him to see the lobster-red hue of her face. "What is wrong with you?" she seethed. "You don't just barge into somebody's personal space and start going through their stuff!" Marching to her closet, she flung the album in.

"Really," he said in that infuriating monotone.

She whirled around to see him staring at her, amused by some private joke, and her stomach turned several lopsided backflips at the sight of him half lying on her bed like that. Black sprawled over pink. She angled her eyes toward the ceiling, trying to get a grip.

"How come you're off the squad?" he asked out of nowhere.

She flushed again, her suspicion that he'd been able to hear her conversation with Brad confirmed. "I quit," she snapped. "I guess since you heard—"

"I heard everything," he said.

He was doing it again. Watching her with that intense, penetrating look, the one she didn't quite get. It made her nervous and dizzy and flustered. Realizing she'd been wringing her hands, she dropped them to her sides.

"Well, then you also heard enough to know you'd better steer clear of Brad for a while."

"Given how much we hang out as it is."

"You know what I mean. I don't know what you did to piss him off like that but . . . well, he's pissed."

"What's funny is," he said, sitting up, seemingly unfazed by Brad's death threats or her added warnings, "neither do I."

He stood, popping the collar of his green jacket, the sudden movement causing her to stiffen. He noticed it too, and paused to stare at her.

She looked away, rubbing her arm. It was just that he could be so imposing sometimes. And unpredictable. And it was just too surreal to see him standing in her room like this.

"Do me a favor, would you?" He moved to her window.

"What's that?"

"Take your own advice."

"What do you mean, take my own advice?"

"I mean," he said, handing her the now slightly runny carton of Banana Fudge Swirl, packing the other away into the nylon bag, "that you should steer clear of your ex for a while."

Isobel tilted her head at him in wonderment. That would be doing him a favor?

"Varen?"

"Isobel."

A chill ran through her at the way he said her name, the way he gave each syllable its own moment, making it sound so regal, so proper. He stood with his back to her, his hands gripping the sides of her window frame. His shoulders remained tense, like he knew what was coming but still held hope that he could escape.

"Why—why did you come here tonight?"

He turned his head toward her, though he didn't meet her gaze. As usual, he didn't answer right away either.

"Because you were right," he said at last. "Yesterday, you were right. And I wanted a chance, deserved or not, to apologize. So . . . for what it's worth, I'm sorry."

Isobel swallowed with difficulty. Had he really just apologized to her?

He ducked his head, lowering himself to straddle her window ledge.

"However, that said"—he looked back at her now, his eyes filled with a dark and secretive mirth—"I can promise that you'll never be right about me again."

Isobel set her carton of ice cream aside on her dresser. She stepped forward and stopped at her window, looking down at him, speaking before she knew what to say. "Never?"

For the first time since they'd met, since they'd been paired together for the project, his gaze was the one to fall away from hers.

Then something on her carpet caught his attention. He frowned, brow furrowing.

"Hey," he said, climbing back inside. He brushed past her.

Isobel's eyes widened, following him as he moved to her bedside. Crouching, he pulled something out from underneath. She felt a surge of panic when she saw the book. He turned to glare at her over his shoulder, holding up *The Complete Works of Edgar Allan Poe*. Isobel stood frozen in place, able to do nothing but gape. He rose, his gaze admonishing as he set the book on her nightstand.

"Little more respect, please," he said, and moved past her again to climb out the window.

"Wait," she called. She hadn't finished telling him about her dream. How could she have forgotten? His presence, it had been like a spell. And now he was leaving and it was too late. He was going to leave her alone with that book. "You can't go yet." She reached out, but stopped short of grasping his arm. "I have to tell you about the dream. I haven't finished telling you what happe—"

"Tomorrow," he said, ducking out. She watched him walk the length of her roof, powerless to call after him. He turned when he reached the end, then climbed down her mother's lattice just as she'd done that day she'd snuck out to meet him. Before she could utter another syllable to stop him, she heard a quiet clink of chains as his boots met with the turf below.

21
Motley Drama

Despite her extra-slow walk to Swanson's class the next morning, Isobel's heart raced in her chest. It thudded against her rib cage and pounded in her ears, the anticipation of seeing him again gripping her more tightly by the second.

She'd had to pace herself, not wanting to arrive too soon and be left sitting there, making it seem as though she was waiting for him. Then again, she didn't want to get there too late and not get the chance to talk to him at all. *Would* he talk to her?

Isobel gripped her books against her chest, as though that could help slow her pulse. She wasn't sure why it felt like such a big deal, anyway. It was just class, right?

Isobel entered Mr. Swanson's room with her head down. She went straight to her seat, chancing only a quick glance in the direction of Varen's chair. It sat empty in its corner.

She took her seat and, even though she told herself not to, watched the door.

Kids filed in. Chairs filled. The clock on the wall measured the minutes. The bell rang.

Varen's seat remained vacant, leaving Isobel with the sensation that a boulder had somehow materialized in the pit of her stomach.

For the first twenty minutes of class, as Swanson scribbled across the chalkboard, she held on to the hope that he was just running late. Her gaze kept straying from her senseless notes to the door. But then, at half past, a sinking feeling overtook her as she realized he wasn't coming.

Over and over she wondered where he could be. Her mind played out different scenarios, most of which involved the wrath of a certain ex-boyfriend.

Eventually Isobel gave up and zoned out. She spent the remainder of the period staring unfocused at Mr. Swanson, her gaze occasionally flickering to Varen's empty seat.

"All right, remember, everyone," Isobel heard Mr. Swanson say when the lunch bell rang, "projects and their presentations are due this Friday, that's All Hallows' Eve, as I'm sure I don't need to remind you." He smiled as everyone began to file out, his voice growing louder over the groans, Isobel's among them. "I hope for your sake, though, that I don't find them too terrifying. And just so you can't say I didn't tell you so, a no-show without a doctor's note equals a no-grade. That goes for both you and your partner."

In the hall, Isobel stopped, looking right and left. At no sign of his green jacket or black hair, her heart sank all over again. Where was he?

Isobel entered the lunchroom with unwavering tunnel vision.

Get in line. Get food. Pay. No eye contact. No talking.

After exiting the food line, she went straight to the empty table she'd ignored last time and set her tray at one end without so much as a glimpse in the crew's direction, or the goths', for that matter. She wasn't going to give anyone the opportunity of shooting her so much as an ugly look today. Instead she'd keep her eyes on her tray and her focus on eating, and she'd direct her mind toward surviving the next twenty minutes.

As she lifted the first forkful of salad to her mouth, another tray hit the table, clanking down right in front of hers. Isobel lowered her fork and looked up.

From behind her owlish glasses, Gwen glared at her. "What's the matter with you?" she asked. Wadding up her broom skirt, hiking it enough so that she could feed her skinny spandex-clad legs under the table, she slid onto the bench seat across from Isobel.

Isobel opened her mouth, not sure what to say. Was Gwen seriously going to sit with her? An overwhelming sense of gratitude welled up inside of her, nearly bringing a sting to her eyes. It was the nicest thing anyone had done for her in more than a week.

"What, were you dropped on your head as a kid?" Gwen railed. "First you hang up on me." She held up a hand and ticked off fingers. "Then you don't call me back, *then* you don't even show up at your locker this morning to say *why* you didn't call me back!"

Isobel chanced a look toward the floor-sitting group that she thought Gwen normally ate with. She received a few curious glances from some scraggly bearded guys and more than a few sneers from the bandanna-wearing girls.

"Hey, Earth to Isobel." Gwen banged her spoon against

Isobel's tray. "Why the snap-crackle-pop didn't you call me back?"

"Oh. I'm sorry. I forgot."

"Well, I'm about to 'Oh I'm sorry' forget to tell you what *I* found out this morning."

"Uh. What?"

Gwen grinned. Looking self-satisfied, she folded her arms. "No, I'm not tell—" but she stopped, her eyes growing round. Something over Isobel's shoulder had caught her attention. "Oh my."

Isobel twisted in her seat. A hush fell over the entire cafeteria. All eyes focused on Mr. Nott, the assistant principal, who'd entered through the double doors, Brad on one side of him, a dark, familiar figure on the other.

"Oh, no," Isobel said. She pressed both hands against the table and pushed herself up to get a better look. At the sight of him, a thrill of excitement mixed with nervousness surged through her. She scanned him, taking an inventory of all appendages and searching for any sign of bruises or blood or evidence of a fractured skull. His face still looked as perfect as it had the previous night, smooth and calm. Brad, however, stood scowling, his shoulders tensed, his hands clenched into fists.

The two boys broke away from Mr. Nott and strode in opposite directions, ignoring each other as well as the countless stares. Brad headed for the crew's usual spot, while Varen, bypassing his own table, moved straight for her.

"Holy granola. He's coming over here," Gwen whispered, hands flapping, knocking over her yogurt cup.

Isobel took in a sharp breath as she watched him approach.

A brown paper lunch bag hit the tabletop. "Mind if I join you," he said. It wasn't a question. Gwen, in a flurry, scrambled to move down one seat.

"Hey," he offered to Gwen as he slid onto the bench next to her, directly across from Isobel.

"Shalom," she said, raising a hand.

"What the hell is that?" asked Varen. He nodded at Isobel's tray.

Isobel sat stunned for a moment, her brain flatlining when she felt his knee brush hers. "Uh." She shook her head. Why couldn't she think straight? She glanced down at the soupy contents of her plate. *Just tell him what it is. Simple. Look at it and say what it is.* "Sloppy Joe," she managed.

"Hmm," he said, sounding doubtful. "May he rest in peace."

"So, I don't mean to be rude," Gwen interjected, "but are you going to tell us what *that* was all about or what?" She jabbed a thumb toward the door through which he and Brad had entered.

Isobel's eyes darted to Varen. Gwen, unlike her, seemed to have the audacious ability to jump in there and ask the hot-button questions. The girl was really starting to grow on her.

Varen sat very still, staring Gwen down in that withering way that always left Isobel wishing she could blend into the furniture. After an immeasurable moment, he blinked slowly and, turning back to Isobel, said, "Apparently, during football practice yesterday, somebody overturned your boy's car in the school parking lot."

"*What?*" Isobel and Gwen shouted in unison.

Several sets of eyes shot in their direction. The three of them ducked their heads and turned to their lunches. Gwen tore her grilled cheese sandwich in half. Isobel poked at her fruit salad with her fork, while Varen pulled a small Tupperware container out of the paper bag.

Isobel leaned forward over the table. "That's what he must have meant last night," she whispered.

His eyes locked on hers, causing a mosh-pit sensation to erupt in her stomach. When he looked at her like that, it was like he was trying to communicate through some form of telepathy. It was a language she wished she held the power to decipher.

"How did I not know about this?" Gwen wondered aloud. "And what? He's trying to say that it was you?" She dipped an apple slice into her yogurt.

"I spent the better part of the last hour in Finch's office being questioned. With your ex and his old man there, let me tell you, it was a real party," he said.

"They seriously think you could have done that?" asked Isobel.

"Yeah, well, I tried to explain that my mind powers don't work on Tuesdays," he said, prompting Gwen to let out a tiny, hysterical, almost fearful laugh. She stifled it quickly by shoving half her sandwich into her mouth at once.

"Didn't you tell them about what happened at the ice cream shop?"

"Wha happwn?" Gwen asked with her mouth full.

Varen shot Isobel a look of warning. "I told them I was at

work when it happened. That should be enough, shouldn't it?" He trailed off. "Hmm," he muttered, his attention caught by something behind her. "Give me just a second." He got up.

"Hey, is that hummus?" Gwen seized his Tupperware container.

"Knock yourself out," he said, and dumped over the paper bag. A Ziploc pouch full of pita bread hit the table.

"Ohh, this looks like the whipped kind Mom used to get from Cohen's Deli back in Brooklyn." Gwen snatched up a piece of pita bread and scooped out a Ping-Pong-ball-size glob of hummus.

Glancing over her shoulder, Isobel watched Varen as he intercepted a dark-haired, Egyptian-eyed Lacy, who, it seemed, had been heading straight for their table.

Isobel felt her blood run suddenly hot beneath her skin. Something about them standing there together like that irked her. And then the girl reached out one lace-gloved, copper-toned hand to brush back a few locks from his ear. She stood on her toes, leaning in *very* close to whisper in his ear as her goddess eyes slid in Isobel's direction.

Isobel whipped around to face Gwen again, balling her napkin into one tightening fist.

She felt sick.

Gwen shook her head, trying to swallow her mouthful of pita and hummus. "Mmm!" she said, gulping hard. "That's what I had to tell you."

A long shadow fell over the table. Gwen averted her gaze and started to nibble on another slice of pita.

"Can you meet me tonight? To work on the project?" Varen asked.

Isobel looked away. She shrugged. "I'm still grounded."

From beneath the table, she received a kick to the ankle. She kicked back, aiming for Gwen's shin, but missed. "But I'll try," she amended in spite of herself.

"Good. Listen," he said, pulling a crumpled red envelope out of his back pocket. It was the same red envelope, Isobel knew, that Lacy had given him that morning after he'd stopped by her locker. "I've got to go return something right now, but I'll find you later."

"Sure," she said. Then, as he turned to walk away, she called after him. "Hey!"

He turned.

"So, for real, we're going to get this project thing done, then?" she asked.

He shrugged, walking backward. "Pending any unforeseen disasters . . ."

She nodded, and he turned to go, a group of tray-carrying sophomores clearing a wide path for him.

"Good," Isobel said, standing. She picked up her own tray, Sloppy Joe remaining untouched. She looked at the cafeteria clock. Almost ten minutes left. It might just be enough.

"Wait a second." Gwen rushed out of her seat and followed Isobel as she went to drop her tray at the dish-washing window. "Wait for me! I still have to tell you—where are you going?"

Gwen at her heels, Isobel hurried through the cafeteria doors. "There's something I've got to do too."

22
Cheer Up

"Hold up!" Gwen piped, pattering after her through the empty hall, Varen's Tupperware container in one hand, the half-eaten bag of pita bread flapping around in the other. "Wait for me!"

"Come on, hurry up. The bell's going to ring soon, and I don't know if she'll give me a note."

"Who? Isobel, listen, they broke up!"

Isobel stopped. Skidding to a halt, Gwen nearly toppled into her.

"What are you talking about?"

"Varen and Madame Cleopatra," said Gwen in a low, drawn-out voice, flicking her fingers dramatically over fluttering eyes. "Happened this morning. I heard it from Trevor, who heard it from Sara, who heard it from Ellen, who said she saw them arguing."

Gwen leaned against a row of lockers, arms folded. "Apparently, though," she said, "they were only pseudo girlfriend-boyfriend to begin with anyway."

Isobel narrowed her eyes on Gwen, then whipped around to stalk through the hallway again. "Sure looked like they were broken up."

She could hear Gwen bustling after her again. "Okay, so I don't know what *that* little moment was all about, but I *do* know for a fact that they're not together. Didn't you see his reaction when she came over? *So* obvious he wasn't about her."

"And I care because?"

"Whatever!" Gwen said. A huge smile sprang to her lips, making Isobel feel even worse. "As if. You *so* got it for him. I mean, can we say, 'Uhm, urh, durh, Sloppy Joe'? Psh. Please. Can't hide it from me. I know *all*—hey, what happened last night, anyway? Are you *ever* going to tell me? And oh my God, Brad's car. Any idea who could have done it? And what's this stuff about the ice cream shop? What happened at the ice cream shop? C'mon, Isobel, you're gonna have to fill me in here—hey, why are we going into the gym?"

Isobel came to a halt outside the double doors and pivoted to face Gwen. "You can't tell anybody."

"What? That we're going to the gym?"

"No," she said. "I mean . . . about Varen."

"What? You mean . . . that you like him?"

"Swear," Isobel pleaded. "You can't tell anyone."

Gwen's expression turned coy. "What, you don't think he likes you back?"

"You do?"

Gwen's smile grew. "You kidding? I mean, did you not see the way he kept sneaking looks at you? No, I guess you didn't. He was very good at it. Kinda makes you wonder what else he's good at." She elbowed Isobel and beamed.

"And why else do you think little Miss Morticia Addams came prancing over? But don't worry, I won't tell." Gwen thrust a fist between them, her smallest finger extended. "Pinky swear."

Isobel paused, an eyebrow raised, but then hooked her own pinky with Gwen's. They shook.

"Come on," said Isobel. Turning, she pushed through the gym doors. Gwen hustled in behind her.

Isobel found Coach Anne in her office, listening to the oldies station and poring over paperwork. She looked up only when Isobel tapped on her open door.

"I want back on the squad," Isobel said.

Coach's curiosity over Gwen faded in an instant; her eyes flashed, then narrowed and locked on Isobel. She leaned back in her chair and tossed her pen onto her desk. She rubbed her face like she was too tired to hear it. Isobel stood her ground, determined to do or say whatever it took to get back into the air.

"You walked off the squad, Lanley."

"And now I want to walk back on," she said. "I was wrong. And stupid. I want to go to Nationals. I want to see us win."

Coach Anne pursed her lips, considering.

Behind them, the bell ending lunch echoed through the gymnasium.

"Get your keister back to class, Lanley," Coach Anne said. "You've got two more hours to prepare your formal apology to the squad, and I want it in cheer format, is that understood?"

"Yes!" shouted Isobel, jumping.

"Go on," Coach Anne said, waiving them toward the door. "I'm not writing any notes. Get your butts back to class."

"Come on!" said Isobel.

Together they hurried out of the gym and took a short-cut through the courtyard, their footsteps crackling through strewn leaves.

"Isssobel."

She stopped and whipped her head around. A breeze washed past them, carrying with it a rush of crisped leaves, the singed smell of autumn.

"What is it?" Gwen asked, jogging up to meet her.

Isobel's gaze darted toward the cafeteria Dumpster, where she thought she'd seen someone. Her eyes snapped to the oak tree in the courtyard's center. She caught a dark blur of something just as it vanished behind the trunk. She heard a low rustle. A group of nearby pigeons, pecking at a pizza crust, took off in a flurry.

She tilted her head back to follow their scattered flight. Shielding her eyes from the sun, she caught a glimpse of several dark figures peering down at her and Gwen from the ledge of the roof.

That couldn't be right.

She dropped her gaze, stepped back to a better angle, and looked again.

What she had first taken for the silhouettes of people's heads, Isobel could now see were crows. They all sat on the edge of the roof, beaks rifling through feathers, heads turning in small jerky movements.

Someone snickered.

"What was that?" Isobel whispered.

"What was what?" Gwen asked. "And what are we looking at?"

Isobel revolved in a slow circle, her eyes scanning the empty courtyard and the vacated cement tables strewn with stray pieces of trash. "Nothing. I just . . ."

Inside, the bell rang.

"Now look what you did. You made us late. Y'happy?" Gwen said. Taking her by the wrist, Gwen led her toward the doors. Isobel followed. Confused, she stared back at the courtyard and up along the building. When they reached the doors at the opposite end, Isobel could see around to the other side of the oak tree and behind the Dumpster.

But there was nothing there.

She was already dressed and ready by the time she walked into the gym that afternoon, wearing a dark blue sports bra and her pair of short shorts with the little yellow megaphone in one corner.

Coach Anne gave her whistle a sharp blow. "Okay, gang," she said, raising her hands for silence, "find a seat, Isobel has something she wants to say."

This was met with murmuring and even one or two arm crossings, but with another short blast from Coach's whistle, the squad complied, piling with heavy footsteps onto the squeaking bleachers.

"You've got to be kidding me," Alyssa groaned.

214 — NEVERMORE

Taking a slow, deep breath, Isobel marched forward to stand in front of her less-than-enthused audience. Alyssa, who'd found a seat next to Nikki, pivoted away with a noise that made her sound like a hacking cat. She leaned back against the bleachers, crossing her thin legs and draping her arms over her lap.

"Whenever you're ready, Lanley," said Coach. With that, she took a spot on the bleachers too. Leaning forward, she braced an elbow on each knee.

Isobel scanned the listless faces of her squad mates. *Well,* she thought, *here goes.*

She straightened, nodded, and brought her arms down sharply against her sides. "Ready? Okay!"

She fell into the movements she'd only had time to practice in her mind, trying to ignore how ridiculous she sounded shouting at the top of her lungs all by herself.

> *"Don't mean to make a ruckus,*
> *Don't mean to make a fuss,*
> *But there is just one thing*
> *I think we should discuss.*
>
> *"I shouldn't try to meddle!*
> *I shouldn't try to fight!*
> *'Cause pushing fellow teammates*
> *Is simply just not right!"*

She turned toward Alyssa now. With one knee up, one

fist at her hip and one arm held high, Isobel brought a finger down to aim straight at the other girl. She beamed her hardest, putting on her biggest, brightest cheer smile. *Wake up, Alyssa. Pay attention.*

> *"I'm sorry that I shoved you!*
> *I'm sorry that you fell!*
> *I'm sorry that I nearly*
> *Kicked your little tail!"*

A chorus of "Oooh!'s" rang through the gym, drowned out only by the raucous laughter that followed. In an instant, Alyssa's smug expression dissolved. Her face reddened. Out of the corner of her eye, Isobel saw the gleam of Coach's whistle as it rose to her lips. Before she could be stopped, though, she plunged forward, still smiling. She snapped into a T position, then hit into a toe-touch. She landed with a nod, pouring as much energy into the cheer as she would in any competition, knowing how infectious enthusiasm could be to those of the cheer persuasion.

> *"I want another chance,*
> *I want to try again,*
> *I want to go to Nationals*
> *And win, win, win!"*

Isobel delivered each "win" with a tuck jump, then threw in a double nine jump at the end just to show off. She finished with a clap, another tight nod, and a forward lunge, her arms extended in a high V.

Breathing hard and gritting her teeth now more than smiling, she awaited the verdict.

There was a general shifting on the stands and some lingering giggles and whispers. A few indecisive, perhaps even apprehensive glances were directed toward Alyssa, who sat glowering, muttering to Nikki, who looked utterly miserable.

Coach stood up. "Lanley, I'm going to pretend I didn't hear that middle part," she said, then turned to the squad and shouted, "Welcome back. You're leading warm-ups."

They'd been working on a pike basket toss when Coach blew the whistle for them to get into formation for the routine. After the run-through with music, Stevie came up beside her. "Don't worry," he said, and leaned in to whisper, "they're glad you're back, even if they're not showing it, Coach especially. Alyssa volunteered to take your spot, saying she knew all your stunts, but she couldn't keep up." He flashed a knowing smile. "Oh, and I think somebody's out there waiting for you."

Isobel's brow furrowed. Her gaze followed the direction of Stevie's nod. She narrowed her eyes at the empty archway. He wouldn't, Isobel thought, picturing Brad standing there during their routine, watching her, waiting to give her a ride, like everything was hunky-dory.

After that, Isobel was only half-able to concentrate on the cooldown stretches as Stevie went through them.

KELLY CREAGH — 217

Her eyes kept flashing nervously toward the door.

What did Brad want from her? Couldn't he take a clue? Or maybe he was just there waiting for Nikki, she thought, though that didn't really make the situation any better. Actually, it made it worse.

As soon as practice ended, Isobel threw on a pair of blue sweatpants over her shorts and pulled on her yellow Trenton T-shirt. Grabbing her gym bag and backpack, she stormed through the doors but stopped when she didn't see anyone. Inexplicably, that feeling crept over her again, an echo of what she'd felt earlier that afternoon in the courtyard. She heard the sound of scuffling gravel and turned toward the patch of warm sunlight that leaked in through the parking lot doors, which someone had propped open. A cool breeze wafted in, and she glanced down as a few dead leaves swept inside, tumbling to a stop at her feet.

The patch of light on the floor flickered. A quick shadow flashed across. Isobel's head popped up, her eyes wide on the open, empty doorway. Outside, she thought she heard a stifled laugh.

Isobel stepped into the door frame. "Brad?"

"Guess again," came a voice from behind her, separate from the laughter.

She turned to find Varen standing with his back against the wall, her own stunned expression reflected in the pair of sleek sunglasses he wore.

"Jeez, you scared me" was all she could manage while trying to kick-start her breathing again.

"I've been told I have that effect," he said in that deadpan way of his.

Isobel tilted her head at him, a new thought dawning on her. "Did you stay after school?"

His gaze fell to his boots before lifting again. He leaned his head back until it rested against the wall behind him. "I do," he said. "Sometimes."

Isobel couldn't seem to help the small smile that edged its way along her mouth.

"Um, how long have you been out here?" she asked.

Stuffing his hands into the pockets of his jacket, he shrugged.

"Hold up," she said, eyes narrowing. "You weren't . . . Were you *watching* me?"

It took him a full beat to respond. "I . . . prefer the term 'observing,'" he said. "The connotations are far less voyeuristic."

"So what, now you speak French?"

That got a smirk out of him.

"Sooo . . . what's up?" she asked.

He said nothing for a long moment, only stared at her from behind those glasses that shielded from her sight the eyes that might have told her more. At last, he pushed off from the wall. "Thought you might need a ride," he said, brushing past her, walking through the open doors.

Doing her best to suppress her grin, she followed after him.

23
Dearly Departed

"So how did you know to look for me at practice?" Isobel asked as he opened his trunk. "I told you I quit."

He took her gym bag and threw it in, then relieved her of her backpack as well. His trunk was remarkably clutter free, she noticed. Besides her stuff, there was only a set of neatly wound jumper cables tucked to one side and a case of CDs, which he traded out for his satchel.

She kept sneaking glances at him out of the corner of her eye while she waited for him to say something, but where it had been hard enough to read him without the sunglasses, with them on, it felt like trying to gauge a block of stone.

He reached into his satchel and retrieved the Tupperware container from lunch. He held it up. "Little bird told me."

Gwen. Isobel found herself smiling at the thought of her newest, most unlikely friend as she climbed into the passenger side of Varen's car.

He got into the driver's seat, sweeping aside his wallet chains and turning the key in the ignition. The Cougar rumbled to life, and the portable CD player sitting between them began to spin. A racing beat surged through the car speakers, complete with electric guitars, crashing drums, and someone screaming a ragged plea to please save their soul.

Isobel picked up the Discman, eyeing the scraped casing and the patch of black duct tape holding it all together. "How do you still have one of these things, anyway?" she asked.

"Because I have car payments," he said. "Seat belt."

"Oh," Isobel mouthed, and deciding to leave her inquiries there, she drew the old-fashioned seat belt across her lap and clicked it into place. He handed her the case of CDs, instructing her to put in "the one with the trees." She flipped through the discs while he toggled the stick shift and put the car in reverse.

Conquering the urge to watch him drive (she'd never thought anyone could make the act of operating a car seem graceful), she finally found the album he wanted, one with a white background and the silhouette of twisted, bare-limbed trees. Isobel recognized the band's emblem right away on the outer rim of the CD. The image was of the same upside-down dead bird on the back of the green jacket he always wore. She pressed the eject button, and for the moment it took her to exchange albums, the car went blessedly silent.

"You're grounded," he said before the new CD could start wailing out a soulful, darkly angelic ballad. "Why?"

Isobel recognized this as an opportune time to lie, or at least practice some good truth omitting. "Because of yelling outside last night," she said. There. She hadn't had to lie at all. She'd just leave out the part about her originally being grounded for returning home past curfew in a strange car the previous Friday—*his* car, to be exact.

She frowned suddenly. What was she going to tell her mom when they got to her house?

"Your parents pretty strict?" He asked this like he already knew the answer.

"I guess," she admitted. "Why?"

She turned to watch him now, glad to have the excuse of conversation. The brakes squeaked as they slid to a gradual halt at a red light.

"I want to ask you something," he said.

Isobel was startled by the abruptness of that statement. It didn't help that his focus remained forward, either. It gave her that plummeting feeling inside, the one she always got when she knew she was in trouble for something even though she couldn't think of what. The light turned green, he shifted, and they were moving again.

"Yeah?" she said. She tried to ignore the flood of internal questions that assaulted her, while at the same time, she racked her brain for anything she might have done or said.

"There's this thing happening on Friday night," he said, "something that happens every year, but not everybody knows about it."

Isobel tensed. She turned her head to stare forward, trying her damnedest to keep from turning either ash pale or fire truck red. There was *no* way this could be happening. He could not possibly be asking her out. It had to be something else. Whatever it was, she knew without a doubt that there was absolutely no way on this earth he could be asking her—

"I want you to go," he said.

Her mouth popped open. She shut it quickly, before he could see.

"With me," he added.

There it was.

He shot her a quick glance before pulling past the fountain and into her subdivision, and it was only when she caught a glimpse of her own dumbstruck expression in his glasses that it occurred to her that he was waiting for an answer.

"I—we have a game on Friday," she said, her mouth seeming to move on its own. The words just jumped out, as though her alter ego, the obsessive cheerleader, had taken upon herself to overthrow all motor skills. For a moment she almost regretted having rejoined the squad that afternoon. Almost.

"It doesn't start till late." He stole another glance at her.

"You mean . . . sneak out?" It wasn't until after she'd uttered the words that she recognized them as composing the most *duh* question of the year.

She thought he smiled.

He pulled up to her mailbox and shifted the car into park. When he still didn't say anything, she knew that for sure must mean yes—it was going to be a sneak-out kind of deal.

He turned off the ignition and reached into his back pocket, tugging from it a red envelope, one just like the envelope she had seen Lacy give him. Like the one he'd pulled out of his pocket at lunch today, only this one was addressed to her. He handed it to her.

"What sort of thing is it exactly?" she asked, opening the envelope.

Inside, she found a cream-colored card, laced with a red ribbon. She recognized it as some sort of ticket, though it took her a moment longer to realize that it had been fashioned to look like a mortuary toe tag. Ew.

"The Grim Facade" it read in ornate lettering across the top. The date was listed simply as "All Hallows' Eve," and below that, on the "Case No." line, it said, "Admit one." Where the tag called for a name she saw hers, printed in his elegant hand (in purple ink, of course), and underneath, she saw his name filled in on the "Tagged By" line.

"It's not exactly a school-sanctioned function," he said, "so think about it."

She looked up from the tag. "Uh, news flash. Your friends hate me."

"They don't know you," he said. Opening his door, he climbed out. He turned back, though, and leaned in on the door frame, peering at her. "Besides," he said, "you'd be with me."

Isobel gaped after him as he shut the door and went around to the back of the car, the tag almost slipping out of her fingers.

Did that just happen?

She stared down at the little card again, at their names printed together like that.

Isobel fumbled for the door handle and let herself out.

She found him at the rear of the car. From the open

trunk, he handed her her gym bag and then her backpack. Then he turned and leaned against the bumper, hands stuffed in the pockets of his black jeans. She stood, watching him, once again faced with his hidden gaze, masked by her own duel reflections. Her heart stumbled. Her mind groped for something to say.

"Are—are you coming in?" she asked, the words sounding so stupidly simple in her own ears, like something a little kid would ask a friend they knew was too cool to hang out with them.

He removed the glasses. His eyes, those jade stones, locked with hers. "I don't know," he said, "am I?"

"Mom!" Isobel yelled into the house. Behind her, she held open the storm door for Varen. He stepped in and then politely to one side, next to the umbrella stand and in front of the coat rack, his hands folded neatly in front of him, where he looked slightly uncomfortable and very much out of place. She felt a sudden lurch of panic at seeing him there like that, her mom's embroidered framed copy of the Lord's Prayer partially visible behind one safety-pin-studded shoulder.

"Mom!" she turned to shout again. "Uh, wait right there," she said. Dragging her gym bag along, Isobel pounded up the stairs to her room.

Her mom wasn't in her room or in the bathroom, though.

Isobel dropped her gym bag off in her own bedroom. Quickly she peeled off her practice gear and wiggled into her favorite pair of jeans. She threw on a clean T-shirt and rubbed on some deodorant. Next, while she was thinking about it, she grabbed *The Complete Works of Edgar Allan Poe* from her nightstand.

It was strange how far away the dream with Reynolds seemed now. She shook her head, holding the book between her hands, suddenly glad she hadn't had the chance to finish telling Varen about the dream, or about the book reappearing, or that she'd thrown it away in the first place. Or *thought* she'd thrown it away.

All that seemed to matter now was that she had the book and that they were going to finish the project. That is, if she could find her mom and tell her not to freak.

Isobel raced back down the stairs. She stopped before she reached the foyer, startled to find the space in front of the coatrack and umbrella stand empty.

She rushed to look out the front door, relieved to see Varen's car still parked outside.

"I actually did a study on Sir Arthur Conan Doyle during my undergrad when I was at Wash U," Isobel heard her mom say as she drew nearer to the kitchen. "But when I found out that Poe's Dupin was the inspiration for Doyle's Holmes, I tell you, I really got swept up in reading Poe's detective stories. I remember wishing I'd done my term paper on him instead."

Isobel stepped through the archway of the kitchen to find her mother at the sink, cutting chunks of boiled chicken with a pair of red-handled culinary scissors. Varen stood farther down the counter, slicing stalks of celery into thin crescent shapes. He glanced up as she walked in and, catching her eye, smiled faintly.

"Oh, Isobel," her mother said, "there you are. I hope you don't mind that, while you left your guest waiting, I enlisted him to help with supper."

Isobel moved farther into the kitchen, not knowing whether to be relieved that her mother hadn't had an atomic meltdown, or mortified that she'd taken it upon herself to play head chef with the nearest thing Trenton High had to a Dark Lord.

Well, at least it looked like he hadn't minded. In fact, Isobel was surprised to note how adept he seemed to be at chopping celery. Practiced, even.

"You'll stay to eat with us, won't you?" her mom asked. Varen flicked a quick glance at Isobel.

"Yeah," she said, "you should stay for dinner."

Could this day get any weirder? She tried to picture Varen at her family's dinner table, and she only hoped Danny wouldn't embarrass the hell out of her. She could just hear her little brother asking all sorts of stupid questions, like if his underwear was black too.

She stepped up to stand next to Varen, placing the Poe book on the counter.

"Varen says you're doing a project together," her mom said. "Isobel's never been a big reader," she added in an aside to Varen, who shot Isobel an amused smirk. She was glad he was enjoying himself so much.

"I was just telling Varen how I studied Poe in college," she continued. "I mostly read his detective stories, though. 'The Purloined Letter,' 'The Murders in the Rue Morgue'—I think I had a crush on Monsieur C. Auguste Dupin," she prattled on, pronouncing the name with the worst French accent ever. Isobel felt her ears go hot.

"Varen, would you like some iced tea?" her mother asked. "I just made some about a half hour ago. Ginger peach. There's some lemonade in the fridge too."

"Mom," Isobel cut in before he could answer, "can we *please* go study now? If that's all right."

"Okay, okay," her mom said, and stepped aside from the sink so Varen could wash his hands.

"Why don't you two go in there on the dining room table so I won't be in your way? There's plenty of room to spread out."

Isobel, her ears still burning, didn't wait for a second invitation to vamoose before her mom could find anything else embarrassing to say or do. Picking up Varen's satchel, which she found on one of the kitchen chairs, she hauled it into the dining room, knowing that if it held his black book, then wherever it went, he would follow.

He was still smiling that "I am silently amused by your quaint home life" smile by the time she set his bag down on one of the tall-backed dining room chairs. She pulled out another for herself and sat.

"What?" she said, waiting for whatever dry quip he'd been preparing to throw at her.

"Your mom's nice" was all he said. He moved his satchel

and took the seat she'd inadvertently designated for him. She found herself wishing that she'd thought to position him closer, but it would look weird if she got up and moved now.

Isobel set the Poe book out on the table between them. She sighed, deciding to get the worst over with first and confess. "I haven't read anything you told me to read," she blurted, proud of herself for looking him straight in the eye while saying it.

He nodded, like a doctor whose suspicions about a patient's diagnosis had been confirmed.

"Don't worry," he said, his fingers flipping through the pages, "skim through the 'Red Death' and write down the quotes you think are the more memorable ones. After that, find the poem 'Annabel Lee' and do the same with it. I've got to finish up the conclusion for our paper, and then we can start organizing the presentation stuff into categories."

Isobel took the book as it was rotated and scooted toward her, too humbled to even try to find the right words to thank him, grateful for his uncharacteristic show of patience.

Eventually she settled into a process where she allowed herself to sneak upward glances at him every time she copied down an acceptable quote in its entirety. At one point, her mom drifted in to deliver a pitcher of her peach tea, two glasses, and a plate of raspberry sandwich cookies, for which Varen set down his pen and stood to thank her, not taking his seat again until her mother was out of the room. He didn't seem to be aware that the gesture had come off as being totally old-fashioned, which made it all the more strange—because it made Isobel realize that he'd done it without thinking.

Almost an hour passed before Isobel finished compiling excerpts, and it was the sound of the front door opening that made her look up.

She saw her dad step in and set down his briefcase. Instantly she stiffened, but she told herself to take it easy. If her mom had been cool about Varen, then why should she expect any different from her father?

"Hey, Dad," she tried, testing the waters.

"Hey, Izzy," he said breezily enough, but when he looked up and into the dining room, something in his eyes darkened. His expression changed.

That's okay, Isobel thought. *Varen's appearance can be a little jarring at first. Just keep playing it cool and he'll relax.*

"Dad," she said, "this is Varen, a friend from school. We're working on a project together for English class." She gestured to their spread of papers and books on the table. *See, Dad? Exhibit A.*

Varen rose again and extended a ringed hand out over the dining room table, toward her dad. "Sir," he said.

Isobel held her breath. Awkward dot com.

Her dad frowned, his face going hard. He stepped into the room, and Isobel watched as her dad grasped Varen's hand in what she thought might have been a tighter-than-necessary grip. Anger shot through her, but she kept her seat, still waiting for the moment of tension to slip away.

The handshake lasted about half a second. Her dad broke from it, saying, "Is that your car parked out front . . . Varen?"

"Yes, sir."

Her dad's hardened expression now deepened with a layer of suspicion. "So then, is it safe to say that you were the one who brought my daughter home past midnight the other night?"

Isobel shot to her feet. "Dad."

"Yes, sir," said Varen, his tone admitting yet, Isobel dared to think, unrepentant.

"Dad."

Ignoring her, her dad brushed past both of them and into the kitchen, calling for Isobel's mom. "Jeannine," he said, "can I talk to you for a second?"

Isobel stared after him, appalled. So, yeah. Hadn't part of last night's lecture been about the treatment of guests? Still dazed by her father's behavior, she became only partially aware of Varen gathering his things and loading them into his satchel.

"Oh, no," she said, having to stop herself from placing a hand on his arm. "Please don't go," she pleaded. "It's okay. He's just—"

"Walk me out?" he said, shouldering the satchel. His words had been little more than a low mutter, which Isobel heard distractedly, her ears half tuned to the sound of her parents' urgent whispers in the kitchen. She thought she caught the word "hooligan" (one of her father's favorites), and, afraid Varen had heard too, she nodded, pressing forward through the dining room, into the foyer, and then outside. She held the storm door for him again, and they stepped onto the front porch. A chilling wind swept up around them, stirring wind chimes somewhere in the distance—a ghostly sound.

Isobel wrapped her arms tightly around herself. They descended through her yard and to his car without words. He opened the passenger-side door and threw in his satchel, then, rounding to the other side, opened the driver's-side door. Isobel stood helplessly by on the edge of the lawn, able only to shiver and watch as she waited for him to climb in and drive off.

He paused behind the car door, holding it open. Standing in the glow of the cab light, he seemed to be waiting for her.

Isobel stepped carefully off the curb and around the car, trying her best to keep her teeth from chattering from the mix of cold and anger. She moved around the car door, not wanting it to be a barrier between them. She kept her gaze downcast at first, drawing as near as she dared, surprising herself as she scooted the toes of her shoes to within inches of his boots.

She focused first on the design of his T-shirt—a wilting rose gripped in the jaws of a skull—and worked her way up to the collar of his green jacket and the light wisps of his hair. "I'm sorry," she whispered. She looked up at him. His eyes, once again partially lost in the dark, jagged recesses of his hair, stared down into hers.

"Don't worry about it," he said.

"Varen . . . I don't think there's any way I can go with you this Friday," she said, blurting the thought out just as it occurred to her. Her throat constricted, and she turned her

---

attention once more to their feet. "I *want* to go," she went on softly, "but . . ." She shut her mouth quickly, before she was able to make herself sound any more pathetic.

"Don't worry about it," he repeated, so gently that she had to look up at him again, to make sure she hadn't imagined the faint note of amusement there. "Listen," he said. He leaned down close to whisper, the sensation of his breath against her cheek nearly causing her eyes to flutter shut. "I've got to go," he said, "'cause right now, your dad's watching every move I make."

Isobel's eyes popped open. Over his shoulder, she could see her dad standing in the orange-yellow light of the dining room, squinting at them through the window like some great ogre, his arms folded, his face grim.

She felt the brush of Varen's knuckles against her jaw. Startled, her eyes returned to his. Then, before she could stop him, he sank away from her and into the driver's seat of the car. He turned the ignition, and the sound of his softly wailing stereo broke the silence.

"I'll see you tomorrow," he said. Isobel stepped back from the Cougar so he could shut the door. Her skin seeming to hum from where he'd touched her. She saw him shift the car into gear and then he drove off, his headlights crossing beams with another car that was just pulling onto her street. Isobel stood and stared after the Cougar until its taillights—like two demon-red eyes—vanished around the next turn. The approaching car pulled into her driveway, and when Danny climbed out from the backseat, she heard him murmur a quick thanks to his ride before calling out, "Hey, Isobel! Who was *that*?"

Her arms still tightly wrapped about herself, Isobel ignored her brother as she made her way toward the house. She stormed through the front door to find her father in the foyer, waiting.

24
The Woodlands of Weir

"Are you seeing that kid?" her father asked, pointing out the door. Isobel tried her best to ignore the fear that flared through her insides, like dry tinder catching flame. Her father hardly ever lost his temper, but when he did, it was totally lair-of-the-dragon-king, complete with fire breathing and fuming eyes.

"*Sam,*" came her mother's voice from the hallway. She appeared in the archway leading to the kitchen, her hands wrapped in a dish towel.

"He's not a kid," Isobel seethed, "and for your information, neither am I. What is your problem, anyway?" She tightened her arms around her middle, bracing herself for the argument. She hated fighting with her dad, and it was such a rare event that it always made her nervous.

"I'm trying to find out if my only daughter is dating a hoodlum, that's my problem!" he railed.

These words were echoed by the bang of the storm door. Danny, clad in his tan Boy Scouts uniform, awe plastered across his chubby face, entered the foyer. "That car was dope!" he announced. "Who—?" He stopped suddenly, looking between Isobel and their dad, his enthusiasm draining. "Ohhhh," he whispered, his voice like a tire leaking air, "should have used the back door."

"Sam, honestly," her mom said, "I don't get what the big deal is. They were just working on a project."

"Did you not see that kid, Jeannine? He looks like one of those gun-toting, school-shoot-out maniacs!"

"Yes, Sam, I did see him! *And* I spoke with him. He was very well-mannered, and if you hadn't blown through the roof, you might have found that out for yourself."

"Who are we taking about?" asked Danny, opening his arms as though expecting rain.

Isobel couldn't believe this. Her dad was freaking out over nothing! He was blowing a gasket because she'd been doing her homework. "You just can't handle it that I broke up with Brad, can you?" she growled.

"Whoa," Danny said, taken aback, "you broke up with Meathead?"

"No," said her dad, starting to shout, "what I can't handle is you being dropped off after midnight by some kid who thinks he's a vampire!"

"And now you're dating a vampire?" Danny asked, intrigued. "You know they bite, right?"

"Danny," her mom said, "go sit in the kitchen." Danny stayed right where he was.

"Oh, please!" Isobel shouted. Spinning away, she mounted the stairs at a run. She was not going to stand there and be questioned like a five-year-old.

"Are we talking about the dude from the phone?" asked

Danny, addressing the room in general.

"Isobel, you stop right there. I'm not done yet!" her dad yelled.

"Too bad," she shouted, stopping midway up the banister, "because I am!"

"How can he be a vampire when he knows so much about slayers?"

"*Danny,*" her mom said, her voice full of warning.

"Just saying." Danny shrugged.

"I said get down here, Isobel! We're going to talk about this or it's going to be another two weeks before you're allowed out of this house!"

"So what else is new!" she bellowed, barging the rest of the way up.

"Isobel!"

"Sam, stop yelling at her!" her mother yelled.

"If this were in Japanese," said Danny, "it could so be an anime."

"Isobel!" her dad shouted again.

She stopped at the top landing and leaned over the railing. "I'm sixteen, Dad! And it's none of your business *who* I choose to date!" She turned and stomped the rest of the way to her room, stopping again outside her door, her anger blazing. "Or who I *dump*, for that matter!" she roared, and sent her bedroom door slamming shut with a resounding bang.

Inside her room, Isobel flung herself onto her bed, unleashing an unbridled scream into her pillow. What was happening to her life? When had everything become so complicated? It was homework! How and when had her life become upended by *homework*?

Quick footsteps on the stairs were followed by a gentle knock at her door. Her mom. Isobel knew it even before she heard the soft voice asking if she would please come down to dinner. Isobel offered no reply. After a moment, she heard a sigh, then the retreat of defeated footsteps.

She lay still for a long time after that, curled up on her side, and tried to ignore the dull ache forming in her head.

She thought about digging her cell phone out of her backpack, but who would she call? She could try Gwen, but Isobel didn't know her number, and since Gwen had called the land line the other night, she wouldn't have it in her cell's directory, either. She thought about trying Gwen's Internet White Pages approach, but that would mean she would have to venture into her brother's room, and right then, she didn't have it in her to face another argument.

For what felt like the first time in her life, Isobel was battling not to hate her father. She couldn't understand how he could be so unfair or so blind, how he couldn't seem to see Brad's other side. Or what it was about Varen that had caused him to go so ballistic in the first place. Why did Varen seem to cause *everyone* around to go ballistic? What about him was not allowed? What made his world so different from hers?

His face, angular and serene, materialized in her mind. The memory of his gaze sent a gentle calm through her. She pictured him just as he had been when they'd been standing outside together next to his car. He'd been so close, she thought, shutting her eyes again, taking in a long, deep breath, as though, if she concentrated hard enough, she might be able to imagine he was right there next to her.

From somewhere downstairs, Isobel heard the phone ring, followed by Danny's shout of, "I got it!" She opened her eyes and rolled onto her back, straining her ears to try to hear whether or not the call was for her, even though she knew she wouldn't be allowed to take it. She heard her brother's voice float up from the foyer, saying, "Hey, Trevor."

She rolled over to stare out her darkened window. Her thoughts drifted back to Varen, and she tried to ignore her brother's heavy footsteps on the stairs and his voice as he spoke loudly into the phone. "Yeah, it's upstairs, let me get it and I'll check."

Now she could see Varen in her mind's eye, just where he'd been in her dream. A far-off form, tall, windswept, framed by a forest of matchstick trees. She was just about to shut her eyes again when there came a quiet knock at her bedroom door. She sat up. "What?"

"Isobel." It was Danny, whispering to her through the bottom crack of her door.

"What do you want?"

"Open up," he said. "It's for you." He raised his voice again, and she heard him say, "Yeah, I got the whole list of codes right here. Which ones do you want first?"

Isobel stumbled out of bed and toward the door. She opened it to a slit and found her brother there, holding the portable out to her. Stunned, she took it.

"Make it quick!" he whispered, and leaning over the banister, he said, "Okay, the first one is for Blood Thirst Traitor Three, and it's to stop the countdown clock on level seven. Ready? Okay—two, two, nine, zero—"

Isobel retreated quickly into her room and cradled the receiver against her ear. "Hello?"

"Okay, so madness runs in the family, am I right?"

"*Gwen!*" Isobel breathed out in a rush, sinking to the carpet on her knees.

"What is it?" said Gwen. "What's the matter?"

Outside her door, Isobel could hear Danny droning on, spouting off made-up codes. She knew there was bound to be a catch to Danny's help, but for the moment she was grateful.

"Varen was here," Isobel whispered, and then proceeded to give Gwen the abridged version of what had happened, all the way from the drive home to the atomic explosion with her dad.

"Are you serious?" Gwen exclaimed, cutting her off before she could finish. Then, as if she hadn't heard a word about the fight, she said, "He tagged you to go to the Grim Facade? Oh my cheese and crackers. Do you even know how major this is?"

"Gwen, are you listening to me? Did you not hear me when I said my dad just finished grounding me for the rest of my natural life?"

"Are you *kidding*?" she squeaked. "Ohhh, you are *sooo* going. You *gotta* see it. 'Course, I've only ever been once myself, but it was awesome. I went the year before last 'cause that emo kid, Mikey, with the spiky hair? You know the one I'm talkin' about? He tagged me. Hey! I bet I could get him to tag me again. If he isn't already taking somebody."

"Gwen, hello." Isobel tapped a finger against the receiver. "You're not hearing me. I can't go. I already told him I couldn't."

"What are you gonna wear?"

Isobel shut her eyes. She rubbed her temple where a headache had begun to set in.

"Look," she said, "it's probably safe to say that I won't be having much social interaction outside of school, at least until New Year's. I'm not going, Gwen. End of story. I'm just trying to figure out a way to meet with Varen this week to get the project done. Can you help me figure that one out? Please? Besides, if I can manage not to get kicked off the squad again, I've got the rival game this Friday anyway."

"Your parents gonna be there?" Gwen asked, a sly edge to her voice.

"At the game?"

"No, at your bat mitzvah—yes, the game!"

"After tonight? Are you kidding? My dad'll probably pick a seat front and center and *still* have binoculars handy."

"Can you . . . *guarantee* that?"

"Yes!" Isobel hissed. "I can!"

"Good!"

"Gwen—"

"Only do me a favor and try not to piss your dad off any more—well, any more than can be avoided."

"But—"

"—is not a nice word, even though we all have one. Now go to bed before your dad finds out you're on the phone and sends you into orbit for nine years. I'll see ya in the morning." *Click.*

Isobel stared at the phone. Now she was completely convinced. Gwen was a mental case. Recent escapee from the Home of Our Lady of Loonies. There was no way she was going to be able to sneak out this Friday. *Hello.* It was *Halloween.* Her parents—at least her dad—would be taking notes for the record if she so much as sneezed.

Isobel jumped when Danny zoomed into her room, snatching the phone out of her grasp. "Abort, abort!" he rasped, rushing back out, practically dive-bombing into his own room, shouting into the receiver, "Yeah—oh, yeah. Detrodon is the best!"

Isobel heard footsteps on the stairs. Her first instinct was to rush forward and slam her door shut, but instead she rose quietly and went to stand in the doorway. She grasped the handle and peered out to see her mother on her way up. Isobel frowned and turned away but left her door ajar. Returning to her bed, she buried herself in covers.

"Isobel," her mom said, her voice soft, coaxing, "I want you to know that your father and I are going to have a talk."

Isobel felt one side of her bed sink down as her mom sat, and then the weight of one warm hand against her arm. "In the meantime, I want you to go ahead and make plans to finish this project, okay? Here, I brought you your book."

Isobel's eyes widened as her mother laid *The Complete Works of Edgar Allan Poe* on the covers right next to her head. She shifted to sit up.

"Do you have somewhere else you two can meet this week?" her mom asked.

Isobel thought for a moment. In her mind, she pictured the ice cream shop. There was also Nobit's Nook, and of course, there was the library if all else failed. She nodded, grateful to have an ally after all. More often than not, her parents stuck maddeningly together on most issues concerning her social life.

"I don't understand," Isobel murmured. "I don't get what his problem is." She traced a finger along the sleeve of her mom's lavender top.

Her mother let her words out in a sigh. "I think he's just afraid."

"Of what? It's not like I was out doing drugs or something. Mom, we were studying."

"I know," her mom said, patting her arm. "I think he's afraid because he sees that you're growing up."

Isobel scowled and twisted around in her covers, huddling to one side. "Well, he's just going to have to deal."

That made her mom laugh. Isobel loved the sound of her mom's laugh. It was light and airy, like something you might expect from a Disney princess. "Your friend *is* a bit different," she said. "I think part of it is that at first, he comes off as a little . . . stark and maybe a little . . . *experienced*. I think that, more than anything else, is what has your father spooked. He

seems like a nice enough boy, though. Just a little eccentric."
Isobel felt her mother's hand brush her forehead, fingertips
stroking her hair. "It won't take your dad long to see that.
He's just . . . I don't know. I think he's so used to Brad being
around all the time."

Isobel snorted into her pillow. "So then why don't the
two of *them* date?"

"Oh, Izzy." Her mom sighed. "Don't be like that. He's
just trying to look out for you. So cut him a little slack."

"Cut *him* a little slack?" Isobel somehow doubted that
her mom could be right about her dad getting over it, though
she hoped he would. She hated fighting with either one of her
parents, but for some reason, things always seemed especially
bad when she fought with her father. Maybe it was because
he was scarier when he yelled. Or more likely, maybe it was
because they hardly ever argued to begin with, let alone outright screamed at each other.

"Izzy?"

"Mmm?" Isobel murmured, thinking.

"Do you want to talk about what went on between you
and Brad?"

Isobel grimaced. She twisted again, trying to straighten the
covers so they weren't wadded around her in a tight cocoon.
"No," she said, "there's nothing to talk about anyway. We
broke up and that's all."

"Okay," her mom said, and patted her side again. It
reminded Isobel of someone trying to put out a small fire.
"Just asking. I'm going to go read now, if that's okay?"

Isobel nodded against her pillow. She wanted to be alone. To think.

"There's some chicken salad left over in the fridge if you decide you're hungry," she said, then bent down and placed a kiss on Isobel's temple. Magically, her headache seemed to subside a little.

After her mother left, Isobel lay staring at the gleaming title on the spine of *The Complete Works of Edgar Allan Poe*. She knew she should probably sit up, prop the book open, and get to reading, but she also knew that after everything that had happened tonight, she wouldn't be able to concentrate on a single word. Especially since reading Poe felt like trying to decode some ages-old dead language anyway.

Besides that, the book still gave her the creeps. Isobel grabbed it and held it out over one side of her bed. She let it drop onto the floor with a heavy thud, then reached an arm over her head and pressed the button to set her alarm. Curling to one side again, she shut her eyes, leaving her bedroom light on.

The trees stretched up high and thin around her, gathered together like innumerable prison bars, all black, all dead.

Withered leaves littered the ground of the circular clearing in which she stood. Still and silent, the woods seemed almost mute. Beyond the trees, a backdrop of deep violet bled through like a glowing cyclorama, casting everything into eerie outline.

She looked up. Above her, beyond the spiderweb mesh

of tangled black limbs, there roiled a storm-purple sky. Snow drifted down around her gently. No, Isobel thought, holding out a hand to catch a flake—it wasn't snow. She rubbed it between her fingers and felt dry grit. Ash.

Like a thin blanket of dust, it coated the forest. It clung to the sides of the trees and collected in the bowl-like bodies of shriveled grayish-purple leaves.

"Where . . . ," she wondered aloud, if for no other reason than to test the silence.

"These are the woodlands known as Weir" came a voice from behind her. Isobel whirled to see him standing just within the perimeter of the clearing, draped in his long black cloak like before, the white scarf swathing his lower face, the fedora hat casting his eyes into shadow. "It is a mid-region. A place seldom consciously reached. One that lies in the space between dreams and all realities."

Startled, Isobel took a step back, her eyes trained on him. Amid all the phantom trees, he cut an even more menacing figure than he had in her room. He even seemed taller, if that were possible.

"So . . . I'm dreaming again?"

"Yes," he said, "and no."

"Ookay." Isobel felt a cold shiver run up her spine. She didn't like it here. What was worse, she didn't like not knowing if "here" really existed. Being in a dream meant that you were inside your own imagination, right? Then why did this feel so real?

Uncertain of what else to do, she continued to walk

backward slowly, her feet crunching over the brittle ground cover. "So, like, when can I get an answer from you that doesn't sound like it's coming from a Magic Eight Ball?"

He shifted slightly, as though there was something about her creating distance that bothered him. His eyes remained on her, unblinking. "Understand that I have no choice but to speak to you in riddles."

"Who *are* you? What do you want?"

"I am not who you may think I am," he said.

"You mean . . . Poe?" she asked. She felt silly saying it out loud.

It seemed to be the response he was looking for, though, because he nodded once, a very slight inclination of his head. He took a step toward her, then another. His feet made no sound against the patchwork blanket of dead leaves and cinders. "Though you should know that he has as much to do with this."

What was up with the way this dude talked? It was like listening to a Grand Master Jedi Ninja Buddhist, only without the enlightenment factor. And why did he keep walking toward her?

"Okay, stop right there," she said, raising a hand. He obeyed only as her heel came in contact with a dried twig, snapping it. They both stood frozen then, listening to the echo.

The forest seeped whispers. Stifled laughter rang in the distance.

Isobel felt panic rise within her. She turned. "What was that?"

"Ghouls," he said, "imps of the perverse. Empty beings

from this world. They have been sent to watch you. They are listening."

"Why? To what?" Isobel began moving back again. She glanced around, searching for a place to run. Every direction looked exactly the same, though, and as far as she could tell, there was no exit sign.

"You must stay close," he said. "They will only keep their distance as long as I stand with you."

Isobel stopped her backward trek. She stared at him, wondering if his suggestion that they use the buddy system was supposed to make her feel better. It didn't, and she folded her arms around herself, fighting a shudder. "How did I get here? More important, how do I get *out* of here?"

"You are here because I brought you," Reynolds said, "so that you will know this place, for I am not the only one who may now transport you here. That is why you must understand that your only hope of navigating this realm is to know it for what it is—to know that it is within a dream that you stand. With this knowledge comes the ability to control. Do you understand?"

"About as well as I understand Swahili."

"Look around you," he said, "and you will see how your friend's actions have already begun to strip the veil." He held out a gloved hand. Ash floated to light on his fingertips. "It weakens, and the night where it is at its thinnest in your world fast approaches. You must—"

A quiet snicker echoed to them from somewhere far off. It was followed by the hissing, static cry of *"Tekeli-li!"*

"What *is* that?" Isobel whispered.

"Quiet," Reynolds commanded. After another moment's listening, there came an answering call of *"Tekeli-li!"* from a different corner of the forest.

"She knows we are here," he said. "I can say no more than I have. You must go." He held his black-gloved hand toward her, palm up. Isobel hesitated, staring at it as though it were the hand of death. *"Now!"*

The urgency in his voice fanned the flame of panic within her. She stumbled forward. He grasped her hand tightly and pulled her through the line of trees, the sound of her steps absorbed into silence by the powder-soft ash.

He sped her through the maze of the dead forest, taking sudden twists and quick turns until the clearing vanished behind them and every direction began to look the same. She didn't know how she was keeping up with him. The trees rushed by her in a blur that made her head swim. It seemed impossible that they could be moving this fast.

You're dreaming, she told herself as they ran. *It's just a dream. Any second now you'll wake up, and it will all be over.*

From somewhere within the woods, Isobel heard a rustling sound and then the whisper of her name. Her head snapped up. In the distance, through the line of trees, a bright light, radiant and ethereal, broke like a beacon through the dimness. Long and slender, the light fluttered beneath the cover of a billowing white shroud, taking shape. Isobel could not help but steal backward glances as they ran. She saw a figure emerge from within the ebbing light—a woman, angelic in form, though her features remained lost in the distance, buried beneath yards of floating gossamer veils.

Reynolds stopped, yanking Isobel to face him. Out of thin air, he grasped a doorknob that appeared just as his hand clasped it. It was as though the door had been painted to blend in with the forest.

"You are her only threat and therefore our only hope," he said hastily, pulling the door open to reveal rose carpeting and a pink bedspread. He pushed her through and Isobel stumbled over the threshold, into her bedroom. There, in her bed, she saw herself—asleep.

"Learn to awaken within your dreams, Isobel," he called after her, "or we are *all* lost."

Behind her, the door slammed shut.

25
Seeing Double

Isobel stared at the sleeping body in her bed. *Her* body.

All at once, the digital clock on her headboard twitched to read six thirty a.m. The blaring sound of her alarm erupted, and with it she felt a quick, sharp tug through her middle.

There came a rushing sensation, like the whir of a carnival ride. Her room blurred into smears of color, and then it all stopped too soon in a jarring slam.

She rocketed up in bed, her chest heaving. Wide awake, she stared at the place in front of her door where she had just been, where she had just stood—*looking at herself*.

Her bedroom door swung open.

"Izzy," her mother said, leaning in, "I'm glad you're up on time but really, do you have to go around slamming doors so early? Besides, your father's already left for the office, so there's no one here for you to make a statement for. Isobel?" Her tone switched from reproachful to concerned. Isobel tried to focus on her mother's face, but she couldn't keep her gaze from wandering over her shoulder to stare down the length of the hallway.

Her mom came into the room and, silencing the alarm

clock, placed a hand on Isobel's forehead. Against her skin, her mom's hand felt like fire.

"Isobel," her mom said again, "you look pale. You're not getting sick again, are you?"

In the hall, Isobel could see yellow light draining out from the bathroom, and Danny's partially open door.

No trees. No forest. No Reynolds.

26
Freak

"Central control to Cadet Lanley. Do you read me?"

By the time Isobel had reached her locker that morning, she'd come up with a neat and (for the most part) logical explanation for almost everything. The forest had come from Varen's black-tree CD, the run through the woods had been her subconscious mind reliving her run through the park, and Reynolds . . . well, Reynolds probably had something to do with her dad. Stick that all in a box labeled "bad dream," tie it up with a dreaming about dreaming theory, and Isobel thought she had things pretty much figured out. Of course, the only thing she hadn't been able to play connect the dots with had been the strange white light, the mysterious ghostly woman. Maybe, Isobel mused, it had been a metaphor for Lacy.

The locker beside hers slammed shut with a bang, causing Isobel to start.

"Yeah, hello," Gwen said, circling a hand around in front of Isobel's face, as though washing sludge from a window.

"What?" said Isobel. She pushed Gwen's hand down.

"What my butt! Did you seriously not hear a single thing I just told you? I said, 'Are you feeling okay?' You're all catatonic this morning. And you look a little washed-out."

Isobel looked away, trying to hide her face behind the locker door. "Yeah, I'm okay. I just didn't sleep very well."

Overhead, first bell sounded.

"Hey," Gwen said, still watching Isobel as though she were examining something in a petri dish. Then her concern softened and melted away, replaced by a wry smile. "Before I forget." She held out a folded slip of paper with Isobel's name printed across one side in deep purple lettering. "I only read it once, I swear."

Isobel gasped and snatched up the note. "When did you see him?"

"Parking lot. This morning. You know, some of us have cars."

"Don't rub it in." Isobel unfolded the note.

Can we meet after school? My house. No parents.
See you in Swanson's class.
—V

Isobel's heart thrummed, turning several loop-de-loops. *His house?*

She grinned, suppressing visions of the Addams Family mansion.

And no parents. No parents?

She reread that line again, suddenly realizing that the thought of being totally alone with him was more than just a little terrifying.

What word had her mother used? *Experienced?*

She refolded the note quickly.

It didn't help to look up and see a grinning, brow-waggling Gwen. Isobel rolled her eyes and tucked the note away in her locker. Then, thinking better of it, she pushed the note into the right pocket of her jeans instead. She still hadn't changed her combination, and it was definitely not a message she wanted Brad to see.

"Hey," said Gwen, backing away to join the traffic of the crowded hall, "I'll see you at lunch, okay? My delicate butterfly nature calls on me to table hop, so expect a visit. And don't look so worried. It's been my experience that the spooky ones usually know what they're doing." Gwen winked, then with a hand cupped around her mouth like a megaphone, called, "And they'll only bite you if you let them!"

Isobel shut her locker, then hustled in the opposite direction, away from all the heads that had turned.

She tried not to smile.

The rest of the morning dragged by, with every minute feeling more like five. Isobel found herself unable to focus on what was going on in her classes. Unlike the day before, when she'd been able to zone out and let time slip away, she felt fidgety and tense. She kept watching the clock, and even though she'd decided to stick with her sleepwalking theory, her second dream encounter with Reynolds kept creeping in through the back door of her mind, shadow-playing through her memory. The only pleasant distraction she found was in the thought of seeing Varen in Mr. Swanson's class and then later that afternoon, though the idea of being alone with him still made her nervous.

After what seemed like nine eternities, fourth period finally rolled around. Isobel stopped by her locker again before heading to class to pick up her English binder as well as the dreaded Poe book. If there was one thing she was looking forward to most about finishing the project, it was not having to tote around Poe's lifework anymore. Besides being creepy and contributing to nightmares, the thing weighed as much as a cement block.

Isobel found her seat in Mr. Swanson's class. A moment later, chains clinking, Varen walked in. She looked up, straightening in her chair, his presence never failing to put her on full alert. But a second later her rigidness crumbled into laughter, and she had to cover her mouth. Several people turned in their seats, looking curiously between them. The T-shirt beneath his jacket read HOOLIGAN in Gothic white lettering. It was the term Isobel's father had used last night. Varen *had* heard, she realized with a stab of embarrassment.

"Shades off, Mr. Nethers, if you don't mind," Mr. Swanson said.

Varen removed his sunglasses in a salute before going to his desk, his wallet chains rattling noisily against the plastic seat and metal chair legs as he sat.

The bell rang, and Mr. Swanson began the day's lesson, leaving Isobel still trying to wrestle the goofy smile from her face. She also had to fight to keep herself from sneaking glances in Varen's direction.

Toward the end of the class, Mr. Swanson began listing project groups on the board in the order of their presentations the next day. Romelle and Todd were going first with Mark Twain, Josh and Amber were next with Walt Whitman, then came the one group of three with Richard Wright. Isobel started to fidget with her pen as the list grew longer.

"And last but not least," Mr. Swanson said, writing her name on the board, "we'll have Isobel and Varen with our Halloween guest of honor, Mr. Edgar Allan Poe. I'm looking forward to that one especially." He smiled and nodded at the two of them.

Way to load on the pressure there, Swanson. She shot an anxious glance at Varen. He gave her what she took to be a "no big deal" shrug, and she thought that must mean that he had a plan. She tried to smile, hoping that was the case, but despite this reassurance from him, the queasy feeling in her middle refused to subside. After all, it was no secret between the two of them that she at least had completed nothing. Well, nothing except scribbling down a few random quotes that, if she read them aloud tomorrow, might prevent them from getting a total zero. Emphasis on *might*.

Isobel shut her eyes, taking a moment to get a grasp on the fact that she could not afford to fail tomorrow. She'd almost lost her spot on the squad once. If she got a failing grade in English, then it would be out of Coach's hands, and no amount of repentant cheers could save her from exile. Her wings would be clipped, Alyssa would take over, and she'd have to wave good-bye as the bus headed off to Nationals.

The bell rang, dismissing them for lunch. Isobel gathered her things and stood, loading the Poe book on top of her binder, now sorry she'd rooted it out of her locker, since they hadn't been given any time to work in their groups that day. When she looked up, though, she no longer saw Varen at his desk. Instead her eyes found him standing out in the hall, talking to somebody blocked by the wall, though her suspicions about who it was were confirmed the moment she caught sight of black hair and a copper-toned, bracelet-lined wrist.

Her eyes narrowed. She shoved her things under one arm and started for the door. She thought, as she drew nearer, that she might have caught the word "bimbo."

Before she could even think to stop herself, Isobel slipped out into the hall and stood next to Varen, touching him gently on the arm. The connection sent a static sensation coursing through her. He turned fast, his eyes on hers, deep green pools of surprise. Through sheer will, Isobel kept her hand steady on his sleeve. Then, for the killer, she leaned in, quietly interrupting with, "Hey, I'll see you after school, okay?"

She didn't wait for an answer. Her gaze slid from him to Lacy, and Isobel took care to flash her a wink-smile combo. The Queen of Sheba stood stunned, her glossy maroon lips parted in awe. Still smiling, Isobel spun on her toes. Putting just the right amount of sway in her walk, she headed toward the lunchroom.

Isobel left the lunch line with the Poe book and her binder both clamped under one arm and tried to keep her tray steady

with both hands. Thursdays were order-out-pizza days at
Trenton, and Isobel, her empty stomach finally catching up
with her, had grabbed the biggest slice of Tony Tomo's mushroom pizza she could find. From there, it was a balancing act
all the way to her table, and she didn't see who was sitting
there until she was ready to set her tray down.

Stevie. He stood up and reached out to take her books.
Isobel noticed that he was wearing one of his usual Trenton
sweatshirts, blue with a big yellow *T* printed on the chest.

"Hey," he said, "mind if I sit here today?"

Isobel shook her head. She slid her tray onto the table,
watching him carefully. She resisted the urge to glance toward
the crew's usual spot, and she hoped Stevie realized what this
would mean for him. But then again, she thought, after standing up for her yesterday at practice, she wouldn't doubt it if
the crew hadn't already given him the boot.

She sat down. "Hey, by the way, thanks for yesterday,"
she said. Maybe if she kept the conversation light, he wouldn't
feel pressured to talk about any falling-out that had gone on.
She picked up her slice of pizza from her plate, famished.

"Isobel . . ."

"Yeah?" she managed, just before chomping down.

"I came over here today because I need to talk to you. I
think Mark and Brad are up to something," he said in a low
voice.

Isobel slowed her chewing. She let the slice of pizza slip
back onto her plate and, wiping her hands on her napkin,
tried to swallow. "What do you mean?"

"I heard Brad and Mark talking about it after third period," he went on. "But they stopped right as I walked up. I only heard Mark asking Brad if he thought you'd tell. Then Brad said something like, 'He won't be able to prove anything.'"

Isobel froze at the word "he." She dropped her hands into her lap, still clutching her napkin, and skimmed the cafeteria with her eyes. She saw Brad, Mark, Alyssa, and Nikki sitting together. She glanced toward the goths' table next, though she didn't see Varen. Or Lacy, for that matter. She frowned.

"Isobel," said Stevie, lowering his voice to a whisper. She turned back to him as he leaned over the table. "Brad won't stop talking about you. Something's gotten into him over this whole thing between you and that guy. I mean, jeez, if he's not talking about you, then he's saying all this stuff about how he's going to mess up this Varen."

Isobel went still as she sat listening. Why couldn't Brad just let it go? Why couldn't he let *her* go?

"Isobel, I think they might do something major. I mean, Brad is *convinced* that Varen's responsible for what happened to his car. Did you know the police found claw marks on his tires?"

"*Say what?*" Isobel leaned in, shaking her head. Stevie was talking so low, she couldn't be sure she'd heard him right.

"All this stuff keeps happening. And I—I think you ought to tell someone that Brad's been acting weird about you before he does whatever he's got planned. Nikki thinks so too."

"*Nikki?*" Wadding her napkin, she tossed it onto her tray.

Okay, now he had to be kidding. Either that, or this was a setup.

"Isobel, listen to me," he said. "The only reason she wouldn't come over here with me today is because she thinks you hate her."

"I don't hate her." The words leaped out of her mouth before she could rein them in. "I mean," she amended, "it's not like she's my most favorite person in the world right now, but—"

"You know the only reason she ever went out with Brad was because she thought it would get your attention. It's killing her that you guys don't talk anymore. Besides that, she and Brad aren't even dating anymore. That lasted, like, two seconds. He just won't let her tell anyone, because he doesn't want you to find out. All he ever talks about now is how brainwashed you are and how he's going to mangle this guy."

Another tray hit the table. Isobel jumped. "Why are we whispering?" Gwen whispered. Isobel looked up to see Gwen lift a length of tailor's measuring tape from around her neck. "Sit up, you," she said, poking Isobel between the ribs. Isobel squeaked and sat up straight. She stared at Stevie, whose eyes widened as Gwen looped the measuring tape around Isobel's waist and drew it snug.

"Gwen," said Isobel, "what are you doing?"

"Just never you mind," she murmured. She stripped the tape away and pulled a pen out of her ponytail to mark the back of her wrist. "Hold out your arms. And don't be rude. Introduce me already. Who's your friend?"

Isobel clamped her arms in against herself like chicken wings as Gwen fussed around her. "This is Stev—*Ow!*" She jolted as Gwen pinched her right on the fleshy part of her underarm.

"Hello, Stev-ow," Gwen said. She nodded to Stevie while she strung the tape around Isobel's bustline.

"Omigod, Gwen!" Isobel's head whipped back and forth to see who might be watching.

"H-hey," Stevie offered with a small wave.

"Oh, I hate you," Gwen grumbled, making a note on the back of her wrist. She pulled the tape away again, this time drawing out one of Isobel's arms to measure its circumference. Scowling, Isobel gave up with a huff, resigning herself to be handled and measured and cataloged. She knew that whatever Gwen was up to, it must have something to do with the Grim Facade. She also knew that no matter what Gwen was planning, there was still no way she was going to get to go.

"Oh my gosh," Gwen said suddenly. She dropped the tape, her gaze locking on Stevie, who froze, a forkful of spaghetti hovering inches from his open mouth. "What are you wearing underneath that?" she asked, pointing at his sweatshirt.

Stevie shot a quick look at Isobel, a loud and clear cry for help.

"Oh, sorry, sorry," Gwen said, hands flapping. "What I mean is that I need to borrow your sweatshirt, and I wanted to make sure you had something on underneath."

"You want to borrow my shirt?" asked Stevie. He pressed

his hands down on his shoulders, as though in an effort to keep the sweatshirt in place.

"Just until after tomorrow. You got a T-shirt on underneath that, right?"

"Well, yeah, but—"

Gwen hopped up and crossed to Stevie's side. Lifting one corner of the sweatshirt, she started peeling it away from the yellow T-shirt underneath. "Thanks a ton," she said as she yanked it over his head. "This is *exactly* what I need."

Stevie sat stunned, his short, dark brown hair alive with static electricity. Isobel gaped as Gwen wrangled the cuffs off Stevie's wrists, then wadded the sweatshirt into a bundle before plopping down next to him. From there, she scooted over her tray, grabbed her pudding dish, and dug in with her spoon.

Isobel rolled her eyes. Shaking her head, she mouthed *Sorry* to Stevie, whose gaze darted from her to Gwen. As he watched Gwen finish off her pudding in three humongous bites, his expression wavered, as though he couldn't decide if he had a good taste in his mouth or a bad one.

"So what are we talking about that's so serious? Oh, that looks so good," said Gwen, pointing at Isobel's plate with her pudding spoon. "I shoulda got the pizza today. Are you finished with that?"

"No!" Isobel snapped. She slid her tray away from Gwen and picked up the slice of pizza again. She bit down just as a long shadow settled over the table.

"Trying to break your own record?" a quiet voice asked.

The pizza slipped from Isobel's hands, tumbling onto her plate, dripping sauce on her chin. She grabbed her wadded-up napkin and pressed it to her mouth, gulping the bite down whole.

Gwen elbowed Stevie, who slid down one space. Gwen slid down too, allowing Varen to take the seat across from Isobel. She caught a faint whiff of his scent, something she had never paid much attention to before, but now tried to analyze. It was peaty and rich, but somehow still delicate. He dropped a clipped stack of papers between them.

"You finished it," she said. She grabbed the essay and read the title page:

The Man Behind "The Raven":
The Life, Death, and Major Works of Edgar Allan Poe
An Essay
by
Isobel Lanley and Varen Nethers

"Wow, it looks great," she said, eyes meeting his again. She'd almost gotten used to finding them within the forest of his dark hair. "You really don't think he'll suspect?"

"Doubt it," he said. "Just be sure to read it over."

Isobel nodded. She thought that maybe reading it more than once would be her best bet, in case Swanson came back around and wanted to know exactly which parts she'd contributed. She opened the front cover of the Poe book and slipped the paper beneath it.

"So, you guys are doing this project on Poe?" Stevie asked, his tone conversational.

Varen turned to stare at him, as though he'd only just noticed Stevie's presence. Stevie, in turn, seemed to shrink into himself, his gaze dropping to his tray, as though he feared any prolonged eye contact might turn him to stone.

"Varen, this is Stevie," said Isobel. "He's on the squad with me." Translation: He's cool. "Stevie, this is Varen."

Stevie raised one hand. Varen nodded, and the momentary razor edge to his demeanor ebbed away. "Yeah," he said, "we're doing it on Poe."

"Hey, wasn't that the guy who married his cousin or somethin'?" Gwen said before chomping down on a Granny Smith apple, half leaning, half scooting in so that her shoulder pressed against Varen's in heedless disregard of his personal space perimeters and unspoken no-touch policy. The table went quiet except for Gwen's horse chewing, which was happening in close proximity to Varen's left ear. Isobel had to press her lips together to keep from smiling. Glancing at Stevie, she saw that his eyebrows had shot clear to the ceiling.

Varen seemed to take Gwen's close proximity in stride. He turned his head slowly to stare down at her, glancing first to where their shoulders connected, and then directly into her intrusive gaze. Isobel waited for Gwen to disintegrate, dematerialize, or melt. Instead she aimed a finger at Varen's nose, the finger belonging to the hand that held the half-chomped apple. "Don't tell me he didn't," she said. She shook her finger at him. "'Cause I know he did."

Varen's stare remained, punctuated by a few slow, plaintive blinks.

Gwen looked thoughtful and added, "And wasn't he the one who sliced off his ear and mailed it to his girlfriend?"

"Van Gogh," said Varen, in a monotone that suggested he might be in pain.

"Van *Gogh*," Gwen said, leaning away, waving the apple. "Edgar Allan *Poe*. Close enough!"

The bell ending lunch sounded. Stevie broke away immediately. As he went, tray in hand, he shot Isobel a pointed look from over one shoulder. She frowned, remembering his warning about Brad and Mark.

"What was that all about?" Varen asked.

She turned to face him as he stood. She should tell him what Stevie had heard, she thought. She should warn him. But didn't he already know? After all, it wasn't like threats from Brad were anything new. And didn't they have enough to worry about as it was? She shook her head. "Nothing," she murmured, deciding that, at the very least, it could wait until after tomorrow, after the project. "He just wanted to sit here today."

"And so the monarchy crumbles in your absence," he mused.

That made her smile, although a little sadly.

"Gwen," he said in acknowledgment.

"Your Darkness-ship," she returned with a bow.

His eyes remained on Isobel as he began a slow backward walk. He was doing it again, speaking to her with his eyes.

She remained trapped in his stare, trying to hear him, to read the underlying message. Finally his gaze broke from hers and he turned away, walking off through the cafeteria doors.

There was a pause before Gwen spoke.

"Let me guess," she said. "Right now, you're trying to decide if that was hot or annoying." She paused, as though formulating her own opinion. Finally she said, "It was so totally hot."

Before lunch was over, Isobel had made sure to stop by the office and give her mom a call to let her know where she'd be, since she wasn't supposed to use her cell until school let out.

She left out the no parents part.

Her mom had been cool. Mostly. At least she hadn't asked too many questions, especially after Isobel had reminded her that their project was due the very next day and that they were behind. Way behind.

She'd assured her mom that yes, Varen would give her a ride home and that yes, she'd be through the front door by ten at the absolute latest.

"What are you going to tell Dad?" Isobel had asked before hanging up. Her mother's response had been, "Let me worry about that," which made Isobel worry even more. She hated it whenever her parents fought. She certainly didn't like being the cause.

After the final bell, she found Varen waiting for her at the same place as yesterday.

"Hey," she said as she drew closer to where he stood in

the open doorway, the autumn sunlight streaming in, outlining one side of him in a rim of gold. He turned toward her, the light casting a glossy sheen against the black of his hair. He smiled, just barely, and the sight of it, the idea that she had induced this rare response in him, sent her reeling.

"Nice job on the paper," she said.

She'd read the ten-page essay during algebra, when they were supposed to be working on the day's problems. She could finish those that weekend, she'd reasoned, since the worksheet wasn't officially due till Monday.

Varen nodded once, but said nothing. They walked out into the parking lot together, Varen slipping his sunglasses into place. It felt good walking next to him. Almost like they were . . . official.

He stopped.

"What?" Isobel asked. When he didn't answer, she followed the direction of his stare.

The words had been carved into the paint of the Cougar, across the driver's-side door and all the way to the rear fender. The message had been scraped out by a key or another sharp object, showing up primer-gray against the once sleek black finish. YOU'RE DEAD FREAK it read.

"Damn it," Isobel breathed. "That's it." She pivoted to march back toward the school, a new kind of rage surging through her, intensifying with each step. Abruptly she swiveled again, changing her mind. No, she thought, she wouldn't go to the office. Brad and Mark were both varsity players with loaded parents, and that's why everyone always looked the other way. She'd go to the practice field instead, right to the source. If she had to kick Brad's ass in front of all his football buddies and get suspended in the process, then fine. So be it. This time, he had gone too far.

"Where are you going?" she heard Varen call after her, and it was like he'd tugged on a string tied around her heart. Her footsteps slowed, but she didn't turn around and she didn't stop. She could hear him following her, but if she looked now, she knew she'd lose her resolve. She sped up again.

Brad was doing this because of her. That meant that it was her job to fix it.

Isobel crossed through the parking lot to the bus loading area, which ran like a wide driveway lengthwise in front of the school.

Yellow buses rumbled, parked in a double line while students wove their way in and out in pairs and groups. Isobel couldn't see the fenced-in practice field just beyond, but she knew the football team would be gathering there, piling on their gear, grunting and smacking one another around about tomorrow's big game.

"Isobel," Varen called, still following. She marched on, stepping down off the grass median, over the curb, and through the line of buses. The smell of hot exhaust hit her, and she held her breath to keep from inhaling it. She crossed the space between the buses and was almost through the second line when she felt a hand catch her arm.

"What?" She whirled on him, flushing pink because she hadn't meant to snap.

"Don't," he said, still clutching her arm, his grip just tight enough to hold her. She looked away from him, toward the field—and saw Brad. Having spotted them in turn, he walked toward the fence, beaming, his helmet dangling from one hand, his shoulder pads and football pants making him look like some hulking comic-book supervillain. His smile broadened and he waved to them, like he would to a pair of old friends.

"Don't you see it's what he wants?" Varen whispered to her, though she could barely hear him over the rumble of the buses.

Isobel watched as Brad stopped waving and pointed straight at Varen. Her entire body tensed. Dread seized her, and she turned to Varen only to find his face as unreadable as ever.

Coach Logan called out to Brad, giving his whistle a short blast. Finger trained on Varen, Brad began to back away, toward where the rest of the players stood gathered, watching.

"Come on," said Varen, releasing her, "let's go." He turned to walk away.

Isobel stood rooted. She stared after Brad a moment longer, still battling the urge to rush out on the field and bash his head in with his stupid helmet. Instead she turned and followed Varen.

Isobel paused in the middle traveling lane, her gaze scanning the windows of the buses. Faces. So many of them turned down on her. *Glad you're all enjoying the show*, she thought.

She looked away from all the eager eyes ready to drink up her life's drama and jogged to catch up with the dark figure ahead of her.

27
The Green Man

They drove in silence.

Isobel stared out her window at the passing trees, the fall colors seemingly neon beneath the gray overcast, and wondered if the plot to deface Varen's car had been what Stevie had overheard Brad and Mark talking about. She also wondered why they hadn't done more—though from their inscribed message, not to mention Brad's ominous pointing, she certainly got the impression that the worst was yet to come.

"Can it be fixed?" she said, finally breaking the silence.

He shrugged, watching the road. "Buff it out. Repaint."

"Will it look the same?"

"Hopefully." She thought he sounded doubtful.

Isobel looked forward again. She wanted to tell him that she was sorry about his car. She wanted to say that she was worried, that she didn't know what Brad was capable of anymore. But she knew Varen wouldn't respond. He'd say nothing and she'd be left sitting there, feeling stupid for having opened her mouth. As much as he was different from other guys, he still had that stupid male pride thing.

"What did you see in him anyway?" he asked, interrupting her thoughts.

Isobel's mouth popped open as though to supply some ready-made reply in her defense. Instead all she could do was utter, "I don't know."

He nodded in that way of his, like he had some sort of private understanding about the way the gears in her mind must work. Like he'd expected as much of her. It made her feel small again, and simple, like he was packing her back into that little box of prejudgments.

"I could just as easily ask you what you saw in that Lacy girl," she said, and leveled a sharp glare at him.

He smiled like he couldn't help it. She couldn't believe it. He was actually *smiling*, teeth and all. Had she ever seen him smile before? No, she realized, because right now, it was such a jarring thing to witness that for a moment it felt as though she was sharing the car with a stranger.

"What?" she said.

"You really made her mad today, you know."

"Well, does she have a right to be?"

"I don't know," he said, his expression sobering at once. "Does she?"

She hate-hate-hated it when he did that. When he turned her every question around and sent her own curveballs flying straight back at her. Folding her arms, she stared out her window again, refusing to play his game.

The car turned off the main road and into a small strip-mall parking lot. Isobel craned her neck to see where they were and was surprised when he parked in front of a store-front, the neon sign reading DOUBLE TROUBLE II.

"Wait here," he said, unlatching his seat belt and getting out. He shut the door behind him, leaving the car idling. Isobel sat up in her seat and watched him step into the restaurant. She could see him partially through the sun-glared storefront glass as he stepped up to the counter and pulled out his wallet. He must have already called in an order, she thought, as the man behind the counter smiled and handed over a plastic bag. It made her wonder, because she didn't think he owned a cell phone.

Varen came out a moment later carrying the bag, which contained several cartons of Chinese food. He opened the door and handed the bag in. She took it, the heavenly scent of egg rolls, moo goo gai pan, and beef with broccoli filling the car. Hunger awoke within her. A growl like that of a ravenous dog snarled through her stomach, and it came loud enough that she didn't bother to humor herself with the hope that he hadn't heard.

"Hope you like Chinese," he said, and shifted the car into gear.

They pulled off a narrow street, past a sign that read ST. FRANCIS COURT. The purr of the Cougar echoed as they drove down one side of the enormous court, which was composed of two long one-way streets, a single row of cars parked along each. A large grass median separated the two lanes, while beyond a wide sidewalk, towering Victorian homes stood on either side, facing one another like dance partners preparing to waltz.

"You live *here*?"

A heavy wind rushed by, causing the leafy heads of enormous, ancient-looking trees to swish back and forth. The sun poked through the clouds, lighting the very center of the court where a huge fountain stood, much larger than the one outside her own neighborhood. Isobel cranked her window down. Crisp autumn air flooded in, chilling her face. She leaned out to get a better look at the fountain as they passed. Water poured from all sides of an enormous green basin, creating a curtain around an elevated base surrounded by graceful swans and solemn-faced cherubs. The rushing water of the fountain created a gentle hushing, the only other sound besides the hum of the Cougar's engine.

At the very top of the fountain, a statue of a voluptuous nude woman looked down on them as they passed. She held a swath of fabric that clung to the lower half of her body and appeared to billow out behind her in a suspended arc.

The car rounded the fountain and headed down the other side of the court. Isobel turned her head, leaning forward to see through his window. A cast-iron lion grimaced at her from atop a stone pedestal. Two rows of ceremonial-looking gas lamps lined either side of the median, all lit with live flames that flickered within their glass holders. Another gentler brush of wind ran through the court, releasing a flurry of a thousand tiny yellow leaves. They fluttered downward, the light catching on their bellies, lighting them up like flecks of gold.

She knew they had to be in one of the oldest parts of town, somewhere in the historic district. It was a part of the city she'd always known existed, but one she'd never had reason to visit before now.

"It's beautiful here," she whispered, unable to decide which window of the car held the best view.

The houses themselves were incredible, each practically a castle in its own right, their facades done up in decorative brickwork and tiling, their fronts accented with small porches, porticos, and verandahs, the perimeters of which were set by carved stone pillars. Some of the homes had balconies, while others had rounded turrets with pointed rooftops. As they passed one gray-toned fortress of a home built completely of stone, Isobel thought she could make out tiny faces set into the facade, their mouths open in an O shape, their eyebrows angled down in fearsome scowls.

"What are those?" she asked, pointing.

"The faces? They're called 'green men,'" he said, slowing the car to a crawl so she could get a better look. "They're a type of goblin or gargoyle. Protectors. They're supposed to ward away evil."

Isobel focused on one of the stone faces, which struck her as being different from the rest. While this green man shared the stern and foreboding expression of his comrades, his eyes, large and almond-shaped, seemed to convey more of a silent dare than a ward-away glower. And where the other faces had leafy beards, gaping mouths, and distorted features, this face bore a smooth and almost human look.

They picked up speed again, and Isobel looked away.

"I can't believe you live here," she said, shaking her head, unable and perhaps unwilling to mask the envy in her voice. He said nothing as they pulled up to an enormous redbrick home, simple only in comparison to the others that surrounded it. Varen shifted the car into reverse and backed into an open slot on the street.

Isobel stared up at the house. It had three levels, the topmost of which she thought might be an attic. The roof met in a peak there, with a little subroof sticking out from underneath the first, framing a rectangular, three-paneled window crosshatched by white Xs.

A small concrete porch led up to the front door, shaded by a simple verandah, which was itself supported by a row of painted white pillars. The front door, done in an opaque gold stained-glass design, shimmered a satiny dim yellow in the late afternoon sunlight.

Varen switched the car off and got out. Isobel got out too, careful not to tip the bag of food. She watched him over the hood of the car as he stepped back to survey the driver's-side of the Cougar, frowning. Before she could say anything he looked away, walking to the rear of the car to open the trunk. They gathered their things and headed down the sidewalk, Varen picking through his keys.

"So where are your parents?" Isobel asked as he let them in.

"Out," he said. "Who knows? They won't be back until late. Some benefit auction event or something." As they entered, their footsteps echoed against the polished wood floor. Isobel craned her head, awed at the incredible height of the ceiling. Someone must like old-fashioned boats, she thought, her eyes finding first the model of what she thought might be a schooner, perched on a long hallway table, and then a large painting depicting an old-time ship being tossed around on a stormy sea.

Their footsteps went mute as they sank into plush gold and black carpeting, which trailed all the way up a grand staircase tucked against the wall to her left.

To her right was an open living room area with tall, sliding wooden doors. Inside, a gas fireplace played the role of centerpiece. The walls were lined with shelves decorated with colorful glass knickknacks and more boats. Tall floor lamps with fancy Tiffany-like glass shades accented the space. The lamps especially, Isobel thought, gave the room a very "look but don't touch" feel.

"You want a Coke?" he asked.

Without waiting for an answer, he slipped from the foyer and disappeared down a narrow hallway.

"Uh, sure," she said. She made to follow, not comfortable on her own, but stopped when she came to a second, larger room to her right. This one was another no-touchy, done in antique gold and soft pinks with hardwood inlay floors, heavy draperies, and fancy old chairs. In one corner, like a squat gentleman in a tuxedo, stood a polished black piano. As she stepped into the room, it felt almost as though she were crossing through a time portal, leaving one century behind for another. She strode toward the piano and set the bag of food down on a low coffee table with spindly legs. She moved to stand behind the instrument, where she let her fingers trail the keys. Picking one somewhere in the middle, she pressed it softly.

The note—out of tune—boomed around her.

Isobel jerked her arm back. Her elbow plowed into the shelf behind her, knocking over a picture frame. She swung around, picked up the photo—and froze when she found herself staring into the intense gaze of a green-eyed, blond-haired boy, ten years old at the most. The photograph, taken from the shoulders up, showed the boy dressed in a gray vest, white dress shirt, and dark blue tie. His gaze seemed to be fixed in an almost-scowl at the photographer, like he was indignant at the idea of having his photograph taken. Faint half circles underlined the boy's eyes, giving him the look of being prematurely world-weary. Isobel brought the picture closer, searching that small face for traces of the boy she knew.

She started when a set of slender, ringed fingers curled around the frame. Isobel let go and spun, suddenly trapped within those same eyes. Her heart did a triple-step as he gently took the picture from her, reaching across her to place it back on the bookshelf with the others.

"You're really a blond," she said, her tone just short of accusatory.

"And if you tell anyone, I will come to you in the night and smote your everlasting soul."

Promise? Isobel turned back to the piano quickly, shocked that she'd almost uttered this aloud. She distracted herself from the thought by allowing her fingers to ghost over the keys again. "So who plays?" she asked.

His eyes fell to her hand, then to the keys. "Nobody. Like everything else, it's just for show. It's not even tuned."

Isobel pulled her fingers away. No, she thought, there was something more here. Something in the way his eyes had traveled over the piano's polished surface before turning inward in thought.

"Nobody?" she pressed.

"My mom did," he admitted, catching her off guard.

"You mean, she doesn't anymore?"

"I don't know," he said. "She might." His eyes returned from their faraway moment, and he handed her a pair of silver forks he must have retrieved from the kitchen. "She left when I was eight," he said.

She blinked. Was he joking? Sometimes it was so hard to tell. "Then who did I—?"

"You talked to my stepmom on the phone." He was serious. Definitely no joke.

"Oh," she said, taken aback. She wasn't sure what to say. "I—uh, sorry," she finally blurted.

"Don't be," he said. "It was a long time ago." With that, he picked up the plastic bag of Chinese food and brushed past her to the hallway. "Grab the Cokes, would you?"

When he was out of the room, Isobel let herself breathe while silence descended anew.

She grabbed the Cokes from where he'd set them on the coffee table and left the room, looking back at the vacant piano seat. She found him waiting for her on the stairs, one hand poised on the banister. The Cokes cradled in one arm, the forks secure in her hand, Isobel mounted the stairs.

She climbed after him, the fingers of her free hand sliding along the mahogany banister. Her eyes focused on the upside-down bird on the back of his jacket, and she tried to resist the urge to say something else, to find words that would make up for the moment in the piano room. But there were none, and so Isobel kept her mouth closed.

It was odd, she thought, that this had been the first private thing he'd ever revealed to her. Watching the black wisps of his hair brush the jacket's upturned collar, Isobel couldn't help but wonder what had happened—what had caused his mother to leave? In one moment she thought it explained a lot about him, but then, in the next, she thought just the opposite.

"This place has a weird layout, I know," he said, waiting for her on the landing above. "It's gone through a lot of renovations. After the Victorian era, it got turned into a nursing home. Then, in the seventies, it was converted into apartments."

"It's huge," she breathed.

After another short, silent spurt of stairs, they reached the second-floor landing, which gave way to a cloister of rooms. When she saw him mount the stairs again, though, she knew this would not be their stop. They traipsed higher yet. Here the carpet ended, and they tromped on naked wood, the sound echoing through the house. They reached yet another tiny landing, a window stamped into the wall to her left. Isobel quirked an eyebrow at the view through this tiny portal, one that showed her little more than the details of the neighbor's brickwork.

"How did you guys score a place like this?" she asked.

They rounded one final corner. With an internal groan, she saw that here, the next staircase, set slightly apart, seemed to slant more steeply and grow even more narrow, the individual steps themselves somehow thicker and taller. This staircase reached up toward a single narrow door. The burn in her thighs intensified as they climbed again. Even Quasimodo in his trek to the bell tower couldn't have had this many steps to climb.

"My dad inherited it," he said, then added, as an afterthought, "These were the original servants' stairs."

"Oh," she puffed, "you don't say." No longer trailing her hand along the banister, Isobel gripped it with her free hand. "You do this every day?"

"Every day I come here," he said, causing Isobel to pause. She looked up, squinting at his back again as he reached the door and twisted the knob. The door creaked as it opened, and without a backward glance, Varen slipped inside.

"As opposed to where?" she called after him.

Reaching the top of the stairs, Isobel stepped over the threshold into his room, an open space tinged with the scent of stale air and incense. Shadows gathered in pockets despite the room's two windows, while above her, the ceiling pitched and slanted upward like the roof of a tent. A time-eaten mauve color wrapped the walls.

"As opposed to somewhere else," he answered. He reached out to the wall beside her, flicking a switch. Light sprang forth from a small chandelier suspended over a narrow metal-framed bed, which had been shoved lengthwise against one wall.

"What, you mean you don't come home?" she asked. She wanted to be sure she had it straight, that he'd meant the house itself and not just this summit peak of a bedroom.

"I said I don't come here."

Isobel shook her head, uncomprehending. "Then where?"

"Wherever," he replied, adopting that biting tone that warned against any further inquiry.

Isobel pinched her lips together and swallowed her next question. She returned her gaze to his bed and the chandelier, reminding herself that he only ever said as much as he wanted, and never any more. He might have opened the door for her, but only a crack.

She distracted herself by studying his chandelier, thinking that he must have rigged it himself, because instead of normal lightbulbs, there were plastic candles topped with red-tinted flame-shaped bulbs. Also, the medieval-looking chain that suspended the fixture from a hook in the ceiling had been intertwined with black electric cords, which trailed down the wall before snaking out of sight behind the headboard.

There was a tiny gas fireplace in this room too, like the one in the living room downstairs, only this one was simpler, studded with plain white ceramic tiles. Isobel doubted if the fireplace was operational, though, because in the space where any fire might have gone, there were instead several small glass vials, each a different color and shape. They stood gathered together like bowling pins at the end of a lane or like potion bottles in a sorcerer's forgotten cabinet. Instead of magical elixirs, though, each little vial held an assortment of dried flowers.

Isobel looked away from the fireplace, casting her gaze around at the walls, which were barren except for one black-and-white poster of Vincent Price. The floor beneath her was dull wood and creaky; a simple white throw rug had been laid out beside the bed. A TV-VCR-DVD unit sat on the floor in one corner, connected to what looked to her like two older-looking gaming consoles. The shelves behind the TV, she could see, were stocked with a handful of video games, some of which she thought she recognized from Danny's endless collection. There were also, she noticed, several DVDs tucked between the games, titles like *Edward Scissorhands*, *Alfred Hitchcock Presents*, *The Tomb of Ligeia*, *The Nightmare Before Christmas*, and *Donnie Darko*. There were other shelves in the room too, all of which seemed to be inhabited by—big surprise—books.

As Isobel drew farther into the room, she passed a folding-door closet and let her fingers brush against the painted white slats. She watched as Varen deposited the food on a simple writing desk tucked beneath a window, one with three vertical panels crosshatched by white *X*s. Isobel immediately recognized the window as the one she'd seen from outside. The other window was smaller, lower to the floor, and on the side wall near the bed, allowing for yet another stellar view of the neighbor's roof.

She stopped when she became aware of a pair of cool blue eyes following her. She turned her head to stare at the cat curled on top of his bed, a plump Siamese nestled on the gray comforter where she could have sworn it hadn't been a moment before. The creature blinked at her slowly, squeezing its eyes shut, then opening them to piercing slivers.

"That's Slipper," she heard him say.

"Oh my gosh, he's gorgeous," Isobel murmured.

"She," Varen corrected.

Isobel drew closer to the bed, then perched on the edge, setting the Cokes and forks aside. She offered a hand to be sniffed, per proper cat etiquette, which Slipper snubbed with a turn of her head.

"Don't let the elegance act fool you," Varen said, drawing out his notepad. "She farts."

28
Ulalume

They'd spread out on the floor to work, sitting on the white throw rug beside the bed. The small red and white Chinese food containers had been opened and passed back and forth between them indiscriminately—neither of them, Isobel had noted, keeping track of which fork was whose.

At first Slipper had watched them from the bed, blinking cool, disinterested eyes. She had waited, it seemed, until they'd become fully engrossed in their work before slinking off the bed and, after making a big show of stretching and yawning, unfolding herself across their papers. From there, she purred loudly and flopped her tail against the floor.

They had decided to divide the presentation into three major categories: Poe's most famous works, his influence on modern literature, and, last but not least, the strange circumstances surrounding his death. Tackling each category one at a time, they thumbed through their combined stack of library books, picking out key facts. Isobel insisted on being the one to copy them down onto numbered index cards, wanting something from the project to be in her own handwriting, just in case Swanson suspected she'd done less than her part. Varen hadn't protested, and even seemed to enjoy this method of locating long stretches of information and condensing them out loud, speaking slowly so that she could finish writing each word. Working like this, it took them a little more than an hour to get to the last category, and Varen, who had flipped to the back of one colossal door stopper of a biography, grew suddenly quiet as he read.

Isobel glanced up from her own perusing and wiggled her pen, waiting for him to prompt her to jot down the next fact. When he didn't, she pursed her lips and tapped her pen against her chin in thought. She glanced to the spread of papers, index cards, and poster board around her, wondering if she should interrupt him with her newest concern. Deciding it couldn't hurt, she lowered her pen and spoke up. "Um," she began, "do you think our presentation is going to be too, I don't know . . . I mean, it's kind of boring, don't you think?"

Without looking up from his book he said, "Seeing as how down to the wire we are, what other choice do we have?"

She nodded, knowing that the same thought must have already occurred to him. She also knew that he was right. Even though this was how things were going to have to go, she still couldn't help but wonder what their project might have been like if they'd actually been able to concentrate from the very beginning. Then at the same time, Isobel reminded herself that she wasn't exactly a Poe enthusiast, and it *would* be a huge relief to have the whole thing over and done with. Well, the project at least. If nothing else, she hoped that whatever they managed to pull together tonight would be enough to keep her on the squad so that she could go back to being a cheerleader for a change.

Isobel sighed. Slipping her note cards between the pages and shutting her book, she diverted her attention to a pile of printouts of pictures from the Internet and a neighboring stack of poster board. There were several pictures left to glue onto poster board, pictures that Varen would hold up at certain moments during their presentation, and then place along the chalkboard tray. Nothing fancy. Very run-of-the-mill high-school project-esque.

She slid one of the printouts toward her, one of Poe himself. After rubbing the back of it down with a glue stick, she smoothed the gloomy-looking portrait onto its poster board and set it aside to dry. Yet she couldn't seem to help but stare at it. And she knew it was because of those eyes, those deep, hooded black holes. They seemed to tunnel through her with their sorrow, something about their expression making it seem as though Poe were silently beseeching the onlooker for something. "Forlorn" was the word that kept forming in her head, repeating itself over and over.

Isobel looked away, fighting back a shudder. She watched Varen as he, with head down, remained engrossed in whatever obscure Poe info he'd stumbled across. Shamelessly, she took the opportunity to study his long frame and how he sat with his back against his bed, his legs stretched out across the floor, boots crossed at the ankles, book open across his lap. With his head down like that, his hair curtaining his face, the only part of his features that remained visible was his mouth.

Her focus narrowed on the curve of the silver ring that embraced one corner of his bottom lip, and she couldn't help but wonder how the metal would feel pressed against her own lips.

A boy shouldn't have lips like that, she thought, and nearly started when he glanced up, catching her stare. She could feel her cheeks flare and knew they must be turning pink. She dropped her gaze immediately and reached out to wrestle yet another black-and-white printout from beneath Slipper, who batted at it greedily. Isobel turned over a portrait of Poe's mother, a young doll-like figure wearing a ribbon-laced bonnet. She rubbed her glue stick over the back.

That's when she started to wonder about what would happen *after* the project. She knew that now they'd at least be friends, she and Varen. After everything that had happened, how could they not? But would he ever ask her out again? What if he thought she really didn't want to go to the Grim Facade when she'd told him she couldn't? What if he thought she was just using her dad as an excuse?

Her movements slowed as a new concern swam into focus. What had she thought before now? That after the project was over, she'd be lucky enough for him to ask her out again? And then another realization dawned on her. What if this was the first and last time they were ever completely alone together? Sure, they would see each other at school, but if she didn't speak up, if she didn't say something now, would that be the end? She could almost see the run of their relationship from that point, dwindling and dissolving into the occasional

and ever-awkward "Hey, how's it going?" before disintegrat-
ing to feeble waves between classes. Without the project, she
couldn't be sure of when they'd ever meet outside of Mr.
Swanson's class or the cafeteria again.

She knew she would have to say something tonight.

Isobel ran a few phrases through her head, trying them all
out, then letting them mellow in her mind. Each one clanged
lamely against her internal ear and sounded vaguely insulting.
What was wrong with her? Why couldn't she just come out
and say she liked him?

Maybe it was because she more than liked him.

Isobel let that thought swirl through her. She set her glue
stick down and let her feelings frighten her because the only
other option was to push them away. Only she was tired of
pushing them away.

Determined, she looked up at him. A jolt of panic ran
through her when she found him already staring at her. Had
he been watching her this whole time?

"Uh, can we take a break?" she asked.

He closed the book and set it aside.

Wow, she thought, that had been easier than she'd expected.
Now what?

In a moment of daring, Isobel lifted herself from where
she sat across from him, scooting around Slipper, whose tail
tapped and twitched in agitation. She repositioned herself to
lean her back against the bed, sitting now less than a foot
away from him, *The Complete Works of Edgar Allan Poe* the
only thing between them.

She stretched her legs out in front of her just like him, crossing them at the ankles, then picked up the book, flipping it open across her lap.

"Why do you like Poe so much?" she found herself asking.

He shrugged. "Why do you like screaming and jumping around so much?"

She sighed, then tried again, "Well, I mean, do you at least have a favorite or something?"

He sat quietly for a moment, then, reaching across her, fingers finding the corner of the book in her lap, he began flipping through the pages, painstakingly, one by one.

Finally he stopped. "This one," he said.

Isobel looked down into the book, at the single column of centered text. She read them to herself in silence:

> "From childhood's hour I have not been
> As others were—I have not seen
> As others saw—I could not bring
> My passions from a common spring.
> From the same source I have not taken
> My sorrow; I could not awaken
> My heart to joy at the same tone;
> And all I lov'd, *I* loved alone.
> *Then*—in my childhood—in the dawn
> Of a most stormy life—was drawn
> From ev'ry depth of good and ill
> The mystery which binds me still:
> From the torrent, or the fountain,

From the red cliff of the mountain,
From the sun that 'round me roll'd
In its autumn tint of gold—
From the lightning in the sky
As it pass'd me flying by—
From the thunder and the storm,
And the cloud that took the form
(When the rest of Heaven was blue)
Of a demon in my view."

"It's so sad," she said, looking up.

"Most of them are."

She frowned, turning pages. "But not all of them, right?"
To this he offered no answer.

From somewhere downstairs, she became aware of the distant ticking of a clock.

"Read me something?" She heard herself say, as though someone else was speaking through her.

He hesitated. Then, after a moment, she felt him slide nearer, causing every one of her senses to become amplified. His shoulder brushed against hers, igniting a tremble that ran through the length of her, and she tried to hide her shaking hands by gripping the sides of the book. He began turning pages once more. She could feel the movement of each sheet with her entire frame, first as it lifted, then as it settled on the other side.

At last he stopped, and she stared down at the printed column of words, unable to comprehend a single one. His hand, warm and steady, wound its way around hers, wrapping it like a spider would its prey. She surrendered it to him, unable to watch even as his thumb traced the place, just above her knuckles, where he had once written his number in deep violet. Isobel ceased to breathe. Her heart pounded in her chest, her thoughts shattering into senseless fragments. All the while, her eyes remained trained and unblinking on the open page. Lines without meaning stared up at her, little more than black sticks in an otherwise white world.

"Ulalume," he began, and the word itself, which he'd pronounced "You-la-loom," flowed from him like a string of soft notes.

> "The skies they were ashen and sober;
> The leaves they were crisped and sere—
> The leaves they were withering and sere;"

He enfolded her hand between both of his, and she felt the silver bands of his rings press into her skin. She turned her head slowly in his direction, though she dared not meet those eyes.

She breathed in, rewarded with that mixed scent that she'd found impossible to pinpoint before. Now that he was so close, she thought she could almost decipher it. Crushed leaves. Incense that had had time to soak into cloth. Worn leather. There was a spice essence there too, sharp and crisp, like dried orange peels.

"It was night in the lonesome October
Of my most immemorial year:"

His voice flowed low and smooth, and she concentrated
on its tone more than on the words themselves as it buzzed
through her like music. With her hand pressed between both
of his, her whole body seemed to hum, and she began to feel
fuzzy from the inside out, like a radio stuck between channels.
Her eyes fluttered shut.

"It was hard by the dim lake of Auber,
In the misty mid region of Weir—"

Isobel's brow creased, her momentary paradise interrupted. Her hand, as though by reflex, tightened around his.
Something in that phrase stirred her from deep within, breaking up the settled debris of her subconscious. Had she heard
him right? She opened her eyes, listening hard for the first
time.

"It was down by the dank tarn of Auber,
In the ghoul-haunted woodland of We—"

A loud crack, like a gunshot, resounded through the
house. Isobel started violently, dropping Varen's hand and
jumping so that the book toppled out of her lap. It thudded
against the floor and snapped shut, just missing Slipper as she
launched herself beneath the bed.

Isobel looked up to find Varen already on his feet, though she hadn't felt him rise.

Footsteps on the stairs.

"No," he muttered under his breath.

Her heart quickened. "What?"

She rose to her knees and then stood, pulling the book after her—heavy as an anchor. She gripped it to her chest. "What? Who's that?"

"They're back early," he said. "Get in the closet."

Fear shot through her. "Varen—?"

Heavy footsteps on wood. Lead feet pounding steps.

He grabbed her by the arm just above the elbow and pulled her across the room. Isobel went, not knowing what else to do, startled by his suddenly iron grip. The pounding grew nearer. She heard a woman's voice now. "Joe," she was saying over and over, like someone trying to calm an angry dog.

Isobel was plunged into darkness, wrapped into a tiny space by the embrace of countless black sleeves. The closet door slid shut, casting a jailbird pattern of light across her trembling form.

She could see Varen's boots through the slats as he backed away.

The door to his bedroom flew open with another bang, causing Isobel to jump and squeak. She pressed a hand over her mouth.

"Did you hear me calling you?" the man yelled. *"I said, did you hear me?"*

Isobel's shaking hand left her mouth, springing up to

shield one ear, her other arm still tightly clutching the Poe book. She only lowered it again when she became aware of a guttural, feline growl coming from beneath Varen's bed. Slipper's wide eyes glowed silver from within the dark space.

She could see another pair of legs now, a man's, clad in black dress pants, his shoes polished to a glossy shine.

"Why do you just stand there and never say anything?" the man said, quietly now, his tone oozing danger. "What's this? What's that mess on the floor? You know you're not supposed to have food up here. Did you have someone over while I was gone?"

"No."

"Don't lie."

"Joe," the woman's voice pleaded from the stairway. "Let's talk about this tomorrow."

"I want this cleaned up now." A pause. Isobel saw Varen hesitate. *"Now!"* He snapped his fingers. "Stop standing there and get down on the floor and clean it up!" He snapped his fingers again, then again, and again. He pointed toward the cartons of food.

Varen stooped, gathering the boxes. His face came into view, though it was unreadable beneath his hair. He did not look in her direction.

"What did you do to your car?"

Silence.

"I said, what did you do to your car? Answer me."

"I didn't do—"

"You think it's cute? You think it's funny?"

"Dad, I didn't—"

"Shut up. I don't want to hear it. I don't want to hear a goddamn word of it. In fact, that's what you're going to do next. After you finish cleaning up this mess, you're going to come downstairs and clean that up too. I'm tired of this act of yours. I'm tired of this black parade you throw yourself—"

"It won't come off, Dad."

"I didn't tell you to talk yet. And you better damn well hope it comes off, because I'm not paying for it to be fixed, and you're not driving that piece of crap around like that. I told you he couldn't keep a car, Darcy. I told you he—"

Varen stood, leaving the cartons. "It's my car. I bought it myself. Bruce cosigned, not you. Or have you been too drunk to remember?"

"*Varen.*" The woman's voice. "Just stop it, both of you."

"That's it. You know what? You're not keeping that pile of junk. You can just ride the damn bus to school, since you can't seem to get a clue. It's not sitting in front of my house like that. And since it's your car and you paid for it, you can pay to have it towed, too. Better yet, call up Bruce and have *him* tow it off! I'll call him up myself—and that's another thing, I don't want you back at that bookshop anymore, do you hear me? I'm tired of that invalid undermining me. I can find plenty of work for you to do here. No more. Is that clear?"

"Whatever."

The man's arm shot out, viper fast, snatching Varen's sleeve in a tight grip.

Isobel pressed one hand flat against the inside of the closet door, ready to push through, but she willed herself to remain, her fingers curling to grip the slats, knowing that it would only get worse if his dad found out she was there.

"When are you going to *wake up*?" the man shouted, shaking Varen, his voice booming again, something about his son's apathy infuriating him more than his defiance. He let go, flinging Varen back. He stumbled but caught himself against the wall, his head down.

"Look't you, you screwup," he muttered, his words streaming together, bleeding into one another. The hard heels of his dress shoes snapped on the floorboards as he walked past the closet door. Isobel swiveled her head as he passed. She heard a drawer from Varen's desk scrape open and saw it hit the floor with a crack, papers spilling. Another drawer joined the first, followed by the overturned contents of a third. Bound portfolios and poems scattered, pens fleeing across the floor. Varen's dad kicked one polished shoe through the rubble. "Look't this waste of time. God, you're just like your mother. Gonna be a screwup scooping ice cream for the rest of your goddamned life if you don't clean up your act."

His dad sighed, and his voice sounded tired now. Spent. He held his open hands over the mess of writing and blank papers waiting to be filled, as though there was no answer for it.

"Joe, that's enough," the woman whispered. "He said he'd clean it up. Come downstairs."

Isobel crouched low, peering up through the slats.

She saw the woman enter the room, though her face remained obscured. She saw her reach out an arm, long, slender, and tanned, her delicate wrist encircled by a glittering bracelet. She touched the man's shoulder.

"Better clean it up," he stammered, "'cause I'll be back up here t' check."

The woman, Varen's stepmother, pulled his father from the room. Isobel shut her eyes. Slowly she rose, clutching the Poe book to her chest. She heard the sound of stumbling. A curse. The door slammed.

In an instant, whispers filled the room—ten people hissing and talking at once.

Her eyes flew open. On the floor just outside, she saw the light dim and then grow bright again, as though the chandelier over Varen's bed swayed on its chain. The echo of footsteps on the stairs grew distant and distorted, as though coming from somewhere far away and deep underwater. Shapeless shadows flitted over the floor and across the closet door, throwing Isobel into moments of complete darkness.

Somewhere in the room, Slipper yowled.

29
Driven

Isobel rattled the closet door. It refused to open. The whispers grew louder; they seemed to seep from the walls. She could no longer see Varen—the space where he'd stood was now empty. Isobel pushed against the door with both hands, the Poe book clamped beneath one arm. She banged against the slats.

The closet door flew open with a crack. She jumped back. The whispers ceased.

He stood there wearing his beat-up satchel, staring through her, his face as cold and expressionless as glass. Behind him, the light hung motionless on its chain, no longer flickering, though she could still hear Slipper growling.

"I'm taking you home," he said.

He spun without another word, and grabbing her backpack, he went to the window against the far wall. Isobel stepped cautiously from the closet, her eyes scanning the floor, the walls, the closet door. Everything was silent.

She watched him grip the window and pull it up. He slipped out into the encroaching darkness, vanishing from sight.

Isobel hurried to the window. She found him standing

just outside, seeming to float on nothing. She looked down, and as her eyes adjusted, she saw the black platform that supported him. An unfolding iron stairway clung to the brick siding, a rust-caked fire escape.

She hesitated. They were so high up. Varen gripped her free hand, giving her no choice. Powerless to resist him, she climbed out into the cold air, her trembling transforming to shivers as a frigid wind rushed up the side of the house, blasting them.

His already fierce grip on her tightened, and when her feet found the metal landing, he pulled her into motion. Beneath them, the rickety stairs groaned and sighed, swaying as they rounded the first corner. Down, around, down, and down. From a rooftop above, an ebony bird sounded a warning, its hoarse call answered by an echoing croak and a flurry of wings.

Varen jumped down first from the ladder that hung at the end of the escape. Quivering uncontrollably, Isobel turned to lower herself one rung at a time, descending one-handed, with the Poe book still tucked under her arm. She felt Varen's hands fasten around her waist. He lifted her and set her on her feet. He caught her hand once more, and she was moving again before she could comprehend how or where.

They reached the curb, and when he let go, handing off her backpack, she knew to get into the Cougar. He rounded the car and flung open the driver's side. Throwing his own satchel into the backseat, he got in, then pulled the door shut behind him.

Isobel fell into the passenger seat, clutching her backpack and the Poe book in her lap.

Should she say something? Would that just make everything worse?

He started the car, revving the engine. Isobel shut her door quickly, afraid he would bolt at any second. He revved the engine again. He must want them to know he was leaving, she realized. Isobel looked back toward the house and saw the porch light come on. His stepmom hurried outside onto the verandah. She was blond, tall, and candle-straight, and she wore a long silver evening dress that glistened like water in the moonlight. She left the stained-glass door open and rushed down the sidewalk toward them, heels clacking, calling to Varen.

The stereo kicked on. Guitars and crashing drums filled the car, somebody screaming more than singing.

The woman stopped when she saw Isobel. For one full second, their eyes locked.

Tires squealed. They pulled out. Isobel's back slammed against her seat as they ripped down the street. He took the first right without so much as braking, the rear of the car fishtailing. Isobel groped for her seat belt and slung it over her lap, fumbling to snap it into place. She saw his hand twist the stereo's volume dial all the way, his face showing little more than the faintest scowl as the sound of rage pumped through the cab.

He took another turn. Isobel yelped.

They barreled down a city street, swerving out of the left

lane into the right as the car ahead of them braked for the light. Yellow flick red. They shot beneath.

"Varen," she said, making her voice as stern and loud over the music as she could. She gripped her seat. "Slow. Down."

The engine growled. He sped up.

"Varen, stop! You're scaring me!"

He ignored her, tires shrieking as he twisted around another sharp corner. Isobel groped for something else to grab hold of. There was nothing.

Buildings and lights streamed by in a blur. Street signs raced past. Isobel's head whipped from side to side, though she couldn't place their fleeting surroundings. Around them, the world bled into one long streak.

Someone screamed at them from the sidewalk. The car rumbled like a beast.

Between the music and the speed, Isobel felt as though her mind might either melt or shatter.

The crashing song fizzed and zipped as they rocketed through an underpass. The lights on the dashboard dimmed and guttered. Static washed over the music while the needle of the speedometer teased higher, then loosened to swing back and forth. A low, dry voice cut through the static of the radio, buried amid a chorus of whispers. Unintelligible, the murmuring grew into a collective hiss.

"*Go away,*" Varen growled between clenched teeth.

At his command, the static rippled, then cleared. The music blared full force once more, and the dashboard lights resumed their dim red glow.

Ice water replaced Isobel's rushing blood. Her fear spiked, crawling its way up from her very depths, paralyzing her. Her eyes slid from the dashboard radio to Varen. Who was he talking to?

"Varen—?"

He turned again, cutting her off. Her shoulder slammed into the passenger-side door, and Isobel pressed a hand to the glass to brace herself. She squeezed her eyes shut and yelled, "You're going to get us killed!"

He wasn't listening.

She felt the buzzing sensation of speed course through her seat and hum through her body. She hated this feeling, of being so totally out of control. This was exactly what she'd always hated about driving with—

Isobel opened her eyes. She slammed her hand on the Discman beside her, killing the meltdown music. "Would you stop?" she screamed. "You're driving like Brad!"

She saw his hands clench on the wheel and had only an instant to regret these words before his foot slammed on the brakes. Tires screeched. The world of buildings, streets, cars, lights, and people gained on them, stuttering into focus as the car squealed and skittered to a stop.

Isobel pitched forward in her seat, then slammed back again, the impact knocking the breath out of her. Around them, horns blared. Cars swerved and went swooshing past, drivers yelling from their windows.

Silence.

She stared at him, her breath coming in heaves. White

headlights pierced the rear window, casting as much shadow as stark light into the car. Black shapes, sharp and quick, slipped over him. They swept their way down his form, retreating to their corners and crevices as a car passed around them, the light vanishing with it. He stared forward, both hands still fixed on the wheel. They sat in silence again, the engine still rumbling, a tension pulsing between them so thick that Isobel thought she might never catch her breath.

He moved finally, leaning forward in his seat so that his forehead almost touched the top of the steering wheel. "Sorry," he said, the word scarcely audible.

Isobel dropped her gaze to her lap. She stared at her still-quivering knees and found herself once more at a loss for words.

He sat back and shifted the car into gear, and they were moving again. He drove with total control, and suddenly Isobel recognized the overpass they turned onto. He was taking her home.

"Varen—"

"Don't," he said.

Isobel snapped her teeth together and set her jaw. Deep down, she knew that it would be better not to say anything. Not when she knew he had never meant for her to see. To know.

30
Projected

Isobel let her bag drop in the foyer as soon as she stepped through the door. She stood dazed, remembering the way the Cougar had shot off the second she'd shut the car door. Just like that, he'd left her standing there in front of her house without so much as a "See you tomorrow." She couldn't even think where he could be headed, but she was certain that he wouldn't go home.

"Wherever," he'd said in the attic.

Isobel frowned, hoping that his "wherever" didn't mean Lacy's house.

She stared at her sneakers and tried, for a moment, to imagine what it would be like not to be able to go home. Then she had to stop, because to her it was unfathomable. And yet she had seen enough of the Nethers household to know she had not witnessed the worst.

Isobel hugged the Poe book to herself. She rested her cheek against the cool, gold-lined pages and black binding, grateful, for once, to have it—her one solid link back to him. Her one tether to his impenetrable world if, after tonight, it proved true that she held no others. If they failed the project— *when* they failed the project—the book would give her one last excuse to see him. To tell him everything, she thought, letting her eyes slide closed. Everything she should have said already. She'd spit it all out, regardless of who was around to hear it. She'd tell him how she couldn't stop thinking about him, how she just wanted to be near him. She'd do the unspeakable. She'd let her hands slide inside his jacket and her arms slip around him.

Brave thoughts, she told herself, opening her eyes. All brave thoughts.

She leaned down to hook her hand once more through one shoulder strap of her backpack. She trudged down the hallway, dragging her book bag behind her like a ball and chain.

The living room was dark and empty, and so were the hallway and the kitchen. Everyone must be upstairs, she thought. She lifted her book bag and slung it onto the nearest kitchen chair, deposited the Poe book on the table, went to the cabinet to get a clean glass, then stalked to the sink to fill it.

Tilting her head back, Isobel drained the glass, then wiped her mouth with her sleeve. She set the glass on the counter and sat down at the table, shoulders slumping.

The dishwasher swished while the kitchen clock ticked.

Isobel stared off in the general direction of the refrigerator.

She felt the remnants of adrenaline subsiding. He'd scared her tonight. After becoming so used to his composed demeanor, his unruffled coolness, to see him like that, so beyond reason, had terrified her. And in that moment, she knew that he'd *wanted* to terrify her. Or at least he hadn't cared. And then, when he'd spoken aloud to the radio, all the warning bells she possessed had blared through her in one unanimous clangor, recalling to her mind all the rumors, all the original forewarnings that had spooked her from day one.

Isobel brought her hands up to her face, rubbing, not caring if she smudged her mascara. That wasn't him. He'd been beyond himself. She might have been too had things been reversed. Anyone would have.

She sighed, feeling suddenly so tired. How had it all come down to this? So much had gotten in the way, and now, after everything, they were *both* going to fail the project.

"You're home early."

Isobel stopped rubbing her face. She spread her fingers and opened her eyes to see her father standing in the doorway, dressed in torn jeans and the red flannel shirt she sometimes liked to steal. His arms were folded, a stance that made Isobel want to reply with something sarcastic. She settled instead on ignoring him.

Opening the zipper on her backpack, she lifted her notebook out, realizing she at least still had her list of quotes, even if their poster-board pictures and index cards had been left on Varen's bedroom floor. Would he remember to bring them? Did he even care anymore?

For a split second, Isobel imagined she could try and fake the presentation for both of them. Maybe she could pull it off. Maybe. If she stayed up all night. But quotes alone wouldn't be nearly enough to get by on.

"Isobel."

The sound of her father's voice irritated her. Couldn't he take the hint? She wasn't ready to talk to him yet. Most of all, she wasn't in the mood for an "I'm just looking out for you" lecture.

"Did you get your project finished?" he asked.

Pretending she hadn't heard the question, she opened the Poe book. She stared down at the tiny words printed in close rows. If she stayed up, how far would she get? Whatever the case, she couldn't hope to get anywhere with her dad standing over her, breathing down her neck like this.

"I said, did you get your project finished?"

"No," she said, "we didn't. How could we when everybody's *dad* keeps interrupting?"

She pushed the notebook away, disgusted, and folded her arms on the table. She dropped her face into the cool, dark space they made. She stayed there, listening to the sound of her own breathing, something about it oddly calming. She heard her father's footsteps and the scooting of a kitchen chair over the tile. As he sat down, she caught a whiff of shower gel and aftershave.

"Something happen that you want to talk about?"

"No," she mumbled into her arms. Definitely not. Besides the fact that she wouldn't know where to start, she couldn't think of anything to tell him that wouldn't just give him another reason to ground her until college. If she even decided to go to college—and there was another argument entirely.

"Well, did you get anything done?"

His tone was curious rather than pushy, and it made her wonder why he was being so nice.

She groaned, rocking her forehead back and forth against her arms, halfway to say no and halfway to clear her thoughts. She was too tired to keep being angry at him. It took too much effort. "It's no use," she muttered. "We're done for."

"That's a bit melodramatic, don't you think? Are you giving up?"

Isobel shrugged. Maybe, since their paper was done, they'd at least get half credit? That way she'd still pass her junior year, even if it meant she wouldn't be a cheerleader when she did. With another pang in her stomach, Isobel thought about Nationals, about the squad going to Dallas without her, Alyssa taking her spot as middle flyer. She released another sigh, this one mixed with a growl, her hands clenching into fists. How was this fair? How was it right when they'd honestly tried?

"Is there something I can do?" he asked.

"Not unless you can work miracles."

She heard the Poe book slide against the table and then the sound of pages being flipped in chunks. Isobel peeked up at him with one suspicious eye, watching as he settled at last on the "Ultima Thule" portrait of Poe.

"He sure was a weird dude, wasn't he?" he murmured, more to himself, Isobel thought, than to her.

She raised her head slowly, staring hard at her father.

"Weird-looking, too," he commented.

Isobel's hand shot out. She gripped her father's arm. He looked at her in alarm.

"Dad," she said, her eyes scanning his face. Her grip on him tightened as she recalled something her father had said before, on the drive home from the library that first day she'd met with Varen. "Dad, do you really want to help? Really?"

His eyes softened, brows slanting. Her own eyes widened. "Yes, Izzy," he said with a nod, sounding almost relieved. "I really, really do."

"Omigod," she said, rocketing out of her chair, pressing one palm to her forehead, a flood of ideas filling her head all at once. She shook her father's arm before letting go, flying to the wall next to the garage door, and taking his car keys off their hook. "I have an idea," she said. "Walmart!" she shouted. "You have to take me to Walmart, right now!"

"Okay, kiddo, okay. We'll go to Walmart." He stood, uncertainty written across his features, and Isobel rushed to him, hugging him, then shoved his keys into his hands.

He spread his arms questioningly. "Well, aren't you going to fill me in?"

Isobel flung open the garage door, clambered down the stairs, and opened the passenger door to the sedan. "On the way," she said. "Get in."

Isobel was late to school the next morning, missing two whole periods. Nobody took class seriously on a big game day, though (nobody but Mr. Swanson, of course), so she doubted that she'd missed anything vital. Carting along her boom box, she moved through the decorated halls hung with poster-board signs and blue and yellow balloons, peeking into classroom doors, hoping on the off chance that she'd catch a glimmer of silver chains or black boots. She had no idea what his schedule was outside of fourth-period English, but it would be a huge relief just to know he was in the building. She wanted to let him know that they at least had a game plan. She could give him a heads-up. Most of all, she wanted to see him. She needed to talk to him.

But that would all have to wait.

Nearing her U.S. history classroom, Isobel decided she couldn't spare the time to keep looking. The rule for all county high schools was that to participate in any after-school functions, like a play, a club, or *especially* a football game, you had to be in school for at least half the day. Isobel wasn't going to push it by waiting until fourth period to show her face. They had a pep rally last period, and she couldn't be certain if that hour really counted or not.

Hitching her bag higher on her back, Isobel grasped the door handle and went in, her yellow late slip crumpled in one hand.

She froze in the doorway as a sudden barrage of hoots, hollers, and desk pounding trumpeted at her appearance. *Oh God*, she thought, *what now?* Then someone from the back stood up, cupping his hands over his mouth, and shouted, "What's up, Tren-*ton*?"

Relief washed over her. Chicken Soup for the Cheerleader's Soul.

She beamed, posing (albeit a little awkwardly with the boom box still in one hand), and shot her fist into the air. Even Mr. Fredenburg put down his chalk to applaud. She'd almost forgotten she'd worn her cheer uniform that day, blue skirt with yellow pleats over blue Trenton sweatpants, yellow turtleneck under her blue-with-yellow-stripes shell top, a yellow *H* for Hawks emblazoned on her chest. This was normal, she reminded herself as she made her way through her personal parade to her seat. Normal, normal, how she loved thee. She was still Isobel the cheerleader. Isobel the flyer. This was what it was all about.

Tonight, even if she failed the project, even if it was for the last time, she would get her spinning lights, her weightless suspension, her gasping crowd — tonight she would fly.

U.S. history ended fast, bringing the bell for the between-class break all too soon. Isobel found herself moving through the throng of blue and gold enthusiasm toward Mr. Swanson's class. A group of sophomores with their faces painted pranced by, laughing together, the girls hand in hand with their letter-jacket boyfriends. Streams of blue Silly String slung out from nowhere, catching in hair and on clothes, spraying the lockers and walls. Lost in the shuffle, Isobel could hear Mr. Nott's cries for order.

The excitement was catching.

A new spirit seemed to have seized and shaken the school, like it always did on a big game day, and Isobel found herself desperately wanting her slice of the fun. Boys hooted as she walked down the hall, a group of them clearing a path for her, shouting, "What's up, Tren-ton?" and banging on lockers between chants. A rhythm of "What's up, Tren-ton!" *bang*, *bang* followed her all the way to the stairwell. Isobel tried to keep her smile in check when what she really wanted to do was get rid of the stupid boom box and turn cartwheels down the hall to the beat of the lockers and the rhythm of shouts. This was her element and she wanted in, the cheerleader inside her screaming and jumping to cut loose. She would, she assured herself. But before she could, there was just one thing left to do: Operation Finish This Poe Thing So My Life Can Go On.

Isobel walked resolutely into her English classroom, her heart fluttering when she saw everyone gathered together in their groups, doing last-minute prep work before the bell. She saw Mr. Swanson and looked away quickly, pretending not to have caught his eye. Varen wasn't there. His chair was empty.

She took her seat, setting the boom box on her desk. Where could he be? Would he seriously leave her on her own? Only now did she allow herself to become fully aware of her jangling nerves. They seemed to splinter all the more now, with her plan unraveling. She remembered Mr. Swanson's warning. Both partners had to be present.

And then he appeared in the doorway. Isobel shot up from her chair, almost knocking over the boom box. He looked a little bedraggled, wearing yesterday's black jeans and, she thought, yesterday's T-shirt turned inside out, his eyes hidden once more beneath dark sunglasses. His hair was more ragged than usual too, giving him a wilder look. The sight of him stirred up something powerful and scary deep within her, the sensation intensifying when she thought about what she'd resolved to tell him that day. Would he listen?

The noise of the room grew louder. She might have thirty seconds left before the bell, thirty seconds left to let him in on the plan. She waited for him, but for some reason, he turned away, moving not toward her, but straight for Mr. Swanson's desk.

Wait. What was he doing?

Isobel tore down the aisle to the front of the room.

"Oh yeah," she said, inserting herself between Varen and Mr. Swanson. "I forgot. We wanted to ask if it was okay if we used a boom box." She flashed Mr. Swanson her most convincing custom-made cheer-ready grin.

Mr. Swanson glanced between them, wearing an expression close to alarm. Maybe it was her cheer uniform next to Varen's undertaker look. Isobel could sense all eyes fixed on them from behind, and she had the childish urge to turn around and stick her tongue out at everyone.

Mr. Swanson shrugged. "Why wouldn't it be?" he said, his expression morphing into bemusement.

"See?" Isobel said, turning to Varen. "I told you." His shielded gaze met hers. She stared at him pointedly, her tight smile reflected back at her through the sunglasses. The sound of the bell filled the room, followed by the scraping of chairs. Time was up.

She leaned in, whispering quickly under the noise cover, "I know you don't want to do any talking, but you have to do the death part, because we didn't get that far. I'll start. Jump in if you can and follow my lead." She slipped away from him, taking her seat on the opposite end of the room.

"Shades please, Mr. Nethers."

Isobel watched as Varen made his way to his own chair. He moved slower than usual and this time didn't bother lifting away the sunglasses at Mr. Swanson's behest. Maybe, she thought, he hadn't heard him ask? That seemed unlikely, though, since lately it had become a sort of start-of-class ritual between them, a show of their mutual respect. Isobel watched him sink into his desk, almost as though this action took more effort than normal. A quick glance out of the corner of her eye told her that Mr. Swanson was watching too. And so, it seemed, was everybody else.

Varen settled into his seat. A moment passed by in which Mr. Swanson seemed to deliberate on whether or not to repeat his request. To Isobel's relief, he did not. Maybe it was Varen's uncharacteristically disheveled appearance. Or maybe Mr. Swanson knew something, or suspected something. Whatever it was, he didn't ask again.

He called the first group. Todd and Romelle popped in a DVD, which turned out to be a music video about Mark Twain's life. It was a good idea, so good that Isobel wished she'd thought of it. It wouldn't have taken that long, and they could have used a song from Varen's collection.

Soon it was the next group's turn with Walt Whitman.

Next, Richard Wright, then Washington Irving. Between each presentation, Isobel kept trying to catch Varen's eye. Why wouldn't he look at her? She thought about passing a note but then decided it was too risky.

"Isobel and Varen?"

Isobel stood, her heart speeding up. She glanced toward Varen, but he didn't need the cue. He'd stood mechanically, and now they both made their way to the front of the classroom. Isobel handed him the stereo and cord. When he took them from her, the little red light next to the control buttons on the boom box lit up. White noise fuzzed, then spiked, and Isobel stopped, confused, because she knew she'd taken the batteries out that morning to make the player lighter to carry.

She stared at Varen as he moved to the front of the classroom, the radio jumping through stations. He set the boom box on Mr. Swanson's desk, and in the moment before he took his hands away, a woman's soft voice broke through. Far-off and fuzzy, it sounded as though it was coming from an old, scratched-up record. " —centrate," it said. "Treat it all like an empty page."

With a stab of unease, Isobel realized that she'd heard this voice before—coming from the attic of Nobit's Nook. It was that day she and Varen had worked together, when she'd gone back to get the Poe book and found the upstairs room empty. Right before she'd gone into the park.

Unsettled, Isobel swallowed. While Varen plugged in the stereo, she brought two chairs to one side of Mr. Swanson's desk, taking extra time to straighten the one closest to where their teacher usually sat. She was glad Varen took the hint. He went to that chair and sat. Trying to forget the moment with the radio, Isobel rounded the desk and lowered herself into Mr. Swanson's swivel seat. Swanson, who had taken an empty seat out in the room, said nothing.

Isobel gathered up her stack of index cards, taking a moment to breathe. This was it.

She smiled at the classroom, reached out, and pressed the play button. Music blared—a catchy, almost game-showish synthesizer tune from a bonus round on one of Danny's video games. Everyone stared, faces blank, Varen's included. The music died down, and Isobel pressed the pause button.

"Welcome to another episode of *Dead Poet Discussions*," she said. "I'm your host, Isobel Lanley, and for this exclusive All Hallows' Eve edition, I have a few special guests in store for you. One of them is with us now. Please welcome Professor Varen Nethers, famous depressed dead poets historian and author of the bestselling books *Unlocking your Poe-tential: A Writer's Guide*, and *Mo Poe Fo Yo: When You Just Can't Get Enough*. Welcome, Professor Nethers."

Isobel hit the next track button, unleashing the sound of applause. Varen's shielded gaze fixed on hers in what she thought might be a pained expression. She gritted through a smile, begging him with her eyes to just play along.

The sound of applause died down. "But that's not all," Isobel plowed on, trying to keep her tone encouraging, the mood upbeat.

"We have yet another very special guest with us this evening," she went on, "all the way from Westminster Cemetery in lovely Baltimore, Maryland." Isobel paused, keeping her smile. She held her arm out toward the door in a presentational gesture, like they did on all late-night talk shows.

"Please welcome to the show Mr. Edgar Allan Poe!"

31
In the Flesh

The door swung open. Isobel depressed the track button again, and another round of applause came from the boom box. Edgar Allan Poe strode into the room. He stood for a moment, his expression a mix of grim remorse and melancholy, one hand held reverently over his heart.

Her mom had done a good job with the white makeup, Isobel thought. His paleness and the circles under his eyes looked too real. Then again, they *had* stayed up most of the night, so they probably *were* real. She thought the black wig they'd gotten from the costume aisle at Walmart looked a little hokey, but she figured she'd done an okay job cutting and styling it. Her father wore the tux he'd gotten married in, and being more than just a little tight now, the pant cuffs hiked up over his black socks like high-waters. A long white dish towel tied around his neck served as a cravat, and a little hair left over from the wig had been glued onto his upper lip that morning with spirit gum. The whole getup (combined with his "woe is me" expression) might have been genuinely impressive, if not for the plush toucan, spray-painted black, hanging limply off his right shoulder, where it had been fastened that morning with Velcro. The bird bobbed stupidly as he strode into the room, prompting an outburst of laughter and applause.

Isobel stood up from the desk and reached out to shake hands with the fake Poe. Then her dad took the open chair next to Varen, who stared, his grip tightening on the armrests of his own chair. Her dad seemed to get the message and didn't offer to shake.

"Welcome, Mr. Poe," said Isobel, trying to get past the tense moment. The room quieted down, everyone eager to see what would happen next.

"Thank you, thank you," Poe crooned in a goofy Southern accent. "Always a pleasure to return to the realm of the living."

Isobel flipped through her stack of index cards to the one she needed first. She'd written almost all her questions out in a backward fashion, giving the facts first, asking for confirmation rather than information. It couldn't, after all, come off looking like her dad had done the work. He hadn't, either, Isobel reminded herself. Mostly he'd spent the night goofing off, parading around the living room, answering every single question with "Nevermore!" and coming up with ways to incorporate horrible Poe puns. Given the way he was currently hamming up the part, Isobel couldn't help but wonder if he'd remember a single authentic thing she'd told him.

"So, Poe," she began, "how've you been these past one hundred and fifty plus years since your untimely and mysterious death in the fall of 1849?"

"Weary."

"And how's Night's Plutonian shore these days?"

"Dreary."

More laughter. Isobel watched as Varen's head turned slowly toward her father. She couldn't exactly tell with the sunglasses, but she somehow knew that he had to be staring down the false Poe with one of his most penetrating "you are the essence of lameness" expressions.

Isobel plowed on. "I would just like to say that we are so glad to have you here on the show today, Mr. Poe and Professor Nethers." She plastered on a big cheer smile. "Mr. Poe, your major works include such stories as 'The Fall of the House of Usher,' 'The Tell-Tale Heart,' 'The Pit and the Pendulum,' and 'The Masque of the Red Death.' All of these feature themes of death and elements of the supernatural. Is it also true that you are considered to be the father of the modern detective story?"

"Oh, yes, of course," said Poe, gesturing loosely with one hand. "Indeed I am. I hear that I am also considered by many in this day and age to be 'America's Shakespeare.'" Her dad beamed at Varen. "Isn't that correct, Professor?"

This was the part that had caused her the most worry. This was the part she'd wanted to warn him about but hadn't gotten the chance. But they'd had to think of *some* way to involve Varen so he wouldn't just be sitting there, some way that he would pick up on. This part, Isobel remembered, had been Danny's one and only contribution, suggested during the ten seconds he could stand to keep his game on pause.

"Uh, yeah," Varen said, shifting in his seat.

She nodded, pressing on, "Perhaps your most famous work, though, was and still is the narrative poem 'The Raven.'

Can you talk a little bit about your success with that particular piece?"

"Indeed," Poe said, crossing his legs, leaning back in the chair. He raised a finger to brush the tarred crest of the limp fake raven. "That poem became more widely read than I could ever have dreamed. My success was, I must say, nothing short of stupendous. I became a sort of . . . literary *Elvis*, if you would."

Varen blanched at the comparison.

"You disagree, Professor?" asked Poe.

"No," he said, "except that Poe never made any money off 'The Raven.'"

Poe sat up, gripping his seat, the bird jiggling. "Certainly I made a profit!"

"Fifteen bucks."

An outright burst of laughter broke through the room.

"That, sir," Isobel's dad said, leaning back in his seat and straightening his jacket, "is beside the point."

"So it's true that you were very poor," Isobel went on, ad-libbing.

"In terms of money, yes, I was poor," her father said, glowering in Varen's direction. "I see that since my death, America has changed little in its obsession with the dollar."

"Is it also true that you drank to excess?" Isobel asked, flipping to the next index card.

Poe scoffed at the question, his response simply *"Nyeh."*

Varen's head snapped so quickly toward her father that Isobel was surprised the sunglasses hadn't flown off.

"Well, sometimes," Poe corrected himself. Shifting, he stooped in his seat.

Varen's stare remained.

"*Often,*" Poe growled, angling away, pulling his already tight jacket around himself even tighter.

This time Isobel thought she even heard Mr. Swanson chuckle. *Good*, she thought. Maybe that meant he'd let this whole thing fly.

"Though you can't say that I wasn't, at heart, a gentleman," Poe argued, this directed outward. "And not to excuse myself, but when I drank, it was only to drown out the sorrowful pain brought on by the blackest despairs of my life, such as the long illness and ultimate demise of my dearest Virginia."

Wow, Isobel thought, impressed, so he had remembered something after all. "After your wife Virginia's death," she said, "you attempted to remarry, correct?"

"Well, for a short while, I courted Miss Sarah Helen Whitman."

"And Annie," Varen interjected.

Poe paused, smiling. He lifted a finger to loosen his cravat. "And . . . Annie," he conceded.

"Who was married."

"See, that's an interesting story indeed. I—"

"And then Elmira."

"And then Elmira, yes, fine." Poe crossed his arms, slumped, and looked away. There came a mix of laughter and several teasing "ooh's" from the back of the class.

"What can I say?" Poe muttered. "Chicks dig the mustache."

Laughter again. Isobel shut her eyes and held them closed, trying to halt the crawl of color over her face. *Take it down a notch, Dad*, she thought toward him, opening her eyes again. Then she grinned in spite of herself, because the plan was working better than she had hoped. As she asked more questions, Varen continued to interject between her father's misty replies, supplying the real facts, eliciting laughter with his dry coolness. Soon they had only one subject left to cover: death.

"Mr. Poe, the details of your end are, at best, cloudy." Her mom had told her to phrase it that way, though Isobel thought it made her sound like a cheesy soothsayer. "No one knows exactly what happened to you on that fateful night. There are theories ranging from rabies to murder."

"Mmm. Murder," Poe mused, "that most hideous yet somehow fascinating of human pastimes."

"You admit that you were somehow involved in foul play?"

"I admit nothing," Poe said. "I enjoy mysteries too much. I invented them, remember? And so I am obliged not to reveal the answer to the riddle of my death." He stood slowly and began pacing, hands clasped behind his back. "Besides, I fear I cannot fully recall what happened to me that night so long ago, so many eons ago. . . ." He reached a quivering hand out toward his audience, his fingers curling into a rueful fist. Isobel rolled her eyes. She never would have thought he had it in him!

"I was on my way from New York to Richmond."

"Richmond to New York," Varen corrected.

"That's right," Poe whispered, bringing his hand toward his brow, bracing his head. "The musty air of the grave! The lull of death's sleep. These things can congest the brain, clog the memory—but you're right. I was leaving Richmond, yes, where I had finally become engaged. I was to be married. Yes, married. But first! First I was to return to my home in New York to collect my dear aunt Moody."

"Muddy."

"That's what I said." Poe stopped then, tilting his head as though listening to something far off. "I remember traveling by train with my trunk full of manuscripts and lectures. The train stopped and then I . . . I . . ."

Isobel let her eyes stray from her father to scan the faces of her classmates. Everyone stared. Even Bobby Bailey, who usually laid his head on his desk, had sat up to listen.

"Perhaps, Professor Nethers," Isobel ventured, "you can enlighten us about some of the details surrounding this mystery?"

Varen, maybe remembering Isobel's whispered plea, took his cue. "For five days Poe went missing," he said, his voice slicing into the stillness of the room. "He was found near a tavern in Baltimore in a state of delirium, wearing someone else's clothing. He was then taken by his cousin and a doctor friend to the hospital."

"Yes, I remember now . . . ," Poe whispered.

"The doctor's reports say that Poe raved for days, talking to imaginary people and invisible objects on the wall."

"Demon!" Isobel's dad shouted suddenly, shooting a finger out to point at the ceiling. With a collective shriek, the entire room jumped in their seats. "Thing of evil!"

A strange feeling stole its way over Isobel. Her brow knotted, and she felt her jaw tighten and set. As she watched her father improvise, her hands pressed down on the desktop while her thoughts and her memory slowly wound around reawakening fears. She remembered now that Varen had mentioned this in the library, that first time they'd met for the project—how Poe had screamed out to invisible beings while on his deathbed.

"On the night before he died," Varen continued in a solemn tone, "he began screaming out a name, shouting it for more than a day, calling for someone no one knew. Someone Poe never reportedly knew, either. Someone named Reynolds—"

Isobel gasped audibly. Prickling white spikes of fear and panic shot through her, freezing her mind and stalling her body. She sat stunned, her eyes on Varen while her memory projected onto her mind the image of a black-shrouded figure.

Isobel had no way of telling how much time trickled by before she registered Mr. Swanson's voice. Apparently, however, it had been long enough for him to guess that this wasn't just another part of the presentation. "Isobel," he said, "are you all right?"

Dazedly she looked for her father, who had all but dropped out of character to stare at her with a "What's going on?" look on his face.

"Uh," Isobel croaked, fumbling for the radio. Flustered,

she pressed play, then pause, then stop. "That's the—all—all the time we have today," she stuttered, pressing play again in an attempt to cover her mangled lines. The tail end of another round of clapping trickled lamely through the boom box before dying out.

Her father made a hesitant bow, now to the live though somewhat sporadic applause of the class, whose attention had begun alternating between Isobel and Varen. No doubt they were wondering what they'd missed.

"I, uh, shall take leave of you now," her father said, backing toward the door. He shot a questioning look at Isobel. She nodded at him. It was all she could manage. "Yes," he affirmed, turning back to the class. "Here I take my leave, to return to this realm—*nevermore*!"

Isobel watched numbly as her father swept dramatically from the room, pausing at the door long enough to jiggle the light switch before ducking out. The bird dropped from his shoulder and onto the linoleum. A black-cuffed hand shot back in and snatched the bird out again. Isobel scowled, vaguely recalling having *begged* him to leave out the light switch part.

The bell rang, ending the class in what felt like a whirlwind. Everyone shot up from their seats, papers flapping, notebooks dropping, laughing and talking. Mr. Swanson rose too, announcing over the clamor, "Okaay, then. Very good job, everyone—and their parents, I suppose," he added with a pointed look at Isobel that normally would have made her gulp. "Papers up front, if you please. Your grades will be ready some time next week and, from there, we're going to talk a little bit more about Mr. Poe, the antebellum era and the Romantics, then we'll pick up on writers of the Civil War era. Have a very safe Halloween tonight, go Trenton Hawks. Pull up your pants, Mr. Levery, I don't need to see your boxers—everybody please stay out of trouble!"

Trouble. Isobel's gaze fell to the swirling grain of Mr. Swanson's desktop, her brain repeating the word. She was in trouble.

Reynolds.

Hadn't he been something purely out of her subconscious? Or could Varen have mentioned him before? No. No, she would have remembered that. Her dreams. Had they been real? It was the only explanation, she realized. It was the only thing that explained everything. The Poe book. She *had* thrown it away. The figure in the door at practice. The image in the mirror. The run through the park. The voice in the attic. She wasn't crazy—or maybe she was? Isobel funneled her focus onto a single black knot in the wood as she tried to recall something else Reynolds had told her. What he'd said about . . .

"Varen?" she asked breathlessly.

She stood abruptly and looked into the seat next to hers. She saw only their paper, bound neatly in a plastic report cover. She watched dully as all the others began piling on top, burying the neat Gothic typeface he'd chosen for the title. She looked up, her eyes locking on his desk in the corner. Empty. His satchel, his black book—gone.

32
Pinfeathers

Halfway out the door, Isobel slammed into her father, the makeshift raven flopping off his shoulder and once again onto the floor.

"Hey, whoa, Iz! I'm still here." He gripped her shoulders to steady her. "How do you think we did? Hey, listen"—he dropped one arm to check his watch—"I better get on to the office so I can be back to pick you up before the game." He bent to get the bird, and before Isobel could utter a syllable, six-foot-something Bobby Bailey stepped between them, blocking Isobel completely.

"Hey, man, that was awesome," he said, engaging her father in a complicated series of handshakes and fist bumps.

"Hey, thanks," her dad replied, navigating through the grips and punches as best as he could. "Uh, glad you thought so . . . man."

Isobel peered down the hall both ways, searching for Varen's familiar dark figure. Not seeing him, she elbowed Bobby aside. "Dad, this is important. Did you see which way Varen went?"

Bobby butted fists with her father one last time before passing on. Her dad, stuffing the bird under one arm, frowned.

"Yeah," he said, pointing, "he took off down that way. Didn't even say hi or, you know, thanks."

"Daddy, thanks. Listen, that was great." She hugged him quickly, then shoved the boom box into his grasp. "Can you take this for me? I gotta go!" She turned without waiting for a reply and ran off through the crowd, jumping up to see over the tops of bobbing heads. It was at times like these that she hated being so short. She also hated leaving her dad like that, standing in the middle of the chaotic hall, still dressed as Poe and carting around her blue stereo.

At first she didn't see him. Then the way cleared, and suddenly he was there. Isobel shoved her way through.

"Varen!"

Hadn't he heard her? She shot after him, almost catching up. She called to him again—why wouldn't he turn around? He rounded the corner without looking back. She swung around the bend right after him—then skidded to a halt.

He was gone.

He'd been right there in front of her not two seconds ago and now, in the space where he should have stood . . . nothing.

Isobel peeked into the nearest classroom. Vacant. She turned again, this time in a slow circle. Lockers slammed. Somewhere in the distance, she recognized the shouts of her favorite call-and-response chant: "When I say Trenton, you say Hawks! Trenton! Hawks! Trenton! Hawks! When I say down, you say Bulldogs! Down! Bulldogs! Down! Bulldogs!" More students streamed by her, laughing and chattering, no one seeming to have noticed one person's total evaporation.

*   *   *

When Isobel entered the lunchroom, she found Gwen right away, sitting at their table. Stevie was there too, which wasn't a big surprise. Someone she hadn't expected to find, though, sitting at one far end, picking through her untouched taco salad, bedecked in cheerful dangling earrings yet still managing to look mopey, was Nikki.

For a moment their eyes met. Isobel resisted the urge to look away, to steal a glance toward where she knew the crew would be sitting. Or, she corrected herself, where what was left of the crew would be sitting. With Nikki attempting to cross over and merge with the light side (if that indeed was what she was trying to do), Isobel figured the crew should be neatly split somewhere down the middle.

At this newest complication, Isobel found herself more annoyed than anything, wishing Nikki had picked another day. *Yesterday*, for instance. She didn't have time for drama right now. She switched her gaze to Stevie, who waved, no doubt on Nikki's side for her attempt at a smooth convergence.

"Hey, Iz," he called, "where've you been?"

Isobel came to a stop beside the table, letting her bag drop to the floor. "Long story."

"You know," said Gwen, after swallowing a mouthful of what looked to Isobel like a peanut butter and banana sandwich, "I've seen that look before. Not on you"—she shook her head—"on somebody else. I think his name was Rambo."

"Gwen."

"Isobel," Gwen said, echoing her tone of seriousness.

Isobel swiveled where she stood, then sat so her knees faced out instead of in. This put her back to Stevie and Nikki. "Listen," she said in a low voice, "can you still get me to that thing tonight?"

Gwen took another bite of the goopy sandwich and smiled. "I thought you said you didn't want to go." The words were barely decipherable.

Isobel frowned. She'd never said she didn't want to go. She *had* wanted to go, only more so now because she had a gut feeling that if she was going to catch up to Varen at all, she would need to find him there, tonight, at the Grim Facade.

"Hey," said Gwen, jabbing a bony elbow in Isobel's ribs, "what's with you? You're doing that creepy stare-off thing again. What made you change your mind, anyway? Not that I was really going to give you a choice in the first place since I got Mikey to tag me. How come you're not eating? Where's your lunch? Talk to me here. Did you guys get the project done or what? And where *is* the Dark One, anyway? I haven't seen him all day."

He should be *here* at this table, Isobel thought, clenching a fist.

A new thought dawning on her, she lifted her gaze to scan the room. She looked toward the goths' table. The congregation there was sparse, probably in aversion to the pep rally and the chaos of rival game day. And it was Halloween. No doubt they were all somewhere getting ready for their *own* celebration, for the Grim Facade. Among those missing from the table, Isobel couldn't help but notice, was Lacy.

"Are you just going to sit there and ignore me?" came a quavering voice. Nikki.

Isobel pulled her feet up, turned around, and slid her legs underneath the table. She wished that she didn't have to deal with this, of all things, right now.

"Just tell me if you hate me," Nikki went on. She propped her elbows on the table and put her head in her hands—a condemned prisoner begging the executioner to hurry up with the ax already. "Tell me off or something." Her chin trembled. "But don't just sit there and ignore me."

Isobel averted her eyes with an actual pang of guilt. "Nikki." She sighed.

All at once, she sucked her breath back in.

"*Omigod, Gwen.*" She reached out, fixing a clawlike grip on Gwen's arm. Her banana sandwich missing her mouth, it tumbled to the side and onto the floor.

"Omigod what? I was so gonna eat that."

"Who's that guy?"

"What guy?"

"*That* guy," Isobel said, her hand tightening on Gwen's arm. "Sitting with Brad."

Both Stevie and Nikki swung around to look.

Sitting right next to Brad was a boy with porcelain white skin, his dark bloodred hair slicked back, sleek yet somehow spiky. His clothes were black leather and chains. Beneath the table, she could see he wore boots, and his pants were covered with buckles and dull silver chains. He had on a thin strap-covered black coat that almost looked like a straitjacket. It fitted snugly against the boy's spindly frame.

"Where?" asked Gwen. "I don't see anybody."

"He's sitting right there. Right next to Brad. Nikki, you see him, right?" Isobel glanced at her former best friend, only to be met with an expression of hurt and doubt.

"Are you making fun of me or something?"

"What? No! I—"

"Iz," Stevie interjected, "Nikki has been trying to say she's sorry."

"No, I know!"

"*Tch!*" Scooting her tray aside, Nikki pulled her ostrich legs out from the table and rose. "I knew you wouldn't listen." Leaving her tray behind, she stalked off, hurrying toward the courtyard doors. With a heavy sigh, Stevie drew himself up. Before turning to follow, he eyed Isobel with baleful disapproval.

She shook her head. "No, this isn't about that! Look!" She pointed. "He's right there! He's sitting right there. He's got . . ." Ignoring her, Stevie turned to head Nikki off at the door. Isobel let her gaze trail after them for a moment until, looking back, she saw that the boy sitting next to Brad had turned to stare at her. She quickly lowered her arm, something in her gut telling her she shouldn't have pointed.

"Isobel," Gwen started, "no offense, but I'm gonna have to go with the cheeries on this one. Not funny."

Transfixed, Isobel watched as the blood-haired boy raised

a thin, abnormally long hand, the tips of which ended in long, red, talonlike claws. He waved at her, and she felt her stomach plummet to the floor. Her mouth went as dry as paper.

They couldn't see him. No one could see him. No one but her. Even Brad, who was sitting closest to the boy, hadn't been paying any attention. He'd been bent low over the table, conferring with Mark, who hadn't seemed to take any notice either. And Alyssa, indifferently listening in, sat coating her nails in polish, oblivious.

"I'll . . . I'll be right back," Isobel mumbled, gripping the table for support as she rose.

"What? Wait a sec, where are you going? Isobel. You're not seriously going over there. Hey! Are you crazy? Sit down!"

She felt Gwen swipe at and catch the hem of her pleated skirt. She pulled free, however, her heart drumming a steady rhythm in her ears as she headed toward the wide windows paneling the wall, walking in a straight line toward the crew's table. She was surrounded by the low murmur of talking, the clank and clatter of silverware and trays. Somewhere behind her, a table erupted into laughter. It all felt so real, so normal.

The muttering between Brad and Mark ceased when Alyssa, with one yet-to-be-slathered nail, tapped the space between them. "Hey," she said, "look who's coming over to chat."

But she wasn't there to talk. Not to them, at least.

Sitting one seat over from Brad, closest to the window, the blood-haired boy leaned forward, turning his head toward her, revealing the other side of his face. Isobel froze, her eyes locking on the jagged black hole that marked his cheek, as though an entire chunk of his face had been knocked out, like a chink in a porcelain vase. She could see straight through, to his hollow jaw and the two rows of red daggerlike teeth within.

Fear pulsed through her, and yet she stood hypnotized. He was horrible and fascinating all at once, like a scorpion prepared to strike, all angles and sharp lines and menace.

Running now on pure nerve, Isobel took up her steps again, determined to prove to herself that this wasn't a hallucination—that she was awake, and this was real. The boy's eyes followed her, eyes that she now saw held no irises, whole only in their blackness.

"Well hey, Isobel," Brad said, greeting her with mock enthusiasm, "what a surprise."

"So you can see me," said the boy. The sound of actual words coming out of his mouth startled her. His voice was quiet, smooth, and acidic, somehow corroded in essence, as though he was speaking through a thin layer of radio static.

It was eerily familiar.

This close, Isobel could see that his hair, which really was more like coarse feathers, grew darker, almost black toward the roots that weren't roots at all, but thick quills sprouting from his scalp. "That's very interesting," he continued, "that you can see me like this." He smiled, flashing a dangerous, dark pink mouth filled with jagged teeth the color of red coral.

Isobel swallowed, clearing the way for her own voice. "Who are you?"

Brad flipped his fork onto his tray, and Isobel jumped at the clatter. She'd almost forgotten he was even there.

"Aw, c'mon, Iz," he said, "don't give me that old 'I don't even know who you are anymore' crap. And don't pretend I didn't warn you."

Suddenly the blood-haired boy moved. Isobel's focus snapped to him as, in a series of quick, jerky motions, like a DVD on fast-forward, he brought an arm across Brad, extending a red-clawed hand toward her. "The name is Pinfeathers."

Isobel drew back half a step, making no move to touch him, staring instead, as though it were a dead rat he'd offered her and not his hand. His nails, more like the scarlet fangs from some deadly venomous snake, gleamed in the light.

"What, you leaving already?" Brad said. "Is that it? You trying to be deep or something? I don't get it."

Pinfeathers withdrew his hand. "Oh, don't trouble yourself with introductions," he said. "I know you. You're the cheerleader." He blinked at her sharply, cocking his head to one side. "Now, you might not realize this," he said, "but you and I, well, we've met before."

Isobel found herself once again staring into the hole in Pinfeather's cheek, her gaze held by the scarlet teeth and the movement of his jawbone as he spoke. There were no muscles, no tendons, no cartilage, nothing to hold him together, only hollow blackness.

He raised a clawed finger to point at the missing portion of his face. "Oh, don't let this bother you. Happens to the best of us."

"What are you doing here?" she asked.

Brad snorted. "I sit here."

"*Duh,*" Alyssa chimed in, smearing another coat of polish onto her thumbnail.

"I like your friends here," Pinfeather said. "Especially the big one." He brought a claw toward Brad's face, poking lightly at his ear. Isobel watched in horror as Brad swatted at the nonexistent fly.

"Stop it."

Pinfeathers drew his hand away, using the same claw to point at her now. "Never pegged you for the jealous type."

"Don't touch him again."

Brad smiled suddenly, broadly. The unexpected expression startled Isobel so much that for a moment she was distracted from the weirdness that was Pinfeathers. "Ah, I *thought* that might have something to do with you comin' over. Haven't seen his face all day, so he must have told you."

Isobel shifted her gaze back to Brad now, her concentration zeroing in with effort on his self-satisfied expression. His inflection on the word "he" could only have meant one person. "Wh-what?"

"Uh-oh," Mark said, biting off a piece of his roll.

Wait, Isobel thought, what had she missed? What was going on? She looked to Alyssa next in her search for clarification, but knew her mistake in doing so when the other girl, returning to her nails, displayed only a knowing smile.

"What are you talking about?" she demanded of the three of them. "What's going on?" she said, this time appealing to Pinfeathers.

The creature winked and tapped his thin white lips with a red claw, like he was letting her know the best part was coming.

"Well," said Brad. He wiped his hands with his napkin, then crumpled it and tossed it onto his tray. "Let's see, Iz." He pushed his tray away and folded his hands on the table. "We caught up with your little bloodsucking boyfriend last night after he dropped you off, that's what. Did he, uh, happen to mention anything to you about it? See, Mark and I had a bet going. I said he'd run to you first thing, but Mark—Mark's giving him the benefit of the doubt."

Isobel watched dully as Mark leaned in to murmur something to Brad that she couldn't catch. Their laughter ensued. Pinfeathers listened too, folding his hands on the table, mimicking Brad's posture.

"We waited for him by your house, and then we followed him," Mark said, as though it were as simple as that.

"I felt we needed to have a talk. A one-on-one," Brad explained, "about the defacement of personal property."

"We did give him a choice," said Mark.

"Yes. We were very diplomatic." Brad nodded.

"He surprised us," Mark said, an almost appreciative note to his voice.

"Yeah, we'd thought for sure he'd pussy out and opt for us trashing his car."

Mark shook his head. "But he didn't."

"Nope. He didn't."

"You'd have been proud of him, Iz."

"Yeah," Brad admitted, "we were impressed."

Her throat tightened. *"You're lying."*

"Nope," Brad said. "No, Iz, we're not." He leaned forward, blocking Pinfeathers from her view, looking her in the eye. He lowered his voice. "And don't go off thinking this was about you, because it wasn't. He deserved it, and you know what he did as well as I do."

At these words, Isobel felt something hot inside of her rush up and snap, like an electric cable.

"Don't you get it?" Before she could stop herself, she lashed out, flipping his Coke over. Ice clattered out of the tall blue cup, liquid splashed over the table. Alyssa screeched and slid away. Brad shot up from his seat as soda cascaded onto his lap. "He didn't touch your car!" she shouted. "And I know you're lying!" He was toying with her. They were just trying to get a rise. She'd seen Varen not twenty minutes ago. He'd been fine.

Or maybe, she realized, her thoughts jarring, maybe that's why he'd sunk so slowly into his chair. Maybe that's why he'd refused to remove his glasses. Maybe that's why he'd avoided her.

"Does this look like I'm lying?" He moved out from the table to tower over her. Her eyes darted briefly to Pinfeathers, who watched unblinking. Lifting his pinky, Brad aimed it at a large blood blister on his upper lip that she hadn't paid attention to until now. Brad was a running back, and she was used to seeing him with scrapes and bruises.

"Hey!" came Mr. Nott's shout from the far end of the

room, followed immediately by the hard, fast jangling of keys.

Brad bent low to speak into her ear. She felt powerless to do anything but listen. "He was a real sport about it. He only clipped me once, but by that time I was done, and I let it go, 'cause I said something I shouldn't have. Somethin' about you, Iz."

Horrified, she recoiled, and Mr. Nott, coming to a jangling halt, stepped into the widening space between them, asking in his deep, authoritative voice the obligatory, "What's going on here?"

"I spilled my Coke, sir," Brad announced over the sudden quiet. A few titters ran through the table next to them. If the whole entire cafeteria hadn't been watching before, they were now. "It was an accident, sir. Pregame jitters."

Isobel returned her gaze to the table, where Pinfeathers watched her. His expression seemed darker now, his humor gone, and the fathomless black of his eyes now threatened to swallow her. "Don't look so lost, cheerleader," he said. "I've watched you watching him—*us*, I mean. I even tried to warn you. But you wouldn't listen. You waited, and now it's too late. For you . . . for us."

"Isobel, did you hear me?" Mr. Nott asked. "I said, go take your seat."

Isobel didn't move. She found her gaze unable to waver from Pinfeathers, from his face as it seemed to struggle and twist between several emotions, finally contorting into a grimace of malice and pain. Why did that make him suddenly so familiar?

"Miss Lanley, are you deaf today? I said, go take your seat."

In one blinking movement, Pinfeathers lunged at her, jaw unhinging, the black hole in his face widening. Teeth bared, claws outstretched, he unleashed an ungodly sound, something between a woman's death screech and a demon's howl.

It happened too fast for her to form her own scream, too fast for her raised arms to do any good. His claws rained down.

Isobel fell back, knocking into the table behind her. A shrieking torrent of jet feathers engulfed the light. His form loosened into violet smoke, and like a demon sucked into hell, he vanished into the floor.

33
Just a Bird

Blood. Where was the blood? Why wasn't she bleeding? Isobel searched her arms for signs of scarlet, expecting the pain to hit her at any moment. Those claws, they'd raked right *through* her. She should be shredded. Still halfway curled into herself, she stood trembling, as though waiting for the moment when she would start to fall apart at the seams. That moment never came, though. There was nothing. Maybe she was in shock.

"Miss Lanley, are you ill?"

It was Mr. Nott who asked this. The quiet tone of his voice made her feel suddenly grounded. It only took her a moment to realize that the cafeteria had grown quiet and looking up, she found the whole world staring at her.

Heat flooded her face.

She drew herself sharply upright, gazing into the faces of those who had been eating at the table behind her, the table she'd knocked into. Spilled cups, ruined lunches, and sopping napkins now littered the surface. All eyed her with expressions wavering between indignation and uncertainty. There was a last beat of silence, one final moment of suspended peace. Then Alyssa's voice, clear and curt, sliced through the stillness.

"Oh my *God*, Isobel, you're such a *spaz!*"

Laughter. A loud burst of it shattered the eerie silence. Horrible, torturous, unforgiving laughter. How could she be living this nightmare again?

Isobel ran for the doors. Grinning faces blurred in her peripheral vision. She thought she could hear Brad shouting after her, but she ignored him. She hurried past her own table without even a sideways glance at Gwen, pushed through the double doors, and ran the length of the hall.

She pushed into the girls' restroom, letting the door bang shut behind her. She drew herself up to the middle sink, placing her hands on either side of the basin. She stood there, trying to regulate her breathing, and fought against the urge to puke.

She was cracking up. She was losing her mind right in front of everyone. There was no other excuse for it. What was *wrong* with her?

She couldn't be dreaming right now, could she?

Isobel brought her reluctant gaze up to the mirror. Staring into the deep ocean blue of her own eyes, she had never felt so alone.

"I *need* help," she whispered. Pallid and haggard, she watched her nostrils flare as she took in a longer breath. She let it out through her mouth and shut her eyes. "I know you're there, listening somewhere." She wondered who she was even talking to. Reynolds? Herself? Varen?

"Look," she said, "I'm sorry I wasn't listening before, but I'm listening now. Please. I don't know what's happening to me. I don't know what's real anymore."

The words were out, and Isobel found her eyes opening, shifting to watch, through the mirror, the space over her
shoulder. She waited for something to happen, for him to
appear in front of one of the stall doors, cloaked and shrouded
as he had done before.

"Reynolds!" she whispered, evoking his name.

She heard a creak from behind and drew herself straight.

The bathroom door cracked open, and Gwen stuck her
head in.

"Isobel, we're going to have to talk about what you're
eating for breakfast, because whatever it is, it's doing nothing
for your social life, I can tell you that. Now I'm only going
to ask you this once. Are you all right?"

Isobel stared at her friend's reflection in the mirror.

"I got your book bag," Gwen said. "Despite your standing ovation in there, I didn't think you were gonna come
back to get it. What kinda books you got in this thing, anyway? Feels like you're schlepping around a hard copy of the
Internet."

"Books?" Isobel swung around. All at once, the sight of
Gwen dragging her backpack through the door brought on
a new thought, something that had not occurred to her until
that moment. In the hall, the bell sounded, ending lunch in a
shrill, nerve-frying clatter. "Gwen! You drive to school."

Gwen stopped her struggle with Isobel's bag. "And monkeys throw their poop. Isobel, you're really startin' to scare me."

"Gwen. I need to borrow your car."

"Are you nuts? What for? It's the middle of the day!"

"Please," she said, holding out her hand for the keys.

They snuck into the boiler room, which Mr. Talbot, the janitor, had left open while he cleaned up in the cafeteria. With Gwen in tow, Isobel hurried past the noise and heat of the boiler and through the back door. She shut it behind them and was certain by the click that it made that it had locked automatically. They'd have to find another way back in.

"This is insane," Gwen whispered. "You're gonna get us both suspended."

"You didn't have to come."

"Oh, right, and let you drive off in my dad's Cadillac with nothing but a permit?"

They stooped, sneaking around the side of the building and through the rows of faculty cars toward the student lot. This would be the toughest part, getting in the car and out of the lot without being noticed. The rear of Trenton was covered in windows. Still, her mind was set. If she got caught, then she got caught. She was fairly sure she could talk Gwen out of any major trouble if she had to, since Gwen was one of the school's four National Merit finalists. Right now, though, she had to find Varen, and after her encounter with Pinfeathers, she couldn't exactly say that Gwen's company wasn't welcome.

There was only one other place she could look for Varen, and right now, she didn't care that it was against the rules to leave school grounds. She didn't even care that she was supposed to be ready to perform with the squad in front of the whole school in little more than an hour.

At least she had a plan. She was pretty sure that if they could get away from the school undetected, and if they waited until the end of fifth period to return, when everyone in the school would be banging on lockers and heading to the gym for the pep rally, they might just be able to pull this off.

Ducking low, they wove their way between the rows of vehicles.

"Could have worn something a little less conspicuous," Gwen grumbled behind her.

"It's a pep rally day. I have to wear this!"

They continued on, making their way across the pavement sideways and crouching, like a pair of crabs moving through a desert ghost town.

"That one," Gwen said, and pointed at an old 1990s navy blue Cadillac hunkered in a middle slot. Compared to the two sporty, brightly colored fiberglass cars flanking it, the thing looked more like a tank. Talk about a getaway car.

"Jeez," said Isobel. "What, is your dad in the Mafia?"

"Actually, he's an orthodontist."

They split apart, crossing the last clear drive-through space, Gwen sidling up next to the driver's door and Isobel to the passenger's. They stayed low as Gwen stuck the key in and unlocked the car. She slid inside and, hunching down in the driver's seat, reached across to raise the lock on the passenger side. Isobel grasped the handle and pressed the silver button until she felt the latch give. She shuffled back to open the door but stopped, catching sight of something in the rearview mirror. There was someone else in the parking lot. She turned her head to see.

He sat no more than ten feet away, perched on the hood of a black BMW, another blood-haired boy, dressed in black like Pinfeathers, only it wasn't him. It couldn't have been, because unlike Pinfeathers, this boy wasn't missing his cheek. He was missing an entire eye. Even from a distance, Isobel could see the gaping space where one eye and half his nose should have been.

The boy hadn't seemed to notice either herself or Gwen. He was occupied with eating something, his mouth scarlet with blood. He held the thing, whatever it was, a bloody gray lump, between both hands, his sharp red teeth biting into it, ripping flesh, tearing feathers.

A bird, Isobel realized with dull horror, almost retching. He was eating a bird—one of the fat pigeons that liked to waddle around in the courtyard looking for morsels, never suspecting that it would one day become a morsel itself.

Isobel swung the door open and climbed in. Shutting it fast, she pressed down the lock.

"Go," Isobel said, "drive."

Gwen stuck the key in the ignition and turned. The car complained with a high, grating whine but then rumbled to life. Isobel checked the side-view mirror again, panic stopping her heart when she saw the creature lower the torn, bloody bird and look up.

"Gwen, we need to go. That would be a *now*."

Gwen fumbled to shift the car into reverse. "Why? Is it a teacher?"

Isobel shifted her gaze to the side-view mirror, watching the thing as he sneered and lowered himself onto the pavement, slowly, one boot at a time. She twisted in her seat to look out the back window, but froze when she saw only the rows of parked cars. He was gone.

To Isobel's relief, Gwen pulled fast out of the parking space and, gripping the wheel with both hands, spun them in the direction of the exit.

The bird hit the windshield with a dull splat.

Gwen screamed. Her foot slammed the brakes. They sat for a moment in shock. Then something moved to block out the sunlight on Isobel's side. There came a quiet *tap*, *tap*, *tap* on her window.

"What was that?" Gwen whispered.

Isobel turned her head to look.

There were two of them now. The first one—the one missing an eye—leaned down to bring his existing eye, black and soulless, close to the glass. It blinked at her, watching her like a shark through a tank. The other one stood close behind, grinning, his face whole but split by a diagonal hairline crack. He had only one arm.

Isobel felt every muscle in her body tense as she stared into that eye, a predator's eye, she thought. Slowly he raised one fist and stuck his thumb out. He aimed it, like a hitch-hiker, in the direction they were pointed.

Isobel pawed at Gwen, who watched the mutilated

pigeon slide down the windshield, leaving behind a gooey streak.

"Gwen," she said. It was a plea.

The creature without the eye grabbed at the door now, looping his fingers through the handle. Had she locked it? Yes, she thought, as he pulled and the latch stuck. Thank God, she had.

Without warning, Gwen's foot hit the gas pedal and they accelerated. Thrown backward in her seat, Isobel heard the creature hiss as it wrenched its hand away in a movement too quick for her eyes to follow. Gwen's tires squealed as they sped out of the parking lot and onto the main road, being caught by school authorities having been bumped down to the bottom of their list of concerns.

Out of habit, Isobel reached behind her and yanked down on her seat belt. She clicked it into place, turning again to look over her shoulder through the rear window. Dead leaves swirled in the wind tunnel they made with their escape, the trees lining the streets receding into the distance. As far as she could see, they weren't being followed. She turned to face forward and caught a glimpse of Gwen's face, pale and frightened.

"I still get the impression there's something you're not telling me," Gwen said, her eyes pinched as she strained to see past the dead pigeon and its belly, open against the glass to display the stark white of its rib cage. Isobel looked away, suddenly glad she hadn't had time to eat anything at lunch. She leaned forward in her seat to try and find the switch for the windshield wipers. The bird looked heavy, but hopefully that would work.

"Turn right at the next light," Isobel said, by accident flipping the windshield wiper fluid release. Sudsy blue liquid squirted across the glass, soaking the pigeon.

"Oh, gross," Gwen muttered, and batted Isobel's hand away. She slowed the car and switched on the wipers, her fingers easily finding the right knob. It took four swipes to get the bird to one side, and then a fifth and final one to scoot it off the windshield completely. It hit the roadside with a wet smack. "Should have stayed home today," said Gwen, taking the turn Isobel had indicated. "Rented a movie. One of those bad romances that make you want to puke. 'Course I already want to puke."

She glanced from the road to Isobel, then back again, her brow furrowing. The silence that followed gave Isobel time to think. At this point she couldn't keep Gwen out, but at the same time, she couldn't justify involving her any further. She thought about Pinfeathers sitting next to Brad in the lunchroom, then pictured him sitting here in her place, next to Gwen, who would just keep driving, never knowing any better. She thought about Gwen driving home. She thought about the Cadillac on the highway, about how it wouldn't take much more than a gentle tug on the steering wheel to send the car careening into oncoming traffic.

"Left here." Isobel pointed.

Gwen put on her signal. She pulled into the left turning lane. The arrow flicked green.

"Isobel, did you really see something in the lunchroom today," she asked, "or were you just playing around?"

Isobel swallowed, not sure if she should answer. How *could* she answer? As far as she knew, the line "I see dead people" had already been taken.

"Did that bird hit my window on purpose? 'Cause you know, I don't think I can take much of that. Not without the promise of sending you my therapy bills later. Are you listening to me, Isobel?"

"Just a bird," Isobel murmured. She turned away from the lie to look out her window.

They passed a group of college students on the right, huddled on the sidewalk, waiting for the crosswalk light to change. Isobel envied them. They all looked so normal in their jackets and blue jeans, scarves lacing their necks, hands stuffed in their pockets, probably talking about their next class or Halloween plans, totally unaware.

"Turn here," said Isobel automatically when they reached the intersection to Bardstown Road. Gwen swerved to make the turn. Either she still had the jitters or she was mad.

"There," she said, pointing for Gwen to pull over. Gwen followed the order. She put the Cadillac in park, turned off the engine, and pulled the keys into her lap.

Isobel grabbed the door handle, and Gwen, apparently not willing to wait in the car, got out too. Together they stepped up to the front of the tiny used bookstore.

Varen had to be here, Isobel thought. There was nowhere else for him to go. If he left school, this was where he would come. He would be here, and she could tell him everything. With that thought stoking her courage, Isobel opened the door and stepped inside. Gwen followed.

She caught that familiar, heavy scent of stale air, and the rusty belt of bells clanked as the door shut behind them.

"What is this place?" Gwen whispered. "What are we doing here? Whoa, is that a first edition?"

Isobel raised a finger to her lips. She led the way, and they wove through the shelves toward the vacant counter, stepping over stacks of books, finding neither Bruce nor Varen.

Then she heard that familiar rattling cough. It came from somewhere at the rear of the shop. Isobel followed the sound across the rickety floor and into the back room, stacked with all the newer-looking nonfiction. Bruce was there between the rows, taking books one at a time out of a cardboard box marked NON-FIC WILDLIFE in Varen's careful, antique scrawl. He brought each book he drew out of the box up close to his face and examined it with a sweep of his good eye before finding a place for it on the shelf.

Isobel stood in the doorway, waiting to be noticed, not wanting to startle him. A distracted Gwen bumped into her from behind, unleashing a muffled *"Oof"* that made Isobel sure then that they were being ignored.

"Excuse me, Mr. Bruce? I'm looking for Var—"

"Not here," he grunted, continuing to shelve. Isobel was taken aback. This was not the kind-if-loopy man she remembered from her last visit.

"Do you know where he is?" she tried, moving closer to him. Gwen remained in place, watching, her car keys clinking between nervous fingers.

"If I did, I wouldn't tell you."

Isobel frowned, unsure where his sudden dislike had come from. Didn't he remember her? "I—I think he could be trouble."

"Could be!" he scoffed. He lowered the book in his hand, finally looking at her. He scrutinized her with his good eye, frowning at her cheer uniform. Then the coughing ensued once more, harsher, mucus rattling in his chest. "I think a bloody nose . . . and a busted lip says . . . that the trouble's already found him. Guess the thing you'll tell me next is that you hadn't anything to do with that."

Brad. He'd been telling the truth. But how could that be when she'd seen Varen only an hour ago? His face—*he* had been fine.

Bruce scowled at her, apparently taking her silence for confirmation of whatever suspicions he'd been harboring. His mouth tightened into a line, quivering with anger. "I told you now, I don't know where he's got to. Hasn't said a word to me since he came in like that this morning. Went upstairs and slept till noon. Missed school. Left a half hour ago. Go upstairs and look for yourself."

Isobel, her mind dulling as it tried to compute the barrage of conflicting information, actually turned to the attic door. She was stopped from making any progress toward it, though, by a soft hand on her arm. "Isobel," said Gwen.

"C'mon. He's not here. We would have seen his car outside. We gotta go."

Isobel turned to stare at Bruce again, trying to gauge if he was telling the truth. If Varen had left only a half hour ago, how could he have been at school to do the project? How could anyone be in two places at once? Maybe Bruce had it wrong, she thought. He was old. Old people got mixed up, right?

"Aren't you supposed to be in school?" He waved them toward the door as though shooing flies. "I'll call the police, if that's what you want."

"Isobel . . ." Gwen's hand on her arm tightened, and Isobel took an involuntary step in the direction her friend pulled. "C'mon," she said, "we'll see him tonight, remember?"

For a moment Bruce's good eye seemed to lighten in surprise. It flashed a glimmer of hope, but like a dying ember, the spark faded, dissolving into bitterness and then defeat. He shook his head. "I'm too old to worry about him like this. You tell him I said that. You tell him . . ."

The coughing again. He was sick. Really sick.

Isobel stood in place and watched him, unable to do much else. The coughing continued, unrelenting in its attack, and without saying a word, he brushed past them into the main room. He hobbled toward the counter and reached for a box of tissues. Isobel trailed after him, torn. She wanted to reach out, to help him to his chair behind the counter, just as she could envision Varen doing. She wanted to tell him that she was sorry and that it wasn't her fault and that she'd find Varen. She bit her tongue, though, knowing that it *was* her fault. She'd seen all of this coming, or at least part of it. Pinfeathers had said as much before he tried to slice her to ribbons. And, in truth, deep down, how could she be certain she *would* find him?

Isobel pushed that thought quickly aside. She *would* find him. She would see him tonight.

She felt it.

Bruce found his chair on his own. He rocked backward into it, as if the joints of his knees no longer worked. Clouds of dust plumed around him, worsening his cough. He glowered at Isobel, as if the sudden fit were somehow her fault. "You . . . don't deserve him."

Isobel's breath lodged in her throat, the truth she feared most let out of its cage in an instant.

"Isobel," Gwen said, pulling at her arm again. "C'mon, we've got to get back."

Isobel shoved away from the counter. She yanked her arm out of Gwen's grasp and hurried through the front door. A burst of cold air hit her in the face, like a splash of fresh water. She took in a huge gulp, sucking as much oxygen into her belly as she brought into her lungs.

Behind her, Gwen emerged from the shop. "Don't listen to him, Isobel," she said, "he's just worried, is all."

"Gwen, I have to find him. I have to be there tonight."

Her face solemn, Gwen nodded, as if she'd come to understand this on her own. "Don't worry," she said, "we'll find him."

34
Caught

They made it back inside the school by sneaking in through the art wing. The sound of banging lockers thrummed, echoed by the approaching drumbeats of the marching band and color guard preparing for their Pied Piper pilgrimage through the gold-and-blue-streaked halls. Kids flooded out of open classroom doors, boys jumping to tap the doorways for luck, girls screaming.

Together Gwen and Isobel melded into the masses, then split courses—Isobel heading to the locker rooms, Gwen joining a group heading down from the eastern stairwell. On the drive back, they'd agreed to meet up again at the game that night. And as Isobel watched her friend go, she offered a small wave, wondering if Gwen would be glad to be rid of her for a while.

She slipped into the locker room unnoticed except by Nikki, who watched her curiously while they went through warm-ups. She sent a tentative smile, which Isobel did her best to return, though she had long since lost her appetite for a pep rally. The whole thing suddenly seemed stupid to her as it never had before, the idea of everyone getting together to scream and act crazy.

Out in the gym, she heard the marching band arrive. The rat-a-tat thumping of the drums traveled into her bones, sounding in her ears more like a funeral march than a rallying call. The squad ran out together as one, the rhythm pulsing through her body and the lights blaring. Everyone shouted as they piled in, feet stomping until the bleachers rattled and squeaked on their steel supports. Balloons waved, banners shook, painted faces laughed. It was like a mad carnival where everyone was oblivious, lost in the bliss of chaos, a throng unaware of a bomb planted beneath the floorboards.

Two hours ago Isobel would have happily been one of them.

She stood in front of the crowd, mechanically clapping and shouting with the squad. She scanned the risers for any signs of a cloaked figure or yet another porcelain-faced demon.

"When I say Trenton, you say Hawks! Trenton!"

"Hawks!"

"Trenton!"

"Hawks!"

The crowd thundered, their voices booming, calling for blood.

As the squad began their stunts, Varen's image continued to haunt Isobel, and more than once, she struggled to keep the count. Stevie, standing as third base, whispered to her almost every time. "All right, Iz?" he asked just before the load.

"Yeah," she said, even though she had never been less right.

Dip. Toss. Isobel popped into the air, propelled high. She opened her legs, hitting a toe touch. The cradle caught her and her sneakers found the floor. The crowd cheered. The squad clapped, shouting a steady rhythm of, "Let's go Trenton, let's go!" Clap! Clap!

Someone announced the football team. Clad in their blue and gold numbered jerseys, they sprang through the gym doors like a herd of oxen and pounded across the gym floor, spreading out like a conquering army, like they'd already won. The stands exploded with riotous shouts of favorite numbers—Brad's number, number twenty-one, prominent among the calls. Isobel saw him then, the last one out of the double doors. Following behind the rest of the team, Brad half jogged, half walked.

Isobel watched him as the team took their place on the bleachers, piling up the rows, but then Henry the Hawk ran by her, flapping his wings, and Isobel jumped, letting out a small yelp.

Coach Anne's whistle blew, and it was time for the squad's routine.

The drums rumbled for action. Isobel walked to her place in the formation. Alyssa bumped her as they passed and leaned in to whisper, "Try not to screw us up, spaz."

The squad gathered. They all brought their arms up, crisscrossed in front of their faces, their hands made into fists. Coach Anne's proud microphone announcement echoed around them, telling everyone how this would be Trenton's routine for the cheer Nationals, the one they'd started over the summer, the one the squad would perform again tonight at the game, and then for real in Dallas in less than two months, the one that would bring Trenton the first-place trophy for the third time in three consecutive years. The crowd filled each of Coach's pauses with screams of enthusiasm. Trenton liked to win.

The music started with a reverberating synthesizer blast that morphed into a fixed beat, electronic and fast. Isobel let her body go to the memory of routine and she was in the air, whirling before she could recall how. Caught, dipped down, then shooting up again, like a stalk through a tangle of weeds. Her body stiff, she raised her arms in a high V; then, extending her leg out, twisted it behind her head, grabbing the toe of her tennis shoe. She went into a Scorpion, her back arching, her rib cage extending out. The stretch felt good.

She felt the dip, and instinctively, on the pop, she went into the tight, spiraling twist of a double-down. Her bases caught her, and Stevie set her back on her feet. Everyone was on the floor now, and the squad wound around one another, in and out like a deck of self-shuffling cards, a montage of blue and gold, their footsteps matching the beat, their arms fanning out and snapping in. They reorganized, the base of the pyramid preparing for the load. Isobel climbed up, one foot sliding into Alyssa's awaiting grasp, the other into Nikki's. Then, extended high, she raised her arms in another V. She felt her foot wobble, and she stiffened. They completed the pyramid within three seconds, almost as tight as Coach had drilled it.

The music ended with the sound effect of a dynamite explosion. The squad held their pose to the eruption of deafening cheers.

Isobel felt her foot wobble again, enough this time for her to glance down. Her eyes locked with Nikki's—two spheres of utter panic, her face flushed pink with effort. Isobel felt a strange pang from somewhere within her gut. Not at the sight of Nikki's distress, but at the white porcelain hand wrapped tight around Nikki's left wrist.

"Hello, cheerleader," she heard a voice say, though she could not tear her eyes away from Nikki, transfixed by her pained struggle to keep Isobel aloft.

Nikki's wrist jerked back, and she uttered a clipped cry. Isobel sank fast.

She floundered, arms wheeling as she toppled forward. The world rushed up around her. She heard the crowd gasp and then someone's strangled cry of, "Catch her!"

Images and silhouettes floated around her, blurred in tints of fuzzy white and muted gray, as though her eyes had gone permanently unfocused. She had the distant sensation of hands pressing against her from behind, supporting her weight, and she could decipher only the formless face of someone she thought she might know. Coach? Even though it looked as though the figure was shouting at her, Isobel could only register a small, indistinct sound, and the shape of her name being formed on those lips.

Then, like a black shadow, another figure drifted into her

focus, this one clearer, though still frayed at the edges. With a surge of terror, she realized that it was one of those creatures.

He smiled jaggedly at her, and Isobel writhed to pull away from the hands that held her. The creature drifted closer, and she found that she could not pull away. Vaguely, she thought she heard one of the gray, muted ghost figures saying her name, instructing her to lie still.

Isobel stared, powerless to break free as the creature's face, a white collage of angles and serrated points, drifted close to hers. Behind him, she saw more shadowy figures collect to line the backdrop of white and gray that resembled the school gymnasium.

She squirmed, her eyes following the creature's movements as he lifted one clawed hand. He reached toward her, his talons—his entire hand—entering her chest, passing straight through her as though she were made of nothing but air.

She felt a clutch in her body and then a heavy, dragging sensation, as though she was being peeled away from herself. For a moment everything went double. The gray shapes and the black outlines multiplied into a sea of forms.

There was a scraping metal sound, followed by the creature's shriek. The angular, disjointed shadow of his presence fell away from her, and a shattering crash sent the remaining black figures fleeing. They dispersed into swirls of black-violet fog, and instantly Isobel was back in the world of nebulous, blurry images.

With another scrape of metal, her savior came to stoop beside her, black eyes set against the white shroud of his scarf.

"You must realize," he said, "that I am not a dog to be called."

"You."

"Yes, me."

"Where am I?"

"Between realms." He looked around. "This is very dangerous. You could become trapped. You must go back immediately."

"What's happening? What are those things? How come only I can see them?"

His eyes returned to her. "They are called Nocs. Ghouls. Dark creatures from the dreamworld . . ." His voice trailed off. "There is no time."

"Where is Varen?"

"Lost."

"No!"

"Isobel, you must go back."

"I won't. Not without him."

"He is yet in your world." He paused. "There is still a chance. All is lost only if you stay. Go."

"What about you?"

"I may reach your world easily now. I will be near."

"Reynolds, wait. You . . . This all has something to do with—"

"Isobel, this isn't the time. They will return. Go now, while you can."

As he swept away, Isobel blinked, and color broke through the whiteness. She blinked again, staring up into the huddle of people around her, the shapes of her squad mates becoming clearer, sharper. The white noise of a murmuring crowd flowed into her ears, like someone turning up the volume on a TV.

"Who's she talking to?" someone asked.

She closed her eyes against the brightness, then, opening them, recognized Stevie's face first, then Nikki's, red and blotchy, streaked with tears, then finally, closest of all, Coach's, pale with worry.

Together their heads made a neat sort of shape with the light, kind of like a lopsided four leafed clover. She sure could use a little bit of luck right about now.

"I'm sorry, Isobel! I'm so sorry!" Nikki blubbered. "I dunno what happened! I—I just—"

Coach turned. "Will someone please get her out of here? Stevie, go take Nikki out in the hall and see if you can get her to calm down. Splash some water on her face. Isobel, sweetheart," she went on, "how many fingers?"

Isobel groaned. Did people honestly do that test in real life?

"Four."

Coach checked her open hand, then craned her neck to squint at the other squad members. "Are you all sure you didn't see her hit her head?"

"I thought she just passed out." It was Jason who spoke that time.

Isobel groaned again and used her elbows to sit up. She glanced around, looking for Reynolds.

"Hold still, Izzy," said Coach, holding a hand out to stay her. "I think you'd better lie back for a second. Four's not quite right."

Isobel sat up anyway. This was utterly mortifying. How and when had she become such a freak show? "Yes, it is," she said. "A thumb's not a finger."

To her surprise and relief, Coach laughed, rocking back on her heels to allow Isobel some space.

"She's okay!" shouted someone from the squad—probably Stephanie. Clapping all around. *Yes*, Isobel thought, as Coach helped her up, then led her off the court and into the locker room, *A-OK, thanks for asking*. She raised a hand to show the masses she'd live.

"You know she's just doing it on purpose" came Alyssa's sour voice from behind as she trailed them, arms folded. Isobel turned to scowl over one shoulder at her as Alyssa added, "She did the same thing at lunch today."

"That's enough, Alyssa," Coach said. "Go check on Nikki."

Alyssa smiled to herself, then spun away with a sweep of her platinum ponytail.

"Iz, are you okay?" Coach asked.

"Yeah, I'm fine. I slipped."

"You're sure?"

Isobel nodded.

"You know," said Coach as she pushed the door open, ushering her into the locker room. She bent to retrieve a water bottle from the cooler and, twisting the top off, handed it to Isobel. Isobel took a long swig, gulping down half the bottle before lowering it again. "I don't know what's going on between you and Alyssa, but whatever it is, I tell you, Izzy, you both had better find a way to patch it up and fast. I'll leave your butts here and we'll go to Dallas without the two of you, and don't think we won't."

Isobel nodded, even though right now, Dallas and Nationals were the furthest things from her mind.

"Certainly Nikki is upset, and I don't think you'd do something like that on purpose—pull a stunt like that—but let me also say that if there's any truth to what Alyssa just said—"

Isobel looked up. "I didn't fall on purpose," she said, her voice rising. She looked down again, not wanting it to seem like she was trying to pick an argument.

"Good," Coach said. "Because I don't have any time for drama queens, and neither does anybody else on this squad. Now listen, you're not stunting tonight, but I still want you at the game anyway. Is that clear? You can join in for the cheers, but I don't want you flying."

Isobel scowled as she was unceremoniously handed the role of benchwarmer. She knew this meant that Alyssa's words had carried more weight with Coach than her own, and the thought of it burned her. But she nodded in spite of herself because there were bigger things to worry about now than her rivalry with Alyssa or her place on the squad.

And far more important things at stake, too.

35
Tell-Tale Heart

The stadium lights glared camera-flash bright suspended above the sea of gathered faces. Isobel sat on a bench on the sidelines, her back facing the crowd. Somewhere behind her, her father sat in the stands, watching the game.

To her relief, her dad hadn't said much of anything after reading the note from Coach about her little trip to the floor. He'd only picked up drive-through fried chicken (which Isobel had devoured in the car, starved from skipping lunch) and asked her if she was sure she wanted to go to the game. When she'd said yes without hesitation, he'd seemed satisfied, and for once he'd said no more. He didn't even mention her supposed "accident" to her mom once they got home. Instead he kept the spotlight of their dinner conversation on the success of the project. Then talk switched easily to the scary movie party Danny was going to with his Boy Scout troop later that night, after trick-or-treating. It seemed that her mom would be going too, since they'd come up short on chaperones at the last minute. Consequently, Varen's name never came up, and it was this one omission that Isobel felt most grateful for.

Even now, though, sitting on the cold bench, watching grass grow as the game played, she couldn't keep him from her thoughts. For the first time in her cheer life, Isobel found that she couldn't care less who they were playing, let alone what the scoreboards showed. Only she knew that she hadn't insisted on attending the game out of some sense of duty or school pride that might have motivated her before, but because this had been the predetermined point of rendezvous with Gwen. She hadn't seen any sign of her yet, though, and the closer it got to halftime, the more Isobel began to fidget.

Every few minutes she scanned the stands behind her, keeping a watchful eye out for more of those creatures—what had Reynolds called them? Nocs? How many of those things *were* there, anyway? Distractedly, she wondered why she hadn't seen any of them since she'd left school. She wanted to think that it was a good sign, but that felt like a false hope.

On the field, the squad disbanded and let the marching band take over. Isobel turned to look toward the stands again, this time hoping to find some evidence of Reynolds's presence. He said he'd be near, but where? Why did he always have to be so cryptic?

"Iz?" She felt the sensation of someone taking the seat next to her. She turned.

Nikki gazed at her, her dark blue eyes wide, her eyebrows knitted together. She cradled her wrist, which had been wrapped tightly in beige gauze.

"Hey, Nikki," Isobel offered. "Let me guess. Coach benched you, too?"

"Yeah," she said, holding up her bandaged wrist. "Sprained. Not too bad, though. Do—do you care if I sit here?"

Isobel shook her head, and they sat for a moment in uncomfortable silence.

"Isobel," Nikki started, "I didn't think I was going to come tonight. But I decided to at the last second because I knew you'd be here. And I have to tell you this. I—I know you won't believe me, but I still have to say it. No matter what you think, I—I didn't drop you today. At least not on purpose."

"I know," said Isobel simply. She turned again to look over her shoulder. She wished the game was over. She wished she could fast-forward through time so that she and Gwen could be on their way to wherever the Grim Facade was surely starting. She wanted to find Varen, to see his face, to know that he was all right. She wanted to know the truth about what was happening. She wanted to know how to make it stop. How to just be normal again.

"No. I mean, I didn't. I swear. I'll swear on anything. It was like . . . It was like something had hold of me." She grabbed her bound wrist for emphasis. "I know it sounds crazy, but—"

"Nikki." Isobel turned to meet her gaze straight on. "I believe you."

Nikki's tortured expression melted into worried confusion, as though she half expected Isobel to take her statement back. This reaction made Isobel realize that Nikki had been spending far too much time hanging around Alyssa.

"Does . . . does that mean you're—that you're not mad at me anymore?"

Wouldn't go as far as to say that, Isobel thought. Wasn't stabbing you in the back and running off with your ex the first two no-nos listed on the first page of the best friend bible? Then again, Isobel wondered—why not? What did any of it matter now if Nikki wanted to make up? She and Brad were over, the crew was over. These days it was starting to seem as though reality itself was over. If the sky was falling, wasn't it better if Ducky Lucky and Loosey Goosey hugged and made up beforehand? Isobel opted for a noncommittal shrug but then, embarrassed by the stinginess of her gesture, added, "No. Not really."

"I miss you," Nikki said. "I miss us."

Looking down between her shoes, Isobel nodded, not certain if she could say the same. She had too much else swirling around in her head. Too much had happened since they fought. Too much that she could never tell Nikki. Nikki and her, well, that all seemed like a lifetime ago. How could she explain to her that she was different? Changed. And that right now she could think of only one person she could truly say she missed.

"I'm jealous, you know."

Isobel's head popped up, eyes angled toward Nikki, who smiled at her. A sweet and sad sort of smile. Isobel was guarded. "What do you mean?"

Nikki shook her head, her eyes glistening. She swept a manicured thumb at each, then laughed instead. "Everyone's jealous of you, Isobel."

Isobel blinked several times, uncertain how to react.

"But I'm jealous because . . . well, because I've never known what it feels like to be in love."

Isobel stiffened. All at once, she ceased to breathe.

"Oh," said Nikki, laughing. She swept at her eyes again, this time with the knuckle of her first finger, trying to save her mascara. "Don't look at me like that. You're not that clueless." She laughed harder then, though, Isobel thought, more in an effort to keep from crying.

"I guess maybe you are," Nikki amended, taking in the stricken look on Isobel's face. "At least for once I'm not the last one to know something." She laughed genuinely now, and her mirth was so contagious, the weight of her words so startlingly plain, that in spite of everything, Isobel found that she had to laugh too.

In love. In love with the stoic, the sullen, the eternally morose Varen Nethers?

He would never allow it.

Isobel sobered quickly. Suddenly the prospect of seeing him became terrifying, because she knew it was true and that the only way she'd hidden it from him before was because she had never allowed herself to put her feelings into words. And Nikki, the least perceptive being on this planet, had seen through it all.

"Hey, Izzy!"

Isobel jumped, nearly bouncing off the bench. She and Nikki both swung around.

Isobel's dad was there, leaning against the fence. He waved her over.

Isobel stood, murmuring, "Be right back," to Nikki, who remained where she was while Isobel jogged to meet her father. She was glad for an excuse to leave the bench, glad for a moment to recover.

"What's going on with you guys tonight? You're choking out there. Major."

"What?" Was he talking about the squad? She hadn't been paying attention.

"You guys are losing. Big-time. Haven't you been watching the score?" He pointed.

Were they really losing? Isobel scanned the scoreboard. Wow. Thirty-one to zero. They *were* losing.

"Hey, what's the deal with Brad out there?"

"Brad?"

"Yeah." He folded his arms over the top of the fence, trying to act nonchalant now that he'd brought up the *B* word. "Didn't you see him drop the ball? Have you been sleeping out there on that bench or what? This is the worst I think I've ever seen him play."

Isobel looked around for Brad now. She saw him standing with the team on the sidelines, filling up a cup of water and pouring it down his shirt, despite the chill of the fifty-degree night.

While the rest of the team headed for the locker rooms, Coach Logan, his face purple, stood two heads below Brad, berating him the way a yappy dog might bark at a squirrel up a tree.

"Sheesh. Looks like Coach is really laying it on thick,"

Isobel's dad said. "Hey, Iz, I'm not trying to get in the middle of things here, but maybe you should go talk to him. See what's going on?"

"Isobel! There you are!"

Isobel turned her head, her eyes narrowing on the blue-and-gold-decked, pom-pom-pigtailed stranger who now bounced toward her along the other side of the fence. Holy cheer catastrophes — it was Gwen.

"Isobel!" she shrieked again, and bounded to a stop beside her dad. She threw her arms over her head, the sleeves of her impossibly huge sweatshirt waggling — no, Isobel corrected as she took note of the yellow *T* — the sleeves of *Stevie's* impossibly huge sweatshirt. Isobel stepped back from the fence to give Gwen an astonished once-over. She'd never once seen her friend in a pair of pants, let alone anything resembling school colors (did Gwen even own a pair of pants?). After closer scrutiny, Isobel couldn't help but notice a certain familiarity about the Trenton sweats she wore. They looked a lot like the ones she herself had shed earlier in the locker room. And then there were the long pigtails, held up by a set of equally familiar blue and gold pom-pom hair-ties. Suddenly it was easy to figure out where Gwen had been all this time.

"Omigosh, is this your dad? Hey, Mr. Lanley!" Gwen slung one wiry arm around his shoulders.

"Um, yeah," Isobel began, not sure where Gwen was going with this, "Dad, this is Gwen. She's, uh . . . she's . . ." *Mentally whacked*, Isobel wanted to say.

"I'm the mascot escort," said Gwen. She flashed her

perfectly straight white teeth in a wide grin. "I babysit the mascot," she added.

"Ah," Dad began. He twisted to look around as much as Gwen's friendly grip on his shoulders would allow. "Where is the mascot, then?"

"Oh, he's around here somewhere . . . molting or something, I dunno. So, Iz, are you coming to my victory party or what? You never answered my Facebook invite."

"Victory party?" her dad echoed.

All at once, Gwen's genius dawned on her.

"Ohh," Isobel chimed in, sounding appropriately glum. "I forgot to respond. I haven't been online much because I've been really busy trying to finish that English project, y'know? Anyway, Gwen, I don't think I can go."

"*What?*" Gwen deflated, her face crumbling in an instant. For added emphasis, she let her arm slip from Dad's shoulders, where it flopped against her side. "Why not? Didn't you get the project done?"

Isobel shrugged. "I got it done. I mean, thanks to Dad. I just . . ." She sent a pitiful glance to her father. *Yes,* she thought, catching a glimmer of indecision in his eyes. They just had to play it up a *little* more. "I just don't know if I can."

"Oohhhh," Gwen said, looking between Isobel and her dad, feigning sudden understanding.

"How can you have a victory party if your team's losing?" her dad asked.

"Wait, we're losing?" Gwen craned her neck in search of the scoreboard.

"Where's this party going to be?"

Isobel sprang on her chance. "Omigosh, Dad, for real, can I go?"

"Yeah, Dad, for real, can she go?"

"I just asked where it was going to be—"

"My house," Gwen said, "all-girls' sleepover, no guys allowed."

"Are your parents going to be there?"

"Oh, they're there right now, setting up the karaoke machine." Gwen mimed holding a microphone and swayed against Isobel's father. "Fame! I'm gonna live forever—take it away, Mr. Lanley."

Isobel's dad set a hand on Gwen's offered fist, gently pushing it down from his face. "Who else is going?"

Gwen pointed at the figure waiting on the bench. "She is."

"Nikki is going?" he asked, looking at Isobel, surprised. "I thought you two were on the fritz."

"Oh," Isobel said. She saw Nikki rise from the bench and start over toward them, probably at hearing her name. Thinking fast, Isobel blurted, "We made up."

"Nikki!" shouted Gwen. "You're coming, right?"

"What?" she called back, eyeing Gwen's getup.

"To the party," Isobel said, nodding, trying to communicate meaning through her eyes. Despite her recent show of perceptiveness, Isobel couldn't see Nikki picking up the clue phone to get the message. "You know," Isobel went on, "the party Gwen's having tonight."

"*You're* having a party?" Nikki asked, studying Gwen. "Hey, isn't that Stevie's sweatshirt?"

Uh-oh.

"Dad might let me go now," said Isobel, nodding again. Lots of nodding.

Nikki's eyes remained on Isobel's, searching, things still not fully clicking. "Well . . . okay," she said finally.

"Someone taking you there tonight?" he asked, checking the time on his cell phone.

Isobel felt a leap of joy in her chest. He was going to let her go.

"She can ride with me," said Gwen. Good old Gwen. Good old brilliant, inventive, industrious Gwen.

"And Nikki can bring me home in the morning," Isobel added.

He sighed, and she knew that his resolve had already crumbled. She launched up into a fit of jumping and squealing, forgetting for half a second that she wasn't really going to a girls' sleepover, that right now she was tricking him, lying to her dad after everything. Again. A stab of guilt grounded her.

"In that case," he said, "I'm going to go ahead and get out of here. It doesn't look like the score is going to change any time soon. Maybe I can catch the end of the U of K game on TV. Think there'll be any candy left on the porch?"

"I wouldn't count on it," Isobel said, trying to resurrect her smile. He held his arms open for a hug, and Isobel reached over the top of the gate and stood on her toes to wrap her arms around his shoulders. "Thanks, Daddy," she said, pulling him tight and kissing his cheek.

"Be good and keep your phone on," he said, shoving his own phone back into his pocket. "And don't forget to check on Brad."

"I won't," she promised.

He turned away and Isobel watched him as he went, blending into the crowd.

She felt her heart sink as she lowered her heels to the ground. She wished she could call him back, that she could tell him the truth. That he would believe her.

"Okay, for real," Nikki said as soon as he was out of earshot. "What was *that* all about?"

After Isobel's dad left, Gwen went off to change and meet up with Mikey in the parking lot. In the meantime, the squad took their position on the field, ready to once again perform the Nationals routine. Isobel, on the sidelines, waited for the music to start before telling Nikki she would be right back and sliding from the bench. She heard the familiar beats blast through the stadium speakers, and she couldn't help mentally tracing through her moves.

She could hear the crowd's cheering escalate (probably for the back tuck the squad did in a fanning wave), and slipped behind the brick siding of the home-side stands. She trailed her hand along the Hawk emblem painted over brick, moving more quickly now that she was out of direct sight, and hurried toward the entrance to the football locker room.

Coach Logan's voice grated loudly from within. Could he *still* be yelling at the team?

Isobel drew up to the entrance and placed one hand on the archway, huddling up close to listen. She certainly didn't have to strain to hear.

"Now I don't know what you ballerinas are doing out there, but that scoreboard better change in this next quarter, or so help me, I'll scout JV for replacements! And, Borgon, I hope I don't need to tell you again that when you catch the damn ball, you're supposed to hold on to it! You got that? Is that clear? Now all of you, get your butts out there and turn this thing around!"

A unanimous scuffling noise came from within, players rushing off their benches. Isobel had to step back as a burst of team members emerged, escaping through the archway like steam from a pressure cooker. They shouldered and bumped their way through the door and past one another. Silent and moody, not a one of them seemed to notice her. She stood to one side, her back against the cold concrete wall. She hoped to remain invisible as she searched each back for the number twenty-one.

Brad's number was not among them, though. He must still be inside the locker room. Isobel waited, and after a moment, Coach Logan came out. He turned and looked right at her, his ruddy face contorting into what she took as a dirty look. Isobel, resisting the urge to glower back, concentrated instead on the space between her sneakers while he stormed off toward the field.

Isobel left the wall. She slipped quietly into the narrow doorway and down the three steps that led into the locker room. The air here turned humid, saturated with the smell of sweat, grass, and dirt. When she took in a breath, the air felt thick in her lungs, as though it held no oxygen. It was like entering a sauna.

Brad sat alone on a bench in the middle, his helmet in his hands, head hung, his hair plastered with sweat to his forehead. Wet, his hair was the color of old pennies.

Isobel stepped toward him, surprised when he didn't look up.

"Brad," she said, announcing herself, her voice even.

His stare remained fixed on his helmet. He turned it slowly in his hands until he was looking into the inside.

"Brad," she repeated, and moved in farther, something about the cooling sheen of sweat over his skin making the blister on his upper lip redden. Or was it that he seemed suddenly so pale?

She stopped to stand in front of him, her eyes falling to peer into his helmet, at the black foam padding lining the inside. She lowered herself to crouch in front of him and placed her hands on his wrists. She looked up, into his face. "Brad, are you okay?"

His eyes lifted to hers, and Isobel felt a surge of terror. Dilated pupils, wide and black, eclipsed almost entirely the bright blue of his irises, so they appeared as no more than thin halos, slim rings of color around two holes of unreflective blackness.

"Don't touch me," he snapped, and shook away from her as he stood. Knocked off balance, Isobel stumbled to her feet. He spun from her, moving for the door.

"Brad, wait!"

"Tell them to leave me alone!" he shouted, and ran up the stairs.

Shocked, Isobel watched him retreat through the archway. She ran to catch up, climbing the three steps, only to find her path blocked. Mark. He glared at her, helmet in hand, his face stern and set, a smear of black paint streaked beneath each eye.

Isobel bounced on her toes and strained to see over the padded shelf of his shoulder. She saw Brad nearing the field, watched him brace one hand to his forehead. The air around him seemed to shift and shimmer. Isobel blinked to clear her vision, but that only served to sharpen the dark, snakelike tendrils of oily smoke that now emerged from nothing. Like clouds of violet ink in water, dark figures took form, pouring into shape through the air around him. All at once, several sets of black boots strode forth. Four white-faced figures fell into stride behind him, two on either side, their sharp red smiles gleaming.

"Omigod, Brad!"

Isobel burst forward, but Mark barred her with a thick arm. She struggled against him. He held her, gathering her momentum, then using it to sling her back. Isobel half tripped, half staggered down the stairs again, catching herself against one wall.

"I don't know what you did," he said, "but just stay away from him."

Isobel stared at him in stunned silence, long enough to watch him turn his back. She waited only one moment more, then rushed forward, up the stairs and out, determined to bolt past him. He must have heard the beat of her sneakers, though, or maybe he'd expected her to try something, because he swung around. Dropping his helmet, he caught her, flinging her back with the full force of both arms. Isobel hurtled backward, her arms freewheeling. She hit the concrete, landing on her rear with a decided thud. Grit bit into the palms of her hands.

She cringed and drew a sharp breath through clenched teeth as the burn set in on her skinned palms. Mark glowered down at her, his expression void of either regret or concern. He bent to retrieve his helmet and then, for the third time, he started for the field.

"Mark, wait!" she called, trying to keep the hurt from seeping into her voice. Even if they weren't friends now, they had been once—at least to some degree.

Isobel struggled to her feet. She caught up to him, hovering a safe distance behind until they were in view of the stands, knowing her chances of getting slugged would be less within the direct sight of parents and coaches. "Listen to me. You don't understand!"

Her eyes darted between his back and the players collecting on the field. The announcer's voice echoed over the sound system, reviewing the score. She saw Brad make his way with the other players toward center field. Securing his helmet in place, he clutched it to his head, gripping either side as though he hoped to block out the world. He didn't look back, and Isobel realized that he could not see the dark forms that trailed him.

"Mark," she said, catching hold of his arm.

"Get off me!" he shouted, jerking away.

"You have to tell Coach Logan to pull Brad!" she insisted. She caught hold of him again. "You have to!"

"I said, don't touch me!" he growled.

"Denson!"

They both looked up. Coach Logan marched toward them, a cold wind whipping his fine white hair, reddening the hard set of his already chapped face. "What's this?" he demanded, gesturing at Isobel as though she were a pet Mark had allowed to follow him.

"Brad told her to leave him alone, but she keeps bugging him anyway," he said.

"Where's your coach? Why are you harassing my players?" Coach Logan growled, the hot-iron color in his face getting deeper by the second. "Aren't you supposed to be over there somewhere?" he asked, gesturing toward where the squad stood regrouping on the sidelines.

Fine, Isobel thought. She'd bypass Mark altogether—go straight to the source.

"You have to pull Brad out of the game!" The words rushed out of her all at once, tumbling one over the other. "Something's not right. You have to pull him," she repeated, pointing toward the field.

Now his face turned purple. His jowls started to quiver, and just when Isobel began to wonder whether he might be having a heart attack, he screamed at her, his voice rough and raw from the back of his throat, like a saw blade through steel. *"Do I tell you how to cheer!?"*

Isobel had to hunker into herself to avoid the flying spit.

"Denson!" he shouted before spinning away to thunder back toward the sidelines, his entire form vibrating with rage. Without another glance, Mark followed, securing his own helmet. Isobel watched their retreating backs. Helpless, she looked searchingly to the field, another cold wind causing her to shiver.

"Well," a quiet voice said. It had come from behind her, soft yet scratchy, with that strange static essence. "That went well."

Isobel turned to see him leaning against the brick side of the stands. His wraith-thin frame partially obscured the painted emblem of the hawk's head. With his arms folded and his hands tucked beneath his elbows, his red claws stretched out on either side like lethal fans. He leveled his black stare on her from beneath the ridge of his brow. A few spikes of coarse, featherlike hair escaped to hang loose over the jagged hole in his white face.

He smiled crimson. "Hello again . . . cheerleader."

36
No Return

Isobel was really starting to hate Reynolds. Of all the opportune moments for him to show his stupid shrouded face, this one would be ideal. He could be so freaking after the fact.

"Call them off," she said, staring straight at Pinfeathers, fists clenched at her sides.

"Ask me nicely," he said, grinning, tilting his head at her as though there was something about her that struck him as quaint.

"Do it."

"Don't I even get a 'please'?"

"What do you want with him?" she piped. "Brad doesn't have anything to do with this!"

His expression darkened, the smile fading. "Doesn't he?"

Her gaze flew toward the field. In an instant, she realized what Pinfeathers had been doing: He'd been trying to stall her—and he'd succeeded. She cursed under her breath and broke away, running full speed toward the fence that separated her from the playing field.

Pinfeathers appeared at her side, his figure unfurling through curling wisps of violet smoke. "I have a message for you," he said.

"And I have one for you. Go away," she snarled, show-ing him the open palm of one hand. Reaching the fence, she gripped the top, preparing to jump it. Could she really stop the play by herself? Or would she just get flattened into cheerleader pizza?

"Don't you even care who it's from?" asked Pinfeathers. He slipped through the fence ahead of her, his body gliding past the metal chain-work easily, muddling, then reform-ing whole on the other side. He lifted two clawed fingers, between which he held a folded slip of white paper.

Isobel stopped, her heart catching in her throat when she thought she saw the silhouette of violet lines, showing like dark veins through pale skin. She snatched the note and in her hand it felt solid and real.

Pinfeathers smiled coyly. Then, as though her acceptance of the message somehow acted as a release, the angles of his porcelain face began to change. His form loosened, and he slipped into the same thick smoke-curls of violet she had seen the other Nocs emerge from. His body, taking on the jagged black edges of feathers, seemed to dissolve and condense at the same time, his face at last sharpening into the wicked spike of a black beak. He croaked at her hoarsely, flapped his wings, then spiraled away.

Her eyes followed him until a separate flying object caught her attention. The ball. It soared from kickoff through the air in a wide arc. It spun toward the open receiver, his knees bent, arms held open. Isobel watched as number twenty-one caught the ball. Clutching it hard to himself, Brad bent forward in a charging run toward the opposite end of the field, his teammates covering the wide space before him, felling tackles. Brad streaked through the opened pathway, the four dark forms slinking alongside him. They grinned like piranhas, gracefully following his every move, almost dancing. Then they closed in on him tighter, steering him at full-force into an oncoming player. The ball hit the ground. Brad followed, disappearing for a moment into a jumbled mix of blue, gold, green, white—and black.

It happened so quickly, in less time than it took to blink. Even amid the shouts from the stands, the clatter and grunts of battling players, Isobel still heard the sharp, merciless snap.

A gasp of shock rose from the stands, a unanimous moan of grief. Isobel could not stop her own hands from flying to cover her mouth. Brad lay still on the turf, his leg bent at far too unnatural an angle. Hissing at their victory, the Nocs vanished into wisps.

Somewhere, a referee's whistle screamed.

Isobel leaped the fence in one easy motion, her hand clutching the note as though she feared it would evaporate. Someone sprang to stop her, but she sprinted around them, running the length of the field to where Brad lay surrounded by teammates and opposing players alike. She shoved her way through, dropping to her knees at his side, trying not to look at the white sliver of bone sticking out below the knee, at the blood soaking through the metallic gold of his uniform pants. Isobel yanked off his helmet. His head rolled and fell to one side. Wet coppery curls clung to his temples and forehead, and his too-handsome face was drained of color.

"Brad!" She pressed one hand to his cool cheek.

His eyes fluttered open, and Isobel felt her breath catch. Only a narrow slice of sharp electric blue showed; the rest of his irises were consumed, blanketed under discs of purest black.

Two coin-size holes locked on her. "They're coming closer," he muttered. The muscles of his pallid face twitched beneath her fingertips. His entire body trembled.

"Brad, it's okay." She smoothed her hand across his brow.

"No, no," he mumbled, "stay back." His quivering intensified.

She felt someone take her arms then. Saying her name, they pulled her back and brought her to her feet. She went, unable to struggle.

"Back up, everybody," someone called, pushing through — a medic. Placing a red case beside him, he knelt next to Brad, who lay on the grass, his eyes rolling into his head, his lids falling shut once more.

"Isobel!"

Someone gripped her by the shoulders, shook her. "Isobel," Coach Anne repeated. Isobel blinked and focused. "You're not going to pass out on me again, are you?"

She shook her head. No. She was wide, wide awake.

"Go on, back to the sidelines and wait," she said. "It's a bad injury, but he's going to be okay. Okay?"

Isobel nodded numbly as Coach turned her away from

the scene. Slowly her legs moved her forward, and her body followed the orders without her mind's consent. As she moved toward the sidelines, she saw Stevie and Nikki. They stood pressed up against the fence, watching, each of their faces a mask of disbelief.

Isobel stopped in the middle of the field. She ran her thumb over the smooth surface of the paper still clutched in her fist. She unfolded it. Under the white glare of stark stadium lights, she read the elegant lines of purple ink.

> *Isobel,*
>
> *This was the only way I knew how to reach you. After tonight, it will all go away.*
>
> *I never meant for you to be pulled into any of this—ever. Please believe that.*
>
> *Somehow I've lost control of everything.*
>
> *I only wish I could see you again. I wish I could tell you everything that I couldn't before. Most of all, I wish there was a way we could start over.*
>
> *Whatever happens now, please believe that I didn't mean for it to end this way.*
>
> *Yours always,*
> *—V*

37
The Grim Facade

After stopping to retrieve her gym bag from the girls' locker room, Isobel slipped out the side doors of the stadium and into the darkened, car-filled parking lot. As awful as it seemed, she'd moved quickly after reading Varen's note, using the distraction of Brad's injury to make a clean getaway. She hadn't wanted Nikki or Stevie (or anyone, for that matter) to catch up to her or ask her where she was going. It had become clear that she could no longer afford any more distractions. Not when she had wasted too much time already. Not when the only thing that mattered anymore was finding *him*.

As Isobel made her way through the parking lot toward the Cadillac, she imagined how her face must look—bleak, colorless.

"What's the matter?" Gwen asked.

A tall, thin boy with choppy black hair stood next to her. He eyed Isobel as she approached, sizing her up, grinning like he found something funny. She glared at him in return, ready for him to say just one thing about her cheer uniform, because she knew he must have pulled the black jeans he wore straight from the girls' rack at Target.

Gwen, having changed out of her phony prep getup, now

wore a black V-neck dress. With enormous bell sleeves and no waist, it looked like a vampire's nightgown. The whole ensemble was almost as ridiculous on her as the oversize Trenton sweatshirt. Under any other circumstances, Isobel might have laughed. Instead she frowned.

She'd already tucked Varen's note into her gym bag, next to her tag for the Grim Facade, not wanting Gwen to see it. After tonight, after seeing what the Nocs could do, what they *had* done, she knew that her promise to herself to protect Gwen from knowing too much was one she had to keep.

"What happened?" Gwen squinted at her as Isobel drew nearer. "We saw an ambulance leave," she said. "Somebody get hurt?"

"Brad," said Isobel. There was no reason to hide that detail. "His leg got broken," she explained, trying not to remember the sight of the jagged bone poking white through the bloody flap of skin.

Gwen winced. "Ouch. He okay?"

Isobel nodded. She moved past them and opened the back door of the Cadillac, tossing in her gym bag.

"*You* okay?"

"Yeah," she said. "Let's go."

Gwen seemed to deliberate. She swayed on her feet, as though not sure which way to turn or what to say. Finally she said, "Isobel, this is Mikey. Mikey, Isobel."

After the introduction, Gwen pivoted and rounded the back of the car. She opened the trunk to scrounge. In the meantime, Mikey busied himself by staring at Isobel. She stared back, her distaste for him growing by the second. Finally he winked and climbed into the driver's seat.

Great. *He* was driving? Isobel scowled but said nothing, not wanting to waste any more time arguing. She slid into the back on the passenger side. From the front, Mikey twisted around to smile lazily at her, his face angular and sharp. Rows of silver stud piercings lined each ear. "Hey," he said.

"Hey," she said, doing her best to smile. There was something about this guy that set off her smarm alert, big-time.

"Scooch," Gwen said, appearing on her side, a long white box tucked beneath one arm. She nudged Isobel, then wrestled in beside her. She threw the box over Isobel's lap.

"What's this?" Isobel asked. "Why aren't you sitting up front?"

"This"—she tapped the box—"is your costume. It's Halloween, remember?"

In the front seat, Mikey cranked down the driver's-side window, stuck his head out, and unleashed a long, loud howl to the moon. Gwen reached forward to grab him by the neck of his hoodie and pulled him back in. He laughed and shoved the key into the ignition. The Cadillac whined, then rumbled.

Isobel looked down at the box in her lap. The last thing she wanted to do when she got there was waste more time in putting on a stupid costume. Even if Gwen didn't know all the circumstances involved, couldn't she understand that she just needed to find Varen? That finding him was the only reason she was even going?

"Just open it," Gwen said. "You know you can't wear what you've got on. They'll kill you."

"Cheerleader meat!" Mikey growled as he hit the gas pedal. The Cadillac lurched forward, throwing them back. The radio snapped on with a fuzz and a pop before jumping through stations. Loud, crashing music blasted from the speakers, fast ragged vocals following close behind. Isobel gripped her seat as the car sped away from the stadium. They turned onto the main road, the rear bumper scraping the curb. She glared at the back of Mikey's absurd hair, which resembled that of a bomb-blasted, smoke-charred cartoon character's.

Next to her, Gwen, impatient, yanked off the box top, revealing folds of lace.

Isobel's eyes widened.

"What?" said Gwen.

"Gwen, I can't walk in there wearing that thing!"

"Why the hell not?"

"It's *pink*!"

"So?"

"Uh—hello—did you not see *Carrie*?"

"Plug it up!" Mikey cried, and banged the steering wheel rapidly in tune to the drums.

Isobel glared.

"You're making a statement," Gwen said, and draped the gown across her own lap, pulling the zipper down.

"I'm not wearing a pink dress to a goth prom."

"These are the shoes," said Gwen, and shoved a pair of rose pink flats into Isobel's lap.

"Gwen, no!"

"Look, it's going to be crowded. Everybody between here and the Indiana underground is coming to this thing. How else is he supposed to find you? Honestly, you'd think I was sending you off as a virgin sacrifice."

"Are you really a virgin?" Mikey chimed almost predictably from the front.

Isobel clamped her mouth into a silent and furious line. Gripping one shoe tightly, she fought the urge to whack him upside the head.

"Besides," Gwen added, fluffing the dress folds, "this thing took forever, so you're wearing it."

"Wait, you made this?" Isobel asked, distracted.

"Altered it," she admitted. She shrugged. "Half off at the Nearly New Shop. By the way, you owe me twenty-five dollars. Oh, and there's a smudge on the toe of the left shoe, but I got them to throw those in, so don't worry about it. Now how do you get this stuff off?" Her hands flew to Isobel, twisting her by the shoulders. Isobel felt the release of her cheer uniform's zipper.

"What are you doing?" Isobel squealed. "I'm not getting dressed in here!"

"What? Why not?"

"Uh, boy!" she shouted, and shot a finger at Mikey, who lifted his chin and waggled his eyebrows at them through the rearview mirror. Isobel made a sound of disgust. Who *was* this kid, anyway?

Gwen leaned forward. Reaching through from the

backseat to the front, she flipped the rearview mirror so it faced the ceiling.

"Isn't that kind of dangerous?" Mikey protested.

"Keep your eyes on the road or you'll be a eunuch before the night's out."

"What's a eunuch?" he asked, chuckling.

"Look it up."

Gwen fell back in her seat and immediately set to work with the dress. Resigned, Isobel let Gwen help wrestle her out of the cheer top, though her eyes never wavered from the back of Mikey's spiked head. If he so much as peeked . . .

They were on the highway now and flying. Her turtleneck was the next to go, followed by her sports bra. Then Gwen, hardly giving Isobel time to breathe, threw the dress over her head and pulled down. Isobel fought through the folds of pink to bring her arms through the tunnel of the cinched waist. The satin lining slid smooth and ice-cold against her bare skin, making her gasp. Her fingers wiggled through, seeking for straps or sleeves, but then, without warning, Gwen yanked the dress into place, and Isobel realized that there weren't any.

"Lean forward," Gwen said, and shoved Isobel over at the waist, knocking the wind out of her. Gwen pulled up the zipper. The fabric drew snug around her body, molding to her perfectly. "Now sit up," said Gwen, and pulled her straight again.

Isobel stared down at herself as Gwen fussed. Even in the dark, she could see that the thing was vintage and frilly. It had a lace overlay, a sweetheart neckline, and a poofy skirt that she thought would frill out and fall to just below the knee when she stood. It was nothing Isobel would have ever picked out herself—almost too pretty, with the pink satin Alice-in-Wonderland ribbon that tied around the waist.

Arms folded, Isobel allowed herself to be dressed and primped. Gwen proceeded to strip her of her blue and gold hair ribbons. Head twisted, Isobel stared out the window. They were moving fast. Too fast. But she found herself actually liking the speed for once, and she urged the car along in her mind, never wincing, even as Mikey swung around one sharp turn after another. Up front, he handled the wheel like a wrestling partner.

Soon the car exited the freeway and traveled along a maze of back roads. Without the aid of streetlights, the darkness outside transformed to blackness. Trees raced by, illuminated by moonlight and the Cadillac's brights, their steady, thickening stream seeming to keep beat with the music.

Isobel felt a bobby pin scrape her scalp, then another. The Cadillac dipped down a hill, and her stomach lurched to high-five her heart.

They would be pretty far out from town now, she thought, watching the trees grow denser, their skeleton shadows more wicked. She hadn't been watching for signs, but she figured they were probably somewhere out in Henry County, or Spencer, though she couldn't be sure.

Then again, could she really be sure of anything anymore? Reality? Reason? Herself?

Isobel looked down at her lap, at her hands. She turned

her left one over, remembering where Varen had written his number on her that first time. Those numbers were gone now, but in hindsight, he may as well have tattooed the moment onto her soul. She clenched her hand into a fist.

What had he meant by not wanting things to "end" this way? Why did it feel as though the note was his way of trying to tell her good-bye? And why had he said everything would "disappear" after tonight?

Isobel squeezed her eyes shut. She wanted to reach into her bag and read the note again. It was as though she hoped the writing there could have changed while she wasn't looking. Then again, why not, when everything else around her seemed to be doing just that?

An unnerving feeling unfurled through her stomach, a poisonous blossom of uncertainty and doubt and fear. She wondered if Varen had known what the Nocs would do. Worse, she wondered if he'd sent them—Pinfeathers, after all, had come bearing his letter. Or were the Nocs part of what he'd meant by having lost control?

"Done," Gwen said finally, dropping her arms. "Now, where's your tag?"

Freed, Isobel opened her eyes. She pulled the tag from her gym bag. Gwen snatched it from her, grabbed Isobel's hand, and looped the red ribbon around her wrist. She tied it there, tightening the knot until the ribbon pressed into her skin, almost to the point of cutting off her circulation. "Whatever you do," she said, "don't lose this."

The Cadillac slowed suddenly, and Isobel had to brace

herself as the front tires bumped over what felt like a log. Gwen bounced as though having expected the jolt, and went to securing her own tag. They shuttled off the last of the long, snake-winding back roads, the tires crunching and popping over gravel.

Mikey switched off the brights, and the Cadillac's normal headlights dimmed to cast a yellowish white light over a wide lot of pale dirt and rock. Dust and grit kicked up to swirl through the two beams like mist. Rows of dark cars lined their path like sleeping monsters. Isobel scooted forward, grabbed the back of Mikey's seat, and squinted through the windshield.

Ahead she saw groups of figures standing outside a long two-story building—something that looked part barn and part warehouse. A pulsing green-to-pink light radiated from within, and distantly Isobel could feel more than hear the low thump of music.

As the car crept closer, its beams passed over a set of tall, pallid figures. Isobel's insides tightened at the sight of them, at the way they stood huddled together beside a black Honda, sharing a cigarette. She pressed to the window, scanning their faces.

Smoke swirled up from the group, and as the Cadillac crawled past, each white face turned to stare. They glowered at her, their sharp noses and starkly painted faces menacing but nevertheless whole. Isobel sat back, taking a moment to breathe, to urge her heart to slow.

"Hey," Gwen said, nudging her. "Look."

Her heart thudding anew, she turned to scan the parking lot. The headlights passed over the rear of a familiar car, and Isobel let out a small cry as she caught sight of the jagged letters against the black finish, the hateful word FREAK spelled out on the side of a Cougar.

Isobel unlatched the door. It swung out, and the Cadillac stuttered to a halt.

"Hey, what gives?" Mikey shouted.

She slipped from her seat into the cool air that instantly latched to her bare shoulders. A shiver ran through her, but the sharpness of the cold felt good—further evidence that she was really here, that she was awake, alive—that Varen must be too.

"Isobel, wait!"

Ignoring Gwen, she ran at full speed for the warehouse, her feet joining in with the thumping, chaotic beat of music. She glanced up at the sky. An almost full moon beamed silver-white through a gauzy haze of cloud cover. Shining like a lazy serpent's eye, it cast the world around her in a ghostly pallor and caused the pink satin and lace of her dress to turn luminescent. Even over the crashing drums that joined in with the drone of bass guitar, Isobel could still hear the quiet rustling of her skirts.

A wide wooden door stood open before her. Inside, colored lights raged. Flashes of violet and red blinked and pulsed, flaring through a writhing throng of black-clad bodies. She slowed her run as she drew into the archway and took in the sea of masked faces. Against one wall a band, the source of the tortured music, played atop a makeshift stage. A boy dressed in a long black coat, his face painted like Death's, screamed into a microphone. He dropped to his knees. The drummer and guitarist behind him thrashed out a violent rhythm while he reached toward his audience, begged them with anguished lyrics to pray for him.

Fighting against every instinct, Isobel drifted farther inward, deciding to try her best to keep back from the carnage that was the dance floor. She glanced up to see pockets of figures standing around a wooden gallery that rimmed the circumference of the room. Like decorative gargoyles and cemetery angels, they stood huddled close to the edges, elegant hands poised on the banisters. She caught a few stares, flinty gazes turning in her direction. She looked quickly away. A flash of black light caught her, turning the pink of her dress deep violet for a fleeting second. She wished that the light could have stayed, could have stained the fabric, hidden her.

She felt someone tap her on the shoulder, and she swung around. A tall boy with an unruly black Mohawk and tiny round sunglasses took her wrist without asking. Black lipstick coated his full lips. A spiked dog collar fastened with a padlock encircled his neck. She jerked away from him, realizing too late that it was her tag he was after and not an open vein.

Annoyed, he grabbed for her wrist again. Isobel let him check her tag this time, knowing better than to try and shout a coherent explanation for her very blond, very frilly presence over the deafening music. He flipped the tag over several times before actually reading it, as though to first confirm authenticity. Isobel stood her ground and watched his face as he took in the purple writing. His eyes flashed to hers, disbelieving. He looked as though he wanted to speak but he didn't, maybe deciding it wasn't worth the trouble to yell.

Isobel jerked her wrist back, remembering Gwen's warning not to lose her tag. The point was that she had one. So what else did he want?

She took a step backward, but he shook his head. It didn't seem as though he was ready to let her go. He crooked a finger at her to come closer, and this time it was her turn to shake her head. He scowled and turned to point at a nearby gathering.

The group he gestured to looked like a stately if not unusual funeral party. There were three young men, two of them with black umbrellas open and held aloft over the head of a girl, her golden-bronze arms coated in black lace sleeves, her thick dark hair piled atop her head beneath bands of silver, secured with large roses and long drapes of black ribbon. She looked like a queen, her full dress a deep bloodred, accented with black.

Lacy.

For a moment Isobel thought about bolting straight into the crowd, but then the other girl saw her and it was too late. Like a mouse paralyzed in the gaze of a cobra, Isobel stood frozen. Lacy's artfully painted eyes narrowed hard on her. She surveyed Isobel for a long moment, a sneer contorting the perfection of her ebony lips. By this time the other members of her party had turned to stare as well, lowering their goblets.

Isobel gulped. They were going to eat her alive.

She silently cursed Gwen for dressing her in baby-girl pink. Why couldn't they have swapped? A little eyeliner, a dash of sullenness, and she could have slipped beneath the radar completely.

Apparently growing impatient with her, Mohawk Man placed a large hand against her back and urged her forward, toward the group. Isobel, not knowing what else to do, went where she was pushed.

The guys with the umbrellas looked like they were in their twenties at least, each of them clad in top hats and long coats. The third had a more edgy look. He wore a leather jacket laced in chains, his hair spiky on one half of his head, shorn clean on the other. Lacy handed off her goblet to Mr. Mohawk and seized Isobel's tag. Her dark eyes narrowed as she read, and when she looked up she stared past Isobel, searching the crowd behind them.

This was the last shred of evidence Isobel needed to know that Varen was present, that he'd been seen, and she wasted no time. She lashed out at Mohawk Man, jerking his arm, causing him to drop Lacy's drink. It splattered on the floor, dark droplets flying onto the skirt of Lacy's dress. She gasped in horror and let go of Isobel's tag. Isobel, seizing her chance, broke away from the group, running headlong into the black throng. She plowed forward, pressing her way through the bodies, weaving between them. Her dress snagged on someone's spiked bracelet, and she had to stop to free herself. She glanced behind her, then turned and spun in another direction. How would she ever find him? Was he down below, or above, somewhere on the gallery?

The farther she wove into the crowd, the more eyes she seemed to attract. Whispers started up around her. Strange faces turned toward her, most of them either porcelain white or covered by masks. She looked over her shoulder, still expecting to find Lacy two steps behind, furious and ready to snatch her bald. Either that, or drain her of blood.

Isobel stepped on someone's toe and looked up. The boy, dressed completely in different versions of plaid, smiled at her. That disturbed her more than if he'd glared, and she turned and pushed through again, the space growing tighter as she wove her way deeper into the crowd. Someone caught her around the waist and she screamed, her voice lost in the noise of the screeching music. She wrenched away. A laughing face fell backward, becoming lost within a haze of colored lights. She stared after it, wondering if she had imagined the hole in his cheek.

Isssobel.

Isobel jumped at the sound of her name. It was as though someone had spoken it from inside her head, the voice metallic and sharp—a woman's.

Someone knocked into her, and she was jostled to one side. Sharp red fingernails reached out from the darkness. She gasped and pulled away, stumbling. Like the face, the hands vanished, leaving her unsure whether they'd been real.

Isobel blinked and watched as the dark figures around began to merge and meld into one another. Becoming one, they moved in on her like a black tide. Blood rushed into her ears and drowned out the music. All sound seemed to drift farther and farther away. She drew her arms in tightly around herself and turned once more, then again, only to find every clear step closed off, covered over by shapeless black shadows.

Isssobel.

That voice again, that same haunting hiss. It caused the hair on her arms to rise and prickle, the thrum in her ears to intensify.

Isssobel, it breathed.

A wave of dizziness washed over her. The room around her shifted on its axis. She lost her balance and threw her arms out to brace herself. She felt people all around her, shapes moving, dancing through the blackness as though they'd been swallowed up just like her but hadn't realized it. Isobel shut her eyes and opened them, but nothing changed. Why did it suddenly feel as though she was slipping away from herself, disconnecting? Why did it feel as though the world was falling away—capsizing?

Was she falling asleep, or waking up?

Isssoooobell . . .

Who was that calling her name? Coach? Mom?

No. It was someone else. Some*thing* else.

This wasn't right. This couldn't be happening. She was here. She was really here. She couldn't be dreaming. Even if this was a dream, she couldn't wake up now. Not when she'd come so close.

Isobel reached out, felt the air shimmer in front of her.

From behind, she felt someone take her hand, clasping hard, pulling her around. She spun sharply, and the force of the movement seemed to shock her into herself.

The world snapped into place.

All at once, the noise of the party spiraled into full volume again. A girl's siren voice now replaced the frayed chords of the skull-faced boy. Her song, backed by the haunting pull of a cello's strings and the gentle thump of percussion, reverberated through the hall. The figures around sprang apart from formless shadows to become people again, leaving in their wake a dark figure that now stood before her, his face hidden beneath a mask of white.

"It's you," she gasped.

38
Out of Space, Out of Time

It was his eyes that gave him away. Despite the phantom's mask that hid his face, she could not have mistaken those eyes. She would have known them anywhere, those two jade spheres, their gaze so sharp it could cut. Framed by the holes in the simple white mask, they blazed into her like they had so many times before, lit now by a strange and unearthly fire.

Isobel could not have stopped herself if she'd tried. Not as she closed the distance between them. Not as she lifted her arms to wrap them around his neck. Not as she pressed herself to his frame, breathed him in, took in the scent of him—a concentrated dose of spice and incense that sent her mind reeling. She clung fast to him, tightened her hold on him, felt the realness of him in the fabric of his familiar jacket, in the warmth of his body.

Unbidden, his arms encircled her, invited themselves around her waist. He drew her in. Isobel's heart crashed against the cage of her chest, beating against his.

She looked up at him and, unwinding one arm, reached to remove the mask. It came away in one easy motion, revealing the darkened, purple bruise beneath his left eye, the angry split in the skin above his lip.

Her brow furrowed. Brad. He'd been telling the truth. And Bruce had been right. But how could that be? She'd seen Varen earlier that day, in Mr. Swanson's class. The contours of his face had been smooth.

Her fingertips reached to trace the damage, but he grasped her hand with his own. He leaned down, far enough that the dark ends of his hair brushed feather-light against her face, caught in her lashes. She had just enough time to take in a breath, to blink, to part her lips before he took them with his own.

Time froze. Her heart ceased to beat. Her eyes fluttered shut.

The cool slip of the small metal loop pressed into her skin as he kissed her. Urgent. Gentle. So slow.

Sweet, soft demolition.

He tasted of cloves and coffee. And of something else. A faraway essence, familiar and yet somehow foreign, too. Something sere and arid. A little like smoke. A little like decay.

Ash.

A tiny sound of alarm escaped her. She pulled back. He gripped her, though, and pulled her to him. Did he think that she might slip through his arms or vanish? Or was his fear that *he* might? He raised both hands to cup her face, to hold her lips against his own. It was as though the moment was a stolen one, as though every second counted, as though this first kiss was doomed to be their last.

Like horrible skeletons, these thoughts reared in her mind, corrupting the moment, frightening her enough to pull away. This time he let her.

A gentle sting played over Isobel's lips, as though they'd just met with a battery's charge. Onstage, the girl continued to croon longingly, though the music behind her began to build and climb, to swallow her reverberation and careen once again toward sure chaos.

"I found you," Isobel whispered.

An agonized expression crossed his features. He gripped her behind the neck, pressed his forehead to hers. His soft hair draped around them, shielded their faces from view. "You shouldn't be here."

Her lips parted to utter a reply, but he released her, taking his mask from her and donning it once more. She watched him, confused as he turned to look behind, to scan the figures around them. He gripped her hand, and she squeezed it in her own. He spun around, and she soon found herself following him through the press of costumed bodies. Where was he taking her? What did he mean, she shouldn't be here? Hadn't he wanted her here? With him?

Fed by the new hard surge from the drums, the dancing turned to thrashing and the costumed bodies closed in, making it almost impossible to keep hold of him as he steered her through the tangle of ghouls, devils, dark faeries, and vampires.

At last they broke through the press of bodies. He led her toward the far wall, where several partygoers stared, their painted features sullen and apathetic. Varen drew her along, moving faster.

She tugged against him, attempting to rein him in. She

was tired of being in the dark, surrounded by shadows and ominous forms that always knew more than she did. She was ready for answers. She tried to loosen her hand from his, but his grip only tightened. She tugged again, and finally he swung around.

"Tell me what's happening."

"Not here." He grabbed her wrist and they were moving once more. He pushed through a gathering of Jack the Ripper look-alikes, and ahead, hidden within a recess of shadows, Isobel saw a door.

They slipped around a pierced couple pressed against one wall, their arms wrapped around each other, their faces molded together, locked in a deep kiss. Varen opened the door. He drew her inside, pulling a string for light, and shut the door behind them.

They were in what appeared to be a small office. At least, the tiny space had probably once served as an office. It smelled of sawdust and stale tobacco. An unfinished desk sat in one corner, a crooked corkboard nailed to the wall above it. A few sheets of paper, still pinned there, yellowed and brittle with age, stirred in the breeze of their entrance. A broken chair, overturned atop a threadbare throw rug, acted as the room's centerpiece. Beyond that and the cord-and-bulb ceiling light overhead, there was nothing. Outside, the music raged on, though muted by the boundary of the four surrounding walls.

Varen, removing his mask and setting it on the desk, gathered the broken chair from the floor and lifted it. He hooked the backrest beneath the doorknob. The action caused Isobel's skin to prickle. What was he barricading them against?

"Varen?"

He held a hand up to silence her and paused at the door, listening.

"Varen—," she whispered.

He swung toward her again, moving fast to her side. "Don't say my name," he hushed. "She can't find you here with me. You have to hide," he said, more to himself than to her.

"She?" He couldn't still be worried about Lacy, could he?

His eyes, wide and anxious, snapped to hers.

She'd never seen him like this. She'd never even imagined him this way. Skittish, fearful—almost fevered. Whatever she had expected to find when she got here, it hadn't been this. His fear, so unfamiliar, doubled hers.

"Tell me what's happening," she pleaded.

He shook his head. "You shouldn't have come."

"Stop saying that." She gripped his jacket, her fingers clutching. "You asked me to come, remember?"

"That was a mistake."

She wanted to shake him, to wake him up, to make him answer her.

"Varen, none of this makes any sense, and then you say something like that! Your letter—why did . . . I don't understand anything that's happening, and it's happening to me, too! Tell me right now what happened to your face. Brad said—but then I saw you . . ." She shook her head, trying to sort out her thoughts, her memory. Did anything fit together?

Which confusion should she start with first? "One minute you were there, the next you were gone. I looked for you but you'd disappeared, just like a ghost! And now you're here and you won't tell me. Why? What are those things? Why are they following me? Why did they attack Nikki and Brad? Where did they come from? What do they want?"

"They want the same thing I want!" he shouted suddenly, yanking away from her. He grabbed the mask off the desk and threw it against one wall. It shattered, shards of porcelain spraying the floor.

Hands quivering, she reached toward him.

"Don't." He turned his back to her, facing the door.

That word had stopped her once before. But not now. Not now that she had glimpsed through the funeral front of Varen's own eternal Grim Facade. Despite all the dark armor, the kohl liner, the black boots and chains, she saw him clearly now. She'd peered through the curtain of that cruel calmness, through the death stare and the vampire sentiments and angst and, behind it all, had found true beauty. She looped her arms around his waist, burying her face against his jacket, against the silhouette of the dead bird. "Please tell me!"

He spun in her grip and pressed his lips to her ear, whispering. "I didn't know it would happen like this," he said. "I only wanted to escape. I don't know if you can understand that. That I only wanted to find a way to somewhere else. Even if it only lasted a little while—even if it wasn't real. But then it *was* real. It was real and I couldn't stop it."

"What? Stop what?"

"Then I met you," he said, his lips hovering close to hers once again. "And the dreams changed."

His breath washed warm against her, and it made her want to surrender to him again, to feel his touch, to hold his kiss, at once petal soft and incinerating. She'd never been kissed like that before—like the shell of her soul had evaporated.

He inched closer, but paused. Outside, the music, the screaming, the voices, the sounds of the frenzied crowd—it all stopped. Silence pulsed. He pulled back, turned to look toward the door.

The room grew cold. Isobel drew in a breath. She hugged herself, shivering as she recalled the night at the ice cream shop, the time they'd spent in the freezer. It felt so long ago.

Seconds passed.

Against the walls, the dull yellow light began to move and sway. The motion threw their twin shadows this way and that against the walls and floor, making the room seem suddenly more crowded. Varen looked up, and her own gaze followed. They watched the naked bulb swing on its frayed cord, as though caught by the gust of a nonexistent breeze. Back and forth it swung, like the pendulum of a clock.

The light blinked, flickered. Darkness teased, threatening to strike.

Hoarse whispers rose up from just outside the door, a sound like dry leaves crackling over a fire.

At first they started low. So low that Isobel couldn't be certain of what the sound was or that she was even hearing it at all. But then the voices became clearer, hissing through the crack at the bottom of the door. Something laughed. A fast shadow moved, darting like an animal.

Isobel gripped his sleeve. "What is it?"

He moved cautiously forward, positioning himself in front of her. "They've found us."

39
Much of Madness

The doorknob rattled.

Isobel watched as the chair holding the door shivered and shook. Something banged into it hard, jarring the door in its frame, and she jumped, letting out a yelp.

All at once the whispers died. The door settled.

A small light, white and crystalline, like the light she had seen in the woodlands, appeared in a wink at the bottom. It traveled along the crack slowly, back and forth, as though probing for a way in. There was a sound on the other side, like the slip of gauze fabric over the wooden exterior of the door, and Isobel found herself fighting the urge to scream. Then the white light blinked out.

Silence. Only the sound of their breathing. And then a new sound. Quiet and distant.

Music.

"Do you hear that?" she whispered, still clinging to him. The tune grew louder. One instrument, one note at a time, it pieced itself together until at last she could place what it was she heard. An orchestra?

"Don't listen," he said, his voice brittle. "Pretend it's not real."

The music grew steadier, firmer, and it *was* real—string instruments sighing out a swirling waltz. A crash of cymbals accented a change in melody. The waltz swelled even louder, so unlike the deafening, crunching goth music. It couldn't be another band, could it? There was no way. She heard no guitars. No tortured vocals.

New voices filtered in from beyond the door, different from the whispers they'd heard a moment before. These voices were more substantial, more alive, the sound of real people laughing and talking and shouting. The voices rose steadily, accompanied now by the delicate clink and tinkle of glassware. More and more voices chimed in, one for every second that passed, until they blended into a unanimous, lively hum. Despite the light laughter, the trilling, swirling tune, Isobel clung tighter to the back of Varen's jacket. It made no sense. All of it felt . . . wrong.

"Who's out there?" she asked. "What's going on?"

"Isobel, listen to me," he said, turning to her. Her stare broke from the door and she looked into his eyes as he spoke. "Look for a way to the woodlands. When you're there, find the door. You'll know it when you see it. Go through it and don't wait for me. Don't trust anything you see."

"What? But . . . I—I don't understand."

He shook her. "Promise me!"

"Varen, I—"

Her voice caught in her throat, seized into silence as she watched his eyes dilate, the pinprick of fear at their core expanding, consuming the green of his irises until nothing remained. Nothing except for two black coin-size holes.

She felt a tremble start all over. She reached for him but stopped short as black-to-purple wisps of cloudlike ink, like a thousand crawling insects, whispered out from behind his shoulders. The darkness surrounded him, growing thicker, clamoring to take hold of him, like the unlimited tentacles of some formless wraith. The wisps wrapped his shoulders, his arms. A pair of blindingly white hands emerged from within the churning void. Like talons, they clung to his chest. A woman's white face appeared in a flash over his shoulder—her eyes two empty sockets.

Panicked, Isobel reached for him. She caught his arm, and for a moment they held each other tightly.

"Find the door," he said. Then he let go.

"No!"

With a hiss of shadows he fell backward, into the open wound of darkness. His arm slipped from her hands despite her desperate fight to keep hold, and then the blackness folded over him, swallowing him, knitting together until it was gone and he with it.

"Varen!"

She rushed through the space that had taken him. She reached the wall, pressed her hands flat to the wood, beating, shouting. "Varen!"

She swung around, searching the room with her eyes. The light overhead continued to sway. Back and forth. Back and forth. Breathing hard, her heart thundering, she watched it, watched it as though, with its next pass, it would bring him back.

She ran to the center of the room and turned in a full circle. She stopped, but around her, the room continued to spin. It turned and turned, revolving faster and faster until everything smeared and streaked into a blur. The light. The laughter. The voices and music. Her legs weakened. Dizziness overtook her. Her body gave in and her knees hit the floor. The room whirred faster. Nausea crept over her. She lowered her head, shut her eyes, and pressed her hands over her ears to block it out.

"Stop!" she said, then screamed, *"Stop!"*

A quiet click noise, like the unlatching of a door, broke through her consciousness.

Isobel looked up.

The room had ceased to spin. Before her, the door stood cracked open. Light shone in—a dim crimson glow. Through the crack, Isobel saw plush ebony carpeting and the corner of thick black draperies.

"Come, let us go," she heard a man say, his accented voice rising over the drone of talk and distant shrill laughter. Small bells jangled.

"Whither?" another man asked.

"To your vaults."

The scent of cinnamon, freshly baked bread, and spiced meat seeped through the door, causing her stomach to clench. She remained motionless, listening, battling the urge to throw up.

When she thought she could, Isobel stood. Shakily she drifted toward the door. She reached an unsteady hand to the knob. The door opened outward, opposite from before, and it moved easily, seemingly more from her touch alone than from any effort on her part to push.

The music washed over her, building and falling, the melody mimicking itself, then starting over again. A chamber of rich ebony lay stretched out before her. Thick velvet draperies spilled from tall windows, like motionless black waterfalls. Phantasmal light played through the stained-glass bloodred panes, setting shadows loose to clamor over the sable walls and coal black carpeting.

"The vaults are insufferably damp," one of the men's voices said. "They are encrusted with niter."

"Let us go, nevertheless," the other voice returned, and Isobel recognized his accent as Italian. The bells on his cap jangled again, and the sound drew her out of the office.

She kept one hand on the door frame as she passed into the room where the smell of perfume and wine mingled with the scent of rich food. She looked up and noticed more black draperies. They hung suspended from the vaulted ceiling. Combined with the deep crimson windows, the space seemed like the innermost chamber of a royal crypt.

But where had the warehouse gone? The goths and the Grim Facade? And why did this place seem so familiar?

"The cold is merely nothing. Amontillado! You have been imposed upon. And as for Luchesi, he cannot distinguish Sherry from Amontillado."

The two men stood just within the doorway opposite her own, one at the far end of the otherwise empty room, their silhouettes surrounded by a haze of dim violet light. Who were they? What were they talking about? And where was she?

The bell-capped figure took the arm of the other. Then that man raised a mask to his face. He drew his cloak in tighter and they hurried off.

Isobel crept forward, toward the archway where they'd stood.

A deep, bold sound arose from behind, halting her steps. The noise vibrated through the carpet, strong enough to stir the curtains. It rolled through Isobel's shoes and through the solid black walls. Dread, like a poison, spread its way through her, and she turned toward the source of the noise.

Like a dark sentinel, an enormous ebony clock now stood in place of the door she'd walked through not a moment before. The clock's face, like that of an unforgiving god, glowed white in the surrounding blackness while the chimes sang out a discordant melody.

The party music died out at once and with it, the voices and all laughter. The clock's song washed clear and haunting through the chamber and the hall, resonating like a false lullaby. When its cry died down, snuffing out at last with a lingering, mournful echo, Isobel could hear nothing but the sound of her own blood rushing through her ears. That, and the quiet turning over of the clock's innermost mechanisms.

She'd been here before, she realized, if only in her mind. It was exactly as she'd imagined it too. Every detail. Down to the clock that now towered over her, real as life itself.

Then the clangs came, dull and droning, and the seed of Isobel's fear grew.

She rushed back toward the clock, but any trace of the door she'd entered through had vanished. In its place, a silver pendulum close to Isobel's own size swung to and fro just as the lightbulb had. It swayed back and forth as the clock chimed the hour.

Four. Five. Six.

Wait. What time was it?

Nine. Ten.

Isobel's eyes rose to the face of the clock. One long spearlike hand aimed at twelve, the other, shorter hand at eleven. She listened as the last chime throbbed around her until it dissolved into nothingness.

There was a beat of pure silence. The gears in the clock finished turning, and then a woman's light laughter trickled from some chamber far away. It was followed by the pluck of strings and the immediate build of voices. The music started again, and somewhere, a champagne cork popped.

No. No. No. This wasn't real. She placed a hand to her forehead, trying to backtrack through her memory, to recall in reverse order the night's events. This couldn't be happening. She was dreaming. She had to be dreaming.

The clock's pendulum sliced through the air like a scythe, reaping the seconds. With each pass, its ornately engraved silver surface flashed a mottled version of Isobel's reflection.

The pendulum passed again, revealing in the circle of

silver the white face of an empty-eyed figure, one which now stood behind Isobel.

She gasped and swung around, nearly tumbling backward into the clock.

There was no one. Her eyes darted, catching the tail end of the fleeting shadows thrown by the flickering light of the bloodred windows.

She looked back at the clock and the pendulum passed again, reflecting only her own image. Isobel took a step back. She looked up at the clock and saw the minute hand twitch. She turned and ran for the violet archway.

Midnight. That was when it had happened in the story. That was when it *would* happen, she realized with renewed panic. Wherever she was, whatever was going on, dream or not—she had an hour. One hour. To do what? To find the door Varen told her to find? Did he think she would leave him? And if she couldn't find him before midnight, *then* what?

Isobel pushed the thought out of her mind and passed through the archway, eager to escape the black chamber. Violet walls hugged in close around her in a short, curving, almost tunnel-like passageway. It funneled her into another room of about the same size, this one sharp violet with windows cut to resemble amethyst jewels.

Where the black chamber had been empty, people stood scattered throughout the violet, dressed like peacocks and jesters, demons and queens. There were feather masks and silk masks, glittering gowns with belled sleeves, top hats and long cloaks. Countless golden ornaments hung suspended from the ceiling, filling the space like a gilded solar system. A young woman decked in white ostrich feathers and diamonds lay stretched on a divan. Her ivory slipper hanging from one toe, a glass of wine in each hand, she laughed hysterically as a tiny man in a green and yellow jester's costume took one false fall after another.

Isobel scanned their masked faces, their forms, looking for anyone—anything—familiar. She pushed through the room and wove her way around groups and couples.

Reaching the archway to the next room, she had to pull herself back to one side to avoid being trampled by a long train of revelers. Hands linked, they rushed past her, screaming and shrieking with laughter. The last person in line, a man wearing a floppy-eared dog mask, reached to grab her hand, to pull her along. Isobel fell away from him, half stumbling into the next room.

This chamber, white as snow and decorated in pastels, opened large and wide around a circular dance floor filled with revolving dancers. Gilt details chased the curved walls and netted the domed ceiling far above. The whole room glistened and sparkled like the inside of a Fabergé egg.

Dressed like iridescent dragonflies, the musicians sat huddled in one corner. They played their instruments feverishly, bowstrings fluttering like the wings of the insects they represented. The rhythm they kept was a steady one-two-three, one-two-three. Dancers turned like dervishes, bead-and-gemstone-encrusted skirts flaring out.

Powdered and pale, the women looked like stale pastries.

Tall and with garish, pointed masks, the men seemed like predators.

She caught a glimpse of a familiar figure. He turned away, locked in dance with a dark-haired girl in red.

"Varen!" Isobel ran onto the crystal tiled floor, dodging between dancers, ducking below gloved arms and snapping fans. She lost sight of them, then saw the couple again and pressed toward them once more. She was sure it was him. His hair, his height and frame—they matched. And the girl. Had it been Lacy?

She ran straight for them, shoving to get through. The couple disappeared and reappeared in flashes through the web of costumed courtiers. They twirled in front of her, glided behind her—then just beside. She felt the brush of the red skirts against her leg as they passed, and she fought to follow them, forcing her way through the linked arms of one couple.

Reaching them at last, she grasped his shoulder. He turned. Black eyes stared down at her though the holes of an equally black bird's mask. The figure smiled, flashing crimson teeth.

"Care to cut in, cheerleader?" Pinfeathers asked. He moved aside from the arms of the girl in red, revealing her dress to be the twin of Lacy's, complete with the stains that Isobel had caused earlier. In fact, everything was Lacy. Everything except for the featureless, fleshy space where her face should have been.

Isobel uttered a sound of shock. Pinfeathers took up her hands, pulling her to him.

"What? No!"

He spun her before she could wrench away, and they coiled in a tight circle. The world blended into a mesh of chaos, color, and noise.

"Stop!" she shouted, but he ignored her, throwing her into revolution after revolution, almost swinging her into another pair of masked dancers who scampered aside, laughing.

"Where's your mask?" he asked. "Everyone is wearing one but you, cheerleader. Are you trying to say you have nothing to hide?" He dragged her through the steps.

"Let go of me!"

"You know, I've been chatting with your friend all evening."

"Varen? Where is he?"

"Really, cheerleader. I'm beginning to think you have a one-track mind." He pushed her away violently, and Isobel stumbled outward, nearly toppling into a pair of courtiers dressed as what she thought must be a pair of black spray-painted toucans. She stared at them confused, and in return, they glared at her until Pinfeathers yanked her once more into the dance. She crashed flat against him and he spun her again.

"I meant your *other* friend," he said. "Then again, you have so many. It's been hard just to keep them all straight! I wouldn't exactly say he's much of a conversationalist, though. Kind of the strong, silent type. At least until he screams. You look beautiful tonight, by the way, have I told you yet?" He smiled.

Distracted by his words, trying hard to read his meaning, Isobel forgot for a moment about the world spinning madly around her, forgot about the dance. She stared at him, searching. Grinning, he stared back as though waiting for her to get the punch line. But she didn't. If he wasn't talking about Varen, then who could he mean?

He swept her into another spin. This time Isobel felt herself twirl effortlessly into the movement. Somehow, while she hadn't been paying attention, her body had picked up the dance. Her feet followed through with the steps. She looked down at her pink slippers, confused at the sight of them gliding over the floor. It was as though she knew the dance perfectly, even though she'd never waltzed in her life.

"There now, that's better," he said, drawing her back to him. "Look at that, you're a natural." They spun again to the trill of bells, and Pinfeathers, tilting his head back, hummed along. Beneath the mask, she could see the jagged outline of the hole in his face, the sharp red teeth within.

Something in her told her to pull away. To run. But her feet remained locked in the dance. He spun her so that her back faced him and linked clawed fingers with hers, one hand at her waist as he guided her into a promenade.

She followed his lead helplessly, her eyes trailing to the white hand that rested on her side, the red claws clutching the pink ribbon. She wanted to recoil, to pull away, but someone's lavender skirt swished against her own, startling her to press back against him. He gripped her tighter.

"Look," he hissed.

Her head popped up. Dancers churned around them like storm-tossed flowers, their heads held to either side as they whirled with abandonment.

"Look at them," he whispered, his voice in her ear. "Have you ever seen anything like it? They have everything, don't they? Everything except a single care to dwell on."

Isobel ripped her hand from his cold clay grasp. He gripped her and twisted her to face him once more, throwing her into a low dip. The world reversed itself, then he righted her too fast, and she came up with her vision swimming. He captured her hands again. His foot pushing hers, urging her back into the dance.

"Don't you see, silly girl? Don't you know that you can do anything here? You can *have* anything."

"It's not real," she said. "None of this is real."

"You're real, aren't you? Try it. Think of something you want. Think of something you want more than anything. Wait. I know . . . but first you have to close your eyes." He stopped the waltz and lifted a clawed hand toward her face. Involuntarily her eyes fluttered shut. When she opened them again, Varen stood before her.

The bruises and the cut on his face were gone. There was no sign of kohl beneath his eyes or the slim silver loop through his lip. And his hair was not the stark black she knew, but a gentle wheat color. He smiled down at her, his eyes somehow warmer, green like a forest. Each difference in him was subtle in and of itself, but combined, the overall change in him was dramatic. He seemed so . . . normal.

She lifted a hand to brush her knuckles against his jaw, as he had done that night outside her house. He linked fingers with her free hand, and she was surprised not to feel the sharpness of his dragon ring or the hard corners of his class ring. His skin felt so warm against her own. She glanced at the front of his button-up shirt. It was blue—her favorite shade—and it looked good on him.

She lifted her eyes, searching his face.

"Trust me," he whispered.

"But I—"

"Just let go."

40

In a Vision

"Isobel, did you hear me? I said, let's go."

"What? Where are we going?"

He laughed, and a dimple appeared that she never knew he had, but it seemed to make sense on him now that it was there. "Swanson's class, where else?" He turned, their hands still linked, and began to wade through the crowd.

Lockers slammed. Around them, kids pulled on their backpacks and grabbed their books. Up ahead, Mr. Swanson stood outside his door, ushering students inside.

They were at Trenton. At school. How had they gotten here?

"Ah, Var-obel," Mr. Swanson said as they approached, "nice to see you make it on time for once. Isobel, I still need that paper on Cervantes. I know there's a game this Friday, but can we get that in by next week?"

Paper. Cervantes. *Don Quixote?* Had she ever finished that one?

"I think she's almost done. Didn't I help you with that one? Isobel?"

Overhead, the bell rang shrill and loud. She looked up in search of its source.

"Okay, okay, I believe you." Swanson sighed. He gestured for them to go inside. "Go. Sit. Learn."

For a moment Isobel stayed. She glanced down the hall behind her, wondering where it was they'd just come from. Why could she not remember sitting through the class before this one? And where did she get these dark-rinse jeans and fitted pink V-neck tee, anyway? Varen tugged her, and like a soap bubble, the thought broke. She followed him in and he led her to their usual spot. Automatically, she took the desk beside his. Why did it feel so different to sit on this side of the room? Hadn't she been sitting here all year?

"Are we still on for dinner at your parents' house tonight?" Varen asked.

Her head whipped toward him. Dinner with her parents?

"I want to ask your dad some more questions about the University of Kentucky. I know he went there for football, but I think he mentioned they had a good English program, too, right?"

"Yeah," she said, thinking she remembered. That's right. They were supposed to have lasagna, she thought. And hadn't Danny been pestering her all week about getting Varen over to help with the game he'd gotten stuck on?

"Okay, kids," Mr. Swanson said, "today is a very exciting day, because we're covering Robert Frost and Ezra Pound. Two of my favorites. You can be sure that means these poems will be ground into the very marrow of your malleable little brains. Don't worry, though. Someday you'll thank me. Now turn to page two-twenty-six, and let's take a look at 'The Road Not Taken.' Can I get a volunteer to read? Emma?"

Emma Jordan's voice broke through from the back of the classroom. "'Two roads diverged in a yellow wood, and sorry I could not travel both . . .'"

Isobel glanced toward Varen again. She watched as he stared down at the open pages of the book in front of him. Sunlight caught on his light hair. This had been how they'd first met, she thought. The first day of school, when he'd sat down next to her and had asked her to write her number on his hand so that he wouldn't lose it.

Isobel smiled to herself, remembering.

He'd taken her out to eat for their first date. A fancy Chinese restaurant. And just last week, hadn't he given her his class ring? Isobel glanced down at her right hand. The thick gold band was held tight on her finger by the soft felt strip he'd wrapped it with so it would fit her. The Trenton blue stone inside glinted in the light, bringing back the memory of the moment he'd asked her to wear it. It had been that day sitting in his car outside her house, the day he'd asked her to go with him to junior prom.

Outside, autumn sunlight winked at her through a fluffy, cotton white haze of cloud cover. She looked forward and watched Mr. Swanson. He leaned against his desk, holding a copy of the textbook open in his hands. His eyes closed, and she watched him mouth key words along with Emma while she read. That was the way you could always tell which parts were his favorites.

When Emma finished the poem, Mr. Swanson opened his eyes and straightened his glasses. "Okay," he said, "now let's talk about what Mr. Frost is saying here. Does anyone have any thoughts on what the metaphor is? Yes, Miss Andrews."

"He's talking about taking different paths in life. Making different choices."

"Yes, good. That's definitely one way to look at it. He's talking about making not just the literal choice of walking down a physical pathway in the forest, but coming to a fork in the road of life and making a decision. We're a product of our choices, wouldn't you say? If the narrator of the poem had taken another path, things would have been different for him, right? Perhaps drastically so. That's the 'difference' he's talking about here. Very good. Anyone else?"

Isobel looked down at her desk, realizing she hadn't taken out her book yet. She leaned over and opened her backpack, pulling out her copy of *Seventh Edition Junior English*. She glanced at Varen's copy to get the right page number, then flipped to a black-and-white portrait of Robert Frost. Next she reached down to get a pencil and her notebook. She stopped, though, noticing the time on her pink locket watch clipped to her bag. The hands read 11:20. But that couldn't be right. Class started at eleven. Was her watch running fast? Or had Danny set it forward as a joke? She unclipped the watch from her bag and held it between her fingers, twisting the tiny dial on one side. The minute hand refused to budge. She shook the small watch, sending the pink liquid glitter within rushing around.

Isobel paused, staring at the watch face as the glitter settled. She focused on the reflection of her eyes in the clear glass.

But . . .

Hadn't she smashed this watch?

Maybe she'd dreamt that.

No. The park. Running. That had been real. The book had smashed the watch. The book. The Poe book. *No again*, she thought. She'd thrown that book away because it had come back. Or did that happen later? But then that really must have been a dream, because books don't come back on their own. Isobel scowled, none of it making sense.

She looked once again at the open pages of her book, at the picture of Robert Frost sitting in his chair, holding out a sheet of paper and reading from a distance.

Suddenly that didn't seem right either. They weren't on Frost yet.

Slowly, carefully, Isobel set her watch on the desktop. She grabbed her book and flipped to the index, scanning. Pasternak, Plath, Pope. What? Where was . . . ?

"Poe," Isobel whispered aloud. Keeping her head low, she glanced toward Varen.

He looked at her, eyebrows raised.

She flipped through the pages of her book. "Where's Poe?"

"Page two-twenty-six," he said, and reached a hand over to help her.

She jerked the book from his grasp. "But we're not

studying Frost yet," she hissed. "We're studying Poe and the Romantics."

Mr. Swanson stopped talking. "Miss Lanley, is there something you'd like to add?" he asked.

She straightened in her chair to find twenty sets of eyes trained on her. Everyone stared at her, and suddenly a creepy feeling stole over her. There was something not right about them. Any of them.

In unison, they all blinked.

"Uh—Poe," she said, and then had to clear her throat. "He—he's not in here," she clarified. She held up the book in one hand. "I thought we were supposed to be studying Edgar Allan Poe." She glanced up—and froze in Mr. Swanson's gaze.

Mr. Swanson lowered his glasses, his eyes black. "Who?"

Isobel whipped her head back to stare at Varen. He watched her with a strange fierceness, frustration in the eyes that had since turned black as ink. His face, now wan and sunken, contorted with anger, scarcely resembled Varen's at all.

That's when she realized that it *wasn't* Varen.

Isobel launched out of her seat. She made a break for the open door. Screams arose from her phantom classmates. Their faces twisted, their expressions demonic. Hands grabbed at her from all sides, but she yanked free and cleared the tangle of desks.

The room stretched and elongated before her like a tunnel. The door in front of her fell farther away. She ran faster, and the door slid back farther. It started to close. The faster she ran, the faster it moved. It boomed shut as she reached it. She groped for the handle but there wasn't one.

"You're always running away. You ruin everything" came a static voice from behind.

Isobel whirled to find herself alone in the classroom with Pinfeathers. His scarecrow figure sat occupying the desk the false Varen had. Slowly he rose, and Isobel pushed herself flat against the door, felt the coldness of it against her bare shoulders. She looked down, finding herself in her party dress again. Outside the door, she could hear music and people.

With quiet steps, he moved toward her, tucking a pencil behind one ear.

"You could have it all, you know. If you'd only let go," he said, danger lacing his tone.

"I don't want a lie."

"Why not think of it as just another version? A better version. Really, no less truthful than the last. Perhaps even more truthful. Think of it as another chance to go back to that road not taken. To see what it would be like. To *live* what it would be like."

"You're not him."

"Aren't I?"

Isobel eyed him, skittish as she marked his approach, even though there was nowhere to run. His words seeped into her, burrowing deep into the recesses of her mind, raising flags of doubt. He stopped at a distance, letting her eyes scour him, his hands folded at his back and his chin turned down, as though posing for a snapshot. Isobel stared in disbelief, unable to deny an underlying shadow-resemblance to Varen that she had never noticed before. Where it could not be found in his face or his demeanor, it pervaded his stature, his height—his very form.

She shook her head, refusing to believe that his words held even the merest fraction of truth. She could not accept that this thing, this hollow zombie nightmare version, could hold any direct link to Varen. "It's not just stalling this time, is it?" she said. "Tell me why you're doing this."

He sighed, eyes rolling. "Blondes, always needing things *explained*."

Isobel glared, hands curling into fists.

He smiled wistfully. "See, this is why I like you. You never give up, even when you should. We need a little bit of your resolve, useless as it is. I think *that's* why, cheerleader. Because the truth is that I don't *want* to kill you. Not if I can avoid it."

He took another step forward. She hitched in a breath, her back smashing flat against the door. Her hand groped for the knob she knew she would not find.

"And that's up to you," he said, his tone softening. "If you'll only play the game, stay in the dance with me a little longer?" His head tilted to one side. He blinked those black eyes at her, the question in them, she was shocked to see, sincere—if that was a word that could be applied to Pinfeathers. That look frightened her more than his words could have. What was it, she wondered, that lurked beneath that monstrous porcelain shell? If it wasn't a soul that animated him, then what? More important, what did it want with her?

He took one step closer, then another. "Only long enough to forget." His face grew serious. "Quaff," he said, his voice hushed, "oh, quaff this kind nepenthe."

He closed the remaining distance between them in a series of movements too fast to see and pinned her to the door. He grabbed her chin, forcing her eyes to his. His nails pressed into her cheek, threatening to break the skin.

She twisted her head away, but he looped an arm around her and yanked her to him. His body felt rigid and hollow next to hers. Empty. His grip on her tightened until she could no longer breathe. He pressed his lips to hers.

Isobel's eyes flew wide. His mouth, smooth, cold, and hard, felt almost sharp against hers, like glass. He tasted of clay and ink, of blood and death.

Bile rose at the back of her throat, and along with it a scream.

He broke away from her, laughing, and released her with a shove before dispersing, unraveling into coils of smoke. Isobel fell, tumbling in a sprawl. Suddenly insubstantial, the floor shattered beneath her. She fell through, and the scream within her broke loose at last. She crossed her arms over her face, shielding her eyes from the jagged shards of emerald glass that winked around her in the blackness, threatening to shred her. She toppled until she jarred to a halt, caught by several sets of arms that dipped her into a low cradle. Glass rained like lethal confetti, a shard embedding itself in her shoulder, another slicing her ankle. She opened her eyes to find a circle of masked faces surrounding her. Above them a shattered stained-glass skylight opened to reveal the swirl of a storm-ridden sky. Ash floated through the opening left by her fall.

The group shouted jovially at catching her, and quickly they set her to her feet. Then the figures disbanded, laughing among themselves.

One look around told her that she was back at the masquerade and that she now stood within the center of a deep green chamber.

Enormous tapestries hung over the walls. A heavy black granite Egyptian sarcophagus stood at each corner of the wide, rectangular room as though on guard. Embroidered pillows and carpets lined the floor, while thick clouds of sweet smoke hazed the air. Lethargic courtiers sat, stooped, and stood around hookah pipes and bowls of smoking incense. A heavy perfume pervaded the space, making her dizzy.

Like a mirage, a dark figure emerged in her blurred vision. It surfaced through the crowd and moved toward her like death itself, face blurred and half hidden from view. She shuddered. It couldn't be twelve yet—could it? Had she missed the last chiming of the clock?

She had no time to pull away or even move before the figure seized her. A gloved hand clamped over her mouth, stopping a shout before it could emerge. He dragged her to one side of the room despite her struggling, and reaching the wall, he pulled back one corner of a heavy tapestry, one that depicted a horse trampling its rider. Revealing a small secret doorway, he thrust her inside.

Isobel rolled across the cold and damp stone floor.

She looked up to find herself inside a hidden passageway, the kind in old murder mysteries where the killer hides to spy on his victims through the eyeholes of hanging portraits. Inside this narrow passageway, a tripod torch burned yellow-orange. Its flame threw jagged shapes across the masonry and against the emerald stained-glass windows, the courtiers on the other side moving across in a shadow play of silhouettes.

Her masked abductor ducked inside and emerged above her, all towering height and grimness. She scampered backward until she met with the damp wall.

"Do you have any idea how much danger you are in?" asked a muffled voice.

Husky and ever sharp with admonishments, it was a voice she recognized immediately.

Reynolds.

And it was about time.

41
Alone

"What is wrong with you?" she exclaimed, removing one of her flats. She threw it at him with enough force to jar her shoulder in its socket. The shoe hit the wall behind him with a sharp smack. Even with the mask and hat, the surprise in his eyes could not have been missed.

"Where the hell have you been?" she raved. Wasting no time, she wrestled her other shoe free and hurled it at his chest. He blocked the slipper with a raised forearm, and it tapped harmlessly onto the floor. She was sorry she didn't have anything else to throw.

Blood oozed from the embedded glass in her shoulder, and she reached up to yank the splintered shard out. She hardly felt the pain, only the blood as it trickled warm down her shoulder to stain the neckline of her dress. She was angry enough to throttle him. Yet at the same time, she could have just as easily rushed him, thrown her arms around him, and buried her face in his cloak. Somehow, though, she figured Reynolds probably wasn't the touchy-feely type, and if you'd asked him beforehand to fill in an option bubble on the questionnaire, she thought he'd probably have opted for the shoes anyway.

"Don't you look at me like that!" she snarled, her teeth chattering. The quaver in her voice betrayed her emotion.

He continued to stare as Isobel struggled unsteadily to her feet. Her knees wobbled.

"This is all your fault!" she shouted. "None of this started happening until you showed up! I don't even know who you are! I don't even know *what* you are!"

"Lower your voice."

"No! I'm not going to lower my voice!" Isobel yelled, incensed. What gave him the right to talk to her like she was a child? "You say you're helping me, but then you just disappear. You show up just to freak me out, and then, when I need you the most, you aren't anywhere, while those other *things* are everywhere!"

"Isobel—"

"So far I've been jerked around, thrown through a window, molested by a monster, and now practically abducted! What do you want from me? Why won't you or anybody else tell me what's happening? Why can't I tell what's real and what's not anymore? Why am I inside this nightmare story?"

"There is no time for this. You should not even be here."

"That's it! The next person who tells me I shouldn't be where I am gets decked! I *know* I shouldn't be here, but I am, and as far as I can tell it's because you—"

"It is because of the boy and his utter carelessness," Reynolds corrected, and with such sudden ferocity that it made her swallow against the anger boiling inside her.

"Where is he?" she asked, quieter now.

"With her," he whispered, as though pronouncing a death sentence.

"Who?" She remembered Varen's earlier mention of a "she." And then those hands that had dragged him into the darkness. She thought about the white light from the woodlands and the figure reflected in the clock pendulum with those black-socket eyes.

"I have no time. You must return to your world immediately. You must seal the link that has been made, because I cannot. Otherwise, your entire world will be forfeited to this one. Come. We must make our way to the woodlands. Hurry."

He held a gloved hand out to her, just as he had done that first night he'd brought her to the Woodlands of Weir.

"I'm not going anywhere with you."

He studied her with those dark eyes, as though trying to gauge the level of her seriousness.

"You refuse?"

"Do you think I would leave him here?"

He stepped toward her, and she had to resist the urge to shrink back. "Isobel, there are countless realities at stake. There are entire existences. You have no idea of the scope. And believe me when I say that whatever in your world does not die from such a merge will surely wish it had. You would sacrifice everything for the sake of one who is already lost? Think of your home. Your family."

As she weighed his words, doubt crept over her resolve. Was he telling the truth? What reason did he have to lie? Then again, what reason did he have not to? When it came down to it, what did she know about him or any of his reasons except that, as far as she had seen, those reasons had always been his own?

Well, two could play at that game. "Tell me how to find him first. Help me and I'll do what you want."

He spoke fast, his words heated. "Do you not see what has become of him? He is no longer part of your world."

"I don't believe you."

"It is true enough," he said. His coldness cut her like a blade of jagged ice. "And if you do not follow me now, it will be too late for you, and all for whom you care."

"Are you Poe?" She surprised herself with the question.

"Edgar is dead. He is the fortunate one."

"Then you knew him," Isobel said with authority, sure of the truth behind that statement as soon as she spoke it aloud. There had already been too much evidence. Too much proof. "That's why you're here now, isn't it? This all happened before, didn't it? To him? To Edgar."

"The past, too, is dead."

Isobel stared at him in disbelief. They continued to stand opposite each other, neither of them moving while an invisible force seemed to pulse between them—an intangible sensation like the push of opposing magnets.

"Fine," she said at last.

He whirled and strode into the passageway on the right again. Clearly he expected her to follow. Isobel did not move.

"I don't need you," she called after him. He stopped again.

She spun away from him and stooped to gather her shoes. "I don't need your secrets." She slipped on the once pink flats, now caked in grit. "I'll find him myself." She rose, smoothing back a straggling strand of hair from her eyes, and turned toward the passageway on her left.

"Stop," he commanded.

She ignored him and kept walking, certain that before her lay new chambers. New nightmares.

"He wouldn't leave *me* behind," she called.

"You are so certain?"

"Yes. Because just like you, he's not everything he pretends to be," she said. "And even though you're saying this now . . . you still didn't leave Edgar, did you? You helped *him* get back, didn't you? So don't tell me there's no way!"

"*Isobel.*" His voice, a whisper, came sharp now. Wounded.

Her stab in the dark had done more than just graze the truth. It had found the very marrow . . . good enough at least to strike a deeper chord in the monotonous dirge that was Reynolds.

She would leave him with that.

She kept her steps steady into the darkness and the dampness. Ahead, through the webwork of shadows, she saw that the passageway turned sharply. Around that corner, she knew she would find herself utterly alone.

"*Isobel,*" he hissed after her. "If you turn your back on me, you leave me with no choice but to turn my own on you. Continue and we are as good as adversaries."

"Then at least now I know."

Determined, she took the turn sharply without so much as a backward glance. Another damp stone corridor stretched before her.

Darkness there, and nothing more.

Her footsteps were her only company now. Even the voices behind the walls had ceased. She did not expect Reynolds to follow. She knew enough about him now to understand that he meant what he said. He had his own agenda. His own ghosts to chase.

Just as there was no way to know what lay ahead, there was no way to know how much time she had left. It was safe to say that midnight was close, though.

But maybe—just maybe, she thought as she rounded the next corner, where ahead she could make out a dim aura of deep purple light—she was closer.

42

A Vow

Isobel came to the place where the next torch stood. Here the dank passageway smelled of kerosene and must. Orange flames cast their glow over a deep purple stained-glass window set into the stone wall, and she knew that beyond it lay the purple chamber of Poe's story.

There was no hidden door or secret nook leading in as with the green chamber, however. At least none that she could find in the wall or on the floor.

Stepping around the torch, Isobel sidled up to the narrow window and pressed her hands flat against the stone wall beside it. She passed her fingers over the grooves and mortar, feeling for some clue to a way in. She leaned her shoulder to the wall and strained to hear either voice or movement. The heat from the fire, warming her face and arms, threw her shadow onto the wall beside her. She heard nothing at first, but soon she sensed a fluttering from within.

She pulled back, lowering her gaze, and focused hard on the purple glass, as though that would cause the rustle from within to amplify. In one corner of the window, she saw a pinprick of yellow light shining through. It was a hole, a tiny dime-size notch missing from the stained glass.

Isobel crouched, careful not to let her shadow catch in the torchlight or fall across the colored pane. At an angle, she peeked through the opening.

She saw the source of the fluttering at once. At the opposite end of the room, a wide casement window stood open. Large purple curtains snapped and stirred in the breeze. Outside this window, a tangled outline of naked black tree limbs scratched at a churning backdrop of ominous gray-purple clouds. Inside the room itself, centered in a pool of yellow light, she could just make out the corner of a plush purple velvet chair.

And the edge of one black boot.

She shifted, repositioning herself. No matter what angle she tried, though, all she could make out were the curtains, the purple carpet, the yellow light, and the boot.

She thought about calling out, but what if it was just another trick? Another illusion? And if it wasn't Varen in that chair, then it had to be one of the Nocs . . . or something worse.

Isobel raised a cautious hand. She wiggled a finger into the hole and waited. With the curtains' next heavy round of flapping, she tugged at the glass. An entire fist-size, diamond-shaped chink broke free from its black-web template, leaving a much larger hole than she'd intended.

She cringed silently and slid back an inch, hoping no one inside had witnessed the chink's removal. Even at a distance, though, she could now see the room in much greater detail. Bookshelves stuffed with dust-caked tomes lined the walls, and she was reminded at once of Nobit's Nook. On a nearby table sat an old-fashioned oil lamp. Dimly lit, it was a partial source of the overlay of yellow light. The other contributor was the bed of fading embers glowing low within the enormous fireplace in front of the purple chair.

Isobel's gaze returned at once to that chair, to the hand that rested on the velvet-covered armrest. A familiar silver ring glinted on a finger belonging to the even more familiar hand. Her eyes traveled up the green jacket sleeve. His head down, Varen sat staring at the purple carpet in front of him, his black hair drawn around his face. Startled at the sight of him, Isobel dropped the slice of purple glass. It *tink*ed against the stone floor.

Varen's head jerked in the direction of the sound. Isobel opened her mouth but stopped just short of calling out to him when the caw of a bird split the silence of the room. Varen's gaze shot forward again, and in that same instant, a quick black thing raced across the room, casting its ghostlike shadow over the fluttering curtains, the floor, the walls, and the rows of bookshelves.

The creature sailed from its high perch into view. Large wings beat against the swirling air as it landed on the back of Varen's chair. Stepping from foot to foot, the bird tucked in its wings. Hunched, it glared through the gloom with beady, coal black eyes.

Isobel ducked low beneath the window ledge. She held her breath in silence and waited.

"What was that noise?" croaked a hoarse voice.

"My imagination," Varen replied, his own voice smooth and dry in comparison, his tone acidic.

"You can't play tricks on *me*," returned the bird.

To this, Varen remained silent. Isobel huddled close against the wall, both hands clamped over her mouth. She shut her eyes, listening hard.

This time a new sound, muffled and distant, assaulted her ears. It had come from an entirely different direction. Someone shouting—screaming. It was a sound of pure terror, and it slashed through her mind like a lance.

"Ah," the bird said with a coughing rasp that might have been a laugh. "Our friend again. It's been over an hour now and he's still at it."

Another tortured yell echoed through the passageway around her. It was followed by the faraway sound of banging.

"Stop it. Let him go. Send him back," Varen murmured.

"Oh, really. Does it bother you that much to hear?" The voice morphed as it spoke, growing deeper, shedding its gravelly tone for a more caustic sound. "Come now," it said, "I would have thought that after everything, you would enjoy it a little. Besides, it was *your* idea."

"You did it, not me."

"Yes, of course I did. But not until *you* thought it."

Easing to one side, her back pressed to the wall, Isobel peeked through the hole again. In the chair, Varen sat nearly folded over, his face buried in his hands, while Pinfeathers's tall form paced in a wide circle around him. His thin shadow, cast from the yellow glow, fell long over Varen.

Isobel looked up to find an added source of the light. It shone brightly from behind the orb-eyed bust of an ancient

Greek warrior, which stared sightlessly down from its place above a set of ornately carved double doors.

Isobel's attention zoned in on those doors. From what she could tell, besides the open window, they looked to be the only way into or out of the room. They probably connected to another colored chamber, she thought. She wondered if she would be able to find some way to get to them from where she was now if she continued down the same passage. If she found her way to those doors, would they be unlocked? After all, even if she could knock out all the glass from the stained-glass window, it would still be too narrow for a person to fit through.

"Funny as it sounds," Pinfeathers said, "you, of all people, confuse me the most in this. I thought this was exactly what you wanted."

"It was."

"But now you've changed your mind."

Varen did not answer.

"Or rather, I should say, *she* changed your mind. The cheerleader. Well, anyway, that's why you're in so much trouble, I'll tell you that. Too many admirers and not enough that's admirable." There was a long beat of silence in which Pinfeathers strode to stand between the curtains. Arms folded, he stared out. "She *is* lovely, though, isn't she?" he continued. "Especially when she gets angry. But you already knew that. Of course, they're *both* lovely. And in such different ways. You know, though, I should probably warn you right now that you and I—seeing as what we are—well, we're bound to have similar tastes. Then again, that's an odd thing for me to say, because the cheerleader isn't much in your tastes at all, is she?"

"Shut up."

"And I think that's part of it. You know—together we seem to have a real problem with wanting things we just can't have. Only now you've got it all. Apparently, it's more than you can handle."

"I said, shut up."

"Though it might cheer you up to know that she *is* strong. Or at least she's got it strong for you. And I mean *you*. I have to admit, it makes me more than a little jealous. But you have to wonder if—are you listening to me?"

"No."

Pinfeathers sighed. "Your dismal moods bore me."

"Then go away," Varen said.

"I think I might. Perhaps I'll go check on our friend again. Tap, tap, tap on his chamber door once more before we carry him out to finish the job. Heh. Though a word to the wise for you. The Mistress returns soon, and between then and now, I think I would change my mind about doing what she asks. At least, I would if I were you. Ha-ha! If I were you—get it?" Isobel watched as Pinfeathers transformed again. He shrank, contorting, his wiry frame turning murky through wisps of violet until he emerged once more as a large black bird. His dry laugh morphed into a croaking cackle. Then he flapped his wings and, circling the room once, shot through the cur-tained window.

When he was gone, Isobel moved the tripod torch aside and positioned herself in front of the stained glass. "Varen," she whispered.

His gaze turned slowly toward her. Through the diamond-shaped chink, his black eyes met with hers. His face, so white, so drawn, seemed like that of a ghost.

"Varen?" she called again, this time louder. "Varen, it's me. It's Isobel."

"Isobel," he said simply, his voice a monotone.

"Yes. It's me."

"Isobel is gone," he said, turning to stare into the fireplace. The fading embers within cast a low orange glow across his face. "I told her to take the door in the woodlands."

"No. I didn't leave. I wouldn't. Not without you. Please. How do I get inside?"

"You can't," he mumbled, "even if you were real."

"Varen. Look at me. I *am* real. I came to find you. It's me— I can prove it. "

All at once, the screams started again. Muffled, long howls of anguish grew louder, accompanied this time by a barrage of brutal banging. Her heartbeat tripling, Isobel looked in the direction of the hellish racket. It was coming from the next chamber over. For a moment, despite its rawness, she thought she recognized the voice, and it spread a sick dread through her.

Brad.

But that was impossible. How could *he* be here?

Isobel looked back to the window and started, her heart leaping almost painfully in her chest. Varen was there, standing before the mottled stained-glass pane that separated them. Through the open chink, his black eyes rested on her. His bruised face, wan and void of emotion, seemed almost alien in the dim light.

"You're a dream," he said, "like everything else."

Isobel frowned. She remembered how Reynolds had told her once that Varen dreamed of her. With that thought in mind, she lifted a fist to knock away more of the glass, not caring if she cut herself. The little pieces fell onto the carpet inside the purple chamber, sprinkling around his feet, and Isobel pushed her hand through the widened hole. "Touch me," she said. "I'm real. Even if this is a dream, I'm not."

She felt his fingers, light as dust, trace her palm. They left in their wake a prickling sensation that made her skin seem almost to vibrate. Seconds passed.

Another scream, louder but still muffled, poured like scalding liquid through the passageway. Isobel withdrew her hand, scanning the stone-walled corridor behind her, trying to determine from which direction the yelling had come. She was sure it had echoed to them from the right, opposite the way she had entered. Her eyes returned to Varen, tracing the split above his lip, and she dreaded having to say the words she needed to now.

"Varen." She kept her voice measured. "Do you hear that? I have to go help Brad."

He lifted his eyes to hers, and, despite their blackness, she could not mistake the hatred that burned within their centers. She swallowed, choosing her words carefully. "They—they're hurting him," she said. "He may deserve a lot, but he doesn't deserve to die. I know you understand that. I'll come back to get you, too, okay?"

"*Why?*" he snapped.

"Because," she said with a gasp, unable to fathom the source of his question, or his tone. "Because I love you, that's why."

He turned his head and looked away from her, back into the chamber.

"Listen." She gripped the window frame. "We'll fix it, okay? We'll find a way."

"It's too late." It was scarcely a whisper.

"Don't say that! There *is* a way. If it's us together, me and you, then there's a way. Okay? We got through the project, didn't we? Even though everything went wrong. Even though everyone stood in our way. Varen?"

His eyes regarded her once more, and this time she searched them for her reflection, for any evidence of light. But they returned only a blackness so pure, so frighteningly bottomless, that it took all of her willpower not to turn away.

"Say okay. Please?" she pleaded.

He stared at her.

Another scream split the stillness. The shrill sound of it ratcheted up her spine and, reaching through her like a clawed hand, seized her heart with a clutching grip. She winced. "Varen, they're killing him. I have to go try to stop it. But you have to say okay first. Please. Say that you know I'm coming back. Just say okay. For me?"

He looked down.

She shook her head. "Don't you believe me?" Her eyes stung with the threat of tears. She could hardly stand to see him this way. It was as though the Varen she knew had been consumed, replaced by this husk of despair, his soul recessed so deeply within that no light could reach it. If there was only some way she could prove that it was the real her who stood before him, and not some phantom imposter. If she only had something to give him, some sort of proof. Or just something to leave with him. A token. A promise. Anything, as long as it was something as real and solid as her.

Isobel ran her hands over her dress, fingers fumbling, grasping for something to give him.

Then her hands stopped on the ribbon tied around her waist. She let her fingers follow the smooth satin fabric to the bow at her back. With nimble fingers, she unlaced the knot and it slipped free from her waist with a soft whisper.

"Here," she said. Reaching through the jagged hole in the window, she offered him the ribbon. "Take this," she said. "It's mine, and I'm coming back for it, so *don't* lose it. You have to hold onto it. You have to keep it safe. For me. Do you understand?"

At first he only stared at the ribbon, but then he lifted one of those elegant hands to touch the fabric. Then their fingers brushed as he slowly pulled the satin free, winding it around his own hand. As she drew back, she saw his fingers curl around it in a fist. Clutching it, something within him seemed to stir. His brow furrowed in confusion, as if there were something about the pink ribbon now encircling his hand that he couldn't quite understand.

"Listen," she said. Around them, Brad's screams continued, building in volume, curdling into a crescendo of utter terror. Isobel struggled to concentrate on her words with the sound of Brad's anguished shrieks echoing in her ears. "Try—try to open the doors. Reynolds—My friend says that if . . . that if you know you're dreaming, then you can control things. So try to open the doors, okay? Try. If you can't, then just wait here for me."

She stood and began to edge backward, away from the window, hardly able to stand the thought of leaving him there, alone. But she had to do something for Brad. She couldn't let him die or continue to be tortured like this. Whatever was happening to him, she had to make it stop.

"Isobel?" Varen called to her in a whisper.

"Hold on," she said. "Hold on and wait. For me." She turned away from him, toward the direction of the screaming, which came now between bursts of a pounding sound like someone beating their fists against a bolted door. She began to run.

"Isobel!"

"I'll be right back, I promise!" These last words echoed through the passageway around her. *I promise*, she thought, repeating her vow over and over in her mind.

I promise.

43
The Oblong Box

The passageway ahead grew colder, narrower, and more maze-like. Her breath clouded in front of her, visible even in the fading light.

She listened again for the sound of screams but heard whispers instead. They seeped through the walls.

Isobel slowed her run and pressed closer to the damp stone, her fingers trailing as she strained to hear. The voices seemed to be moving along beside her, through whatever room lay on the other side.

She hurried along the passageway, struggling to keep up with the lingering sound of a long, low moan, one that had issued from the midst of the hissing snickers and low cackles. One she knew belonged to Brad.

She rounded the next bend, suddenly finding herself within a large circular room. Dark doorways lined the walls, each like the gaping mouth of a monster. Knowing there was no time to deliberate, she took one on her left, a tunnel-like entrance. This snaking pathway of stone, mortar, and dampness seemed to take her down and down. So far that the whispers and groaning faded. Along the walls and clinging to the stone overhangs, Isobel could make out the edges of a crystallized white substance. She hesitated, wondering if she should turn back, if she'd taken the right way. Was there a right way?

She pressed forward, lured through the blindfold of darkness by the promise of a glimmering, uneven light that danced against a portion of the stone wall far ahead. Shoulders hunched against the damp and cold, she passed one hand along the gritted wall to guide her. Something hard crunched under her feet, and Isobel willed herself not to look, not to even imagine what sort of matter covered the floor.

She stepped into the pocket of dim light, which illuminated a bridgelike portion of the passageway, one that overhung a vast and open vault of catacombs. Her eyes followed the orange-yellow flickering to its meager source—a torch. There, far below, a man worked in solitude. Divested of his cloak and coat, a trowel in one hand, he busied himself in laying a brick wall across a gaping black archway.

A clanking echoed from within the hole, as though from chains. A tingling of bells issued forth, and Isobel froze, her eyes widening with the realization that there was someone inside the recess. At once she recalled the pair of men she'd heard when she had first stepped through the doorway that had transformed into the ebony clock. There had been one with a mask and a cloak, and hadn't the other worn a hat with bells?

The man working to wall up the hole paused, a brick in one hand. Slowly he turned his head until his eyes met with hers. She fell back with a gasp, then plunged headlong down the darkened path.

She ran, the floor snapping and popping underfoot.

Around the next corner, at the end of the long corridor, Isobel saw a shaft of soft blue light. It streamed through an open archway, and she sped toward it. Her footing slipped on the jagged edge of something hard, and she tripped forward, slamming onto the stone, sending up a rush of dust.

The light confirmed her worst fears. Bones and ash scattered the floor.

Her fingers curled in the grit as she pushed herself onto her knees.

No, wait, she thought. *Not bones at all.*

Hand shaking, Isobel slid her fingers beneath what had looked to her a moment before like the cap of an ancient skull. It was, instead, the broken sliver of a porcelain face, the curve of a cheek all too evident in the outline. All the pieces were similarly identifiable. Broken fingers, like tiny tombstones, lay scattered in the dust. Half of a hand here. Part of an arm there. A jaw. An ear.

Isobel flung the shard aside. She stood, wiping her hands on the folds of her grime-caked dress, then pressed them to either wall to steady herself. She continued through the passage, finally stepping past the shaft of blue light and through the narrow archway. She drifted over the threshold and down one step, finding herself suddenly within the confines of a large marble crypt.

Slats of blue-gray light funneled down from high square windows, each no larger than a letter-size envelope. Inside, the smell was dry and sharp, like burnt paper. Countless broken and misshapen faces stared sightlessly down at her from their perches along marble shelves lining the four tall walls. More hollow and intact appendages littered the outer edges of the space, strewn like the remnants of discarded marionettes.

At the front of the crypt, an iron door stood ajar. Backed by blue-tinted stained glass, the door was the source of the sapphire light, which fell like a translucent gauze over the crypt's centerpiece—an elevated stone tomb. Atop the tomb, chiseled in polished marble, lay the carving of a beautiful woman, her eyes closed in death, her cold stone hands fastened around an equally frozen bouquet of roses. Isobel knew she had seen that face before, had watched it emerge from the unfolding blackness that had claimed Varen.

The woman's hair, like that of a sorceress, lay spread around her head. It draped over the sides of the sarcophagus in long, coiling tendrils. Her marble dress, heavy and flowing, like the inaugural gown of a queen, spilled from either side of the elevated tomb while the embellished train fell in gentle folds along the stairs leading down from the base. The pleats and endless ripples in the marble garment gave the illusion of softness, her face the illusion of life. It was as if at any moment Isobel could expect to see her chest rise and fall with the intake and release of breath. Perhaps the most disturbing element about the tomb, however, was that the impossibly heavy lid had been shifted open.

Isobel didn't dare climb the steps and peer inside, knowing that the only thing worse than finding a withered body within would be not finding one. She waded instead through the carpet of broken faces and parts until she reached the crypt door.

"Mistress?"

At the sound of the voice, low and grating, she halted.

"Mistress, is that you? Have you returned?" the voice asked, curious.

Isobel's hand stopped short of the iron-and-glass door. She pulled back and, with careful steps, drew to peer around the other side of the sarcophagus.

He sat slumped against the far wall, half of him lost in shadow. A Noc. He looked up, his dark gaze focusing on her. "Ah," he said, grinning, "now there's a surprise. Tell me, what demon has tempted *you* here?"

He was different from the other Nocs. This Isobel noticed right away. Instead of a dark red to black, his hair was deep black to blue-violet. As he lifted his head from the wall, his hair spiked up from his skull like the feathered crest of a bird. His teeth, pointed like the tips of countless sharpened pencils, gleamed an unsettling indigo. Though his face was whole, he was missing nearly half of himself on one side, including an arm from the shoulder down, part of his abdomen, and his leg from the knee. A thin layer of dust coated his dark pants, evidence that he'd not moved for some time.

He wore no shirt or jacket, which was what revealed the most unusual thing about him.

Scrolling designs covered much of his exposed skin. His chest, sculpted and smooth like a Greek statue's, depicted

KELLY CREAGH — 459

minutely detailed tattoos of sailing ships, tossing waves, and foam. A long-haired mermaid graced his existing shoulder, her scaly tail sweeping the length of his arm. An entire portion of the sea epic vanished into the pit of his missing side, and though the pictures themselves might have been beautiful, Isobel was too distracted by the fact that they had been chiseled into his skin like carvings. That thought, combined with his demonic grin, the garish white of him, and the jagged gaps in his body, made them somehow vulgar.

"Who are you?" she asked.

"Not who"—he wagged a blue-clawed finger at her—"*what.*"

"Fine," Isobel obliged, "what?"

"Baffled," he replied, "at how you, fetching though you are, could have cost me an arm and a leg."

Isobel stepped out fully from behind the tomb, eyeing him warily.

"If I had known about your masked friend," he continued, "and his way with a sword, I'd have let Pin go first in the chase."

"Chase?" she asked, her voice echoing through the crypt.

He grinned and pointed at something behind her with a detail-swirled finger of his existing hand. "Be a doll," he said. "Show your worth and hand old Scrimshaw that empty limb over there."

Isobel glanced over her shoulder, where against the side of the open tomb lay a hollow arm, complete from shoulder to wrist, though missing its hand.

Her head whipped back to him and she stared in disbelief, all other questions forgotten. She watched as, with his
remaining hand, he rooted through the pile of dust beside
him and pulled free a large shard. He held it against his gaping
body, like someone trying to determine where a puzzle piece
might best fit. With horror, Isobel realized what he was doing.
He was piecing himself back together. Was that possible? She
took a step back, her footstep crunching.

He looked up. "No?" he said.

She took another step back from him.

"There's gratitude," he muttered, the shadows overtaking
his form once again as she receded. "Ah," he said, and began
to sing softly to himself in a lilting tune.

> "Can it have been the woodlandish ghouls—
> The pitiful, the merciful ghouls—
> To bar up *your* way and to ban it
> From the secret that lies in these wolds—
> From the *thing* that lies hidden in these wolds—?"

Isobel turned and ran for the iron door. Behind her, he
laughed, the lyrics of his dreadful song rising in volume.

> "Well *you* know, now, this dim lake of Auber—
> This misty mid region of Weir!"

She grasped the side of the iron and tugged inward. With
a screech for each pull, the door gave inch by inch until it

yielded a space big enough to slide through. She eased out, a panel of lace ripping free from the skirt of her dress.

"Well *you* know, now this dank tarn of Auber,
This ghoul-haunted woodland of Weir!"

Isobel pushed the door shut behind her, blocking out his voice with one last shriek of iron and rust.

Outside, gray ash coated the ground of a silent cemetery. Flecks of white sifted from the purple sky, falling through the arid atmosphere to gather like snow atop the countless crooked tombstones that pockmarked the grounds in crowded patches. They leaned into and away from one another like scattered, broken teeth. Stone angels and grim, robed figures wept and grieved at the sides of aboveground tombs, while in between it all stood several of the same thin black trees as from the woodlands. Beyond the cemetery, the jagged edge of a cliff split the sky from the ground, stretching in a serrated rift spread as far as she could see.

Behind her, attached to the crypt, loomed the cathedral-like castle, the abbey from Poe's story within which raged the masquerade. Its spires pointed toward the ashen sky, jagged and wicked, like the spine of a slumbering dragon.

The view was all stillness and quiet, like some creepy charcoal etching brought to life.

Until the sound of loud knocking shattered the sanctuary quiet.

Isobel kept close to the side of the crypt, pressing one

hand to the cold marble wall as she moved away from the stained-glass door. Soon the Nocs drifted into view. She counted six of them altogether as they exited from the iron doors of another vault.

They bore aloft on their shoulders what she recognized at once as a long wooden coffin. Her heart jarred at the sight of it, fear tightening her chest.

A shout arose from within, followed by the clatter of more knocking.

On top of the coffin, like a king, perched a great black bird. In between dry croaks, it pecked at the lid, as though in answer to the knocks coming from within.

Pinfeathers. He made seven.

Another anguished cry for help came from inside the oblong box, and now she was certain. It was Brad inside that coffin. But how had they brought him here?

Isobel remembered how, on the playing field, Brad's eyes had turned black. Just like Varen's, they'd lost the vibrancy of color within the beat of an instant. But when Brad's eyes had changed, his body had remained on the field, unconscious. How, then, had he been transported here?

Isobel slipped away from the crypt. She followed them, venturing through the tangle of trees, ducking behind monuments and tombstones. She stopped at the side of a tall winged seraph weeping into her stone hands, and watched them from a distance.

Like bizarre pallbearers, they carried the coffin along toward a misty clearing encircled by more black trees.

Nearby, a mound of dirt awaited, pricked by the spade ends of several shovels. Their handles, like needles in a pincushion, stood erect from the pile, ready to be put to task.

In front of the mound, as a marker, loomed a tall, shrouded statue. A long hooded robe concealed the form's entire head and swathed its arms, which were held open over the gaping maw of the black grave.

Isobel squeezed her eyes shut and opened them again. But she didn't wake up. The scene remained. The screaming remained. It was all the same, only now the Nocs lowered the coffin from their shoulders.

"Let me out!" Brad shouted.

The Nocs laughed and together heaved the coffin into the hole. Pinfeathers squawked and fluttered up from the lid while the box landed with a crackling thud. A rush of ash burst forth from the grave. Brad howled.

Isobel drew in a sharp breath, her heart pounding so hard that it started a ringing in her ears. She gripped the base of the stone angel that hid her as if, somehow, it could give her strength.

This was insane. They were going to bury him alive, and she couldn't do anything about it. Why had she followed them out here? What did she think she could do to stop them? What could she do to stop any of this? It was just her. And the Nocs.

They would shred her to bits.

"Please! Let me out!" Brad screeched.

Isobel forced herself to look again. She watched

Pinfeathers morph out of his bird form. He took shape standing at the foot of the grave, staring down. Like buzzards, the
other Nocs gathered in, positioning themselves around the
opening.

"Please!" Brad shrieked, banging again, scratching.

Unable to bear it any longer, Isobel burst forth from
her hiding place. She had no plan. She had no idea what she
could possibly do to save Brad. Up until the moment that
she reached the grave, she had nothing but the pure rush
of adrenaline. Then, without thinking, she snatched up one
of the shovels from the mound. Brandishing it like a club,
she swung the shovel blade-first into the back of one of the
unsuspecting Nocs.

The shovel hit its mark—and kept going. The blade
swiped cleanly through him, caving his body with a crash.
The creature shrieked before toppling into the grave, where
he burst apart against the coffin lid.

Isobel stared at the place where the Noc had shattered,
shocked at her own actions.

A collective howl arose from the other Nocs. In turn, each
of them loosened into their purple-smoke selves, re-forming
into the shapes of maddened birds.

Isobel swung the shovel freely amid the frenzy of feathers
and wild flapping. The murder of crows screeched and cawed.
She batted at them blindly. Panicked, they scattered. Isobel
twirled, raising the shovel again. Something jarred it in her
grasp.

White hands clasped the shovel's handle on either side of

hers. Pinfeathers towered over her, his bloodred shark's teeth gritted in rage, his porcelain face a mask of fury.

"You!" he bellowed. "You're not supposed to be here!"

That was *it*. Detaching one hand from the shovel, Isobel reared a fist back and let it loose. Pinfeathers arched away from the attack, releasing the shovel. Thrown backward, Isobel felt herself tip into the open grave. She hit the lid of the coffin inside with a bone-jarring slam.

Over the lip of the grave, Pinfeathers's wiry frame appeared.

"Why did you come back?" he seethed.

Isobel spat ash from her mouth. She wiped sweat and grit from her eyes and leveled a defiant glare up at him.

"Time and again!" he snarled, livid, yet somehow . . . concerned? "You should have left when I gave you the chance!"

Isobel tightened her hand around a wad of dirt. She unleashed it at him. He hissed, recoiling as the spray caught him in the face.

Somewhere in the distance, a bell tower began to chime the hour. Loud, brazen bongs ricocheted through the cemetery. It was a sound that gripped her, wrung her with its meaning. Midnight. It was midnight.

"*Help!*" came a raw gurgle from the pine box beneath her.

Isobel whirled. Hands and knees on top of the coffin, she cleared away the top layer of dirt and broken bits of Noc.

"Cheerleader!"

Isobel turned to glare over her shoulder.

Pinfeathers knelt down at the edge of the grave. He

stretched one clawed hand out to her. "Take my hand. Leave him!"

Isobel grabbed for the shovel that had fallen in with her and, grasping it, swung it at Pinfeathers. He caught it easily, his forearm stretched firm along the handle.

"Stop fighting me and come!" he growled.

Isobel snarled between gritted teeth. She kept her grip on the shovel, and placing one foot against the wall of the grave, she twisted, pushing off, wrenching the shovel handle like a lever. A sharp crack echoed through the graveyard, followed by a howl. Isobel fell free, landing on her backside atop the coffin while Pinfeathers's snapped arm toppled limp into her lap.

He recoiled with a long hiss. His frame loosened once more, and he became a mix of wisps and bird. He floated above the grave, a dark mass emitting hoarse croaks and inhuman wails. His wings beat at the air with a broken rhythm, his bird's body twirling in a spiral, struggling to gain the purchase of flight. His face appeared through the vapor, long enough to roar at her. Then, as violet mist, he swept away, black plumes escaping his wings, flitting down like fallen leaves into the open grave.

In the distance, the deep chimes of the hour continued to ring, and there was no way to know how many remained to be announced. Isobel threw the hollow, broken arm to one side and returned to the coffin, which had grown silent.

"Brad!" she called. She pulled at the wooden lid. It budged only slightly. Isobel whirled, looking for the shovel.

She snatched it up and drove the blade against the side of the coffin. The wood cracked, but not enough. She tried again.

"Brad!"

She hacked the blade against the wood again, and this time a portion of one corner splintered off. Isobel dropped the shovel. She shoved her hands into the hole and pulled upward. The coffin lid came slowly. She conjured all her strength, pulling until at last the lid came free, clattering to the side just as the bell tower's final chime bonged through the cemetery.

It was twelve midnight exactly.

Inside the coffin, Brad lay silent and shaking, his eyes fixed heavenward. He was dressed in a clean hospital gown, his broken leg bandaged in a thick blue cast. Isobel reached for him, but her hands swept cleanly through, as though he were a hologram.

"Brad!" she shouted.

His shaking intensified.

"Is-Isobel?" he murmured. His eyes stared sightlessly past her, focused on something above her.

She tried grasping for him again, but once more her arms ghosted straight through him.

Something thick, wet, and warm splattered against her arm, stopping her. She looked to see a bright crimson starburst of blood glistening on her forearm. Had she been hurt?

Another splatter came, this one straight into the open palm of her questioning hand.

Isobel looked up. Blood oozed from the statue looming above her.

Great streaks of red coursed the length of its robes, sliding down the folds of its stone gown, pooling in the dirt.

"Isobel!"

Brad flew upward and past her, his limp form yanked
from the grave like a rag doll, plucked by an unseen force.
He swept up, distorted and stretched, elongating as he was
sucked one inch at a time into the visage of the statue. It drew
him in, arching the moment it absorbed him completely,
Brad's screams snuffing into silence.

Within the darkened hood, two pinpricks of ruby light
sprang to life.

Stone gave way to spilling folds of brilliant crimson.
Blood soaking through the stirring fabric of its robes, the
figure moved. It turned its head and stepped down from the
anchor of its granite base. Isobel stared in motionless horror
as the specter rounded the gaping hole in the earth, its blood-
dabbled robes fluttering about its shape as it floated more
than walked.

A heavy train of red fabric followed the form. It dragged
through the ash, causing a cascade of red-stained grit to spill
over her.

Isobel coughed and fell back, sprawling into the now
empty coffin. She squinted through a haze of dust, mesmerized as she watched the dripping thing drift around the outer
perimeter of the open grave.

"Brad?"

The figure stopped. Its glistening, fiendish gaze fell on
her. From within the drape of its sleeve, it raised a hand over

the open grave, over her. The blood-drenched, bone-thin fingers curled one at a time into a slow fist. Beneath her, she felt the ground tremble, then shudder. Above, the edges of her enclosure quivered, dirt and rock loosening until, at last, they broke forth in a tidal surge.

Earth poured over her in rushing waves from all sides. It fell against her body in heavy clods, a suffocating weight that fast became crushing.

"No!" she screamed, flailing. She thrashed, battling to loosen herself from the raining soil and ash that threatened to consume her. She fought to stand, causing the dirt to press more tightly around her. It claimed her legs, trapping her. She reached with both arms toward the edge of the grave, toward the open sky, but the earth gushed, building to her waist, to her chest. It piled past her shoulders, her head, and now raced to consume her arms, swallowing the light one fragment at a time. With it went the vision of the trees, the gravestones, the ashen sky, and the scarlet, blood-drenched visage of the Red Death.

44
Red Death

The growing silence seared her mind. Isobel arched against the constricting earth, the enclosing darkness. Her dirt prison shifted in answer to her movements, compressing.

Out! She needed to get out!

With her mouth clamped shut, she unleashed a scream from the back of her throat. But who would hear? She couldn't move her arms. Her legs. Anything. Panicked, she realized she'd been holding her breath. The packed dirt squeezed her chest, crushed her lungs. She couldn't breathe!

She gasped involuntarily and was rewarded with a mouthful of coarse grime. She swallowed and her body convulsed at the acrid taste. Her lungs burned for air. Her heart knocked hard against her rib cage, begging for release.

If she didn't get out, she was going to die. She knew it. She was going to die.

Varen. She thought his name over and over in her head. *Varen, where are you?*

No answer came to her, and gradually she grew still again. Locked in the earth's suffocating embrace, she listened to the flutter of her heart, the only sound in her ears as, beat by beat, its rhythm began to slow. Its thump reminded her of the sound of a clock, one that was winding down, about to stop forever.

At least she'd gotten to see him, she thought, to tell him how she felt. At least he knew. At least she'd tried. Tears pricked at her eyes. How could she die when she'd promised to come back for him? When he was waiting for her? She squeezed her eyes and felt the tears leave her, stolen by the absorbing dirt that had taken her breath, and with it, her final hope.

Something cool grazed the very tips of her fingers. That was when she realized that they must be the only bit of her still above ground. Her waning consciousness told her it was the wind. The sensation came again, and Isobel flexed her fingers—and felt the soft brush of . . . fabric?

All at once, the crushing pressure pushing down on her lightened. Something drove into the dirt, and Isobel latched at once to the arm that plunged to grasp hers. It pulled, and she felt herself being dragged up one inch at a time. The dirt fell away, releasing her from its death grip. Her head broke the surface. She gasped. Someone was there, pulling her free.

Coughing, Isobel sucked in cool gulps of air, her lungs battling to expel hunks of dark gray soot.

"Varen?" she choked, groping for the arms that pulled her from the grave. "Varen!"

"Why *will* you not heed my words?"

The gloved hand clutching hers tightened. She opened her eyes.

From behind the white scarf, Reynolds's dark gaze

tunneled into hers, anxious, angry, and . . . fearful? He shook
her. "Why do you not *listen* to me? If you would only take
control!"

The world swam. Above him the sky churned to a deeper,
more tumultuous violet. The ash fell heavily now, catching
like snowflakes on her eyelashes. She blinked them away.

"Varen," she croaked. She released her clutch on Reynolds
and fought to sit up.

Ahead, through blurred vision, she could see the doors
of the masquerade palace open. That *thing*—the Red Death—
had gone inside.

Isobel pushed against Reynolds, who held her still. She
struggled to stand, but he gripped her hard, holding her
steady by the shoulders. "You will not find him there."

Her eyes snapped to his.

A long, low moan of wind stirred the edges of his cloak,
the gale picking up speed. It whisked a cascade of falling ash
between them in a whirlwind.

"What are you talking about? Where is he?"

"Escaped. If I am discovered in this, his release could
cost what is left of my soul. And yours," he added in earnest.
"In truth, it could cost everything. Do not let it have been
in vain."

Isobel shook her head, trying to understand. "How?"

"I followed you," he said, his tone clipped. "You left me
no choice. I knew how to enter the purple chamber. May it be
that I was not witnessed. If he was not intercepted, then it is
on the other side, in your world, that he now waits."

Isobel hesitated, gripping his sleeve, wanting to believe. "You said there was no way!"

"In truth, there is no real escape for him—for anyone," he said. "Not unless the link he has created is destroyed. As long as it remains, this world shall always lay claim to him."

He drew back, and from within his cloak, he brought forth a gathering of coarse green cloth. A familiar jacket—Varen's. There was the emblem of the bird pinned to the back, and the patches of all his favorite bands sewn to the sleeves. Startled, Isobel reached for it. She took it in her dirt-caked hands and knew from its scent that it was truly his.

"How did you get this?"

"He bequeathed it to me as a token of testimony, because you had mentioned me as a friend. And so now, as your friend, I beseech you." She looked up from the jacket and saw that the plea within those black eyes was real, filled in equal parts with pain and desperation. "Help me to honor my vow as I have helped you to honor yours." The fluttering ash began to fall more heavily around them. "The world of dreams and the world of your reality have already begun to merge. All that you know is in danger. The fusion has only just begun. It is incomplete, and so there is yet a small chance. As long as that hope remains by your side, so shall I. But you *must* end this now."

Her eyes strayed down to the churned soil, to the thick, black liquid trail of blood, the ominous path left by the Red Death.

"What about Brad?"

"His spirit, stolen by the Nocs, exists here in astral form alone, trapped between realms. As long as he is held by forces here, his body will remain in your world while his mind, his essence, lingers here, imprisoned. A torturous link, which only death could sever. It is what happened to Edgar."

He stood, and Isobel felt herself being drawn to her feet.

"But how can I free him when I couldn't even touch him?"

"You mustn't touch him now. He has been cast in the role of the Red Death—a figure whose sole function, you well know, is to destroy."

"What do you mean? Cast by who—or what?"

"There is no more time for questions. If you wish to save either of them, then you must take action now. You must change the dream, Isobel. It is here, in this realm, that you hold the ability to control your surroundings, as long as you do not allow them to control you first. That grave"—he pointed—"you could have flown out of it."

Isobel stared at the sunken ground, disbelieving.

"Come," he said, releasing her. "We must go at once to the woodlands." He started away. Following the path of blood, he moved in the direction of the abbey.

"Wait!" she called after him, gripping Varen's jacket to herself. "First tell me why you came back. Why did you change your mind?"

"I didn't," he said without turning. "You did."

She took a wobbly step after him. "But you said—how do I know I can trust you?"

Calling back, he did not stop. "As I have been left with

no choice but to place my faith in you, Isobel, so it seems have you been left with no choice but to place yours in me."

She glared after him, a shudder running through her. He was always talking in circles like this, always leaving her with more questions than answers. It made her want to scream at him, to demand one single cut-and-dry, yes-or-no reply.

But she knew he was right. Time had run out. It had slipped through her fingers, like sand, leaving her with no other choice but to trust him. This person, this entity who she knew nothing about yet at the same time knew enough to have called him a friend. He had warned her from the beginning. He had saved her. He'd tried to save Edgar. And now he was trying to help her save Varen.

She moved to follow him, and her feet wobbled unsteadily beneath her, her knees weak. She paused to slide her muddied arms into the sleeves of Varen's jacket. She drew the fabric close around her and turned up the collar as she had once seen him do. His scent washed over her, expelling from her mind the bitter taste of dirt and the coppery smell of blood. Now each of them held in their possession something of the other's. Something to return. A double promise. Affirmation that there was still a chance. That they would see each other again when, at last, the nightmare ended.

When *she* ended it.

Ahead, Reynolds turned, waiting, his black cloak fluttering around him as he watched her through the screen of falling ash.

She ran to catch up, her footfall sure once again.

45

A Door

They found the double-doors of the palace open, a long smear of blood leading them inside to the first chamber—the blue chamber. Crystal snowflakes hung suspended from a vaulted ceiling, wavering ever so slightly in the eerie stillness that now replaced the once feverish chaos of the masquerade.

The revelers had since stopped their antics and had receded from the center of the floor. They stood in a mass of confusion and fear, masks lowered, eyes darting in the direction of the open doors leading into the purple chamber. Following on Reynolds's heels, Isobel rushed into the room. Or rather, into the space where the purple chamber should have been. Instead she found herself back in the warehouse—at the Grim Facade—the raging goth music blasting at full volume, the sudden noise of it startling her so much that for a split second she'd thought the world truly had ended.

Confused, Isobel turned to look behind her. The archway to the chamber remained, freestanding in midair, all the courtiers watching her, their faces as stunned as hers. She glanced down. Between her feet, a long wet smear of blood marred the floor.

She followed its path with her eyes, her gaze stopping on the hem of a scarlet-stained robe.

The Red Death. It glided amid the other costumers, who, Isobel noticed, began to consist of goths and dream-revelers alike. And the two worlds were only just starting to notice each other.

Reynolds appeared suddenly at her side. "Look out," he growled, shoving her.

A hissing sound pierced her ears as a Noc came sailing between them. Reynolds, his arm as quick as a striking cobra, grasped the Noc by the neck and slammed the creature to the floor, where it shattered on impact, a look of shock registering on its face the instant before it smashed apart.

Several masqueraders and goths squealed and shrank back from the commotion.

"Reynolds!" Isobel gasped, pointing. Behind him, another Noc formed through a cloud of violet murk. Reynolds whirled, taking a swipe with one arm, his movements precise, practiced. His attack sailed through the violet mist, and, laughing, the Noc slid away. Another swooped in to take its place, snatching Reynolds's hat from his head and placing it on his own, while yet a third formed through the air, its crimson claws raised.

Isobel rushed the Noc that was poised to strike. At the sight of her, it screeched in terror and dissipated. She heard an echoing shriek from somewhere to her right, followed by another smash. Then the head of the Noc that had stolen Reynolds's hat, now free of its body, rolled to a stop at her feet, its eye sockets hollow and void. Isobel brought her foot down, crushing the face in.

The remaining Nocs wailed in terror, and as one, they receded, flitting apart as they took their bird forms. Their dark wings whisked them up and higher, until they reached the banisters of the gallery, where they perched. There they squawked and hopped, their caws ringing in their throats like curses.

Isobel glanced down in time to see Reynolds replace his hat over thick, dark, and smoothed-back hair.

Somewhere in the crowd, a girl screamed. The goth music ground to a slow halt, and the moaning singer's voice died out. Everyone began to take notice, to shrink back from the visage of the Red Death. At its feet lay one of the dream-revelers, her silver dress spotted with crimson. Beneath her dove's mask, her face oozed, glistening red from the pores.

"It is happening," Reynolds said. "You must go to the woodlands now, find the door with the signs. You'll know it when you see it. The link between our worlds is there inside. You'll know that, too, when you see it. Godspeed, and beware the white one."

"What—but I don't even know how to—"

"Go," he said. "Only you can change the dream. Only you can sever the link."

She hesitated. "What about you?"

"I will fight here."

She shook her head. "That's not what I meant."

His eyes locked with hers. Surprise lit their darkness

from within. And then he laughed, a bitter sound. "For me, the worst has long since been done. Now go."

"But—!"

"I cannot vanquish the Red Death. Not without killing the boy whose soul it imprisons. I can only hold it at bay, and only for so long. Then know that I will do what I must."

"What? Brad? No! But—but I don't even know how to get to the woodlands from here!"

"Make a door, Isobel," he said. "When there is no way, you must make a way." His hands disappeared beneath the folds of his cloak. There was a scrape of metal, and in the next moment, his gloved hands emerged. In each, he now brandished a short curved blade. A pair of silver cutlasses. They glinted in a pass of strobe lights. Without a further word, he turned from her. His gait measured and assured, he walked a straight line for the figure of the Red Death.

As though alerted through some extra sense, the glow in the phantasm's eyes brightened like hell-fire, and Death turned to greet him.

Isobel watched on as, for a single moment, the two figures from the dreamworld stood opposite each other, like knights on a chessboard. One robed in black. One in red.

When the tension between them broke into movement, it was like watching a battle for light between moths. Cloaks whispered and curled. A blade flashed. Like jagged leaves stirred by a storm, they swept round each other, neither landing a blow, yet each of them whirling in a perpetual fury of motion.

One of Reynolds's blades caught the cloak of the Red Death. The crimson-soaked fabric fell partially back, revealing a head and torso that might as well have belonged to a skeleton. Ribs strained to break the tight yellow skin that clung to the creature's body like wet cloth. Blood dripped from its sunken eyes, from its shriveled mouth, and from the tips of its outstretched fingers.

The space cleared for them by the crowd once more widened with a collective retreat. The goths lowered their masks to watch, their stark faces appalled, afraid, confused, and then, finally—excited.

Then someone actually cheered.

Typical, was the only thing Isobel could think. Even given the circumstances, she couldn't help but roll her eyes. The goths—they thought it wasn't real. They thought it was all a show. And why not, when this sort of twisted crap was just their thing?

Above, along the gallery, an audience of Nocs crowed and rasped frenziedly in their bird forms. They hopped the length of the banister and followed the fight with their beady, bloodthirsty eyes, as though anxious to join in yet too afraid to swoop down and add their own blows.

A *whoosh* sound, a great rushing of air, came from the center of the open space. Like a house of cards, the Red Death collapsed in on itself, swallowed whole by the floor. It left in its wake a dark and ominous stain. In the next instant it emerged from behind Reynolds, rearing over him like an all-consuming shadow.

As though by magnetic force, Reynolds's blades were swept out from his grip. In midair they turned on him, and Reynolds whirled just in time to accept the thrust of both into his chest.

A collective scream arose from the mass of onlookers, Isobel's shrill cry among theirs.

She broke forward in a run as the Red Death drove Reynolds forcefully back. He plowed hard into the floorboards and slid, unconscious, to a halt at Isobel's feet.

"Omigod!" she screeched, landing on her knees at his side.

What should she do? Her hands fluttered uselessly over him, like stupefied butterflies. She reached for the blades but then snatched her hands back. Her gaze fell to the white scarf covering his nose and mouth. Was CPR even an option at this point?

His eyes popped open, and she yelped. He glared up at her past the brim of his hat and, with each hand, grabbed both blades by the hilt. He yanked them from his chest in one clean motion. Gray ash poured out from the would-be wounds like sand. Then the openings closed over, and all traces of damage vanished into the blackness of his clothes.

Isobel gaped.

"Why are you still here?" he growled, then launched himself up from the floor. Blades crossed, he charged, then drove them into the Red Death's back, stopping its approach toward a group of retreating girls dressed as fallen angels. The demon arched and howled—a sound like a hundred baying hounds. In a wrenching motion, Reynolds uncrossed the blades in a clean swipe. They sliced neatly through, and the bloodied figure dispersed with a shriek, transformed into a syrupy red-black liquid that slapped the floor and sent a slash of bright crimson to mar the clean white of Reynolds's scarf.

There was no moment of reprieve.

The liquid on the floor pooled and writhed. It gathered itself, and like a phantom emerging from its grave, the robed form rose, whole once again. Its ruby eyes flashed rage.

Like everyone else, Isobel stood rooted to the spot, mesmerized by the otherworldly battle taking place before her. At least until one of Reynolds's blades sailed in her direction. It pierced the floor right next to her foot. She jumped, staggering back.

"Go!" he boomed.

Thinking she shouldn't wait to see if he'd send the other one after her, she turned and sped pell-mell through the throng of hapless spectators. She shoved and nudged her way past countless empty stares from innumerable masks.

But where was she going?

The answer came when something caught her foot, and she tripped. She met the floor palms-first with a smack.

"Whoops. Need a hand?"

That voice. Isobel twisted around to find him hovering over her, the hollow, jagged portion of his lost arm held out to her. "Oh, wait," Pinfeathers said, withdrawing the lacking appendage. "Already gave you one of those today, didn't I?"

Isobel pushed up from the floor, ready to run. He shoved her down again with one foot. She fell with a sharp gasp of pain, and he flipped her to sprawl flat onto her back. A squall of fluttering appeared behind him, and one by one, the other Nocs took their true forms until, like a flock of ravenous vultures, they encircled her.

With one black boot, Pinfeathers trapped her outstretched arm against the floor. With his remaining hand, and to the delight of the other Nocs, he lifted something curved, sharp, and gleaming to rest on his shoulder. Isobel's eyes widened at the sight of Reynolds's cutlass, the one he'd thrown at her. Only now did she realize that he must have meant for her to take it, only now did she see how stupid she'd been for leaving it there, open for grabs.

"Well." Pinfeathers sighed, twisting the blade, letting it catch the light. "You know what they say—eye for an eye and all that."

The Nocs barked with raucous laughter.

"No!" She twisted at the waist, sending a fierce kick into Pinfeathers's side. To her surprise, her aim landed true, and under the snug fabric of his jacket, she felt part of his torso cave in with an audible crunch. He roared at her, though more out of fury, it seemed, than from pain.

The other Nocs, their laughter transforming into sympathetic hisses, writhed and withered away from her, cringing and clutching into themselves like snakes.

"Hold her!" Pinfeathers ordered with a stern point of the cutlass. As one, the other Nocs obeyed. Cold clay hands fastened to her free arm, claws dug into her legs as they pinned her.

Isobel wrenched and thrashed beneath their grip, her gaze darting. But there was nothing she could grab, nothing to use as a weapon, no one who could help her.

She held her breath and shut her eyes, braced for the pain. In her mind, she groped through her thoughts and formed the image of a door. She thought of one that would take her to the woodlands. *Make a way,* Reynolds had said. She pictured the door behind her, right at her back, pressed against her the way the floor was now. With the hand held closest at her side, she felt with her fingertips for the doorknob in her imagination . . . and touched something solid.

She gasped, her eyes springing open.

In a split second, the cutlass came down, whistling as it divided the air in its path. Isobel clenched every muscle, ready to feel the severing of her arm from her body. She gripped the doorknob that it was now too late to turn. The blade rained down, and with a clank, she felt it—break?

Low whispers erupted from the Nocs, the sound of suspicion and fear. They released her and shrank back at once, unanimous in their recoil.

Isobel had to raise her head from the floor to look, to make sure that her mind hadn't simply blocked the pain. It was the cutlass that lay broken and detached, though, and not any part of her. Her widened gaze shot immediately to Pinfeathers, who, still looming over her, raised the fractured hilt to his scrutiny.

"Hmm," he said, "I was afraid that might be the case."

Isobel took her chance. She grabbed the doorknob she'd

made in the floor and twisted it. The ground beneath her swung free, and they toppled through.

Taken by surprise, Pinfeathers tumbled past her, while Isobel held tightly to the knob. She opened her mouth in a silent scream as her body jerked to a halt and she dangled above a world of ash, of withered leaves and black charcoal trees. She looked down between her feet in time to see Pinfeathers dispel into thick spirals of ink before he could shatter against the ground that lay no more than ten feet below.

It had worked, she realized, casting a quick glance around her. She was back! She'd made it to the woodlands.

The heads of the other Nocs appeared in a circle around the open door above her. Their whispers continued, and they turned their heads to look at one another, though not a one of them made even the slightest move to grab her.

Isobel's grip on the doorknob began to slip. She let go and, prepared for the drop, landed squarely on her feet. Pinfeathers gathered himself once more into his humanoid form. He stood at a distance from her while other Nocs, morphing into birds, poured themselves through the open doorway. They lighted on the barren, swaying branches of the skeletal trees, watching, waiting.

Ash rained around them, heavy and thick enough to collect on the shoulders of Varen's jacket. By now, Isobel's hair had become completely unraveled, and it whipped about her face in a flurry of cold winds.

The purple sky overhead swirled and roiled like the eye

of a hurricane. The door that hung open and suspended in the sky swung shut with the next gust of air. She peered through the trees, and there she saw another door. This one was narrower, familiar to her, and she knew it at once as the one she sought. It was almost, she dared to think, as if the door had been seeking her.

Or lying in wait.

As she approached, her eyes went to the two signs taped to the door's surface. The words on the signs were written backward, but she didn't need to read them to know what they said. She knew that the top one read DO NOT ENTER, while the one below it warned the reader to BEWARE OF BESS.

46
Bedight in Veils

Isobel came to stand just in front of the door. Behind her the Nocs called and rasped wildly. Winds pulled and jerked at her hair, at the jacket and at the hem of her tattered dress. The paper signs taped to the door twitched and stirred in the bluster, threatening to blow away in a wind that was fast becoming violent. She reached for the doorknob, which was on the left side of the door this time, backward from what she remembered from the door in Bruce's shop, just like the signs. There came a rustle at her side and she stopped, turning her head sharply to catch Pinfeathers's jerky approach.

"Don't," she warned him.

He froze, leaving a distance of several feet between them. The other Nocs silenced and stilled themselves in the trees as Pinfeathers eyed her warily. She glared back coolly. It seemed that they now both understood what she was capable of.

"I know what you're thinking," he said, that static voice taking on a smooth, diplomatic tone. His gaze darted to the door, then back to her. "And so I'll offer you that same warning."

She narrowed her eyes on him. There was something very wrong about the way Pinfeathers worked. Hadn't he tried to skewer her only a moment ago? So now why was he turning all Jiminy Cricket? And why, after fighting with her so fiercely in the graveyard, had he changed at that last second and offered her help?

That he'd wanted to toy with her had been evident right from the start. But it had become more than that. There was something else to him, a deeper secret lurking behind the hollow mask that was his face. Her thoughts went back to the purple chamber, to Pinfeathers and Varen's strange conversation. What were they to each other?

Isobel knew it would be a dangerous question to ask the creature standing before her, and so she would keep it locked away, along with so many more, for Varen. She had other questions, though, for the apparent ringleader of the Nocs. "What will I find behind this door?" she asked.

"The other side of what you know," he answered, with a laugh. "Just like me." His smile faded.

A chill ran through her. "What do you mean?" She tried to make the question sound demanding, but even she couldn't ignore the note of uncertainty and fear in her voice.

"Oh." He sailed through the distance in quick, twitchlike motions until she became aware of him standing just behind her. His remaining arm wrapped around the front of her, across her chest, "I mean that you might not like what it is you find in there, that's all."

Stiffening, Isobel tolerated his closeness. At her side, her hands balled into ready fists. "You can touch me, but you can't hurt me," she guessed.

"Which works out," he said admittedly. "Because, remember, I don't *want* to hurt you. But you have to understand, Isobel, there is always that fine line." As he spoke, his hand trailed up her collar, his touch featherlight. "Between doing what we want . . . and doing what we're told." Cold, his fingers wrapped around her throat.

Isobel gasped and grabbed for his hand. It dissipated at her touch, and her fingers clutched at her own skin. He swept around her, coils of violet and black mixed with the churning ash. He reassembled to block the door, his form shimmering into solidity.

"Open this door, and no matter what, you'll never close it," he warned.

"Kind of like you and your mouth," she snapped, and went to push past him. Fear flashed in his eyes and he loosened again, slithering aside. She grasped the handle, and at this, the Nocs in the trees renewed their frenzy. She could hear them flitting and rustling.

"You're going to need a lot more in there than backflips and cute tricks, cheerleader," Pinfeathers called. He slid away with a fearful whisper that sounded like *"Tekeli-li!"*

The cry was taken up immediately by the other Nocs. In hoarse, rasping croaks, they echoed the call. *"Tekeli-li!"* they shouted with their parched voices. She had heard it before, that first time she had found herself in the woodlands. But what did it mean? They took flight from the black branches and fought the turbulent air with their wings, carrying off the strange word with them until they vanished into spells of violet.

Left alone, Isobel turned her attention back to the door. She took in a quick breath, then twisted the knob. The door creaked as it opened inward. As she crossed the threshold, it felt as though she was moving through a screen of static. The electric sensation lingered over her skin like pins and needles as she passed into the small space of an enclosed staircase landing. Immediately the wind at her back silenced. She glanced behind her to watch the world of ash and charcoal whip and toss. Traces of static blipped the scene, and it was like watching the whole thing on a muted television.

The air inside the stairwell was musty, like an old closet. Cold slats of gray-white light streamed down from the square window above the narrow wooden stairs. Dust particles filtered in and out of the stark light like tiny lost beings. The staircase itself, sandwiched between two wood-paneled walls, led up into what Isobel knew to be an attic.

Ash slipped from the sleeves and cuffs of Varen's jacket as she moved forward to take the first step.

Isobel placed a hand on either wall. She took the second step, and it creaked low underfoot. In her chest her heart began to pound, rushing blood to her ears and adrenaline through her system. She could *feel* the presence in the room upstairs. It was like a tight vibration humming in the air or a tuning fork set off deep inside her. She glanced over her shoulder to see that the storm outside had intensified. The tangled boughs of the twig-trees scrambled back and forth, clawing wildly at one another. The ash swirled in wild cyclones and blustered in sandstorm clouds. Still, no sound of the chaos reached her.

When Isobel came to the final step, it was to find herself alone in the attic. The table and chairs that she had once sat at with Varen now hovered in the air. Several books, too, and the threadbare rug drifted about in lazy suspension.

She looked out the window at the top of the stairs, which she now stood in front of. It should have shown her the brick side and the windows of the next building over. Instead there were only the tempest-tossed woodlands below. It was the same story with the other window, the oval one above the table that in the real world would have overlooked the street. This was the place where she had first read Poe, and standing there, staring at it all, the distance of time felt like years.

Isobel's gaze traveled to a slim, familiar book floating near the table. She recognized it at once as Varen's black sketchbook and went to snatch it out of the air. She held it between her hands and let her fingertips trail over the book's surface, then hook beneath its cover. She opened the book, flipping through the pages crammed tight with his beautiful handwriting. She stopped at a spread of drawings, suddenly realizing that she'd seen them before. Roughly sketched faces stared up at her, faces with whole pieces missing. In the middle, she saw Pinfeathers's familiar countenance, though he was not labeled by name. She remembered these pages from the day in the library, the first time they'd met to study. Isobel turned the book sideways, noticing a poem that stretched vertically down, crammed in between the artwork and the page's edge.

> *The Nocs*
> *The Nocs*
> *They live in the floor*
> *The Nocs*
> *The Nocs*
> *They knock on your door*
> *The Nocs*
> *The Nocs*
> *Where there's one, there's more.*

Isobel felt a rush of ice creep its way through her veins. She turned to the next set of pages, then the next, each strewn with words that seemed to flow into one another. She flipped faster, the pages seeming to whisper their contents. Her. Dream. Sleep. Return. She. Real. Need. Run.

She stopped, reading from the top of a page somewhere in the middle of the book.

> *He stood in that place again, the middle*
> *realm, the forest between worlds, and waited*
> *for her. She came, her white skin illuminated*
> *to a ghostly pallor in the flashes of lightning.*
> *The sky swirled, her black hair loosened and*
> *tumbling around her ivory shoulders. Gray*
> *ash sifted from the sky.*

"My prison," she said, "it disintegrates.
When, at last, will you write my ending?
When, my love, shall you set me free?"
"Midnight," he whispered. "On that night
of all nights in the year."
"You have done well." She drifted toward
him. For the first time, she kissed him. Her
lips, pale and cold, sealed his and so bound
them together.

Isobel flipped the page again, and here the handwriting morphed, changing from elegant script into unintelligible scribbles and scratched-out starts. At the bottom, she read the only bit of writing that she could make out.

This should make him happy. This should
change him. But it doesn't. It can't. He's
been changed already. And I don't know
what to write anymore, because I'm afraid of
what it will be. Because I can't think, and she
asks me to write, but I don't know what to
write and I can't think because I don't know
what to write. I can't think. I can't think.
Isobel. Isobel. Isobel.

A warm coursing rush lit her skin and spread through her. She stood staring in disbelief at her name scrawled so desperately against the snow-white paper. She brought the sketchbook closer, trying to imagine him sitting there, writing this. When? There was no date. After her name, repeated three times, the page went blank, blank except for a small blot of red on one bottom corner. Blood?

A quick, sharp *bang* ripped into the silence. Isobel jumped, nearly dropping the sketchbook. The other books, the table, and the chairs all clattered to the floor with a resounding clunk.

The door.

Isobel turned to find she was no longer alone.

At the top of the stairs stood a woman. Layers of glowing white draped and clung to the curvatures of her slight though tall frame, and it was as though the fabric itself was made from moonlight. A gauzy veil of white covered her head, like a cerement of the grave. She was beautiful. Luminescent, like a sliver cut from a dying star. Trails of gently curling hair, thick and raven black, tumbled past the length of her fingertips, a stark contrast to the white. Behind the veil, two large onyx eyes stared fixedly at her.

It was a moment before Isobel could speak. "Are . . . are you Bess?"

"I have many names," the specter answered. Her voice was deep and throaty yet wholly feminine. "I am Lila. I am Ita and *Li-li*. I am Ligeia. I am Lilith."

Isobel swallowed, her mouth gone suddenly dry. Schizophrenic much? She thought the age-old and ever-popular "Are you a good witch or a bad witch?" might be the ideal follow-up question but then decided against it. Bess or Lady

Lilith or whoever didn't exactly strike her as the joking type. And despite all the white, she didn't strike Isobel as the good-witch type either.

"Ligeia . . . ," Isobel murmured. She hugged the black book close to her, and her mind went back to the lyrics of the song she'd heard in the ice cream shop, the one Varen had played over the sound system while they'd cleaned. "But she's just a character in a story."

The woman lifted her arm to hold out her hand. The motion was sudden and unnatural, and Isobel had to fight the urge to take a step back. "Are not we all?" she asked.

With every warning signal inside her blaring, Isobel watched a gauze sleeve slip away to reveal the woman's hand. Her open palm was whiter than the draping fabric, her skin as flawless as marble. Hadn't Reynolds warned her to "beware the white one"? Remembering these words, Isobel felt her jaw tighten. If she ever saw him again, she'd have to thank him for providing her with such useful, detailed advice.

Isobel's gaze went from the figure to her outstretched hand. The silent gesture was one that suggested something be exchanged or handed over, and Isobel held all the tighter to the sketchbook. Why did she want it?

The woman took a step toward her, the train of her veil whispering against the floor. This time Isobel did not argue with her instincts. She backed away, bumping into the table behind her. She lowered one hand and, keeping the other clutched around Varen's black book, steadied herself.

"You yourself, Isobel," the woman continued, "could be

nothing more than a shadow, someone else's dream who is, themselves, someone else's."

"I don't think that makes much sense," said Isobel, only because it was the first thing that sprang to her mind. If she could keep the chatter going, maybe she could make it to the staircase, to the door. But then, she couldn't leave yet. Where was the link between realms Reynolds had told her to find? Wasn't that the whole reason she was here in the first place? Why hadn't she found it yet? Hadn't Reynolds said she would know it when she saw it? And even if she did find it, how the heck was she supposed to destroy it?

"I have been watching you," the woman said, "ever since that night you first entered his dreams."

Her back pressed flat to the wall, Isobel inched her way toward the stairwell. The woman pivoted where she stood, and the white gauze swirled tighter around her form, like the garb of a mummy. Through the screen of the veil, the black pools of her eyes followed Isobel's every movement.

"At first you were just another coal added to the fire. Fuel for his hatred, and I'd have had reason to thank you. Then his dreams changed." Underneath the gauze, her head tilted to one side and her delicate brow knitted, as though she did not quite understand this observation. "Uninvited, you invaded the corners of his subconscious and intruded on *our* time. Your mere image became a nuisance, a *distraction*." Her open palm snapped shut into a hard fist. "In this room, it was not *I* who was the ghost, but you. And so I sent them for you while they still could obey. You were, after all, yet an uncertainty in his thoughts. They would have had you that night too, if not for the aid and protection of your masked guardian."

It took Isobel only a second to realize that she was talking about the night she left the bookstore, the night in the park. She recalled what the blue Noc from the crypt had said. Had he been there that night too? Only then she hadn't been able to see the Nocs. And the voice that had whispered for her to run? Hadn't the blue Noc also mentioned her "masked friend"? Of course. It only made sense now that it had been Reynolds trying to warn her.

"In the end, however, you shall have little to thank your secretive friend for," Lilith said. "In time I shall discover him as well, and he will soon find that I have a special fate for those Lost Souls who betray me."

"Why are you doing this?" Isobel demanded. "Why Varen?"

"He is not like others, is he?" she asked almost wistfully, and floated to the oval window. Through it, Isobel detected new light, warm and orange, like a streetlamp. "He is special, even in regard to those who have come before him," Lilith continued. "Like them, he holds the ability to receive and interpret the shades and shadows of the dreamworld, to bring life and body to new ones, such as the Nocs. What is more, though, is that energy within him that drives him to destroy as much as he creates. The only thing he lacks is control. That in itself is what makes him so perfect. Tonight he is to finish my story. Tonight, when you are gone for good, he will set me free."

Uh-oh, Isobel thought. *Say what? Rewind.* What was this "gone for good" business? Isobel flashed a forced smile as she fumbled backward, edging farther and farther toward the stairwell. Apparently, despite Isobel wearing his jacket, Lady-Lovely-Locks didn't quite seem to get that Varen had left the proverbial building. It was about time for Isobel to make her exit too, link between worlds broken or not.

That was when the thought hit her. Instinctively she clung tighter to the sketchbook. The answer came to her in a flash, and suddenly it made all the sense in the world. It was all there. Varen's doorway into the dreamworld. Lilith's story. The Nocs. This was the bridge between realms, his way in, on its way to being *her* way out. The link Reynolds had told her she would know—she held it in her very arms!

Lilith, too, seemed to see the light of realization in Isobel, because she turned and stared through her with those hole-black eyes. "It's too late," she said, "for you to do anything. He cursed you the night he wrote your name within those pages, for now you are part of the story. That is how you are able to see us fully in your world. Or did you not wonder?"

"If I destroy this book," she said, "this will all go away. You and everything else will go back to where you came from."

"And where will you go, Isobel? You who now has a foot grounded in both realms? You would rip yourself asunder? You would perish for the sake of one who is doomed already?"

"What—what are you talking about?"

"Did your masked guardian fail to mention your own

fate? I am not surprised. I suspect he is selective in what he chooses to share with you. It would be an inconvenience for him, I think, if you were able to make too many decisions of your own. But it doesn't have to end this way. It appears to me that we have been pitted against each other by men. Why? When we both have something the other wants."

"I'm not giving you this book," she said. Her footsteps took her backward until her heels found the edge of the top stair.

Lilith laughed, a soft and almost melodious sound, haunting and even beautiful. "Do you not see that you yourself are now something of far greater value?"

"What?" Isobel blurted, her mind unable to wrap around Lilith's meaning.

"However unwittingly, *you* have become a link between realms. Your name in those pages has transformed you, has made you better than a poor lost boy's sketchbook, for you are not a link to power, but power itself. Together we would have free rein over all, for I know all routes and you, dreamer, hold the ability to traverse them. I would no longer need an ending. Why, when we would live forever? Bound as one with you, I would no longer have any hold over your Varen. He would be released, free to be with you, with *us*."

The woman moved toward her, the veil falling away from her face as she drew closer. She was dark beauty perfected, her cheekbones high and regal. Her skin held the sheen of stardust and her hair, dark, massy waves of silk, seemed to float about her like a black halo. It was her eyes, though, almost alien in essence, that held Isobel so completely transfixed. Fringed with dark lashes, twin wells of bottomless ink, they trapped her, and she found herself no longer able to blink. "Take my hand," she whispered, and raised her white palm once more. "Come with me."

Isobel felt her hand lift.

The pull of those eyes was magnetic, a force that couldn't be fought or resisted. She was so beautiful. Isobel paused, her fingers hovering just over the cold set of white ones.

This was how she must have lured Varen.

The thought came to her suddenly, buoying to the surface through a deep and cloudy sea of confusion, doubt, and longing. How easy it must have been for her, she thought. She'd made promises to him just like this. Only she had promised *him* more. So much more.

Like a serpent, this demon had coiled and nested into those empty and cavernous spaces of his heart. Like a harpy, she had preyed on his absolute aloneness—on his need for a "Lenore."

You could never be Lenore, Varen had once told her.

In her mind, Isobel imagined the future. A future void of herself. But also void of the creature before her. She pictured Varen safe at home. Sitting at his desk, he filled the pages of a new sketchbook by candlelight. His purple-inked poetry packed the crisp white sheaves of paper, her name printed more than once within those lines of elegant handwriting. In the company of soft, feathery drawings, those lines would be his last farewell to her.

Would he write about her? She liked to think that he would. About how, forevermore, the syllables that made up her name would continue to drift to him on the wings of his dreams—dreams now free of the ghouls and demons that had once haunted and stalked his mind. Finally, in this small way, she *would* be his Lenore.

She blinked at last. Her fingers twitched and retracted.

This witch had nothing to offer her. She had no spell to cast, not while Isobel knew Varen was safe, in her world. When the link was sealed, it would be that way forever.

Isobel's gaze fixed directly with Lilith's. "Didn't anyone ever tell you three's a crowd?"

Those black eyes widened in shock.

"It's too late," Isobel whispered, "for you to do anything." She brought both arms tight around the sketchbook. It was still her dream, even if it meant she went with it when it ended. She squeezed her eyes shut tight.

"What are you doing!" shrieked a voice like a screech owl's.

At first Isobel focused the heat in her chest. Guided by her mind, it traveled into her arms and then burst into flames over the sketchbook.

Someone screamed. Was it her? She opened her eyes. White heat engulfed her, consumed her. She was grateful not to feel the pain. A gift perhaps from her subconscious to her conscious? Like a hallucination, the vision of the white, black-eyed figure dropped away. The lamplight through the windows grew brighter—or was that the reflection from the fire?

She looked down to see fire course the length of her arms. It danced over the sketchbook held close to her, and she watched the edges of the paper curl and turn from orange to brown to black—taking on all the hues of autumn.

Everything died in the fall.

The book in her arms collapsed, tumbling into ash. The fire snuffed into blackness and with it, the world.

47
Surcease of Sorrow

She had smelled this smell before. It was that too sweet, deep scent of decay. Dead roses. The aroma of it was so much more potent than she remembered. It wasn't a bad smell, but it was too strong in such a concentrated dose. Oppressive.

She tried to turn her head from it but for some reason found little room to move.

She wondered if she was dreaming. Or still dreaming . . .

Or was she dead, locked away forever in a flower-filled casket?

Did the dead dream?

She became aware of a pressure across her shoulders and behind her knees. Pain, too, invited itself into her brain like a bad memory, pervading her entire body.

The next sensation that occurred to her was that of movement. She was moving. Cold air prickled the tiny hairs on her arms. She wanted to open her eyes to see where she was, what it was that transported her, and where she was going, but at the same time, she didn't. Why, when it would be so much easier to drift away again, to settle back into the cocoon of sleep, that blank place between dreams and reality, where the word "nothing" found its true definition?

She felt the press of something like fabric against her cheek and gathered beneath her curled fingers. Her hair tickled her brow in the wake of another breeze, and through her eyelids, she sensed light.

By now she had surfaced to consciousness enough that it was too late to fall back into the deathlike chasm of rest. Against her will, she became more and more aware of herself, of the seemingly limitless aches in her body, and finally of that steady one-two rhythm of movement beneath her. Her thoughts broke through the muck of oblivion, and she stirred.

She opened her eyes to the sight of a black cloth vest, so close she could count the stitches. A silver chain leading out of a small waistcoat pocket glinted in the light, and Isobel saw that she grasped the loose cloth of what she thought must be someone's black cloak. That was when she realized that the pressure at her back and behind her knees was the pressure of arms, arms she currently occupied, arms that carried her.

His body felt neither cold nor warm next to hers, solid, but somehow not alive. She listened, but he never breathed. Her gaze trailed up to the chin and nose covered by a blood-marred scarf. She squinted, trying unsuccessfully to peer through the shadow cast over his face by a wide-brimmed hat.

Stars dotted the sky around the edges of him, visible through tangles of knotted limbs that could not have belonged to the same trees as the woodlands. Their leaf-dotted boughs were too peaceful, too normal.

Could it be possible she was back in her own world?

At first she didn't say anything, because she was too

afraid to hope. She wanted to suspend time and just be still for another moment, to let her tired mind and sore muscles rest. The stale, moldering odor that clung to him didn't bother her as it had before, and against him, she felt almost comfortable. Safe.

Isobel released her grip on his cloak and, curious, let her fingers spider-crawl their way to the glinting chain that had caught her eye. She pulled at it, and a small ticking pocket watch came free in her hand. She turned it over, her eyes following the light as it chased across the polished surface. She opened the watch. It had a simple white face encircled by roman numerals and three black hands. There was a name engraved in cursive on the inside of the little circular cover. Isobel traced her thumb over the name. "Augustus," she read aloud. Her voice came out small and hollow-sounding, as though it had been a long time since she'd last used it. "Is that your real name?" she asked. "Augustus?"

"I dare think," Reynolds said as, over his shoulder, the pale slice of moon became visible between the knit of branches, "that not half so much trouble would find its way to you if you would only learn to leave things that are not yours alone."

"Okay, Augustus."

He sighed. "Augustus is dead, long since."

"Oh . . ." She closed the watch and slipped it back into his pocket. "And you're not?"

"Not quite."

"Am—am *I* dead?"

"You, strange puzzle of a girl, are very lucky."

"Where—where are we?"

"We are nearly through the park behind your home," he said.

"And—and Varen?"

"He is . . . home now, as well."

Home, she thought with a sudden pang of yearning. She pressed her lips together and felt her face pinch with sudden emotion. She fought the sting that threatened her eyes and instead forced herself to laugh. The sound that came out of her was more like a choking bark than anything else, and it rocked her body with a tight tremor. How? How had they managed to survive when their demise had been so certain?

Isobel shut her eyes again and released a long breath. Her sore muscles relaxed. Safe. He was safe.

"I had a home once. A family, too," said Reynolds, interrupting her thoughts. Isobel looked up at him, surprised by this uncharacteristic sharing of information. "Never one of my own, mind you. I never married," he said, as though reading the question in her silence.

"Like you, I had a mother and father," he said, "and a grandfather, with whom I was particularly close. It has been so long, and yet I remember them just as they were."

The light around them grew brighter, and Isobel became aware of the heads of streetlamps, their glow warm and promising, and she knew that they must have just entered the rear of her neighborhood.

"You must miss them," she heard herself say.

He sighed. "Sometimes I fear I shall never forget them."

"Why would you want to forget them?"

At first he didn't answer. The moon drifted out of sight again behind the brim of his hat, and the glow of the stars lessened as the streetlights and houselights around them grew brighter. Isobel turned her head enough to see the approaching outline of her house, the dark windows and drawn shades. Everyone inside must be asleep, she thought.

Candy wrappers littered the street along with scattered leaves. A white ghost's mask lay far off in the grass, like the broken face of a Noc, left behind and forgotten. Reynolds's footsteps made no sound on the gravel walkway that led to her back porch. He carried her to the door, but instead of setting her to her feet, he laid her gently on the cushion of her mother's long wicker bench. As he stepped back from her, Isobel sat up, worried that he might leave her without another word.

He paused, though, and crouched down next to her. "Isobel," he began, "it is naught but pain and regret when we think of the things and people we will never have, the opportunities we may never get. Would you not agree?"

She frowned, not sure where the question had come from and even more unsure of how to answer it.

"But to pine for those we have had and loved and once held but will never clasp again," he continued, "it is a torture of an unbearable degree. It is the worst pain possible. Enough to drive you away from yourself . . . as it did with Edgar."

"Why are you telling me this?" she asked. "Am I dead after all?"

He chuckled, and Isobel realized that it was the first time she'd ever heard his laugh. It was a soft and husky sound, like the opening of a rusted gate. Slowly he rose, sending her another waft of fermented roses. He drifted away to the edge of the porch, where he stood with his back to her. He raised an arm and curled one gloved hand around a wooden support beam. A breeze blew past, rustling his cloak.

"Edgar." He looked down, speaking the name as though it were one he did not often allow himself to say. "You are right that I knew him well. Despite our list of differences, we were two sides of a single coin. Different, yet inherently one and the same. He was my friend."

Isobel listened. It was strange to hear Reynolds talk this much. And he was always so vague. Usually you could turn around everything he said and it would make just as much sense.

"What really happened to him?" she asked.

"He died," Reynolds said. "He perished partly by his own means and partly by the means of others. It is best left at that."

"You mean Lilith killed him?"

"She was . . . responsible," he said.

"I don't understand," Isobel said breathlessly. "I burned the book. Why am I still here? Why didn't I die?" It was the question she had been waiting to ask, one that now fought its way through a crowd of others.

"Ah," said Reynolds, "that is something I do not fully comprehend myself, though I suspect that it was somehow your friend's doing."

"Varen? But how could he—?"

He turned toward her. "Allow me to attempt to explain with an example I do understand. The Nocs. They are part of *his* imagination, part of Varen's story, and so, part of him. If he would not hurt you, then it only makes sense that they would not be able to do so either. They are the deepest parts of his subconscious. Shrapnel of his inner self. As you might have learned, they have the same desires and conflicts as their maker. As separate pieces, freed from the soul and from the confines of a human conscious, however, they develop minds of their own. And, as demons created in the dreamworld, they are compelled by law to answer to its queen. That is why they attempted to harm you but in the end could not."

"That doesn't explain why the fire I made didn't burn me."

"You created the fire in a dreamworld that is subject to the rules of its queen, yet influenced by the imagination and desires set in motion by an outside force—your friend. Therefore, the same power that protects you from the Nocs perhaps also protected you from the fire. Furthermore, when you destroyed the link—the book, I should say—you also destroyed the page that held your name. Your sole connection to the dreamworld was broken, and you existed here fully, in your world, once more. And finally, because the fire was created by you in the dreamworld and was, in essence, a dream itself, it also ceased to exist the moment the link was severed, the moment the two worlds parted."

"She asked me to join with her," Isobel blurted.

"Then," he said, sounding unsurprised, "I suspect that she knew of the power that protected you. Invulnerability in a physical form caught between two realms? There is no greater power she could wish for."

"What about you?" she prompted. "Did you know about the protection?" She asked this, already knowing the answer. For a long moment, the question hung between them like a dead thing. A knot of discomfort deep in her stomach tightened to the point that she felt sick, and she wished that she hadn't spoken the question aloud. After all, he wouldn't have had to guess at why she was still alive if he had known all along that she'd been under Varen's protection.

"A long time ago," he said at last, "I made a vow to a friend that at all costs, I would not let the events that led to his death threaten his world or any other again."

Isobel blinked long and slow. She glanced down at her hands in her lap and past them to the tattered and stained ruffles of her once pink dress.

"So . . . I was the cost," she said finally. "You thought I'd be done for if I did what you said. That's what Lilith meant when she said you hadn't told me everything." Her eyes flicked to him, and it was his silence that told her she'd hit the mark.

He watched her, and in return, Isobel studied the portion of his face she could see, just that strip of skin around the eyes. They were young eyes. Misleadingly young, she thought. Who knew how old this guy really was? Older than Christmas, probably, especially since he seemed to have the moral code of an Aztec priest on sacrifice duty. She looked down at her hands in her lap again. She shrugged, doing her best to pretend that it didn't bother her. "You could have told me, you know," she said. "I—I still would have . . . If—if that was the only way to—to save him."

She waited for him to say something. To tell her that he hadn't really believed she'd die. Instead he said, "I . . . am not sorry that you survived."

She laughed, but the sound came out hollow. It was funny, because she could tell he'd meant it. And saying so was probably a lot coming from him. She swallowed with difficulty. In truth, the realization that he'd sent her off to become barbecue without so much as a heads-up was not something that sat well with her. Still, he'd come for her after it was all over. He'd helped Varen return. And he'd brought her home, too. He'd cared that much at least, right? "What are you, anyway?" she asked. She thought she might as well, as long as they were being blunt.

"It makes no difference."

"Lilith said you were a Lost Soul."

"I suppose that is one way to view my existence," he replied.

"Is that what would have happened to Varen? If I hadn't . . . ?"

"Possibly," he said. Then he glanced away, amending his answer by adding softly, "Yes. At least . . . eventually."

She tilted her head toward him. In that moment, he had sounded so terribly sad that she couldn't help herself from asking her next question. "What does it mean to be a Lost Soul?"

Perhaps it had been the note of sympathy in her voice that he'd found so deplorable, or maybe it had simply been the underlying shift in focus from Varen to him. Whatever the case, she had apparently overstepped her bounds by asking. He turned toward her suddenly, his tone sharpening once more. "Isobel, after tonight, you will not see me again."

Her mouth clamped shut. She knew that this was his way of snapping the shutters closed on that particular topic and all others. But she had too many questions left to stop now. She blinked up at him. "Where will you go?"

"I will return and continue my vigil, as promised."

She smiled at him sadly. "The party never stops for you, does it?"

She'd meant it as a joke, but he didn't laugh. Instead, he pivoted on his heel and took his first step down from her porch, the hem of his cloak brushing the weathered wood.

"Wait!" she called after him, rising. For a moment, she wobbled on her feet and her vision swam. She staggered forward and, not trusting her knees to support her, gripped the beam he'd held only a few moments before. "There's one last thing, please. It's about Varen."

She had expected him to keep moving, maybe even to vanish into thin air before her very eyes. But he stopped. Maybe he had heard her stumble? Whatever the reason, he still did not look back at her, only turned his head ever so slightly in her direction, a gesture that seemed to say that even though he was willing to listen, willing to humor her one last time, he still, as always, retained that infuriating right to answer her with silence.

"Yesterday," she began, speaking to his back, hurrying as though there was some element of him that was part hourglass. "Before this all started, I saw him. I hadn't seen him all morning. I don't think anyone had. But he came to Mr. Swanson's class to do the project. Then, after class, he disappeared. Later, I found out he'd been at the bookstore the whole time, asleep. Then, when I saw him late last night, his face . . . He looked different, but . . . I don't understand." She shook her head. There were too many details to fit them all into a single coherent question. She tried anyway. "How . . . how could he have been in two places at once?"

To her great shock, Reynolds swiveled abruptly to regard her, something about her words having piqued his interest. "You say he'd been asleep?"

"Yeah. That's . . . what Bruce said." She looked at him curiously.

"You're sure you saw him?"

"Yeah," she said, confused by the question. "Everyone did."

He drew rigid at this response, his black eyes actually widening. Until that moment, Isobel would not have thought "surprise" belonged to Reynolds's limited gray-scale palate of conveyable emotions.

"What?" she said.

He stood and watched her very closely now, so closely that she would have given anything at that moment to have been able to read the thoughts streaming through his head.

"Perhaps this is a question better suited for its subject," he answered.

Bam. She could almost hear the door of conversation slamming shut in her face.

"But . . ."

"I must leave you now," he said.

Of course you must, she thought bitterly. She crossed her arms, her gaze dropping to her ragged shoes, the same ones she had flung at him earlier that night. In that moment, she was half tempted to find something else to throw at him. Preferably something heavier and more solid, like one of her mother's garden gnomes. *Fine, then,* she thought. She *would* ask Varen when she saw him.

"Isobel?"

"What?" she snapped, not bothering to look at him. He could make her so mad sometimes. Even now, after everything, after he'd saved her, after he'd brought her home, after he'd rescued Varen.

"It is best for all if you remember what I've said tonight," he told her. She just shrugged at this, glancing down at one hand, turning it over in the dim light to frown at the dirt caked beneath her fingernails. "And know that if for any reason it should occur to you to seek me again, I will not be found."

At this, she scowled and kicked at the support beam with one foot. Eyes rolling, she said, "Like I would even *think* about calling you to hang out, Ren. You have the social grace of an undertaker."

The porch light flipped on, and, squinting, she looked up.

Danny stuck his head out the back door. "Who are you talking to?"

Isobel glanced at the place where Reynolds had stood. He was gone. She looked toward the corner of the house, almost expecting to see the furl of his cloak disappear around the edge. There was no sign of him, though, and it was hard to say how she felt about him being gone from her life for good. Annoyed mostly, she thought.

"What the hell happened to you?" Danny asked. "You lose a fight with a Weedwacker?" Her little brother stared at her with eyes round as manholes. "Mom and Dad are out looking for you, you know," he said.

Her stomach dropped at these words, and she turned to gape at her brother as he said, "You're in a crap load of trouble."

48
Invisible Woe

It was Gwen who had called Isobel's house. When neither she nor Mikey had been able to find her, they'd used Isobel's cell, which Gwen had found in her gym bag.

At the mention of the fight that had broken out, her dad had phoned the police. Then he and her mom had gotten into the car and started for Henry County. They'd left Danny behind to wait in case Isobel showed up at home. When she did, Danny recounted the drama, and Isobel reluctantly forced herself to dial her father's cell.

There had been lots of yelling, and in the background, Isobel could hear her mother sobbing with relief.

When she hung up, Isobel felt exhausted to the point of passing out. Still, she managed to fumble through a shower and change her clothes before her parents got back. She put on jeans and long sleeves to hide the bruises and cuts, and stuffed what was left of the pink dress into the bottom drawer of her dresser. Then she folded Varen's jacket and hid it away within the deepest recesses of her closet, where it would wait until she could return it to him.

The lecture she'd received that night had been long despite how late it was and filled with scathing questions of the rhetorical kind as well as threats both empty and loaded. That she would not be allowed to go to Nationals was among the emptiest. That there would be no car for her birthday, however, would most likely turn out to be true. That she was grounded until further notice was a given. Number one on her father's list of restrictive punishments, though, was that she was not allowed to speak or communicate in any way ever again with Varen outside of school, or in school if it could be helped.

She was given no room to argue, and this time her mother did not intercede.

Finally she was exiled to her room, and she had only reached the stairs when she was stopped again by her mother's voice. She told Isobel how Brad had undergone emergency surgery on his knee that night. That he'd had an allergic reaction to the anesthesia, that he'd suffered delirium and had almost gone into a coma.

Isobel thought back to the coffin, the graveyard. The screaming.

"Is—is he okay?" she asked. She turned back, taking in the sight of her mother's wan face and drawn features.

"Okay considering," she answered. "He'll be out of school for a while."

Isobel nodded once. She started up the stairs again.

"Izzy."

She stopped.

"His mom called to tell me tonight because . . . because while he . . . she said he called out for you."

Her hand tightened on the banister. She felt her shoulders go rigid.

"I think you should go see him when he's up for visitors," her mom said. "I'll take you if you want."

Again, Isobel only nodded. She couldn't tell her mother that she doubted that Brad would ever want to see her again, and she had to wonder how much he remembered. Would he recall being in the dreamworld at all? Or becoming the Red Death? At the very least, Isobel thought he would not forget what had happened on the football field.

Eager to escape, she hurried up the stairs. In her room at last, she collapsed under the overwhelming weight of her exhaustion. Her body gave her no choice. She slept.

Isobel awoke late the next morning to the sound of knocking. The noise echoed in her head, starting her from sleep, causing her to rocket upward. She felt her chest tighten as her heart leaped into triple speed.

She gasped and scrambled out of bed, gripping her comforter beneath her with clawed hands, surprised when she did not feel the coarse dryness of dirt or the brittle bite of grit. She grew still and listened, her gaze darting.

There were no tombstones. No dead trees or black birds. No phantom figures or looming shadows. Only cold, white daylight. Lurid but still midmorning hazy, the light streamed through her window, bathing her powder pink walls in a translucent glow, giving each object in the room its own thin halo.

Isobel squeezed her eyes shut before letting them flutter open again.

To her relief, her surroundings remained. Her breathing slowed, and she allowed herself to believe that she was really home. Safe.

As she relaxed, the painful aches in her frame seeped into the forefront of her consciousness, bringing with them the memory of last night. It all rushed back to her in a series of flashes. The game. Brad. The Grim Facade. The dreamworld. Reynolds. Lilith. Varen . . .

The knocking came again, louder this time, more insistent. Her body tensed once more, an automatic response.

The sound was coming from downstairs. That's when she realized that there must be someone at the door.

Varen.

Isobel was still clothed in the long-sleeved shirt and jeans she had thrown on the night before. She tore out of her room and onto the landing, swinging around the banister, her bare feet thudding on the carpeted stairs.

Midway down, she stopped.

Her dad stood at the base of the stairway, his back to her. He held the front door open, allowing in a gust of cold morning air. Before him, on the porch, right in the space where she had fully expected to find Varen Nethers, there stood two men Isobel had never seen before. Each of them wore a starched white shirt and a dark tie. Both were clad in long, brown overcoats, their faces set with blank, unreadable expressions.

Confused, she watched as the taller, dark-haired man

flipped his wallet open for her father to see. There, in the center of the bill fold, she caught the gleam of a silver badge.

Police? What were the police doing here?

She edged farther down the stairway, staying close to the wall, but halted again when the tall man's gaze shifted suddenly from her father to focus on her instead.

"Detectives Scott and March," the man said, and flicked his wallet closed. He eyed her as he stuffed the bill fold into an inside pocket of his coat. "Are you Isobel Lanley?"

Her dad swung around, seeming surprised to see her standing there, frozen on the stairs. He glanced between her and the two detectives, his own expression darkening with uncertainty and suspicion. "Can I ask what this is about?"

Isobel felt her knees giving, her legs losing the strength to support her. Dread welled in her chest. She shook her head, willing the scene to stop. She wanted to wake up again and for everything to start over before it could go wrong. But it was too late for that. Something *was* wrong. Horribly wrong. She sensed it, like an invisible presence in the room.

It was the shorter, red-haired detective who spoke next. "We're investigating a missing persons report that we believe your daughter may have some information about."

"Who?" asked her dad, but Isobel already knew who. Like the missing piece of a puzzle, the horrible truth clicked into place.

She suddenly felt dizzy, nauseated. The room seemed to go fuzzy in the corners of her vision.

"You *are* Isobel, I take it?" asked the red-haired detective. His eyebrows arched as he regarded her, his chin tilted downward, as though he were trying to prompt her, to remind her of her own name.

Stunned, she stared straight through the space between the two men. Like an illusion, the detectives, the foyer, the harsh morning light, and her father all melted away until each of them became no more than a distant pinprick in her awareness. Her mind freewheeled backward through the chaos and hell that had been the night before.

Reynolds. In the graveyard. He had lied to her.

He'd lied.

In that moment, the truth of it seemed so simple to her, so simple and so glaringly obvious. But then how could it be true? How, when he had brought her Varen's jacket? Varen had given it to him, hadn't he?

Her jaw fell slack. Of course. If he'd lied to her, then there would have been nothing to stop him from lying to Varen, too. He could have told him anything, and even now, Varen could be trapped there, still waiting.

For her.

Reynolds's words rushed back to her. *He is . . . home now, as well.*

She covered her mouth with her hand. She heard those damning words again and again, his voice ringing clear in her mind, like the reverberating drone of a funeral bell.

She sank down onto one step, feeling herself disconnect from reality.

He had called her a friend. He'd saved her, and because of that, she had wanted to believe that he had saved Varen too. And so she had drunk down every word as truth. She had swallowed his poison so easily. How could she have been so stupid? She should have known that he would have said whatever he had to, whatever it would take to get her to destroy the link. To part the worlds.

He had meant it when he'd called her his enemy.

Isobel felt her body hitch as she drew in an involuntary gasp of air. She hadn't even realized that she'd stopped breathing.

Lilith had been right, she thought with a sudden pang of bitterness. Reynolds had kept the truth to himself the whole time. He had tricked her and sent her in on her own, with false hope, fully expecting her to die.

A barrage of emotions coursed through her all at once. Hurt, anger, betrayal.

Loss.

So *this* was what his speech on the porch had meant. His last soliloquy before his grand vanishing act. *I won't be found,* he'd said.

"Miss Lanley," the tall detective pressed, "do you know anything about the whereabouts of Varen Nethers?"

Distantly, she registered this question.

Yes, she thought. *Yes, I do. He's in a horrible place where no one can reach him. He's in a world of ash and black trees and broken people, held hostage to a demoness who will possess him for eternity.*

She shook her head slowly. No. No. No. This couldn't be happening.

"Isobel." It was her father who tried this time. "I thought Varen brought you home."

Isobel shook her head. *No more words. No more words, please.*

"Are you saying he didn't give you a ride home? Isobel?"

"No," she whispered.

She wanted everything to stop. She wanted the police to go away. The walls and the foyer, the too-bright morning light and the realization—everything—to just go away.

"His father reported him missing early this morning. He didn't come home from school yesterday, and apparently he went to a party last night and was seen there with your daughter. You're aware, I assume, that there was a bust?"

"I made the call," said her father.

"Ah, well, that makes sense. Anyway, after everything cleared up, they found the boy's car, still in the parking lot, but there's been no sign of him."

"Isobel?" her dad asked. "Do you know anything about this?"

She said nothing. She didn't want to talk, she couldn't. It would do no good. Slowly, methodically, she shook her head no.

"I'm sorry," she heard her dad say. "We . . . Well, we had a long night. All of us."

"I understand," the taller detective said. "In that case, I'll leave you with my card, and maybe we can try you again another time. If you think of anything in the meantime, though, please don't hesitate to give us a call. But, you know," he continued, his tone changing, as though he were aiming these next words at Isobel. "I wouldn't worry too much. We're always on cases like these, and ninety percent of the time, the kid shows up. Besides, we get the impression this isn't the first time. Like your daughter, he probably got spooked by the sirens and just hitched a ride with someone else."

Isobel heard her father say good-bye to the detectives. Then he shut the door, blocking out the cold air and the stinging light, casting them both into shadow. For a long moment, he stood with his back to her, his hand still on the doorknob, as though he were trying to think of what to say. Or to decide how he felt.

Isobel rose to her feet. She wavered, waiting until her father, at last, turned to face her. Then she did what she thought would be easiest for the both of them. She took one look at him, and turned away.

"Isobel," he called.

She paused, but only for a moment. Drifting up the stairs like a ghost, she vanished into her room.

49
Obscure and Lonely

Isobel returned to school on Monday, walking the halls with her body, but not with her mind. It was like her whole awareness of the universe had somehow become inverted. Words became indecipherable. People morphed into objects, moving automatons that floated through the space around her as meaningless, formless shadows. Hours elapsed without her being aware of their passage. All the while, her thoughts never changed, never deviated from that place where she had last seen Varen, locked in the purple chamber where she had asked him to wait for her. Where she had promised to come back for him.

The image of his despair consumed her.

In Mr. Swanson's class, his vacant chair haunted her. Even though she knew it was empty, she kept stealing glances toward it, as though he might somehow materialize.

She did not return to the cafeteria to sit with Gwen, Stevie, or Nikki at their hodgepodge table. Instead she spent lunch in the gym. There she turned flip after flip. She drilled herself on her layout, on her back handspring and round-off. She went through the motions over and over until the repetitive action and the necessity of focus caused the world to condense. Until she didn't have to think, until it was just her and the floor.

Still, there was no reprieve from the ghost of his memory. He followed her everywhere. She felt him on her skin, sensed him in everything, in the books she carried, in the paper she was forced to write on.

She skipped practice that week so she wouldn't have to face Nikki or Stevie, and she did her best to evade Gwen at every turn, going to her locker at odd times and taking longer routes to class, not caring if she was late. While Stevie and Nikki seemed to take the hint, Isobel's allusive behavior only goaded Gwen into taking more extreme measures. She called Isobel's house every night, even though her father had repeatedly made it clear to her that Isobel wasn't allowed to take calls. After that, Gwen resorted to disguising her voice, though she knew Isobel's parents had caller ID. Almost every one of these calls had ended with a direct hang-up from her dad, who had since taken to calling Gwen "that Northern girl."

For once in her life, Isobel was grateful for the excuse of being grounded. She couldn't stand the thought of being barraged by questions she didn't have answers for. Or to be reminded again of how she had failed Varen. Of how she had left him there, waiting in vain for her to return because she had promised to come back for him. She had *promised*.

At Trenton, rumors connected to Varen's disappearance began to build and circulate through the hallways in hisses and whispers. While most people thought that he had simply run away, others buzzed about how he'd been murdered by his weird one-eyed boss, his body boarded up beneath the floor of Nobit's Nook or buried somewhere in the park. There had, after all, been neighborhood reports of strange lights and sounds coming from the attic of the bookstore the night he disappeared, as well as one account of a cloaked figure seen exiting through the rear entrance, a limp body held in his arms.

At the end of the week, Swanson handed back their project papers. He went through the aisles, dropping them off at every other desk. When he placed her and Varen's paper in front of her, Isobel thought that he might have lingered for an extra moment or two before moving on. She stared through the clear glossy report cover at the B- they had managed to pull off.

"Good job," he'd written on the title page in red. "Next time, though, ask about parent participation instead of stereos, okay? Also, I've attached an Internet article from the *Baltimore Sun* that the two of you might find interesting. By the way, nice bird."

Below that, Swanson had added something else. This note appeared in blue ink, and in a tighter, more compact version of his loopy cursive. "P.S." it read, "if you need to talk, I'm here."

This tiny gesture, so very unobtrusive and kind, struck a chord deep within her, inducing a surprise moment of lucidity. It brought a sad smile to her lips, because it didn't matter that she could never accept the invitation. She just liked knowing that Swanson had added it because he liked Varen. And that, in turn, made Isobel like her English teacher more than he would ever know.

She slid the paper off of her desk and shoved it into her backpack, putting Varen's name out of sight so that the world could go mute again. Mute and void, colorless except for that one empty chair in the corner.

That afternoon Isobel made the mistake of going to her locker.

She had just finished shoving her binder, notepad, and English book inside when Gwen sprang up behind her, sending the door to her locker slamming shut.

"You," she said, jabbing Isobel right in the shoulder, "are a terrible friend."

Isobel scowled and kicked the corner of the metal door so that it popped open again. Her notebook slipped out and fell to the floor, loose papers scattering. "Thanks," she muttered. "I needed that."

She stooped to gather the spilled papers, but stopped when Gwen stepped forward, pinning them to the floor with one foot. "*No,*" she barked. She sent Isobel's locker slamming shut again, this time with a decided bang. "What *you* need is a reality check. You've been wandering around in this little bubble of solitude and sulk long enough. Now, I don't know what happened that night, but I know that you do. I know it was weird. I was there, remember? I saw that fight with my own eyes, but unlike everybody else, I knew it was real. I also know that you disappeared on one side of town only to reappear on another. You might be fooling everyone else, but you're not fooling me, Isobel Lanley. If he's dead—"

"He's not dead!" Isobel shouted suddenly, her voice piping with panic. She grabbed Gwen tightly by the arm, shaking her. "*Don't* say that."

Gwen pulled her arm roughly away. She took a step back, and, for a long moment, the two of them stood there and stared at each other.

"I'm tired of chasing after you," Gwen said at last. "And if you're not going to do something, then I'm not going to cover for you. Those two detectives came to school yesterday. If they come back, if they ask *me* what happened, I'm telling them what I saw."

Isobel gaped at her friend. "*Do* something?" she repeated. She shook her head, uncomprehending. "Do—do you have any idea—"

"No!" Gwen snapped. "No! I don't. I have *no* idea! In fact, the only thing I *do* know is that it looks like you're giving up."

Isobel blinked, suddenly speechless, stung to the core by the accusation of those words.

Gwen glared at her, unrelenting, her eyes lit with intensity. "Don't look at me like that. I saw you there with him that night. And I know you know where he is."

Isobel's lips parted with a tremble. She started to speak, to deny it. But the truth was that she *did* know where he was. There was just no way to reach him. How could she tell Gwen that it was impossible to save him because the link

between worlds had been destroyed? How could she expect
anyone else to understand any of it when she'd scarcely been
able to grasp what had happened herself?

A glower hardening the normally soft angles of her face,
Gwen turned away to dial the combination to her own locker.
She opened the metal door and, reaching inside, grabbed
something from the top shelf, shoving it into Isobel's hand.
Her pink cell phone.

"There. Now it's your turn." With that, Gwen looped
her purse strap over her head, her movements fast and jerky.
"When you figure out how to use one of those again, well . . .
I logged my number in at the top of your address book. And
here," she added, yanking out Isobel's gym bag. She let it drop
onto the floor between them, right on top of the smattering of
papers. "My locker's not a storage unit."

With a flip of her long hair, Gwen stalked off, leaving
Isobel to stand there, staring at her rumpled gym bag, wondering how it was possible that she could feel any emptier.

Mechanically, she sank to one knee in front of her locker
and with slow, deliberate movements, began to gather her
things.

Then something about one of the papers made her pause.
Her cell phone slid from her grasp. It cracked against the floor,
but Isobel hardly seemed to notice, too distracted by the black-
and-white photo mixed within the spread of loose white sheets.

She grabbed one corner of the printout, tugging it free
from the others. Isobel's eyes scoured the page, certain that
she had to be imagining what she saw there.

At the top of the paper, the header read *Baltimore Sun* in bold block letters, and she knew it was the article Mr. Swanson had wanted her and Varen to see, the one he had handed back with their paper. There, in the middle of the page, Isobel focused on the dim and misty black-and-white image that had first drawn her attention. Head bowed, a man knelt before a large gravestone. On the headstone itself, she could scarcely make out the outline of a carved raven. The man, however, she could see more clearly.

He wore a dark coat, and a black fedora covered his bowed head. In his hand, he offered flowers to the grave. Roses? Around the lower part of his face, a white scarf concealed his features.

Isobel read the caption:

> The only known photo of the "Poe Toaster," taken in 1990 for *Life* magazine. This mysterious figure visits Poe's Baltimore grave during the early morning hours of January 19, marking the poet's birthday each year with roses and a toast of cognac. First observed in 1949, the ritual has continued over the years, though the Toaster's identity, along with the details of how he enters the locked cemetery, remain a secret to this day.

"Reynolds," she hissed, gripping the page until it crumpled in her fist.

Isobel stared with sheer disbelief. She gawked at the image of Reynolds, kneeling in front of the headstone, paying homage before Poe's grave, blatant and visible to all who dared to watch, imprinted forever on film.

She looked up and, at the far end of the hall, caught sight of Gwen's swaying broom skirt. Something inside of her clicked on, and for the first time since she had found out that Varen had never returned, her mind switched to life. Her awareness spread out. Suddenly, the external world reentered her sphere of existence. She heard the lockers slamming around her, and people laughing and talking. Sneakers squeaked by on either side of her, everyone heading for the buses. Clutching the article in one hand, Isobel fumbled for her phone. She flipped it open and turned it on, thankful that she still had some battery life left. She thumbed through her address book, highlighting the first entry before pressing the send button.

Even from a distance and with the clamor in the hallway, she still heard the trill of Gwen's cell phone. Through the net of interweaving students, she saw Gwen stop, and watched as she reached one hand into the patchwork purse slung at her side. Isobel studied her friend as she fished out her ringing phone and eyed her view screen, as though trying to decide whether or not to pick up.

Isobel stood.

Please, she pleaded in her mind. *Please. I need you.*

Slowly, Gwen lifted the phone to her ear. Then Isobel heard her voice just as she saw her lips move. "So, you let me get through that whole spiel, my entire tirade, but you weren't going to let me have the dramatic walkaway, were you?"

"Baltimore," Isobel blurted. "January nineteenth. I have to be there."

Gwen turned to face Isobel. Phones pressed to their ears, they stared at each other from across the expanse of the clearing hallway.

"*What?*" Gwen asked, already starting back toward her again, shouldering her way through clusters of stragglers.

Isobel lowered her own phone. She held the article out at arm's length.

Closing in, Gwen snatched it from her. "Hey!" she said, "It's that guy! From the Grim Facade . . ."

Gwen suddenly grew quiet, and Isobel watched her eyes grow wide behind her glasses as she scanned the brief paragraph. Meanwhile, Isobel allowed her thoughts to spiral backward to the moment when Reynolds had laid her on her mother's wicker bench. With that memory, a new thought occurred to her, one very important detail that, until that very instant, she had managed to overlook entirely. Despite what he had said about the separation of worlds and the destruction of the link, *he* had still stood there, in her world, fully real and tangible.

And hadn't Varen created the link in the first place? Wouldn't that mean that Poe had done the same?

Isobel's eyes narrowed. Her gaze slid back to the article in Gwen's hand, just as she was lowering the paper. Gwen's eyes met with Isobel's, and her face held a wondering expression, one that went through several quick changes as the wheels of her brain spun to catch up, to draw the same conclusion that Isobel had already decided on.

Isobel was going to Baltimore. One way or another.

And contrary to what Reynolds thought, she *would* see him again.

Of that she was now certain.

50
From Out That Shadow

That night, Isobel waited until everyone was asleep before sneaking down the hallway to Danny's room. She pressed in on the door, and it creaked slightly as it opened.

Her little brother lay in his bed, snoring, huddled to one side, his arm slung around a giant Transformers pillow. Drool pooled on the robot's plushy shoulder. She shook her head, taking in the scene. If her mood had been any different, she might have risked snapping a blackmail photo. Instead, she crept inside, tiptoeing around the minefield that was his bedroom floor.

Quietly she slid into his computer chair. It squeaked as it swiveled into place, and her ears pricked up as she heard Danny stir behind her.

She ignored his groan and wiggled the mouse, causing the sleep screen to disappear. The PC hummed to life and, when the window for Google popped up, she started typing.

"What are you dooooing?" Danny moaned. "Get out of my roooooom."

"Shh," Isobel said. "Go back to sleep."

The web page for University of Baltimore popped onto the screen.

It had been Gwen who, despite her reluctance concerning Isobel's plan, had thought of using the excuse of visiting colleges to get to Baltimore. After Nationals, if Trenton won the championship this year, then there would be no way her mom and dad could deny her the request. Especially if she happened to utter the word "university" all on her own.

Of course, that meant Trenton would *have* to win.

From there, things wouldn't get truly difficult, until she was in the city, in Baltimore. It would be sneaking off and getting into the locked cemetery that was going to be the tough part.

"I was having a good dream," Danny mumbled. She heard him roll to face the wall. "I was an only child."

"So go back to sleep."

Isobel typed "Athletics" into the search field. The only return was for an athletics club. "Damn it," she hissed. She pressed back and, returning to Google, typed, "University of Maryland + Athletics." When the page loaded, she clicked the first option, and the sports page splashed onto the screen in a flash of red, yellow, and black. And there, dead center, was a photo of the football team.

"Home of the Terrapins?" she whispered aloud.

"It's two a.m.," Danny whined. "Aren't you still banned from life?"

Isobel squinted at the little image of the mascot. Apparently, a terrapin was some sort of turtle. Weird.

She went to a drop-down menu and clicked "Spirit Squad." The page went black before the Terrapin cheerleaders flicked onto the screen. Girls wearing big ear-to-ear smiles and bright red uniforms trimmed in black dominated the monitor. A few of the pictures showed squad members suspended in midair, doing high-difficulty stunts. *Not too shabby*, she thought.

She scrolled down and there, just below a championship portrait, was the info she needed. Yes—they competed.

"Turn the screen off!" Danny growled. "You suck."

Isobel closed out of the page. She powered off the monitor, then stood.

Stepping around Danny's beanbag chair and kicking aside his school shoes, she lowered herself to sit on his bedside.

"Guuuh," he snarled into his pillow. "What do you *want?*"

Isobel pulled up her knees and lay down on the edge of her brother's narrow twin-size bed. Turning to face his back, she looped an arm over him.

"Get *off* me," he growled, but made no move to pull away or push her off.

For a long time, he let her lay there, and she stared at the back of his head, at the part in his dark hair, and then at the wall, at the Darth Vader poster that loomed over them.

"You're a freak," he muttered.

"I know," she whispered.

The hum of Danny's computer slowed and went out, the PC going back to sleep.

"I'm sorry your boyfriend's still missing," he said, his words startling her, catching her off guard.

She felt a sudden straining pinch behind her eyes. Her throat constricted, and she swallowed against the impulse to cry. She shut her eyes, and despite her best efforts, a warm tear tumbled from her cheek, hitting the sheets beneath her.

"I hope they find him," he said.

"Yeah," she managed, the rust of emotion caking her voice, "me too."

Danny grew quiet again, and beneath her arm, she felt his breathing deepen. She watched and felt his side lift and lower. The steady motion rocked her arm and, like a balm, smoothed the pain back down.

Carefully, Isobel unfolded herself from Danny's bed, doing her best not to wake him again. She put her bare feet onto the carpet and wove her way through his room to the door. She slipped down the darkened hallway and into her own room, taking care to ease the door shut behind her, turning the knob to silence the click of the latch. Then she did what until that very moment she had forbidden herself to even think of: She retrieved Varen's jacket from her closet and, sitting with it on the edge of her bed, clutched it to her chest.

She pressed the collar to her lips, breathed him in. The coarse fiber still held his essence, reminding her of the moment they had been so close. She traced the length of one sleeve with her fingertips, remembering the feel of his body pressed against hers and the taste of his lips.

Isobel pulled on the jacket, threading her arms through one sleeve at a time. The weight of it settled onto her shoulders. She hugged herself, imagining that it was him who now held her and not this vacant shell, this last remaining relic.

She felt, and heard, the right pocket crinkle.

Isobel froze.

Without looking, she slipped a hand inside . . . and touched the edge of smooth paper.

She pulled free the folded slip. A note.

Its ash coating powdered to nothing at one pass of her thumb. Lips parted, she gaped at it, half expecting it to dissolve from her touch.

It didn't.

She slowly opened the paper, handling it as though it were a wounded sparrow. She could tell from the uneven, crushed folds that it had been crammed into the pocket, hastily stowed away by its author, as though to put it out of sight before it could be seized.

Purple writing, *his* writing, dominated the page in quick yet beautiful curves and loops. Her eyes traced the lines, soaking up each sentence, one word at a time.

In the shadows of the dreamland, he waits.
He watches the gaping window to the world
he had so longed to open. Now flown wide,
bleak and empty, ravaged—like him—it
grants his wish. He belongs.
    It cannot compare to the memory of her
eyes. Blue azure, warm as a summer sky.
    If he could but fall into their *world.*
    Would that he had.
    Now he writes the end to the story that

*past its Midnight Dreary—that too late
an hour—has its own without him. It was
always, he knows now, meant to end this way.*
      *Like that circle that "ever returneth into
the selfsame spot."*
      *My beautiful, my Isobel. My Love. You
ask me to wait. And so I wait.*
      *For all of this, I know, is but a dream.
And when, in sleep, at last we wake,
I will see you again.*

Isobel stared at the paper in her quivering hand, able to
do little more than trace and retrace, through her searing
vision, the deep violet ink that comprised that final line.

Despite its literal meaning, she knew that he had meant it
to say "good-bye."

Never, she thought, trailing a fingertip over the swirl of
those carefully crafted letters. A thousand times never. They
were entwined now, irrevocably. Ever since that day he had
set his pen to her skin. And if this rift that stretched between
them now extended beyond the confines of time and space,
of dreams and reality, she still had to believe that there was
a way to cross it, still a way to keep her promise. There had
to be.

Slowly, Isobel lowered the note, lifting her free hand to
brush away the tears that fell.

A chill of ice air rushed up behind her, causing her to
start. The breeze stung her dampened cheeks and combed

cold fingers through her hair. She twisted to peer over her shoulder.

Her window. It was open. She frowned, unable to recall having raised it.

The lace curtains fluttered and whispered in the brisk wind, the white gauze of their fabric slipping and uncoiling against the panels of her wall with every swell, creating a sound like the rush of distant waves.

The winds picked up again, growing fiercer, with a hint of the sharp, bitter tang of the oncoming winter. The breeze tugged and jerked at the note in her hand, as if to snatch it from her grasp.

Refolding the paper, Isobel stood with a shudder. She pulled the jacket tightly around herself, wrapping her arms in close. She rounded her bed and went to her window, but paused at the sight of its reflection in her dresser mirror. There, around the square of black and empty night, she watched the white lace curtains flutter and snap. They waved at her like twin ghosts in the wind until, she thought, one took the shape of a familiar figure—a shrouded, translucent form—with skin the perfect whiteness of snow.

Epilogue

He stood on the farthest edge of the cliffs, boots caked in ash.

Like clawed fingers, the black rocks jutted out over the torpid waters far below, pointing toward the distant horizon. A vast motionless sea, canvas white and still as death, spread itself wide and long before him. It met, in the distance, with the thin black line that separated it from a torn violet sky.

At his back stood the skeleton ruins of the once-grand palace, now a crumbling structure forged of forgotten words and thoughts long since given to slumber.

Varen closed his eyes, allowing the dead nothingness around him to numb his mind and still the rhythms of his body until all he knew was the buzz of static, that dull vibration, as familiar to him now as breathing. His concentration drew to the cool, soft sensation of the pink satin ribbon wrapped around one hand, held tight in his fist.

"Is that why you return to this place each night?"

At the sound of her voice, musical and deep, Varen opened his eyes, though he did not turn. If he looked, then he would only be trapped again, lured by that ivory seraphim face framed by those endless waves of black.

His gaze narrowed on the horizon. He held his silence as

the winds stirred, brushing his hair from his eyes. It flicked cold fingers at the bare skin of his arms.

"But do not forget that it was she who left you here."

Far below, the frost white seas began to churn. The waters turned choppy until restless waves lapped at the rocky cliffs, as though to test their resolve to stand.

There was a billow of white gossamer to his left as she floated to stand beside him. The gales picked up with yet more speed, whipping her hair wildly about her face.

Below them, the sea's voice rose from a whisper to a roar. Waves crashed, throwing themselves as though in suicide upon the pointed rocks.

The wind howled past them, lifting her veils into a violent dance. The satin ribbon rippled and snapped. Varen clutched it tighter.

"Standing here, so *alone* for so long . . . Do you not grow cold?" he heard her ask.

He stared forward, unblinking, as a knife of blue lightning sliced the sky.

"No," he said.

Acknowledgments

There are so many people to whom I owe a wealth of gratitude. A huge thanks and many hugs go to my ninja agent, Nadia Cornier. Thank you as well to all of my friends at Simon & Schuster and Atheneum; to my superhero copyeditor, Valerie Shea; and to my amazing editor, Namrata Tripathi, for her brilliance, for being my sounding board, and for pulling things out of me I didn't know I had.

I would also like to thank all of my partners in crime from Spalding University's MFA in Writing program, especially my Writing for Children peeps; thanks for your insight, your friendship, and for being my cheerleading squad. Splvoe and Spuddles, always. Thanks also to my Spalding mentors who helped me shape and form the first draft of *Nevermore*: Louella Bryant and Luke Wallin, with special thanks to Joyce McDonald, who believed in this story when it was just a spark and who encouraged me at every stage to go full speed ahead.

I have so many spectacular people who have played an integral part in my life while writing *Nevermore*, and I want to thank you all for being there as both my friends and my early readers. Thanks to Amy Ameno Blew, for reading along and for pointing me firmly to Poe (you were right).

Thanks to Marcus Wynn, for reminding me to check my batteries (judo chop! *Force field*), and to Nick Passafiume, for listening to me jabber and for helping me to laugh at the absurdity that is me. Thank you to my dear friend Jenny Haskell, for meeting me at the Grind and for continuing to answer my ceaseless research questions. I would also like to thank Melody Molito, Angela Cook, and Jeannine and Laura Buhse, for their infinite patience, friendship, and for steering me through the occasional midnight dreary. (On that note, I would like to offer double thanks to M-Pony and J-Pony, for standing outside of a certain Baltimore, Maryland, graveyard after midnight in the middle of January, shivering and watching the snow flurries fly while waiting for that guy with the scarf and hat to appear. You guys must really, *really* love me.) And to A-Pony—I fear I would still be lost within the woodlands if you hadn't taken me on that long walk and talked me through that one scene (you know the one).

Additional thanks goes to Susan Luka, Jackie Marrs, Judith Robin, and Megan Evans. I heart your faces (for days). And I can't forget Michael Luka (a.k.a. Freddie Jo), for the prank calls and for being my football coach.

More thanks goes to all of my friends at the Louisville Free Public Library. Thanks for the constant encouragement and making such a fuss over me.

This novel took a lot of research, and I would like to thank Mr. Jeff Jerome, curator of the Poe House in Baltimore, for taking the time to chat with me and for all he does at the Poe House. I would also like to thank the staff of the Poe Museum of Richmond, who answered all of my questions with lightning speed and for making my visit unforgettable. Additional thanks goes to the Poe Society of Baltimore, for their extensive and informative web page and for their dedication to all things Poe. I would also like to include a special thanks here, if I may, to the Poe Toaster. I admire you so. (And I hope you don't mind that I put you in the story.)

A very heartfelt thank-you goes to my family. I love you all. Thanks for understanding, for being so supportive, and for cheering me along. And, Mom, without you, this would never be. Thanks for insisting all those years that I was really a writer. You were right. Thanks for believing in me no matter what; for helping me put the binding on that first book, *Pink Lettuce*; and for being my best friend.

Lastly, I would like to offer thanks in memory of Edgar Allan Poe. His legacy and writings continue to inspire me as well as countless others. Thanks, Eddy. Evermore.

Nevermore
by Kelly Creagh
Reading Group Guide

1. Early in their work on the Poe project, Varen discusses the identity of Lenore with Isobel, calling her the love of the narrator. How is this notion of the narrator's lost love an important element in the story? In what other ways do Isobel and Varen's initial work on their project foreshadow events to come?

2. In addition to his interest in Poe, Varen knows a good deal about dreams and their relationship to real life. What clues in this scene suggest that Poe also knew much about the nature of dreams? What does Isobel learn from talking with Varen and how does she relate their conversation to the frightening experiences that happen in her bedroom?

3. How does Reynolds first enter Isobel's consciousness? What important information does he give her about dreaming? Initally, do you think Reynolds is Isobel's friend, enemy, or something in between? How does that change over time?

4. When does Pinfeathers first appear to Isobel? Why do you think none of her classmates can see or hear the Nocs? What

important messages do the Nocs convey to Isobel in the course of the novel?

5. When Isobel finds herself in a dreamlike version of Mr. Swanson's class, she reads Robert Frost's poem, "The Road Not Taken." Why is this poem apt for the moment in which Isobel finds herself? How does Mr. Swanson's comment about choices relate to Isobel's experiences with Varen and Brad?

6. What is the Red Death? How is it related to the white-veiled woman? To the Nocs? How do you know the Red Death has been involved in what happened to Brad, and why do you think Brad has been chosen for this torment?

7. When Isobel escapes from the Grim Facade, she returns home to startling news about Varen and Brad. If you had found yourself in Isobel's situation, what choices might you have made about answering police questions, confiding in Gwen, dealing with Brad, and trying to find Varen?

8. While Isobel sees elements of the dream world Varen has created in her real life, she ultimately maintains a stronger hold on reality than he does. What makes her able to keep a distinction between her world and the dream world? What do you think makes Varen more susceptible to being engrossed in this alternate dimension?

9. Varen once told Isobel, *"You could never be Lenore."* Yet, does the epilogue imply that Isobel has become Varen's Lenore? Do you think there remains any hope of Isobel rescuing Varen? Does Isobel herself need rescuing?

10. In *Nevermore*, Varen tells Isobel that "Alone" is his favorite work by Poe, and he reads the poem aloud to her. Read "Alone" and discuss how this poem relates to Varen's life and to his character. How does this poem relate to the novel's epilogue? What imagery is shared?

11. Discuss how the author uses parallels in the novel. For example, the real world and the dream world, Isobel and Bess, Varen and Pinfeathers. What do these parallels represent, and what does their existence say about the characters in the book?

12. Read at least two of Poe's works mentioned in the novel ("Alone" or "Ulalume," for example) and consider the way he ends his stories and poems. Are the resolutions what you expect? Are they satisfying? Compare the endings of Poe's stories to the ending of *Nevermore*.

WHAT'S IN STORE
FOR ISOBEL AS SHE
DREAMS OF LOVE,
AND VENTURES
FURTHER INTO
POE'S WORLD OF
NIGHTMARES?

Enshadowed

A NEVERMORE Book

KELLY CREAGH

Turn the page for a special look at part two of Kelly Creagh's series,
available from Atheneum Books for Young Readers

Prologue
Washington College Hospital
October 7, 1849

"Edgar?"

Speaking softly, Dr. Moran leaned over his patient. His eyes traced the wan and pallid countenance of the famous poet, Edgar Poe. But the man who lay on the hospital bed before him now, bathed in the dim yellow lamplight, bore little resemblance to his dignified portraits. He seemed, instead, more like a ghostly shell of that man, a wasted imposter, his cheeks shadow-sunken, his skin waxen, white as the sheets beneath him. Dark lashes fringed his bruise-purple lids, serving to blacken the deep crescent-shaped hollows beneath each eye. Sweat glistened on his broad brow, his hair plastered to his temples, less from fever and more, the doctor knew, from exertion.

Rain pattered against the vaulted Gothic windows, glittering crystal beads that quivered into long streaks against the backdrop of darkness.

Though morning approached, the shadows of night pervaded inside the otherwise empty room.

Outside, the wind moaned while the clop of horse hooves and the rattle of carriage wheels echoed from the alley below.

"Edgar," Moran spoke again, "can you hear me?"

Poe's eyes drifted lazily open, glassy and distant, like the sightless eyes of a child's doll, black as inkwells. He stared at the ceiling.

Moran reached to check his patient's pulse, his thumb and finger clasping the clammy skin of the poet's wrist. There, a racing throb marked the seconds.

The doctor hesitated. He did not wish to send his patient into a frenzy yet again. Still, he could not help but press for another moment of lucidity, another brief glimmer of the man locked within the mania. Another clue to the puzzle of what had happened four days ago when Poe had been brought into his care, delirious, covered from head to foot in ashen grit, insensible, dressed in another man's clothing and unable to relay a single coherent detail as to where he had been—or whom he had been with, for that matter.

"Do you remember where you are?" Moran asked.

The doctor shifted in his seat. The old wooden chair creaked beneath him.

Suddenly Poe's arm shot out. He grasped for the doctor, locking his wrist in a grip that held all the strength of rigor mortis. "Who is it?" Edgar gasped, a rattle sounding in his chest, his voice husky, raw from the hours of screaming. "Who is here?"

"Be calm," Moran urged. He allowed Edgar's rigid, clammy grip to remain, hoping that the physical contact would somehow ground him, that it could bring him back, tether him to reality.

"Reynolds?" Poe whispered. His hand tightened around

Moran's arm with unbelievable strength, quivering with urgency. "Reynolds . . . tell me that you've come at last."

The doctor swallowed. He wetted his lips, which fought to form words before he knew what to say. "It is Dr. Moran, Edgar. Your physician. As I'm sure you remember."

Poe's face contorted. His eyes squeezed shut. His mouth opened, the corners collapsing in silent anguish. He released the doctor, his grip falling limp. "I should have known," he moaned, every syllable dripping the blackest despair, "that you would leave me here. Like this."

"Edgar," Moran whispered, "I wish only to help. Can you tell me what happened? Can you tell me how you came to be in Baltimore?"

"But I am not." Poe muttered, rocking his head back and forth against the damp pillow. With these words, his breathing turned shallow and quick. A shudder ran through him, causing the bed itself to tremor.

Moran frowned at his patient and groped for what next to say, for whatever words might keep Poe's mind present, distracted from hallucination, from the entities he claimed he saw slipping through the walls in swirls of black smoke. "Mr. Poe, you mentioned yesterday that you had a wife. In Richmond. Can you tell me—"

"Almost," Poe whispered. "Almost. But then, Reynolds, I *have* a wife." With these words, he traced his fingertips lightly across his chest, over a place where a portion of his shirt lay open. "Here. All the while," he murmured. "Locked within this feverish heart. All the while."

"Who is this Reynolds you speak of?" Moran asked, "A friend, perhaps?"

"Perhaps," Poe murmured, his hand falling away, his eyes fixating upon the ceiling. "We shall see. The shadows gather. Can you hear them whispering? *She* is coming. And so we shall see."

Poe's eyes grew wider then, their centers expanding, black as pitch.

Moran watched, transfixed. He had treated delirium many times before. But what was it about this man's condition that made him want to steal a glance at the barren walls that encircled them? What about this man's ravings made him want to look—to follow his gaze and be certain that there was truly nothing there?

Edgar gasped. His body went rigid. He wrenched against the bed, arching his spine. He threw his head to one side and howled, writhing as he gripped the bed beneath him, twisting the fabric of the matted bedclothes with quivering hands, crying out, "REYNOLDS!"

Moran shot to his feet.

"REYNOLDS!" Poe screamed again, renewing the cry that had carried him through the night, his voice grating raw and ragged.

"Edgar!" Moran shouted, grasping for his patient's hand. "Edgar, you are *safe*."

The hand that clamped his in return felt like that of a skeleton's.

"REYNOLDS!"

"There is nothing here that can harm you. Edgar, listen to me! It's over. Do you hear me? Whatever has happened, it is over!"

Poe froze in that moment, his teeth gritted, his face rigid with agony, beads of sweat sliding down his temples.

Then something in him changed. He seemed to return to himself all at once, like the flickering flame of a candle that had managed to steady itself after a gust of cold wind. His body, saturated with a dead yet almost graceful heaviness, sank slowly into the bed.

For the first time, his eyes turned to lock with Moran's.

The doctor stared, unblinking, stricken as he watched the blackened centers of Poe's eyes recede, like clouds from a storm-ravaged sea, revealing the bright rims of two blue-gray irises.

Poe stared at him with sudden intensity and intelligence, present for the first time. "Is it?" he asked.

As he exhaled, Poe's grip on the doctor's hand eased. "Lord, help my poor soul," he breathed, even as the glow within those bright and glittering eyes dimmed, fading as fast as it had come.

"*Edgar,*" Moran called.

But it was too late, for the eyes that stared up at him now, wide and sightless, held their strange light no more.

Pulse It

Did you love this book?

Want to get access to the hottest books for free?

Log on to simonandschuster.com/pulseit

to find out how to join,

get access to cool sweepstakes,

and hear about your favorite authors!

Become part of Pulse IT and tell us what you think!